HIGH PRAISE FOR RAY GARTON!

"*Live Girls* is gripping, original, and sly. I finished it in one bite."

—Dean Koontz

"The most nightmarish vampire story I have ever read."
—Ramsey Campbell on *Live Girls*

"It's scary, it's involving, and it's also mature and thoughtful."

—Stephen King on *Dark Channel*

"Garton never fails to go for the throat!"
—Richard Laymon, author of *Flesh*

"Garton has a flair for taking veteran horror themes and twisting them to evocative or entertaining effect."
—*Publishers Weekly*

"Ray Garton has consistently created some of the best horror ever set to print."

—*Cemetery Dance*

"Ray Garton writes horror fiction at its most frightening best."

—*Midwest Book Review*

"Garton is, simply put, one of the masters."
—James Moore, author of *Blood Red*

Standridge, *City Slab Magazine*

BESTIAL

"Over the top? You betcha! And Garton being Garton, we wouldn't have it any other way. . . . For his devotion to delivering serious horror without taking the horror too seriously, he's one of the most reliable brand names in modern fright fiction."

—Bookgasm

"*Bestial* moves at a blistering pace. Where *Ravenous* succeeded by instilling a creeping sense of horror, *Bestial* triumphs in its intrigue as the werewolves spread their surprising influence throughout Big Rock."

—*Shroud Magazine*

"This is a book any fan of hairy, horny monsters and B (as in breast) -movies will be happy to sink their fangs into."

—Fear Zone

RAVENOUS

"Hurley is a sheriff to root for, and Garton's well-paced horror novel reworks the werewolf myth to great effect."

—*Publishers Weekly*

"*Ravenous* is Ray Garton's most disturbing, affecting, and ferocious novel since *Crucifax Autumn*—which is to say, he's going to cost you a lot of sleep with this one. There are images and sequences in this book that only a frontal lobotomy will make you forget."

—Gary A. Braunbeck, Bram Stoker award–winning author of *Far Dark Fields*

"Witty, warped, and steeped in blood, this novel of hungry horror tumbles toward a delicious finale that will only leave you wanting to read more and more . . ."

—Douglas E. Winter, author of *Run*

"Expect nothing more than thrills and chills . . . Fans of wild horror will want to make it No. 1 on their to-read list . . . with a (silver) bullet."

—Bookgasm

With the cup of coffee in his right hand, Stuart turned back to the landscape of bobbing, swaying heads. His eyes settled on one head in particular, and his heart skipped a beat.

The oblong head stood well above the others, a few inches higher than Stuart's. Bald and pale and veiny. A stethoscope hung around the skinny neck and drew attention to the large, pointy Adam's apple in the throat. Small round glasses framed the deep-set eyes, which looked directly at Stuart.

He was grinning, as if he had been standing there watching Stuart all along, waiting for him to turn around. His oversized teeth appeared in that light to be a smoky gray.

There was a break in the crowd between them, and Stuart saw that Dr. Furgeson wore a long white coat. Right hand in the pocket, elbow slightly bent. The doctor removed his hand, held it up beside his grinning face. The silver scissors flashed with the dull reflection of a spinning red light atop a nearby video game.

Stuart could no longer breathe. His mouth hung loosely open.

Dr. Furgeson slowly tipped his head and turned it to the right, as if to reveal his ear to Stuart. It was an exaggerated movement, the gesture of a clown silently telling a child to listen.

Snick-snick-snick. Snick-snick-snick.

Other *Leisure* books by Ray Garton:

BESTIAL
RAVENOUS
NIGHT LIFE
LIVE GIRLS
THE LOVELIEST DEAD

RAY GARTON

SCISSORS

LEISURE BOOKS NEW YORK CITY

For Dawn.
I live and write
because of you.

A LEISURE BOOK®

February 2010

Published by

Dorchester Publishing Co., Inc.
200 Madison Avenue
New York, NY 10016

ISBN 10: 0-8439-6186-4
ISBN 13: 978-0-8439-6186-7

Visit us online at www.dorchesterpub.com.

SCISSORS

CHAPTER ONE

In his nightmare, Stuart is a little boy lying on a table in a doctor's office examination room. He is tense and stiff and his fists clench as the doctor removes stitches from the right side of his groin. The area around the sutures is numb so Stuart feels no pain, but he can feel the dull tug of each one being pulled through the holes in his flesh.

"Looks like I forgot to cut something off while I had you on the table, Stuart," Dr. Furgeson says.

"*What?*" Stuart cries as he tries to sit up. Hands on his shoulders hold him down. Stuart looks up at his mother's upside-down face.

"Just hold still, honey," she says, smiling down at him with too much lipstick, bright red hair still smelling of that morning's permanent. "It'll be over before you know it."

"I hope you'll take this like a big boy and not give me any trouble," Dr. Furgeson says. "Gotta make sure you can pee right, Stuart." He takes something from the cupboard over the sink. He tears open its wrapping.

Stuart lifts his head for a moment. Eyes widen when he sees the long hypodermic needle.

"This will hurt, Stuart. You may scream, if you like." Dr. Furgeson grins down at him.

He lifts his head again as the needle is stabbed into the head of his penis. The pain is exquisite and radiates through his body, all the way up to his throat, where it threatens to cut off his scream. His penis becomes numb, but the throbbing pain lingers deep.

Something else is ripped open. Stuart looks up to see

Dr. Furgeson removing a pair of scissors from the wrapper. The three-inch blades glimmer beneath the fluorescent lights as Dr. Furgeson opens and closes them: *Snick-snick-snick*.

"You won't feel this at all," the doctor says as he leans over Stuart.

Stuart struggles and his mother pushes his shoulders down harder as she says, "It has to be done, Stuey, honey, you won't feel it, and it'll all be over before you know it."

He lifts his head, still screaming, just in time to see the scissors close with a metallic *snick*. In time to see the head of his penis pop into the air, then drop between his thighs as dark blood bubbles up and dribbles down his penis, over his groin. Blood spurts into the air in jets of red, spattering Dr. Furgeson's white coat.

Dr. Furgeson, grinning around large white teeth, says, "It'll be good as new in no time."

Stuart thought he was screaming when he sat up in bed, but he only gasped for breath. His face and neck were slick with perspiration. He turned to see if he had disturbed Amelia.

She lay on her side, bare back to him, and softly snored, undisturbed. The waves of blonde on her pillow were all gone, and for a moment, Stuart thought he was in bed with a stranger.

He sighed as he remembered the haircut. He slid his legs over the edge of the bed and waited for the residue of the dream to evaporate, but it would not. Stuart stood and wondered if he was getting up for awhile, or just going to the bathroom. He decided he was up, put on the ratty old paint-spattered gray sweatshirt and baggy sweat pants he kept on a chair by the bed. Stuart did not own a robe. Never had gotten the hang of them.

The house was cold and one or both of the cats had absconded with his slippers again. He went to his open closet and felt around the pile of clothes on the floor with a bare foot, found his flip-flops and slipped them on. He tried not to let them slap his heels too loudly as he shuffled past the bed, looked back at Amelia one more time.

She had allowed some vile little man who called himself Romeo to cut off that thick, glorious mane of golden hair. Now it was short, chopped, blocky. Stuart was not bothered by the appearance of the new hairstyle—it was not unattractive, once he had recovered from the shock of seeing it for the first time—but it smacked of being hip. He loathed hip.

Downstairs in the kitchen, he turned on the fluorescent light over the sink, above the small window that looked out on the backyard. He found one of his slippers in the sink, abandoned there by Hieronymus or Hermione, his manx cats. He dropped it to the floor, leaned his elbows on the sink's edge and let his head hang low for a moment, then looked out the window. The fluorescent glare on the pane against the black night outside allowed him to see nothing but his own reflection. He was still shaken by the dream.

The incident in the doctor's office exam room had not happened exactly as it had in the nightmare, of course. But what really had happened seemed almost as bad when he thought about it, replayed the vivid memory in his mind.

Eight-year-old Stuart had been a little too enthusiastic in helping his uncle move a piano into the house. His mother had bought the piano on the condition that Stuart would take lessons and practice, practice, practice. He was so eager to get started, he had given himself a hernia. The surgery went smoothly, and he had gone home three days later. On the day Dr. Furgeson removed the stitches, he realized he had not performed a procedure he had intended to perform on the operating table while Stuart was anesthetized. The words in the nightmare had been Dr. Furgeson's. So had the voice. Stuart's mother had been there, and had held him down. She had not been as garishly made-up as she was in the dream, but she had worn just a touch more makeup than usual, and she'd had her hair done that morning. They were to attend a church potluck lunch right after Stuart's doctor appointment, and she had dressed in her Sunday best, even though it was Wednesday.

Dr. Furgeson had explained that the opening of Stuart's urethra was smaller than it should be and slightly misshapen. It needed to be enlarged so he could urinate properly. Stuart saw the hypodermic needle. The pain from the injection that was to numb his penis was exquisite, indeed, every bit as excruciating as it had been in the nightmare, and worse.

Everything had happened just as it had in the dream except the actual cutting. Dr. Furgeson had not cut off the head of Stuart's penis. But he had cut off the very tip. And Stuart remembered lifting his head just in time to see that tiny piece of flesh pop into the air as it was snipped off, followed by a glistening red bead of blood.

Stuart remembered Dr. Furgeson's teeth being very large and white, and when he spoke, his lips had to do a little extra work to speak around them. It seemed the doctor had been smiling all the time, as if the size and position of his teeth would not allow him to stop.

A stool scraped over the wood floor as Stuart scooted it up to the bar between the kitchen and dining room, reached over and turned on the twelve-inch television. He found a Three Stooges short and made himself a bowl of Cap'n Crunch. He watched what remained of the short and sat through the next, chuckled as he chewed his cereal. And he tried to forget about the dream and get the metallic whisper of those scissors out of his mind. *Snick-snick-snick. Snick-snick-snick.*

Hermione wandered into the kitchen. Stopped and looked up at Stuart with wide eyes, as if to ask what the hell he was doing up at such an hour.

"You think you could find something to drag around the house besides my slippers?" he muttered, looking down at the gray manx.

Hermione meowed her denial, blamed it all on Hieronymus, then sniffed around the cupboards. Making her rounds, Stuart forgotten.

By four thirty, Stuart was feeling sleepy again. He rinsed the bowl, turned off the television. He went back to the sink, reached up and switched off the fluorescent light.

Dr. Furgeson grinned at him from the window. He held up his small shiny scissors in his right hand, level with his shoulder, blades open wide. His back was stiff, large teeth a bright white in his mouth.

At first, Stuart thought it was a reflection in the glass and spun around with a gasp, expecting to see the doctor behind him. He was not there. Stuart turned to the window again in time to catch a glimpse of the doctor's white coat as he ducked out of view just outside the window.

His hands trembled and he put them on the edge of the sink, clutched it hard. He thought something was thumping loudly somewhere in the house, but it was only his heart beating in his ears. His mouth hung open as he stared wide-eyed through the glass at the darkness.

That's impossible, he thought.

For an instant, Stuart felt the pain of the injection in the tip of his penis, felt it all the way up to his throat, just long enough to make him press his thighs together reflexively.

He saw a flash of gray in the darkness outside—Dr. Furgeson's white coat as he hurried across the backyard diagonally, the coat's clean bright white muted by the darkness. He bent at the waist, ducking to stay out of sight.

Moving against the cold, powerful gusts of fear that sent gooseflesh over his body, Stuart rushed through the shadows to the back door. He grabbed the long black Mag-Lite flashlight from its hook beside the door. He reached over to flip on the outdoor light but remembered he had not yet replaced the bulb that had burnt out a couple days ago, and went outside. The flashlight was heavy enough to serve as a weapon if necessary, almost too heavy for his shivering hand as he turned it on and aimed it ahead of him. He tucked the butt of the light under his right arm.

It had rained all day the day before and the early morning was cold and damp. Dark, the moon hidden behind clouds. The wet grass brushed against his feet, unprotected in the flip-flops.

Stuart stopped several feet away from the house. He swept the flashlight slowly over the small yard, over Amelia's rosebushes hunched along the six-foot-tall wooden fence that surrounded it. He turned, went to the gate beside the house. Beyond it, a narrow strip of grass between the house and fence led to the front. The gate was closed and latched.

His heartbeat still throbbed in his ears. But it was not loud enough to prevent him from hearing the whispery *snick-snick-snick* of scissors somewhere in the dark. He spun around, shone the light in the direction of the sound.

There was no place to hide. The yard was empty, no one there but Stuart.

He went to the side fence, thinking perhaps the sound had come from the next yard. He stood on his toes to peer over the top. The house next door was vacant and for sale. The yard, thick with weeds, was empty.

Stuart turned around and came face-to-face with a figure in the dark. The figure said, "What're you—"

He cried out in strangled fear, lifted the flashlight to strike.

"*Stu!*" Amelia took a step back, stared at him with round eyes and a slack jaw, right hand pressed to her chest. She wore a blue velour robe and slippers, face white in the darkness. The newly short, spiky hair made her look momentarily unfamiliar, a total stranger in the dark.

"What're you doing in the backyard at four thirty in the morning?" she asked. Her voice was high and soft with sleepy surprise.

"I . . . I'm sorry," he said. He sounded hoarse and winded. "I thought I, um, saw someone. Earlier. Out here."

"Well, they're probably in the house by now. You left the

back door wide-open, the cats could've gotten out." She forced a small laugh to cover the tremble in her voice, but it was too late.

"I did?"

"Yes, you did. Are you through? I mean, are you coming in, or do you want to wander around out here in the dark awhile longer?" Another hollow laugh.

Stuart looked around the yard one more time. He knew he had not imagined it. He had seen Dr. Furgeson outside the window, grinning—flesh and blood, not an apparition, not a fuzzy hallucination. He had done enough acid in high school and college to know what hallucinations looked like. The doctor had darted across the yard bent over to avoid being seen. Would a hallucination try to duck out of sight?

"Stuart?" Amelia stepped toward him. She sounded concerned now. "Are you all right?"

He forced his lips into a smile. He did not want her to know what he was feeling. He was not too sure what he was feeling himself. He only knew he did not like it.

They went inside and back to bed. But Stuart did not go back to sleep.

CHAPTER TWO

At work the following day, the snick of the scissors haunted him, distracted him, and he got very little done. He had gotten very little done for weeks—enough weeks to make up months. When he started work in the morning, his mind seized up, yielded nothing. His hand worked on its own, looked busy to cover for him.

Stuart was always afraid he would come to work only to be told he no longer had a cubicle, that his services were no longer required at Carnival Greetings. That fear took the bus to work with him every morning, straddled his shoulder and gnawed at the base of his skull. He smiled at everyone, kept quiet, stayed in his cubicle and hoped no one would notice him until the work started flowing again, until everything had blown over.

If Owl-Man had worked, he would not have to do that. He was pretty sure if Owl-Man had worked out the way everyone had hoped—the way Stuart had always known it would *not*—they probably would have given him a promotion, a paid vacation, and a trip to someplace exotic. But Owl-Man had failed miserably. Stuart was a perfect scapegoat, and with each passing day, he wondered why they were withholding the ax, why they continued to put it off.

That's probably part of the punishment, he thought. *Knowing it's going to happen sooner or later. Having to wait.*

That would not have happened on Allen Cohen's watch. When one of Al's projects failed—Stuart knew of only two—he took responsibility for it, and treated it as a personal challenge, which he met by succeeding brilliantly with his next project. Allen was that way about everything, not just work, and Stuart had liked that about him. A true optimist, but one who kept it to himself. He was, in fact, rather grumpy. A curmudgeonly optimist, no "have a nice day" from Al, but he was there with support when you needed it. Owl-Man would not have happened on Al's watch if he worked there for a hundred years, because Al was incapable of coming up with such a stupid idea.

But Al was gone. Two years ago, Carnival Greetings had become a member of the CorpAmeritron family of companies. Allen's old office was occupied now by a quiet but jittery guy in his early thirties named Adrian Chalmers. The door to his office was always open—something Adrian called his "open door policy"—to show his willingness to listen to employees at any time. On his first day at Carnival, he assured everyone that his door would remain open as long as he was there. Betting began immediately. No one believed he would leave his office door open all day, every day. If he did, he would not do it for very long. But he did. Adrian Chalmers left the door of his outer office open at all times. The inner office's door was always closed, of course. To get through that door, you first had to get past his secretary, Myrna, and you had better have an appointment, too, and if you don't, you'd better make one, otherwise you can just march yourself back out that door and quit wasting the precious time of busy people, thank you very much.

Chalmers was not a responsibility-taker, he was a blame-placer, and he placed the blame for the entire Owl-Man fiasco on Stuart's shoulders. Those exact words had not come out of his mouth, or anyone else's, but Stuart knew it and so did everyone else at Carnival. The blade of the guillotine had begun its descent. It was only a matter of time now.

The entire situation chewed away at Stuart's insides like maggots at dead flesh on a carcass.

* * *

It seemed Stuart had been born with a pencil in his hand. For as long as he could remember, he had always been happiest when drawing or painting. Before he could speak his first word, he could communicate a simple but distinct idea with a picture. His mother had saved everything he had ever drawn or painted while growing up. She had boxes of them. Each had a small piece of paper clipped to the top left corner which gave the date and time the piece was done in large, round numbers. Some of the attached slips included brief notes about Stuart's state of mind at the time. Much of what Stuart had created early on was not as bright or cheerful as might be expected from a child. Some of it was quite dark and violent. His mother had monitored carefully what he read, what kind of music he listened to, and what he watched on television, prohibiting anything remotely violent or sexual, or anything that dealt with the supernatural (the last including everything from *The Twilight Zone* to *Bewitched* to *Scooby Doo, Where Are You?*). The appearance of violence and brooding images in his drawings and paintings disturbed her, because she knew he had not been exposed to such things.

She told the stories to this day to her church friends— "The Girls," she called them. "Oh, the things he drew when he was just a chubby little toddler," she'd say with a click of her tongue. "What he put me through. I got so worried that for awhile I even considered taking him to . . . you know . . . one of those doctors. A *psychologist*." She always whispered the word. Wouldn't want anyone besides The Girls to hear such a thing. Betty Mullond's church had always believed psychiatry to be the work of Satan. Having more than its fair share of nuts in the pews as well as in the pulpits, the church's stance had softened out of necessity over the decades, but going to a psychologist or psychiatrist was still considered a last resort, and then only to a psychologist or psychiatrist who had graduated from one of the church's own religious colleges, and whose approach to each patient was Bible-based and Christ-centered.

Some of Stuart's early drawings and watercolors, even a few from his Crayola period, still hung on her walls in attractive frames. But the dark, sometimes even bloody pictures he had created were shown to no one. They remained in boxes, put away in the crawl space she referred to as the attic, or in a closet. They were not the work of a healthy Christian boy who sang in the church choir and got consistently good grades in every class at church school. What would people think?

Stuart's father, Delbert, had harbored no interest whatsoever in his son's work, and therefore did not care if he drew smiley faces or sex organs.

At no point could Stuart remember ever wanting to do anything with his life besides draw and paint. He had not entertained the idea that he was an artist until high school. It was so much a part of him, he did not think of it as something that could be labeled—that would be like naming his fingers and toes. It was not something he chose to do, but simply who he was.

In junior high, Stuart made up his mind to work in comic books when he got out of school. He had read comics throughout his childhood, teen years, and even later, as an adult. He'd spent hours studying the colorful panels, the actions of the characters, the backgrounds. Finally, he created his own comic book superhero. The character was based on a photograph of an owl he had seen in a *National Geographic* magazine. The owl had been dark and sleek, sinister, with an ominous depth in its round eyes. Stuart had created Owl-Man. Knowing how his mother would react, he had kept his Owl-Man work tucked away under his bed. She did not approve of comic books and would not let him read them. He had sneaked across the street to read Daryl Fitch's comic books. It was Daryl who had introduced him to them. Stuart was fascinated by their fluid, action-driven images, and in the case of the horror comics, deep shadows and funereal mood. He went over to Daryl's almost every day, devoured one comic book after another and then reread them. His mother had no idea, of course. Not only were comic books forbidden by the church, but Stuart was not supposed to be spending time with Daryl at all. The boy was a known troublemaker, and the Fitches were Catholic.

His mother had found all his Owl-Man panels, of course. Before telling his dad, she had asked why Stuart had drawn them. When he told her he planned to do that for a living, her lips had trembled and her eyes had filled with tears. He'd known precisely what was on her mind. She was wondering what people would think if Stuart were to do such a thing. It had always been his mother's hope that he would go into the ministry. Stuart supposed it could not have been much worse had he told her he preferred kissing boys to girls. Even after his first exhibit, right after graduating from college, Stuart's parents had still asked, now and then, what kind of work he planned to do.

Everything seemed to have come full circle. Owl-Man had gotten him into trouble again. First as an ominous and violent comic book superhero who flew silently above the city's streets at night with hang-glider wings that slid out from beneath his cape, then as a chubby figure of fun, a doodle. This time, of course, there was no tearful, righteously indignant response from his mother. No, this time he would have to hang around Carnival and eat human waste for awhile, then lose his job. They were just waiting to get the final numbers from the Owl-Man disaster so they could hold them over Stuart's head.

Barbara McNab, who worked in the cubicle across from Stuart's, was still home with the flu after two days. That made the day quieter than usual, and the quiet left Stuart open for distraction. Barbara muttered and grumbled to herself as she worked. He had grown so accustomed to her muffled voice, he hardly noticed it anymore, until now that it was gone. In the unusual quiet, he heard the snicking of scissors.

The hours till lunch seemed to stretch on forever. After lunch, more of the same as he discarded one sketch after another of a cartoon moonscape he was working on.

Sometime in the afternoon, Stuart's ex-wife Molly would drop their thirteen-year-old son James at the house before running off to spend a couple weeks with her rich and handsome ski instructor at his lodge near Lake Tahoe. That was the only good thing he could think of about being at work that day: avoiding Molly. He looked forward to seeing his son, though.

James seemed to be going through some changes when Stuart had last seen him about three weeks ago. And not all the changes appeared to be good ones. Until he started thinking about scissors and a certain doctor from his past, Stuart had been preoccupied with worry about his son. He hoped things went better between them this time. But he was not in the mood to exchange pleasantries with his ex-wife. He seldom was, but even less so now.

As his right hand rounded off a crater, he frowned down at his work and muttered, "Happy skiing, or . . . break a leg . . . or whatever the hell they say on the slopes."

Even better, he would not have to sit around and listen to Amelia and Molly get along so well, like a couple of old ladies working on a quilt. Stuart found it unnatural, and it gave him the creeps.

Stuart had told Amelia everything about his years with Molly. They had married as soon as Molly became pregnant. James was not planned, but they were both thrilled by the news and drove to Las Vegas that night. They were wed in a small, overlit, all-night chapel by a man with a pronounced stutter. Their witnesses had been an old woman in a sequined magenta dress and a midget in top hat and tails. Their families were furious that they had not been included, so a formal ceremony was held later for their benefit. Stuart had no choice but to get a steady job, and began his work at Carnival Greetings, while Molly worked as a legal secretary. He put his own painting aside for the time being to pay as much attention as possible to James. The first seven or eight years were better than Stuart ever could have hoped. After that, things changed, gradually but steadily. Molly began to go out with her girlfriends. Stuart did not mind at all, until it began to happen three or four nights a week. She stayed out later and later, came home swaying from liquor. They fought about it repeatedly, and each fight was louder than the last. She was bored, she said. He said they would go out more, they could leave James with her mother or sister. But that was not what she meant. It took a few years to figure out what she really meant—she was bored with him, with being home all the time and having to live her days around James's schedule and Stuart's schedule. He asked why she had married him in the first place.

"I don't know," Molly had said. "It was a mistake. My mistake. I'm not a wife, Stu. I don't have it in me. I just wasn't wired for it. I've been unfaithful to you. At least . . . several times. I think we should get a divorce."

They agreed to remain civil for James's sake and to share custody of him. James was free to go back and forth between them as he pleased, and he spent equal time with each. But lately, he was happy with neither of them. That was another problem altogether.

When Amelia and Molly hit it off like two high school girls at a slumber party—it happened the moment they met, as if they had known each other for years, as if Amelia knew nothing about the way Molly had treated him—it felt to Stuart like a betrayal. He never said so to Amelia because he knew how it would sound—like he was simply being too sensitive, something he had been told all his life. He was too sensitive. He heard it from his parents, teachers, friends. He let little things gnaw at him and big things eat him alive.

His grandmother used to tell him, "You're gonna age yourself ahead of time, you keep that up. You want hair as white
as mine when you're in college?" Stuart hated hearing it, no
matter how it was put. He would never admit it, but he knew
it was true. As willing as people always had been to point it
out to him, though, none of them ever told him what to do
about it. He had been unable to figure that out on his own,
so he had learned to keep it to himself. He was no less sensitive, he simply did not express it. Good thing Grandma was
gone and could not see the strands of silver in his chocolate
brown hair.

In the quiet, his pen's scrape was loud as he sketched. In
the texture of that sound, Stuart detected another smaller
sound:

Snick-snick-snick. Snick-snick-snick.

CHAPTER THREE

Amelia was most productive in the morning, and as usual, she started working as soon as Stuart left the house. Like Stuart, she was an artist. Unlike Stuart, her work had been dismissed by the art snobs. But her pieces sold steadily on the Internet, and for good money. She had started out by posting a few things on eBay. They had sold so quickly, she started her own website. Each piece was made from the disassembled parts of obsolete technology: a mobile of rotary dials from old telephones, a dinosaur constructed of the guts of an old adding machine, an abstract piece made of parts from a Betamax VCR. She spent a couple hours tending to orders, then went to work on a bouquet of flowers made of old television tubes.

At two o'clock, an alarm clock went off in the bedroom she had converted into a studio. She had set the clock that morning to remind her that Molly would be bringing James over. Before starting work, she had eaten a banana with her coffee, and by the time the alarm went off, she was hungry again. She made some tuna salad, enough for three, in case Molly and James were hungry. She was making a sandwich for herself when the doorbell rang.

"Oh, my God, your *hair*!" Molly exclaimed as she came in, putting a palm flat against each cheek.

Even James gawked at her, openmouthed. There was genuine sadness in his eyes. "It's gone," he said quietly.

Amelia's eyes widened when she saw that James had shaved his head. His hair was a shadow on his skull. "You should talk!"

"Yeah, isn't that nice?" Molly said. "This is what I get for letting him go get his own haircut. Chemo chic." She took off her coat and tossed it over the back of the sofa.

Amelia offered tuna salad sandwiches, but they declined. James removed his coat and went straight to the computer in the corner of the small dining room, but not before telling Amelia in a low, morose voice that he thought she had made a big mistake with the haircut.

"You are definitely your father's son," she said.

Amelia and Molly sat at the tiled bar between the kitchen and dining room. Amelia nibbled on half of her sandwich and some baby carrots, and they both drank Diet Dr Pepper on ice. They talked about Molly's handsome, wealthy ski instructor for awhile, before Molly looked at Amelia with a troubled expression.

"I'm sorry, but I can't adjust to your hair," Molly said. She asked hesitantly, "Are you sure nothing's wrong?"

"Wrong? What do you mean?"

"Cutting your hair off like that, all of a sudden." Molly shrugged. "I don't know, it just seems a little severe."

"You mean, like in some kind of emotional half-drunken breakdown, or something? Maybe in front of a mirror? Like something out of a fifties Bette Davis movie?"

Molly shook her head, laughing. "No, nothing like that. But you said it's been long like that all your life."

"Too long. I've been thinking about cutting it for months. But I had no idea Stu would react the way he has."

"He isn't happy with it?"

Amelia made a laughing sound, but it was not quite a laugh. It was hollow, chilly. She lowered her voice, even though James was completely engrossed in whatever he was doing at the computer. "I thought he might be disappointed. But the way he's taken it, the way he's behaved . . . I think he's getting over it now, but it's almost like I've had a mastectomy, or something."

Molly leaned forward over the bar and said loudly, "Because you cut your hair?"

She shook her head uncertainly. "I don't know." She took another small bite of her sandwich and chewed for a moment. "Something's been wrong for awhile now, my haircut is just part of it. I think. Actually, my haircut probably has nothing to do with it."

"Uh-huh," Molly said. It was a knowing sound. She took one of the baby carrots from Amelia's plate and snapped it between her teeth. "What's he doing?"

"It's nothing he's doing. He's just . . . not here. Know what I mean? He's somewhere else most of the time. Inside himself. You look at his face and there's a lot of activity there, like he's listening to an intense conversation in his head. Sometimes, you have to shout at him to get his attention. A couple times, usually." She told Molly about finding Stuart in the backyard the night before. About the almost child-like expression of terror on his face when he nearly hit her with the flashlight.

Molly took the untouched half of Amelia's tuna sandwich from the plate and took a couple bites, chewed slowly, frowned. "Hmm. I've never known him to walk in his sleep, that's new. But I told you he was moody."

"No, it's not a mood thing. Not exactly. It's something else." Amelia frowned, sipped her cola. Wiped her fingers on a paper towel. "It's like there's something else going on."

"Another woman?"

"No, nothing like that. I mean, like there's something going on somewhere else and he's missing it. I don't know. It's hard to describe."

"I know what you mean. Maybe moody is the wrong word. I may not know what to call it, but I recognize it." She took a couple more bites of the sandwich.

"What is it?"

"It's him. The way he is. If I'm not mistaken, I warned you about it the first time we spoke."

"Yeah, you and your warnings. I'm not complaining,

Molly, I'm worried, that's all. If there's something wrong, I want to know about it. And help, if I can."

Molly finished the half of Amelia's sandwich, licked her fingertips. She stopped suddenly and looked at Amelia. "He's not having nightmares, is he? Recurring nightmares?"

"Not that I know of."

Molly sighed and nodded her head once, as if perhaps she were relieved. "He'll tell you what's on his mind when he's ready. He never talks until he's ready."

"You want me to make another sandwich?"

"Nah. I'm not hungry."

"I don't mind that he keeps things to himself," Amelia said. "He always talks sooner or later. In fact, we talk a lot. More than you probably think. But I'm afraid this is something serious that he isn't telling me. Maybe something he doesn't *want* to tell me. He's been working out."

"What? Stuart?"

"Yeah. Joined a health club and everything. He goes two or three times a week, sometimes before work, sometimes after. Lifts weights. He just started taking a class in Thai kickboxing. Before that, he took a class in something called Modern Arnis, some kind of Phillipine martial art. In fact, I think he's still taking classes in that." A small laugh slipped out. "He looks fabulous, Molly, and he's so limber these days. You wouldn't believe it if you saw him."

Molly's mouth curled downward, lower lip curled out. She made a *hmph* sound. "He jogged for awhile when James was little, but it didn't last. He's always been careful about his diet. Used to go on walks. But a health club? He hates people who belong to health clubs."

"That's why it surprised me. I'm not complaining, believe me. It's just odd. I didn't think it would last, but he's been at it all year."

"Is he still upset about that . . . what was that character he did for Carnival? Owl-Man?"

Amelia closed her eyes at the name. "Oh, God, that thing. It's been awhile, but yes, that's still bothering him. He's waiting for the ax to fall."

"The ax? You mean, he might lose his job?"

"I don't think he will, and I've told him that. But he seems to think it's coming."

"Whoa, wait a second, what did I miss? When did this get so serious?"

"Didn't I tell you all about it?"

Molly shook her head. "This is the first chance we've had to sit down and talk for . . . jeez, I don't know, months."

"You've been too preoccupied with your ski instructor."

"James told me a little about the situation. That Carnival had poured a lot of money into a cartoon character Stuart had come up with and the whole thing flopped. Is that about right?"

"It's accurate, but not true. Owl-Man was an accident, and Stu was opposed to the whole thing from the beginning. It was just a little character he doodled. You know how he's always doodling things? No matter where he is or what he's doing?"

Molly nodded.

Amelia finished her Dr Pepper, took the plate and glass to the sink and rinsed them as she talked. "Well, Owl-Man was just a doodle, not something Stu was doing for work. It was a character he'd come up with when he was a kid. He was doodling Owl-Man before CorpAmeritron came along and took over the shop." She put the plate and glass on the drain board and dried her hands, left the kitchen and went to the computer desk in the corner, opened a drawer. "Excuse me, James."

Slouched in the chair, James held a joystick in his lap. Slender black headphones covered his ears. His intense eyes did not move from the monitor. Amelia was gone before he knew she was there.

She handed Molly the dog-eared sheet of beverage-stained binder paper she had taken from the desk drawer. "He'd leave me notes with Owl-Man doodled on them. Sometimes they were cartoons with captions, sometimes just absent-minded doodles. I always thought he was cute. Owl-Man, I mean."

Doodles of varying shapes and sizes—faces, a human hand, an odd-looking long-necked bird—were scattered over the page, but a large one near the center stood out. A short, tubby, befuddled-looking man in an ill-fitting owl suit with a cape and hood dangled from a ledge by one hand, and the seat of his costume had ripped open to reveal his round butt.

"He *is* cute," Molly said.

"Chalmers thought so, too. Remember, Stu doodles at work, too. Chalmers happened to see an Owl-Man doodle on Stu's desk one day and went berzerk for it. At the time, he was looking for something they could build a whole line of merchandise around. Instead of going through the process of licensing something from a movie or television show that everyone was already familiar with, Chalmers decides they'll come up with something in-house that's all their own. Something they can put on cards and calenders, sweatshirts and coffee mugs. And right away, he decides Owl-Man is that character."

"Shit!" James barked as he slapped a palm on the desktop.

Molly turned to him and shouted, "Hey! If you don't want to be sociable, you could—James, take off those headphones!"

He took them off, but did not turn to his mother.

While Molly told James at length to watch his language or his computer game privileges would be revoked, Amelia left the bar and put a kettle of water on the stove for tea.

"If Stuart didn't like the idea, why didn't he just say no?" Molly asked as she turned back to the bar.

"He couldn't. He'd doodled Owl-Man at work, and that made it the property of Carnival Greetings."

"So, they just took Stuart's character and did whatever they wanted with it?"

"Not exactly. Stu decided if they were going to do it no matter what, he wanted to make sure it was done as well as possible. When Chalmers asked him to head up the project, he said yes. It wouldn't have mattered, though, they would have done it without him. Want some raspberry tea?"

"No, I've got shopping to do and tea goes right through me."

Amelia got a mug from the cupboard, a tea bag from a box on a shelf. She dropped the tea bag into the cup and set it on the counter. As the red kettle on the stove began to whisper with heat, Amelia leaned against the edge of the counter and faced Molly at the bar.

"Last year, they launched a line of Owl-Man back-to-school supplies, and they sat on shelves untouched for—well, you know this, right?"

Molly nodded. "James told me about that part. But that's all he told me." She glanced over her shoulder at her son. "He doesn't talk much these days, and when he does, it's usually profanity or computerspeak." She frowned at Amelia. "Why didn't they do some test marketing first?"

"That *was* the test marketing. The research department determined that Owl-Man would be most appealing to children of a certain age. That's when they decided on back-to-school supplies. They were launched in selected parts of the country. And they didn't sell. People ignored them in droves. Even worse were the back-to-school greeting cards. Stu said nobody knew what to do with them. Were parents supposed to give them to kids? Were teachers supposed to give them to students? Actually, they were for students to give to each other, but since greeting cards don't come with instructions, nobody knew that. Carnival tried a different approach in their advertising, but by then, it was too late. They even hired actors to make appearances as Owl-Man at stores carrying the Carnival back-to-school line. Stu still has one of the costumes upstairs. One of the Owl-Man guys overdosed on heroin and choked to death on his own vomit in his Owl-Man suit. I think that was in Seattle. Stu doesn't know how they did it, but they managed to keep it out of the news. The whole thing was a disaster, top to bottom. Then, as if all that wasn't bad enough, the guy in research? The guy who told them Owl-Man would appeal to children of a certain age? He went completely nuts one day and ran up and down the corridors naked and crying like a baby. He urinated all over the candy machine. He'd been coming to pieces for months, but nobody knew. His little boy had been run over and killed by a dairy truck, his wife had left him, and he was unraveling like a ball of yarn. Turns out only a small fraction of the research that was supposed to have been done on Owl-Man was actually done. The rest was . . . management used the word 'manufactured.'"

"He made it up?"

The kettle began to whistle. Amelia took it off the burner and poured steaming water into her mug. "Yep, he made it all up."

"But how could Stuart possibly be fired for this?" Molly asked.

Amelia put her tea on the bar and sat on the stool again. "You think Chalmers will take responsibility for it? Even though it was his idea. Stu's afraid they'll either fire him or make his life miserable. They've been doing that already. He gets nothing but the crappiest assignments."

"No wonder he's so upset."

Amelia frowned as she dipped her tea bag absently. "It's not that he's upset, exactly. And I don't think Owl-Man was the cause of it, either. It made things worse, but he started behaving differently just before that. Right after he started painting again."

"He's painting again?" There was a spark of surprise in Molly's eyes. "He's painting regularly?"

"Yeah." Amelia removed the spoon from her tea and put the bag in its bowl on the bar. "I thought it was great at first. But he disappears into the garage at night, stays in there for hours, and when he comes out, it's like he's been jogging in the desert. He always looks so drained and sweaty."

"What kind of work is he doing?"

Amelia shrugged as she sipped her tea. "He doesn't show me anything. I've asked, but he says nothing is ready. Why? You look bothered."

Molly frowned and chewed her lip thoughtfully. "He's always been that way when he's working on something. First, it was when he was working on something of his own, but later, he got that way with some of his Carnival work, too. He says he's never happier than when he's painting, but it sure doesn't seem that way. Painting seems to make him miserable. And a real pain in the ass to live with."

"You should talk," Amelia said with a smirk.

"I know, I know. I was the one who screwed everybody from here to the Silicon Valley. But I was always easy to live with. And all I needed was a little therapy and a divorce. I don't think it'll be as easy to fix him, though."

"You talk about him like he's a lunatic, or something, Molly, and he's not. In the—what is it? Three? More than that—in the years we've been together, he's been great. That's why this worries me. It's not like him. Usually, he's wonderful to be with, I don't know what your problem was."

Molly nodded slowly, stared at the bar for several seconds. Sadness moved over her face, like the shadow of a passing cloud. "Maybe I exaggerate. Maybe." She spoke quietly and did not look up to meet Amelia's eyes. "He's an artist, and there are no mentally healthy artists, they don't exist. Mentally healthy artists are like military intelligence and Jews for Jesus. Oxymorons. For me . . . he was tough to live with. But that's mostly because of *me*. I was never cut out for marriage. Just took me fifteen years to figure it out." Finally, she looked up. Smiled a little, but not much. "You're a lot more laid back than I am, I guess, more accepting. And more giving. That's why you're much better for him." She grinned, but the passing sadness had remained in her eyes. "Let's go see what he's working on."

Amelia's mouth dropped open, but her eyes were smiling. "No!"

Molly laughed. "Oh, come on, you know you want to. I bet you've gone out to that garage half a dozen times to see what—"

"I have not!" She laughed, shook her head. "I've wanted to, but I haven't. I'm anxious to see what he's doing, but if he says it's not ready, then I don't want to see it. Like a Christmas present, I guess. I can't wait to see what it is, but I don't want to peek early and spoil the surprise."

"Aren't you the romantic."

"What do you mean?"

Molly put a hand to her suddenly heaving bosom, tipped her head back. With breathy, mock passion, she said, "Your love has ressurected the artist in him, the passion you've brought to his life has reignited the flame of his creativity and—"

"Oh, knock it off," Amelia said.

"C'mon, let's go take a look. I'm serious."

"No. It wouldn't feel right." She lifted the mug to her lips, blew on the tea again, sipped.

"Might make you feel better. Maybe you'd stop worrying about him so much if you knew what he was doing. Might even save your life."

"Save my—what are you talking about?"

"Think about it. If Shelly Duvall hadn't waited so long to take a look at the manuscript Jack Nicholson was working on all the time in *The Shining* and had seen it was about a thousand pages of the same sentence over and over, she might have had time to grab the kid and—"

"You are so mean today, Molly!"

Molly's head dropped forward and her shoulders bobbed with laughter for a moment. She lifted her head, took a deep breath. "I'm only half joking, Amelia. It might be good for you. Wouldn't you feel better if you knew he was working on the most beautiful thing he's ever done, and he's just got his mind wrapped around that?"

Amelia hesitated this time, just for a moment, then shook her head.

"Okay, tell you what," Molly said as she stood, smiled. "I'll go take a look by myself, then you won't have anything to feel bad about."

Amelia winced. "I wish you wouldn't, Molly, really."

"I'll just take a peek, I'll be in and out." She walked past the bar and crossed the kitchen, went through the door into the hall. Her footsteps on the hardwood floor faded to the other side of the house.

It felt wrong to Amelia, and she was a little angry at Molly for doing it. But what could she have done to stop her? Stuart would tell her to get angry and kick the crazy bitch out, but Amelia was incapable of maintaining anger. When it came, it passed over her like a chill—as it did when Molly ignored her request to stay out of the garage—and then disappeared completely. Even when she wanted to hold onto it and make it last awhile, it slipped from her grasp like water. She could not stay angry long enough to kick anyone anywhere. Anger in others made her tense, and she usually walked away from it as quickly as possible. She could not keep Molly from going to the garage, but she would never tell Stuart about it.

Amelia's eyes turned to James at the computer. He was on another planet. He looked heavier. Something else for Stuart to worry about. He had obsessed about it the last few times James had stayed with them. It occurred to Amelia that James's gradual weight gain might have been part of Stuart's inspiration to start working out. It probably reminded him a little too much of his own years as the fattest kid in the room. He had given her no other reason than, "I just want to get into better shape."

Whatever his reason, it was the kind of thing he would

not have hesitated to share with her a year or so ago. Not anymore.

At the sound of Molly's footsteps coming back up the hall, Amelia turned on the stool, thinking, *That was fast.*

"There are no paintings out there," Molly said.

Amelia frowned at her. "There's got to be something. Nothing on the easel?"

"Nothing."

Although tempted now, Amelia decided not to go look for herself. There had to be paintings out there somewhere, and she did not want to see them until Stu was ready to show her. But where were they?

"Unless he keeps them locked in that big wooden cabinet," Molly said.

"The one against the wall?"

Molly nodded.

"Oh, there's nothing but junk in that—*locked?*"

"Yeah. There's a big padlock on it."

"You mean the one with the sliding accordion door? It doesn't have a lock."

Molly's eyebrows rose as she shrugged. "It does now."

Amelia left the kitchen and walked down the hall at a quick pace, Molly behind her, through the door that opened off the small laundry room.

When Stu had decided to start painting again, he had cleaned up the messy, cluttered garage, stacked everything neatly on the high shelves and in cupboards and in the large wooden cabinet against the wall. But now, the things once stored on the deep cabinet's broad shelves were stacked in a front corner of the garage. A large toolbox, unused tennis racquets, a rusted old tackle box, several cardboard boxes filled with Christmas decorations, others containing assorted junk. The four adjustable wooden shelves that had held them had been leaned against the side of the cabinet. The cabinet's door—narrow, hinged slats of wood that folded up when the door was slid open—no longer latched and always stood open an inch or so. Now it was closed tight, held by a large silver padlock on a hasp.

Amelia walked over to the cabinet slowly, tugged on the lock. It was secure. She looked around the garage, her mouth open slightly. The easel stood beside a table covered with brushes and painting knives. A crumpled smock had been tossed over the corner of the table, smeared with paint.

"When he first set this up," she said quietly, "he only came out here two or three times a month. But in the last few months or so, he's out here all the time. Every night. Sometimes late."

Molly nodded at the cabinet, hands on her hips. "Maybe he's got a woman in there, you think?"

Amelia said nothing as she continued to look around slowly, brow creased.

When she saw the worry in Amelia's eyes, Molly said, "Hey, like I said, he's an artist. So he keeps his paintings locked up in the cabinet, big deal. I wouldn't worry about it if I were you."

"Yeah. You're probably right. Nothing to worry about." But Amelia worried, anyway.

CHAPTER FOUR

When Stuart stepped into the dining room and saw the back of the bald figure seated at the computer, a bolt of fear shot through him—the kind of fear that buckled knees and soiled pants. It lasted only a couple seconds, but hit him so hard, he stepped backward and leaned his shoulder against the edge of the dining room's arched doorway, wondering if Amelia was okay. He was certain, for those few seconds, that it was Dr. Furgeson who sat at the desk. The doctor had come into Stuart's home, made himself comfortable, and had done God only knew what with Amelia.

But, of course, that was not the case. The head was bald, but with a shadow of returning hair. The shoulders were fleshy and rounded, and the thick neck was creased with the beginnings of fatty rolls in back.

James has shaved his head, Stuart thought as the fear quickly receded. A tremor lingered in his hands and knees as he took a deep breath, pulled himself together.

On the bus ride home, Stuart had prepared himself to greet his son. He practiced smiling. Others on the bus probably thought he was a lunatic, but he did not care. Stuart had not been doing much smiling lately, but he wanted none of the darkness inside him to be evident to James. He did not want to give the boy any reason to distance himself further from Stuart, from everyone.

James was being eaten alive by computers, by the Internet. Role-playing games, space battle games, chat rooms, and Stuart could only guess what else. James did not talk about it. He did not talk about much of anything, because he spent all his time there, slouched in the chair, head craned forward slightly. For the last two years, Stuart had watched his son crawl inside himself and shut everyone out. The only people he communicated with regularly were the ones on the other side of that glowing monitor screen.

Stuart crossed the dining room, smiled as he put a hand on James's head and brushed it over the tiny, whiskerlike bristles of hair. "How come nobody told me you had brain surgery?" He knew it was the wrong thing to say before he finished saying it. It sounded sarcastic, in spite of his friendly tone, and reminded him of something his own father would have said. Stuart laughed to cover it up. He meant nothing by it, but knew James probably would read something into it.

James jerked his head away from Stuart's hand. He did not remove the headphones or take his eyes from the monitor. He wore a black T-shirt with Godzilla blowing a stream of radiation—not the computer-generated American Godzilla, but the original Japanese monster, the guy in the rubber suit.

Stuart pulled a chair over from the dining table and took a seat beside his son. James still did not look at him, or even acknowledge his presence. Stuart cleared his throat loudly, reached over and lifted the headphones off James's ears, put them on the desk. He smiled at the boy.

"Thought I'd say hi," he said.

"Hi." Still gazing at the screen.

"So. What's up with you lately?"

After a few long moments of moving the joystick back and forth quickly, James said, "Nothin'."

"Think you could play that later?"

"If I stop now, I have to start over." A quick glance at his dad. "Can't we do the father-son shit later?"

Stuart flinched, lifted a brow. He had never heard James swear before. Most surprising, and troubling, was not the word "shit," but the casual way in which James used it, as if he said it a thousand times a day and it no longer had any meaning to him.

Of course he does, he thought. *So did I at that age. But not when I was talking to my parents.*

Stuart reached over and pressed the button on the top edge of the keyboard that severed the Internet connection. "No, we're going to do the father-son shit now."

James slouched even farther in the chair. He let out an angry breath as he put the joystick on the desk.

"Do you talk to your mother that way?"

"Yeah. She doesn't notice 'cause she never listens to me. Besides, she talks that way all the time."

"How many times have I told you not to look to your mother as a good example? Of *anything.*"

"What do you care how I talk?" James asked quietly, staring at the dead screen.

Stuart leaned forward, elbows on his thighs, and whispered, "What's the matter, James? The last time you were here, you barely said a dozen words the whole time. And the time before that. Something's bothering you. I wish you'd tell me what it is."

James stared down at the keyboard. He folded his beefy arms across his chest and said nothing.

Stuart said, "Are you angry with me? Is it something I've done?"

Still nothing.

"You know, I can't apologize if I don't know what I've done." When James still did not respond, Stuart leaned back in the chair and sighed. "Okay, how's this. You tell me when you feel like it, as long as it's before you leave here and go back to your mother's, okay?"

James nodded once.

"Promise?"

Another nod.

"Where's Amelia?" he asked.

"She went out to get groceries for dinner."

"Okay. After dinner, we're going for a walk, so don't make any plans."

"But it's raining outside."

Stuart smiled. "That's why God made umbrellas."

When she got home, Amelia made fireman's stew, a favorite of Stuart's and James's. But they showed no enthusiasm as they seated themselves at the table to eat. James, of course, had to be pried away from the computer. It was a quiet dinner. Stuart tried to make conversation with James, but without success. So he and Amelia chatted quietly about their day in low monotones. She did not seem to be very talkative, either. Stuart ate little, picked at his food, and finally pushed the plate away half finished.

After dinner, Stuart managed to keep James away from the computer long enough to get him out of the house. Amelia asked where they were going and Stuart simply said, "For a walk." She looked at him with a worried expression, which he had little time to consider. James was already on his way to the front door, slipping on a black denim jacket—as if he wanted to get it over with and go back to whatever he was doing online.

Stuart grabbed two umbrellas from the brass stand in the foyer and handed one to James as they went out the door.

The rain had died down to a drizzle. Stuart turned right on the sidewalk and they walked along Lake Street.

"How's school?"

"It's school."

"Uh-huh. But how is it?"

"I thought I didn't have to talk about this until I was ready."

"Oh, no, that only applies to you telling me what's wrong. It doesn't cover talking about school. Or anything else, for that matter." Stuart felt a mild ache in his chest when he saw how tall James was. He was growing up fast. Growing up and in directions that took him increasingly further away from Stuart. "Are your grades okay? Are you being abused and molested by your teachers?"

A laugh slipped through James's tightly pressed lips.

"Ah, so there *is* a human being in there!" Stuart shouted.

James kept laughing, and hearing it made Stuart feel so good for a moment that he laughed with him, loudly. Their laughter upset a couple dogs, and the barking echoed up and down the street. "Doing any better in math?"

"Math sucks."

"You won't get any argument from me about that."

"And I'm not doing any better in it."

"Don't you have any friends who are good in math? Somebody who could help you?"

No response. Stuart had suspected as much.

"I'm lousy at it, but I'd be happy to help you," he said. "Amelia would, too, I'm sure. And chances are, she's better at math than I am."

They walked in silence for awhile, and when they started talking again, it was about things that did not matter. Movies, music, television, sports.

It occurred to Stuart how easy it was to bury real problems under shovelfuls of nonsense, trivia, and small talk. What bothered him most was that he did not know what problems they were burying. To the best of his knowledge, he had done nothing to anger or hurt his son, and yet he felt a nagging guilt, as if he had. Maybe it was just James's age. He was leaving his childhood and entering unfamiliar territory, uncertain of what was expected of him. When Stuart thought back to the beginning of his teenage years, he could unearth no pleasant memories. Maybe the best he could do was continue to let James know he was there for him and let the boy handle things his own way. But still, there was the gnawing sense that something was not right, that somewhere along the way his son had taken a wrong turn.

"What exactly do you do on the computer?" Stuart asked curiously. "You're on that thing a lot, you know."

"I know. I like it. I play games. Chat with people."

"People you know, or people you've met online?"

"Both."

"What kind of games do you play?"

"Quake. Doom. Void. All kinds. Online, I can play with other people from all over the world."

"Ever have any language problems?"

"No. Some of 'em don't speak English very well, but it don't matter while we're playing games."

"*Doesn't. Doesn't* matter." In the rainy darkness, Stuart could sense James rolling his eyes.

"Where're we going, anyway?" James said.

They had turned off Lake and started up a steep hill. James was already winded and when he spoke, his words were punctuated by gasps for breath.

"A new video game arcade just opened a couple blocks up," Stuart said. "I thought you might like to check it out. And I thought you could use a little exercise. You know, sitting at a computer all the time . . . that's not very healthy."

No response. Stuart had not expected one. James's sedentary lifestyle concerned him. He was not a big overeater, but his mother couldn't cook a healthy meal to save her life, and James's diet contained a lot of junk food. With no exercise, he would no doubt continue to gain weight. The unfamiliar territory he was entering—his teen years, high school, dating—would be even more hostile if James did not do something about his weight. Stuart knew that from first-hand experience.

They said little the rest of the way. James was too busy trying to catch his breath.

The arcade was called Game Zone, and they could see its glowing red and purple neon sign through the drizzle well before they reached it. The building seemed to be made mostly of glass. Inside, it was dimly lit and the darkness throbbed with multicolored light that oozed from the screens of video games lined up in row after row. The door stood open and a symphony of electronic bleeps and roars and explosions spilled out onto the street. Loud music pounded from speakers mounted overhead and clashed harshly with the sounds of the games. Everyone was forced to shout to be heard, raising the noise level even higher.

In spite of the fact that it was Wednesday, a school night, the arcade was crowded. The narrow aisles between rows of video games were clogged with teenagers. A snack bar in the back offered soft drinks, candy, hot dogs, and nachos.

"When did this place open?" James asked once he had caught his breath.

"About a week ago."

They went to a change machine and Stuart slid a five-dollar bill into the slot, put all twenty quarters into James's hand. "You lead the way," he shouted, then followed James into the shadowy mass of teenagers.

Stuart frowned at the sight of a few grown men here and there hunkering over the controls of video games. All of them appeared shady—unshaven, tattooed, in old clothes that looked unwashed—and Stuart hoped the management kept an eye on them.

James led him to a game with an unpronounceable name. Stuart did not bother to ask for clarification. He leaned his umbrella against the side of the game next to James's.

"You wanna play a game with me?" James asked.

"Maybe after I watch you play a game or two."

James dropped a couple quarters into the slot, gripped the triggered joystick with his right hand and spread the fingers of his left over a panel of four large buttons. His hands moved with great economy as he guided the muscular male figure in a metallic pseudomilitary uniform down a filthy alley littered with toppled garbage cans and overflowing Dumpsters, graffiti on the filthy brick walls. As the game character walked, villainous street scum dropped from fire escapes and appeared from behind Dumpsters to attack him. With James's pudgy hands and fingers to guide him, he fought them off using his fists, feet, and knives. It was a gory game. Blood splattered the walls of the alley, and the killing machine controlled by James did not just dispose of his assailants, but dismembered them as well. It was enough to make Stuart wince.

He leaned toward James and shouted, "I'm going to get something to drink. Want anything?"

James shook his head once, but never took his eyes from the game.

Stuart shouldered his way up the crowded aisle. He stood taller than most of the others. Ahead of him lay a narrow stream of heads and caps, none of which held still for more than a second or two at a time. He was not fond of crowds or loud music and felt a twinge of claustrophobia as he made his way to the snack bar. He tossed a look back over his shoulder.

Each game was occupied by more than one person. Girls stood by and watched their boyfriends play, friends played each other. James was the only one who stood alone, attention riveted to the screen.

James was always alone, and it worried Stuart. It was hard to make friends when all you did was stay inside and sit at a computer. But it appeared he did not even have friends at school. Stuart had been overweight at that age, but he had not been a loner. He'd hung out with other outcasts. A fat girl, a stutterer, an effeminate skinny guy. They still exchanged Christmas cards every year. But James appeared to have no one.

Working the snack bar was a paunchy, bearded man in his midforties with dark hair pulled back into a ponytail. Wiry strands of silver kinked wildly over his ears. The man smiled, nodded.

"A cup of coffee?" Stuart said.

"We don't sell coffee," the man replied. "Damned kids spill it all over each other, then we gotta lawsuit, which I need like I need a case a leprosy. But I got a pot on in the back. I'll getcha some."

The man returned a moment later and handed over the counter a waxed-paper cup with a lid on top. When Stuart reached into his pocket to pay, the man shook his head.

"Nah, take it. On the house."

A favor from one middle-aged guy to another, both drowning in a sea of youth.

"Thanks." Stuart peeled back the perforated wedge in the plastic lid. "Are you the owner?" he asked the man behind the counter.

Half the man's mouth turned upward and he said, "Owner, janitor, chief cook, and bottle washer. You bring your kid?"

Stuart nodded. "My son. He lives for these games."

"Don't they all?"

"Thanks again."

"Just be careful with it, okay?"

With the cup of coffee in his right hand, Stuart turned back to the landscape of bobbing, swaying heads. His eyes settled on one head in particular, and his heart skipped a beat.

The oblong head stood well above the others, a few inches higher than Stuart's. Bald and pale and veiny. A stethoscope hung around the skinny neck and drew attention to the large, pointy Adam's apple in the throat. Small round glasses framed the deepset eyes, which looked directly at Stuart.

The arcade's darkness shimmered with light of all colors from the video game screens. The colors moved over Dr. Furgeson's long, narrow face, oozed into the valleys beneath his pronounced cheekbones, danced on the lenses of his small round glasses. He was grinning, as if he had been standing there watching Stuart all along, waiting for him to turn around. His oversized teeth appeared in that light to be a smoky gray.

The music became garbled and warped in Stuart's ears and the voices struggling to be heard in the dark arcade sounded suddenly far away.

There was a break in the crowd between them, and Stuart saw that Dr. Furgeson wore a long white coat. Right hand in the pocket, elbow slightly bent. The doctor removed his hand, held it up beside his grinning face. The silver scissors flashed with the dull reflection of a spinning red light atop a nearby video game.

Stuart could no longer breathe. His mouth hung loosely open.

Dr. Furgeson slowly tipped his head and turned it to the right, as if to reveal his ear to Stuart. It was an exaggerated movement, the gesture of a clown silently telling a child to listen.

Snick-snick-snick. Snick-snick-snick.

The small, sharp sounds cut through the underwater gargle of music and technology. A frozen-hot pain shot into the head of Stuart's penis and he pressed his free hand over his groin reflexively, closed his mouth so hard his teeth clacked together. The pain, which had never really been there in the first place, disappeared instantly, but Stuart's hand remained over his fly. He heard a low grunting sound and realized it came from him. Then another sound, from another source. It sounded like sandpaper being jerked spastically over the surface of a chalkboard. It was the sound of Dr. Furgeson laughing. At him.

The man at the snack bar was saying something to him. It sounded far away, like a fading memory.

"Hey. Hey, buddy. Somethin' wrong?"

Dr. Furgeson held his head up now, and his smile was gone. Lips together, his mouth took on the appearance of a simian muzzle over his prominent teeth. He turned and moved into the crowd, away from Stuart. He carefully stepped around a girl with tiny rings and studs in her pierced eyebrows and a squat, long-haired boy who had a silver ring in his right nostril. Dr. Furgeson moved between two of a group of three boys who were laughing at something. He disappeared around a brightly colored machine filled with small stuffed animals, and down one of the narrow, crowded aisles.

The pounding music, young laughter, and electronic sounds of the video games became loud and immediate again in a sudden rush, as if Stuart had just stepped into the arcade from outside.

"Uh, hey!" the guy at the snack bar called. "You okay?"

Stuart heard him, but did not move or respond. He took his hand away from his crotch, watched the top of Dr. Furgeson's bald white head, which was visible over the tops of the video games. Realization was a fist in the gut and his lungs emptied, knees weakened.

"James," he croaked dryly.

"Whatsamatter?" the guy asked at the snack bar behind him. He sounded irritated now.

Stuart bolted into the crowd clumsily, slammed into a short, pudgy boy of about fifteen. He heard the boy curse, but ignored it, moved on, pressed through the crowd. Teenagers shouted at him, closed in on him. A foot hooked his shin and tried to trip him. Someone clutched his right elbow and tried to hold him, but he jerked his arm away. The cup of coffee almost slipped from his hand. He clutched it to keep from dropping it, and the lid popped off. Hot coffee sloshed from the cup and a high, shrill scream of pain erupted in Stuart's right ear from the girl with the pierced eyebrows. Coffee had splashed over her face and chest. He pulled away from the sound with clenched teeth, nearly tripped, and fell against someone—a large, broad-shouldered teenage boy, nearly as tall as Stuart. Some football coach's favorite student, no doubt, with buzzed hair and a granite jaw, and enraged eyes.

"What the fuck's your problem, dude?" the boy asked.

The girl was still screaming in pain, and the man from the snack bar shouted angrily at Stuart, his voice getting nearer. Stuart turned from the football player and pressed on between two rows of video games. He could not see Dr. Furgeson ahead of him, but neither could he see James.

"Goddammit, what did I tell ya?" the man from the snack bar shouted. "Hey, come back here! I'm not payin' for this!"

The girl's screams had dissolved into sobs and wails.

Heads turned to him and people began to move aside, get out of his way. Eyes followed him, some mocking, some angry, others afraid. The arcade had become oddly quiet. Music still played, the games still made their sounds, but the loud voices had dropped to a low mumble.

By the time he reached the game James had been playing, Stuart was winded. Not from exhaustion, but fear. His umbrella still stood against the side of the machine. James's umbrella was gone. The game had not been played through. It was waiting to start another round.

"James!" he shouted, looking around frantically.

The proprietor was still shouting at him.

A hand clutched his shoulder, spun Stuart around and slammed him against the machine. It was the boy with the silver ring in his nose, lips pulled back, eyes on fire. The sides of his head were shaved clean, with long, floppy hair on top, dyed black.

"The fuck you think you're goin', asshole?" the boy asked angrily. "You just spilled hot coffee all over my fuckin' girlfriend! I'm callin' the cops." He turned his head and shouted to no one in particular, "Somebody call the cops!"

"Hey, hey, c'mon now," the owner said. "Let's just everybody calm the hell down, okay?"

Stuart barely understood what they were saying and pushed away from the machine. He could think of nothing but finding James. He called his son's name again, louder this time, as he walked away from the pissed-off haircut.

Hands grabbed his shoulders from behind, pulled him back.

Without giving it a thought, Stuart threw himself backward hard into one of the machines. The boy cried out in surprise and pain, but only gripped Stuart's shoulders harder. Stuart swung his right elbow back, felt it connect solidly with the boy's rib cage. The boy grunted, let go, and Stuart hurried away, calling, "James? *James!*"

"Goddammit, come back here!" the owner shouted. Then, over his shoulder, he bellowed, "Hey, Petey, call the cops!"

The girl with the pierced eyebrows continued to wail and blubber.

Stuart spun around, faced the owner. He spoke in a hoarse, tremulous voice. "My son, he's gone. He was just here. Playing that game, right there. The bald man." His eyes scanned the faces staring at him. "Did any of you see the bald man? With the little glasses? Did anybody see him with my son? Scissors, he had a pair of scissors, he was standing right over there—" He pointed past the faces. "—holding up a pair of scissors."

The voices fell silent. Eyes burned him from all directions. Several kids stood up on the fronts of video games to see Stuart over the tops of the other machines.

The owner waved an arm angrily and shouted, "Get down from there, goddammit, you know how much them things cost? You probly won't make in your *life* what one of them costs." When he turned to Stuart again, his expression softened and he stepped forward cautiously. "Look, buddy, I'm sure your kid's around here someplace. He's prob'ly in the bathroom. You wanna go check?"

Stuart knew James would hold his water until he played a game through. Words bottlenecked in his throat. He spun around, eyes searching, searching. He looked over heads to the front windows, at the night outside. It was raining hard again. "*Jaaames!*" he shouted.

A hand came to rest on his shoulder and beside him, the owner said, "C'mon, buddy, we'll find your kid. But you poured scalding hot coffee all over that girl back there and she's—"

"He's gone," Stuart said with a note of finality. He was

certain Dr. Furgeson had taken James out of the arcade. He jerked his shoulder from the owner's hand and plunged through the crowd, roughly knocked teenagers aside, then pushed through the glass door into the chilly rain.

The owner shouted angrily after him, but Stuart did not hear him.

CHAPTER FIVE

There was no sign of James or Dr. Furgeson outside the arcade. Stuart looked in all directions. It was raining again, hard enough to make it difficult to see very far with any clarity, but the sidewalks were empty in both directions, on both sides of the street. Nothing there but evenly spaced pools of illumination cast by streetlights. He had left his umbrella inside, leaning against the video game James had been playing. His hair was soaked flat against his skull in seconds.

"James?" he called, walking hurriedly back the way he and James had come. His voice reverberated up and down the street. He called again, and again.

There were sounds of activity behind him. Voices, footsteps on the wet concrete. Stuart ignored it, until someone said, just loud enough for him to hear, "There he goes!"

Stuart was too busy with other thoughts to care—thoughts of James with Dr. Furgeson, of what the doctor might do to his son with those sharp, shiny scissors.

As he broke into a jog, the phantom pain stabbed through the head of his penis for an instant. It was only a memory, really, not an actual pain—the memory of what Dr. Furgeson had done to him. A stray thought occurred to him, bounced through his head like a rubber ball on its way downhill: *Who will hold James down?* It was followed by a nightmarish image: His mother standing over James in the doctor's examination room, hands on his shoulders, pressing him down as she smiles and says, *I did this with your father when he was just a little boy.*

Running down the hill, he realized James had not had

enough time to go back the way they had come and already be out of sight. It was a straight shot to Lake Street, and Stuart could see no one ahead of him on either side. He would recognize James in spite of the poor visibility, his walk, his shape. He would recognize Dr. Furgeson, too. But he saw no one on the sidewalk or in the street.

He slowed his pace and looked down a dark alley between a laundromat and a closed furniture store. The alley dead-ended and was too dark to see anything in the narrow space between the buildings, so he stopped, went to the mouth of the alley. He took a few steps into the blackness.

"James? Are you there?"

Nothing. Not a sound, other than the pouring rain.

Suddenly, Stuart heard footsteps rushing up behind him and he started to turn, but not quickly enough.

Stuart recognized the voice of the boy with the nose ring: "Son of a bitch." He drove his fist into Stuart's left kidney. Pain exploded at the point of impact and shattered through his back and abdomen. Stuart continued to turn as he fell away from the boy and saw two others with him. One of them was the short, pudgy boy he had run into earlier. The other was the beefy football player.

No time to wait for the pain to go away, they were coming fast, close together, silent. Stuart spun his body to the left, shot his right leg out, and kicked Nose Ring in the stomach. He dropped like a bag of groceries to the ground.

As Stuart kicked, the football player moved in, a broad, slightly hunched sillhouette that quickly swallowed up the glow from the streetlights beyond the alley. Stuart stepped forward to meet him with an extended right arm, elbow locked, fingers straight and rigid. Unable to see the boy clearly, his aim was off. His fingertips knicked the boy's chin before stabbing into his throat. It was effective, nonetheless. The football player made a miserable gagging sound and fell away, knocked a garbage can over and sent its contents across the alley.

The short, pudgy boy took three quick steps backward, then turned and ran. Stuart ran after him. The boy turned right, Stuart to the left. In the black alley behind him, Nose Ring vomited noisily while the football player gagged and wheezed. The garbage can still rolled over the gritty pavement.

The slap of Stuart's walking shoes echoed abruptly, almost as if someone were chasing him, keeping rhythm with his steps. But when he looked over his shoulder, there was no one there. No one but a couple backlit figures standing at the top of the hill, watching him run.

"James!" he shouted. As usual, he expected no answer from his son. His gut told him James was gone. But he kept calling his name, anyway. Dogs barked at his voice and heads appeared in windows.

In his mind, as he ran, the scissors kept time with him. *Snick-snick snick-snick snick-snick* . . .

All the way home.

He went up the concrete stairs two at a time, slammed into his front door. It was locked. It was always locked. As he fumbled in the pockets of his trenchcoat, he realized he was still calling for James. His fingers found the keys in his right pocket, removed them, promptly dropped them. He bent over to retrieve them as the front door opened.

"My God, Stuart!" Amelia said, eyes wide. "What are you doing out here? Are you drunk?" She wore peach sweats and moccasin slippers and carried the *TV Guide* in her left hand.

"James," he said as he pushed her aside and stumbled into the house. Dripping on the floor, he went down the hall, saw James through the doorway. He was seated at the computer, but turned his head and looked over his shoulder, lips parted and eyes round as he stared at his father.

Stuart ran into the dining room, clutched James's upper arms, pulled him out of the chair to his feet, and threw his arms around the boy.

"My God, James!" he shouted, crushing his son to him. "Dammit, where the hell did you go? You scared the shit out of me!" He released his hold on James, moved back, but held his arms. He lowered his voice, nearly whispered. "Did he talk to you? Did he touch you, James?"

The boy glared at Stuart, struggled against his grip. "Let go of me!" James cried as he broke free. "Did who touch me? Jeez, what the fuck is wrong with you?" His face quickly turned a dark red as he screamed the last three words at the top of his lungs.

"What is going on?" Amelia asked, her voice getting louder with each word. She had a palm pressed to each ear and her face was screwed into a tense grimace.

"The bald man in the arcade, the doctor," Stuart said. "He had on a long white coat and there was a stethoscope around—"

James flopped back into the chair and laughed. Nothing on his face coincided with the laughter. It came through a dropped-open mouth and was not reflected in his wounded brown eyes. "You really *are* crazy," he said. His eyes glistened with tears. "Mom says it all the time, but I've never believed her, not really. She's right, though, you're crazy, you're out of your fucking—"

Stuart's flat palm connected with James's round cheek with a loud smack.

Amelia gave a surprised yelp, then: "Stuart!" she said. "What are you—"

He held up a hand, palm out. "Not now, Amelia," he said.

She froze and their eyes locked. After a moment, Amelia backed away—physically and, somehow, inwardly. He saw it in her eyes.

"Answer my question, James," he said.

James shouted unsteadily, "There was no bald man!" He stood so fast, he knocked the chair back against the desk as a single tear rolled down his cheek. "There was no fucking doctor!"

"There *was* a doctor!" Stuart shouted. "He was there, I saw him."

Even louder, James said, "Well, I didn't see him. I was too busy watching you act like a crackhead!"

"If you didn't see him, then why did you leave?"

"Because you were acting fucking crazy!"

Amelia held out her hands, palms down, and bobbed them slowly in the air as she said in a low, almost threatening voice, teeth clenched, "Will you please . . . stop . . . shouting."

Her eyes moved back and forth between them as they stared at one another. After a long silence, Stuart quietly spoke again.

"What did you see, James?"

"You," the boy said. Quietly, but with an underlying rage in his voice. "I decided I wanted a Pepsi, so I left the game for a minute to tell you. I saw you standing by the snack bar." His upper lip curled back in a sneer. "Playing with yourself. Grabbing at your dick. I went back to the game and thought about leaving. I didn't want to be seen with you. Then, when I heard a scream, I just *knew* it was because of something you were doing. So I left. I went a block over so you wouldn't see me and walked back here."

Stuart's eyes widened and his neck became hot. He knew he was blushing, but could do nothing about it. How could he explain himself? "I wasn't . . . I-I wasn't *playing* with myself. I was . . . I saw him in there. He turned around and headed straight for you. Then when I couldn't find you, I was . . . afraid." Suddenly, he felt exhausted, drained, and moved slowly to the dining table. He pulled out a chair and dropped into it.

Amelia stood across the table from him, leaned forward and pressed her hands to the tabletop. She looked angry, confused, and a little afraid. "Who are you talking about, Stu?" she said. "What happened?"

Stuart did not doubt what he had seen in the Game Zone, but knew how he would sound if he tried to explain. It would make no sense to either of them. He was not sure it made sense to him, but that did not change what he had seen.

He stood, ran a hand back through his wet hair.

James left the room.

"What's going on, Stu?" Amelia asked.

"It's . . . I don't know, it's . . . I can't explain it. Let's just drop it, okay?"

"I can't drop it. Something's been wrong for awhile now, and I don't think it's just work. You're a million miles away most of the time, and you hardly ever talk to me about—"

"Just drop it!" he shouted, and regretted it immediately.

Amelia flinched, stared over the table at him with large, hurt eyes.

Stuart sighed. "I'm sorry, sweetheart, I just can't—"

She stood and hurried out of the dining room.

A surge of anger passed through him, and for a moment, he wanted to pick up something and throw it, break it, stomp on its pieces. "Screw it," he muttered, before going out to the garage to see if he could get any work done.

CHAPTER SIX

Stuart went to work the next morning after only an hour or so of dozing. He'd nodded off on the sofa in front of the television after spending the night painting in the garage. He had not gone to bed because he was afraid he would see Dr. Furgeson again in his sleep. He also feared he might see him again while awake. He was unable to shake the incident in the video game arcade the night before in spite of his efforts to bury it with work.

It was utterly useless work, he had known that from the beginning, nothing he could ever show to anyone, not even Amelia. The paintings were for him alone. But it was work he had to do, was compelled to do. It was fueled by dreams he'd been having for months—not the dream about Dr. Furgeson, but others—by the images that burned in his head until he put them on canvas. The dreams had gotten him to pick up his brush for the first time in years, that was something. And the paintings had restored some of his confidence in his abilities as an artist, in himself.

In an odd sort of way, the paintings were a private joke, a secret thumbing of his nose to Carnival Greetings. Each painting was darker and more ominous than the last. They took on more depth as he went along, and the figure that occupied them became more imposing in each painting. It was a figure that had gone through many changes over the years—from heroic to whimsical to brooding, from tall and muscular to short and fat, and back to tall and muscular.

Stuart had changed as well. He had started working out,

getting in shape. The roll of fat around his waist had melted away. Muscles became etched into his arms and legs and chest, his abdomen became flat and firm. Martial arts classes had given him coordination and speed he had never before possessed. He had a new body that was still improving. He told himself he simply wanted to get into shape, but there was something more to it, something that compelled him to improve his physique.

He had changed inside, too. That had taken longer, had been more gradual. And it had not been for the better. Once, he had been in love with painting, had bubbled with confidence in his abilities as an artist, a husband, and a father. But Molly's infidelities had beaten him down, each one a crushing blow more difficult to recover from than the last. By the time his marriage began to collapse beneath Molly's restlessness and dissatisfaction, a cold distance had grown between Stuart and the work he loved. He'd enjoyed working at Carnival back then, but the drawing and painting he did there was empty compared to his own—junk food that left him hungry for real nourishment. The only bright spot in his life was his relationship with James. As a youngster, James had adored him. Stuart spent every spare moment with his son. They drew and colored with crayons and painted together, went for long walks, laughed at cartoons on television together. Although she never said so directly, Molly seemed to resent Stuart's close relationship with James. But she made no attempt to grow any closer to the boy herself. As he got older, James grew inward, and a wall was slowly built between him and Stuart. When Stuart and Molly divorced, he was unable to spend as much time with James as before. As hard as Stuart tried to keep it from happening, they had gradually grown apart.

Now, James seemed to think he was crazy. Amelia had taken him to school that morning in the car. The house had been very quiet as Stuart got ready for work. Neither of them had spoken to him until he was about to leave the house, then Amelia had said quietly, "We really need to have a talk this evening."

"About what?"

"About everything."

She had not sounded angry, but then, Amelia never did. She did not get angry, only quiet and hurt.

His relationship with Amelia was the only solid thing in his life now, especially since things had fallen apart at Carnival. But he felt it gradually slipping as well. That frightened him. He would talk with Amelia that night. Most importantly, he would listen.

Unable to focus on his work, Stuart stood and went to a mirror mounted on the wall of his cubicle. It was a car's rearview mirror he had picked up at a yard sale one Sunday out with Amelia. He stood at the mirror, looked at his reflection. His face was drawn, with puffy gray crescents beneath his eyes. He barely had gotten through his workout that morning. He had a kick-boxing class that night after work, but if he felt then the way he felt now, he doubted he would make it. Some sleep would help, but there was the nightmare. He did not look forward to living through that experience with Dr. Furgeson again, even if only in a dream.

At his drawing table, he went back to work on the spaceship he was drawing. When he was finished with it, the spaceship would be landing on the surface of the moon beside two green bug-eyed aliens in party hats, one holding a cake, all against star-sprinkled blackness. It was to be a birthday card for preschoolers—simple lines, bright colors. Nothing complicated or challenging. It was shit work, empty and dismal and mind-numbing. But it was among the better assignments he had gotten lately.

Stuart came to a sudden, nonsequitur decision. It entered his head with the inappropriateness of a machete. He decided to go see his mother. He had a few questions for her.

"If you're sick, you should be home in bed," Betty Mullond whispered.

Unaware he was whispering, too, Stuart said, "I didn't say I was sick, Mom, I said—"

"Oh, you look horrible, Stuart. Would you like to lie down?"

Stuart's whispering voice became tense. "I'm fine, Mother, I'm not sick."

"You look sick. Do you take any of the vitamins I give you, Stuart? Those are very good multiple vitamins," she whispered with a confident nod of her head. "Elvita Baker told me about those, and since I started taking them—"

"Mother, I'm not sick." He strained to keep his voice low. "I just said I was sick at work so I could leave."

Her shoulders sagged with disappointment and she tipped her head to the right. "Oh, Stuart, you shouldn't do that. That's lying."

He rolled his eyes behind closed lids. He could have spoken the words along with her, even a beat ahead of her, because he had known exactly what she would say before he finished speaking. He could have spoken it with precisely the same weary, moral sadness as she, had she been speaking aloud. But she was still whispering.

"Why are we whispering?" he asked in his normal voice, irritated.

They stood in the small foyer of Betty Mullond's cottage-like house on Duprey Street in Redwood City. Stuart was enveloped by the strong, cloying odor from the containers of potpourri his mother kept scattered throughout the small house. She was playing one of her cassette tapes of what Stuart had always called simply "church music"—dirgelike hymns played on piano or organ or both, sometimes with mournful vocals that sang of blood and crucifixion and an abandoned tomb. She wore a gray and blue dress and her silver hair looked newly coiffed. At seventy-four, she was pear-shaped but in good health, and as always, the smile almost never left her round face.

"I have company," she whispered. "I'm on the recreation committee at church and we're having a meeting. We're planning a trip to Marine World for the spring, and we—"

"Could we talk for a few minutes?" Stuart stepped around her to go into the house, but she put a hand on his arm and leaned toward him.

"Oh, please don't say anything about lying at work," she whispered.

"Say anything to who?"

"Sh-shh. To the girls." She took his elbow and led him through the living room, past the stereo playing "Bringing in the Sheaves."

The house was immaculate, as always. Never a thing out of place, nor a trace of dust anywhere. And yet she never stopped cleaning, never stopped moving through the house doing what appeared to be housework, cleaning up, even though there was never anything to clean up, never anything to put away. She had been widowed a decade ago and there was no one else around to make any messes. The worst it got was when her cat, Jester, shed during the summer or burped up the occasional hair ball on the carpet. She went through all the motions repeatedly, regularly, every day, with as much vigor as ever, as if she were afraid that if she stood still too long, she would disappear.

"Where are they?" Stuart asked.

"In the kitchen."

Stuart stopped walking and pulled his arm from her. "Well, if they're in the kitchen, why are you *taking* me to the kitchen?"

"They'll want to see you," she whispered, as if it were obvious. "I'm sure they've heard you by now, so—"

He lowered his voice a bit, but did not whisper. "I don't want to see them, Mom."

Her gray eyebrows rose above her large glasses. "What will they think if you don't—"

"I don't care what they think, Mother. I didn't come here to see them, I came to see you." Against his will, his voice grew loud, words became clipped and sharp and tense. It was a part of himself he hated, over which he had no control. The change in his behavior was automatic and quick. Frustration became anger, and the anger stiffened his posture, made his voice louder, made him bark words at the little old woman like a drill sergeant. He always felt bad about it later and apologized to his mother. This time, Stuart was determined to keep it from going that far.

He drew in a deep breath, let it out slowly as he massaged a closed eye with two fingertips. "Look, Mom, I just want to ask you a couple questions, that's all," he said quietly. Gestured toward the sofa. "Can we sit down?"

"You go ahead, sweetie, I'll be right back." She spoke over her shoulder as she went on into the kitchen.

Stuart took a seat at the nearest end of the sofa. He knew his mother would be giving The Girls some long, rambling explanation for why she needed to step out of the kitchen for a few minutes. It probably smelled of lavender and rosewater in there. That, and something else, an aroma that sneaked around amid the treacly smell of potpourri. His eyelids lowered and nostrils flared as he inhaled the smell of his childhood. His mother had made cookies. Judging by the strength of the aroma, he guessed they were still warm.

When she returned, his mother handed him a yellow paper napkin with four warm cookies stacked on it.

"Lucky you came today," she said, still whispering. "I made your favorite. Macadamia chocolate chip." She lowered herself to the sofa beside him. Her movements were not as quick as they once were—she used to move around as if she were fleeing a housefire. Now she moved carefully, slowly, and her joints popped now and then.

Stuart bit into one of the cookies and closed his eyes. He hadn't had his mother's macadamia chocolate-chip cookies in years. They were still delicious, and he told her so. He was halfway through his second cookie when he remembered why he had come.

"Do you remember Dr. Furgeson, Mom?"

Her slightly magnified eyes squinted behind the large glasses. "The urologist?"

"Yeah. The one who took a pair of scissors to my penis. Remember him?"

She clicked her tongue and sighed, rolled her head back in a half circle. "Stuart, honey, that's not what happened."

Whenever the subject had come up in years past, Stuart's mother always insisted the doctor had performed the procedure quickly and painlessly with a scalpel. Of course, his mother's memory was hazy on a lot of things, particularly bad things. She remembered unpleasant things very pleasantly. It was the Mullond way, always had been.

"Look, I don't want to argue about it," Stuart said. "I just want to know what he's up to. I went by his office building before I came here. His name isn't on the sign anymore."

"Oh, I'm sure he's retired by now."

"Do you know if he's still in the area?"

She shrugged. "I couldn't tell you. Why? What's wrong?" Her wrinkled face darkened with concern and she leaned close to him, put a hand over his. "Is your prostate okay?"

"My prostate?"

His voice rose on the word and she stiffened, winced as she glanced toward the kitchen doorway. "Ssshh, Stuart, please. They'll hear you."

He gestured toward the small tape player on a shelf above the television and said, "Not over that, they won't." He stood and went to the player, turned it off. "I'm sorry, Mom, but I just can't think with that stuff playing."

When he returned to the sofa, she looked hurt, as if he

had said something personally insulting. "You used to *sing* that stuff when you were a boy," she said quietly. "And very beautifully, too."

Stuart had spent his entire adult life so far trying to forget his boyhood and teen years. It was all his mother could think about.

She smiled. "You were the youngest member of the church choir. Mr. Hinkle thought you were an outstanding tenor. He said you—"

"Mom, Mr. Hinkle was an asshole."

The profanity made her gasp. "But I thought you liked Phil Hinkle."

"I couldn't *stand* Phil Hinkle." His voice dropped. "He was always making fat jokes about me."

"You never told me about it!" She looked hurt.

"Mother, I've told you a dozen times or more."

"But not then, when it happened."

"What would you have done? You wouldn't have done anything."

"Well . . . your dad probably would have."

"Oh, yeah. He probably would've gone over to Hinkle's house in the middle of the night and hit him in the face with a shovel, or something. That would have made me real popular."

"If you didn't like him, why did you stay in the church choir?"

"Because Miss Tanner—remember her, the redheaded woman who used to run the Sunday school nursery?—sat right next to me in choir practice, and she had the biggest breasts I'd ever seen in my life."

His mother leaned back in the sofa and groaned, face twisted with disgust. She reacted as if he had just stood, turned his back to her, dropped his pants, bent over and exposed his anus.

"Those pews we sat in were so crowded," he continued

with a gentle smile, "sometimes we were bunched together and one of them would press against me."

"*Stuart!* I'm going to wash your mouth out with soap!"

"And it made you so happy, Mom. I stayed in the choir because I thought you wanted me to."

"Well, you can't blame me."

"I'm not blaming you, I just wanted—"

"You should have said something. It's your own fault."

It was always his own fault. Stuart's parents had never made a mistake in their lives. That was the way they had always behaved, anyway, the attitude they had maintained. He had never known them to apologize to anyone for anything, ever, because as far as they were concerned, they did not make mistakes. There was always someone else to blame. He supposed that made them the perfect Christians—Jesus would not have to go to all the trouble of forgiving them for anything before letting them into Heaven.

"She died, you know," Betty Mullond said as she sat up straight again, gently patted her hair.

"Who died?"

"Miss Tanner."

Stuart felt a sharp pang in his chest.

"Must've been, oh . . . coming up now on four years ago," she added.

Deep creases lined his forehead. "How did she die?"

Her eyebrows rose. "Breast cancer. A shame, really."

"Was she married?"

She sniffed. "Never married."

Stuart leaned back into the sofa's fat, pillowy cushion and finished off another cookie. He put the remaining two on the end table to his right. Chewing, he muttered, "Miss Tanner. Breast cancer." Shook his head. "One of life's cruel ironies."

"What are you talking about, Stuart?" she asked suspiciously.

"What *were* we talking about, Mother? Before we skipped down memory lane."

She tilted her head back and sought the answer on the ceiling. "Let's see, now. . . ." Her head dropped again. "Oh, that's right—you were going to see Dr. Furgeson about your prostate."

Stuart put both hands over his face, massaged his temples with his thumbs. He was not sure when his head had started throbbing. "No, Mother, I'm not going to see Dr. Furgeson. If my prostate gland was on fire and Dr. Furgeson was the last doctor on the whole planet, I wouldn't go to him."

She clicked her tongue again, rocked slowly back and forth, shook her head. "That's not very nice, Stuart."

"Not very nice?" he snapped. As he continued to speak, his voice grew louder with momentum, and his mother raised a hand, palm out, and shook her head. "What do *you* think, Mother? I mean, Jesus Christ—"

"Oh, *ssshhh!*" she hissed. "Stuart, please—"

"—the son of a bitch took a pair of scissors to my penis—"

"—they'll hear, just, please, lower your voice, Stuart, *please*—"

"—while you held me down!" Stuart shot to his feet.

She pulled back as if he had taken a swing at her and gasped loudly, right hand flat against her chest. She stared at him silently as he paced, her mouth open wide.

He had stood because he could see the tears beginning in her eyes. They appeared whenever Betty Mullond found herself faced with more than a brief, passing glimpse of anything unpleasant or disquieting. But she would get over it quickly. Stuart knew if he mentioned this conversation to her next week, she would have no memory of it. It had nothing to do with the usual memory loss that accompanies age—she had been like that all Stuart's life. His dad had been exactly the same way. They remembered only what pleased them, or aided them, and the rest was rewritten or thrown out entirely.

He often wondered if that had been the only thing that held them together for so long—their common view of the world.

"Stuart, I was there only because I thought you wanted me there," she said, voice thick and quavering, nose sniffly. "You always said you were afraid of doctors, so I always went with you. You know, there are plenty of parents out there who stay in the waiting room while the doctor takes their little ones into the back to do whatever he wants with them, would you have preferred I do that?"

He flopped into the recliner that faced the television, leaned it back with a muted thump. Talking to his mother was always so exhausting. It drained him, aged him, made him feel like hugging her tightly until she stopped.

"I didn't come over here for this," he said with a sigh.

"Well, fine. What did you come over here for? You say that every time, you know. You come over here and start something, and then you say you didn't come over here for this. So what did you come over here for?"

Stuart felt so heavy, he feared he would never get out of the recliner. "I wanted to know if you knew anything about Dr. Furgeson."

She softened a bit. "Why?"

"Just curious."

"Well, why are you curious? Do you want to contact him, or something?" Her shoulders sagged and she seemed to shrink. "Oh, Stuart, you aren't going to do something dumb, are you?"

He lifted his head and frowned across the room at her. "What do you mean, *dumb*."

"Ssshh!" She glanced at the kitchen doorway. "I know how you can hold a grudge."

He blurted a single loud laugh as he sat up in the recliner. "Oh, yeah, I'm holding a grudge all right. For this guy? You bet. The son of a bitch showed up in my backyard the other night. Four thirty in the morning, he's outside the kitchen window with a pair of scissors. Yeah, he thinks he's real funny, the first stand-up urologist."

"Scissors? Why would he have scissors? I've told you, Stuart—how many times have I told you this?—he didn't use scissors. He used something that looked like a small scalpel. He wouldn't use scissors for something like that."

"Okay, okay, I'm not going to argue." He stood stiffly, stretched his arms with his fists behind his head, elbows jutting. "I just wondered if you knew anything about him."

"Well, I can find out for you. I'll make a couple calls this evening and let you know."

"Could you e-mail me?"

She stood, too, knowing he was on his way out. She pressed her hands between her breasts and hunched her shoulders slightly. "Oh, Stuart, I don't know what I'm going to do— that machine! No matter what I do, it's always wrong. I've been following the instructions, but no matter what I do, a little window pops up with a number on it, or it says I'm doing something illegal—what does that mean, illegal? Can I get in trouble for—"

"No, Mom, it doesn't mean that kind of illegal. I'll bring James over this week, he'll set you up and teach you in an hour more than I've learned in my whole life about computers."

"James is with you?"

They moved together slowly toward the front door.

"For a couple weeks," Stuart said. "Molly's out of town."

"Oh, I'd love to see James. I haven't seen him in ages."

Stuart heard the kitchen door open and turned to see The Girls spilling through the dining room and into the living room. Some of them looked familiar. He remembered their faces being much younger, before age had ripped them new ones. Half a dozen of them, all smiling and laughing as his mother introduced him. They moved in on him, hugged him in turn. Cool, perfumed, tissue-paperish skin shriveling around decaying muscles and fluid sacks of fat that swayed from brittle bones. "Oh, I remember you, don't think I don't!" one said. Another laughed as she shouted, "I used to kiss your little rear end when you weren't much bigger than a loaf of bread!"

Stuart sighed and relaxed a little. He decided to forget about leaving, for a little while, at least. His escape had been thwarted. But he found comfort in his mother's macadamia chocolate-chip cookies.

CHAPTER SEVEN

"How would you like to go to the movies?"

"What? Now?"

"Sure. I found a theater showing a couple Abbott and Costello movies this afternoon. I've got just enough time to pick up James at school, and I thought you could meet us there."

"Where are you?"

"A pay phone."

"Why aren't you at work?"

"Because I left. They said I looked sick, so I said I was, and then I left. So, do we have a date, or what?"

Amelia was silent for a moment. "Stu, are you all right?"

He laughed. "No, not really. I went over to Mom's today."

"Today? How long ago did you leave work?"

"Oh, I don't know, who cares."

She sighed. "Why did you go over there, Stu?"

"I had to ask her about something. But, of course, it took forever to pry the information out of her."

"Oh, honey, you've really got to go easy on your poor mother. I mean, you're the one with the education, you know what I mean? Can't you . . . I don't know, talk down for her, or something? She really loves you, you know. She doesn't know any better, that's just the way she is, and you've got to stop expecting her to change, because it'll never happen."

"My God, I call to ask you to the movies and I get a lecture."

Stuart did not sound angry. He sounded more defeated than anything else. But there was a dark undertone to his voice that made her uncomfortable. Depression? Repressed anger? Whatever it was, she did not like the sound of it.

"I'm sorry for lecturing," she said. "I didn't mean to. It's just that I feel bad for your mother sometimes. She has such good intentions."

"I know. And sometimes I hate myself for being so impatient with her. But . . . I don't know, I just can't help it."

"I don't think I'm in the mood for Abbott and Costello today. I want to finish the piece I'm working on by tomorrow, and I'm kind of behind." Amelia imposed deadlines on her work to keep herself from tinkering endlessly with one piece.

"Okay. I guess we'll be home in time for dinner. He may not want to go, either, I don't know yet."

He sounded so disappointed, and suddenly distant. She frowned and asked, "Are you sure you're okay, Stu? I can come if you really want me to, the piece isn't that important, really, that deadline's just so I won't—"

"No, no, I'm fine, really. Go ahead and work. I'll pick James up at school, see if he wants to go. If not, maybe I'll drag him through the Exploratorium. Haven't been there since James was knee-high."

After saying good-bye, Amelia left the messy room she called her studio and went to the kitchen. She put the cordless phone back on its base by the small TV on the bar and looked in the refrigerator for a quick, light lunch. She was not hungry—especially after talking with Stuart—but knew if she did not eat now, she would go back to work and forget all about it until she had a headache. She removed a plastic bowl of fruit salad with a white plastic fork taped to the lid, clicked on the radio, and ate while leaning back against the counter's edge.

She wished there was some way she could get Stuart and his mother to get along, but knew it would never happen. She had never met Stuart's father, but according to Molly, Betty Mullond was a light spring breeze compared to her late husband. Betty was frustrating, but she meant well. Delbert Mullond, by all accounts, had been nearly intolerable. He had died of prostate cancer about ten years ago.

"Yeah, but it wasn't just prostate cancer," Molly had told her one day over frozen yogurt in the Stonestown Galleria. "Remember, he was almost twenty years older than Betty. By the time the cancer got him at the tender age of eighty-two, he'd already had four heart attacks, three strokes, God knows how many operations on one thing or another, from his back to his testicles, and he used to fall off his house or out of trees once or twice a month. Eighty-one years old, this guy was, and he was still climbing up on the roof to work on the swamp cooler, or climbing trees in the backyard to prune them, or just to see what's going on in the neighbor's yard. Sober as a judge he couldn't walk a straight line on flat ground, but he climbed like a spider monkey."

"Well, bad health and falling out of trees are no excuse for abusing his family."

"Oh, yeah," Molly had said with a nod. "Sometimes I forget he was like that. See, when I met him, he'd already had two strokes and one heart attack. Stuart said he'd already changed a lot. And that's what changed him. All those strokes and heart attacks, I mean. That's what Stuart says, anyway. Before that, he says his dad was impossible to live with. Completely unpredictable. Wild mood swings, temper tantrums. He'd go into a rage over the smallest things and break something, or knock a hole into a door with his fist. Which he would then bitch about having to fix. Those strokes and heart attacks sedated the bear."

Amelia had nodded. "I've heard they can leave you very emotional, with everything right on the surface."

"Oh, yeah, Delbert used to cry at the drop of a hat. Especially when commercials for local convalescent hospitals came on television." Molly had laughed then. "He didn't raise his voice anymore, and he was always hugging everybody. But Stuart thought that was only half of it, that over-emotional aftereffect. He said the rest was fear. He figured Delbert was thinking about all the people he'd pissed off and treated like shit now that he was weak and vulnerable. Especially Stuart, who conceivably could have ended up taking care of him. And he wasn't that little kid anymore that Delbert used to blame for everything but the weather. He used to drag Stuart through the house by the hair, kicking him and calling him names. All of a sudden, the tables were turned, and Stuart thought that scared the shit out of Delbert. He hoped it did, anyway."

"Has Betty changed since he died?"

"Not a bit. She used to wait on him hand and foot, and not just when he was sick. All the time, from what I can tell, ever since they got married. Now she's got time to relax, do whatever she wants to do, but does she take advantage of it? Nope. All she does is housework and church stuff. Same as before. She's led such a sheltered life, she's probably afraid to try anything else. Something new in her routine would probably traumatize her. I think she's afraid of the whole world."

Amelia meant it when she'd said, "It's amazing Stuart turned out so normal."

Molly had barked a laugh. "Stuart? Normal? Honey, don't forget, Stuart's an artist. Artists aren't like normal people. You'll see." She'd grinned. "You just haven't lived with him long enough."

As much as Amelia liked her, she took everything Molly said about Stuart with a brick of salt. The divorce had been messy and ugly and a great deal of hostility remained between Stuart and Molly. They were often unsuccessful in their efforts to remain civil, and it was only for James's sake that they did not pounce on each other like professional wrestlers. Later, once James grew up and found his own life, Amelia imagined Stuart and Molly probably would pose quite a physical threat to one another if not kept apart.

Finished with the fruit salad, Amelia dropped the empty

plastic bowl and fork into the trash can and took a Diet Dr Pepper from the refrigerator.

She did not think Molly would ever lie to her about Stuart, but neither did she know to what extent Molly exaggerated the truth. Stuart and Molly talked about one another the way the nefarious villains of Gotham City spoke of Batman and Robin the Boy Wonder. Both remained bitter, and both shoveled it pretty deep on the topic of their marriage. One night a couple weeks ago, Amelia and Stuart had been lying in bed, an open book facedown on each of their chests, when the conversation somehow had landed on Molly, and Stuart had launched into a quiet but vicious rant about his ex-wife. Amelia listened, and listened. Sometimes, it became difficult to remember that he was talking about her friend, Molly. Amelia was well aware of her friend's faults, and there were plenty of them. But none of them made Molly the monster Stuart described.

"It's like she's got multiple personality disorder," he'd said. "One minute, she makes you feel like the most important person in the world. The next minute, she's making somebody else feel the same way. On a nightly basis. My God, she was disgusting. She probably humped the furniture when she was alone in the house. Jeez, it's a good thing we didn't have a dog."

"Stu, honey, do you ever listen to yourself when you talk about Molly?" She had turned to him on the bed, moved a bit closer.

"I know, I know," he'd said with a groan.

"No, I'm serious. Because maybe you're not hearing yourself the way I hear you, the way everybody hears you. Maybe you're not aware of how hateful you sound sometimes."

"Not aware of it? Are you kidding? I cultivate it."

"But I know you're a kind and loving person. You can't hate her that much. You just sound like you do."

"Well, I learned from the best. My dad."

Stuart was not alone with his problems. Molly was not

exactly a mental health role model, either. Her promiscuity alone, practiced joylessly and desperately throughout much of their aborted marriage, was a therapist's wet dream. And she was prone to depression.

"The depression I got from Stuart," she'd said. "He depressed the hell out of me. Which is why I had all my little adventures."

But the problem had been her own, not Stuart's, and they both knew it, just as Stuart knew he was not free of guilt. He was in no hurry to admit it, but he knew it. Amelia could see it in his eyes every time he apologized to her for something, any little thing at all. When he said, "I'm sorry,"— and normally, he did not hesitate to do so when he was wrong—his eyes looked desperate to go on, to keep apologizing, over and over, to her, to everyone, for everything.

She thought of the lock on the cabinet in the garage, wondered what Stuart was trying to hide from her.

Go take a look and find out, silly, Molly said with a laugh in Amelia's head.

It would feel like a betrayal of Stuart to sneak through his things. But the padlock felt like a betrayal to her. She was sure he would keep the key to the padlock somewhere in the garage. He knew as well as she did that if he took it out of the garage with him, he would set the key down in some obscure place and never be able to find it again, and would have to break into his own cabinet. It probably would not be very difficult to find.

Amelia sipped her Diet Dr Pepper, gave it some thought. She whistled along with a car dealership jingle on the radio.

If she could find the key, she decided to look in the cabinet. But without the key, she would give it up, forget all about it, because the only remaining option would be to break in. She would leave no sign that she had been there. If Stuart found out, he would be hurt, and Amelia would not be able to forgive herself.

She finished the soda and crushed the can in her fist,

dropped it into the recycle basket under the sink. She left the kitchen, went out to the garage, and looked for the key to the padlock. Amelia found it in under two minutes. It was in a small compartment in an old tackle box that stood open on the old card table, next to his painting supplies. The box was full of junk that might one day come in handy: paperclips and staples, a few spools of thread and a sewing needle, pens and pencils, erasers, tiny pencil sharpeners, a large pair of black-handled scissors, a roll of postage stamps, and in a rectangular compartment, beneath a pocketknife and a lifelike rubber lizard, was the small gold key she sought. She hoped.

Amelia went to the cabinet. The key slipped into the lock, turned. The heavy padlock opened with a sturdy click. She put it on the floor next to her and swung the accordian door open.

It was a large cabinet and covered a good portion of the garage's long outer wall. There were about twenty paintings inside, separated by large sheets of sturdy white paperboard. She went through them carefully, jaw slack.

She made a sound similar to a laugh, but much tighter and without any joy. Then she became silent as she stared, mouth still open. Her eyebrows slowly drew closer together just above the bridge of her nose.

Is this a joke? Amelia thought.

She wondered if Stuart were planning some kind of practical joke on someone at work. She could think of no other possible explanation. But she did not quite believe that, either. Surely he would not go to so much work for a mere practical joke. The paintings were too good. They were beautiful, unlike anything he had ever done before, and maybe the best work he had done so far.

But the paintings made absolutely no sense, individually or together, and Amelia was honest with herself about them: As beautiful as they were, they seemed obsessive and frightened her a little.

Her back slammed against the edge of the cabinet when the telephone chirped in the house. She quickly closed the cabinet and fumbled with the padlock. Her hands shook, as if she knew Stuart were in the hallway, bearing down on the half-open door, about to step in and catch her.

With the cabinet locked, Amelia hurried across the garage, up the steps. She pulled the door closed behind her and rushed down the hall, but stumbled to a halt, padlock key still in hand. The telephone continued its impatient trilling as she went back into the garage, replaced the key exactly as she found it.

The answering machine picked up.

Amelia was in the hall when the machine beeped. There was a lot of background noise coming from the other end of the line. Was Stuart calling from a pay phone again?

"Um, this is James. Just wanted you t'know I'm gonna come home a little later than usual. I'm s'posed to meet up with some friends after school. Prob'ly be gone a couple hours. I'll be home in time for dinner."

She picked up the phone the moment the connection was severed with a click and heard only a dial tone. She frowned at the answering machine as she punched the replay button, listened to the message again. But even the second time through, she could not concentrate on what James was saying. She could not get her mind off the astonishingly dark, vivid, richly textured paintings of Owl-Man, who was no longer a doodle.

CHAPTER EIGHT

Stuart was furious when he got home with James. He led James into the dining room, waved at one of the table's chairs and said firmly, "Sit down." He sat across from his son, tried to calm himself. He told himself he wasn't going to get carried away with this. It was the scare more than anything that had upset him. They had not spoken all the way home because Stuart had been too angry to speak. Now that he knew James was okay and the boy was with him, Stuart knew he should be able to handle the rest of it calmly. But he was not so sure he could.

Amelia came into the dining room, frowning. She stopped, darted her eyes back and forth between them.

"Would you rather I step out for this?" she asked.

"Oh, no, have a seat," Stuart said coldly. "This should be good for a laugh."

James released a loud, angry sigh.

Stuart folded his arms on the table, leaned forward. Quiet anger bubbled in his level voice. "Before you make that extremely irritating sound again, you're going to tell me where the hell you were all day, and why. And once you've answered all my questions to my satisfaction, you *still* won't make that irritating sound again, do you understand?"

Eyes on the tabletop, James nodded once.

"Okay. Where were you?"

James shrugged. "Out with friends."

"Instead of going to school."

Another nod.

"Can you tell me why?"

Another shrug. " 'Cause bein' out with friends is . . . more fun than bein' in school."

There was no sarcasm in the remark. It was an honest answer, and it almost made Stuart laugh. Some of the tension left his body and voice, but he remained edgy and very serious. "Okay, that was a stupid question. But fun isn't what we're talking about now. When you're in school, *most* things are more fun. But when you're past all that, later in life, you look back and wish you'd paid more attention, worked a little harder, showed up more often. Because without going to school, you end up not going to work. You end up washing dishes at Denny's the rest of your life. Or sitting on a bench somewhere with a cardboard sign that says, WILL WORK FOR FOOD. You want that?"

James released a weary but cautious sigh, still staring at the tabletop. He shook his head back and forth once.

"Look, I'm trying to be honest with you," Stuart said. "I'm not giving you the standard bull about how school builds character or that you get out of school whatever you put into it. Those might be true, but they're useless, pointless things to say. The hard cold fact is that school isn't fun for most people, and some never recover from it. But it's necessary. It's one of those things you have to do, and those who choose not to end up wishing they had. But that's only part of the problem here. You can't just run off and roam around the city without telling anybody whether you're going to be in school or not, or where you're going, or when you'll be back. I mean, if something happened to you, we'd have—"

"But nothin' happened, Dad."

"Something *could* have happened. If not this time, then maybe next time, or the time after that. How would we know where to find you? We'd have no way of knowing where you were, how to get to you. What were you thinking? I mean, I don't understand—how could you just—have you done this before?"

James sucked his lips between his teeth, still averting his

eyes. He clearly did not want to answer, but there was real anger in Stuart's voice, and finally, James nodded once.

Stuart stood and paced the length of the dining room. Small, explosive breaths came from his mouth. "I can't believe this! Does your mother know about this?"

A deep breath, a slow sigh, then James said in a hoarse, whispery voice, "School's called her a coupla times."

Stuart stopped pacing and turned large round eyes to James, then to Amelia. "Can you believe that?" he asked. Back to James. "What did she do?"

The boy shrugged. "Grounded me a coupla times." He fidgeted in his chair, clearly itching to stand and leave the room. "Look, I won't do it again, 'kay?"

Stuart laughed. "Is that what you told *her?*"

James bowed his head lower.

Stuart sat at the table again, and said quietly, "James, are you . . . are you really hearing me, here? I mean, do you understand why I'm so upset? Because, if not, maybe, I don't know, maybe I could explain it a little clearer."

James said nothing.

Softening his voice a bit, Stuart said, "I really want to know, James, I'm not just being a hard-ass. Do you understand why I'm so upset?"

James nodded.

"Now, you can't do this again. You *will not* do this again. If I have to, I'll go to school with you and stick to you like glue all day long."

That ought to put the fear of God in him, Stuart thought.

After waiting for James for about fifteen minutes in front of the school, Stuart had gone into the building to look for him. He'd asked a portly, unsmiling, middle-aged woman in the administrative office where he might find his son. She looked in an open folder before her, told him James had not come to school that day.

"What do you mean?" Stuart had asked.

"Didn't someone call you?"

"Call me? At home?"

"Yes, at home." She did not look up from the folder.

"I've been out all day."

"This is his second in a row." She looked up at him, her face a lumpy, drooping mask of abject boredom. "We always call the parents the day after an unexcused absence. If we don't hear from them first. This is his second in a row, so you should have gotten a call today."

"In a row? Two absences in a *row*?"

"Are you hard of hearing, sir?" Her hair was a synthetic auburn, or a shade meant to approximate auburn. It seemed frozen on her head, a curly, wavy helmet.

"No, no. Is it possible the school called his mother? My ex-wife? Because she's out of town."

"Would you like to speak to the assistant principal?"

Stuart had not known what he wanted, or whom to call, where to go. James was in school during the day. When he was not in school during the day he was . . . where? Where would he go?

His real fear, which he had not allowed to take shape in his own mind yet because he did not want to contemplate it, was that James had been taken—not by just anyone, but by Dr. Furgeson. Stuart wondered where someone like Furgeson would take someone like James to do what Stuart knew the doctor would do. Where would he go to do his work in peace?

That just opened the floodgate on all the other questions Stuart could not answer. Why was Dr. Furgeson doing this? How was he doing it? What possible reason could he have for going after James? Had Dr. Furgeson lost his mind? Had he developed some kind of psychotic fixation on that one ugly procedure, on Stuart's in particular? Insanity was the only explanation Stuart could imagine for Dr. Furgeson's apparent interest in James.

He called Amelia, who told him about James's message on the answering machine. Stuart told Amelia to call Molly's cell phone and ask if she had any idea where James might be. For the first time in his life, he wished he carried a cell phone. He'd had to wait in the administrative office for Amelia to call back, which she finally did with a few names, phone numbers, and addresses.

"Molly says to try the first number on that list first," she had said. "It's a friend of James's, or a couple friends who live together, or something, I'm not sure. Molly was talking so fast, I could barely understand her. Anyway, she says that's probably where he'll be."

"Jesus," Stuart barked, "does the cunt *know* he does this?"

The bored woman, seated at her desk behind the counter, said, "If you don't mind, sir, this is a school, not a Martin Scorsese film."

Stuart lowered the telephone from his ear and leaned as far as he could over the counter. "Oh, like they all don't talk that way already," he snapped.

The woman was overwhelmingly disinterested at her desk.

When the image of a smiling, cackling Dr. Furgeson rose up in his mind—holding scissors that went *snick-snick-snick*—a deep shudder moved through Stuart's body. It caught him off guard, surprised him. He was so angry at Molly and so worried about James, his hands shook as he put the telephone receiver to his ear again. He felt as if something deep inside the machinery of his mind was about to snap, then and there, causing the whole thing to shut down right there in the administrative office, right there in front of—he squinted his eyes slightly at the rectangular nameplate on the woman's desk—right there in front of Mrs. Edith Mandable. Stuart realized he was breathing too rapidly as his body tensed in anticipation of his entire life crashing down on him like the enormous, charred parts of an airliner that had exploded in midair. But it did not happen. He rubbed his eyes with thumb and fingertips, composed himself.

On the telephone, Amelia sounded tense when she said, "Bitch about Molly later and go find James now."

He had called the first number and was surprised when James himself answered.

"Where the hell are you, James?"

"Um, a-at a fr-friend's," he stammered nervously. "How could you, um . . . call me . . . if, um, you don't know—"

"We'll talk about it later," Stuart said. "Right now, I want you to go outside, to the street, in front of whatever building you're in, and wait for me to show up. You are not to move from—"

"Can't I wait inside and—"

"No! I want you in the rain and miserable when I get there. And if this address is where I think it is, you better hope to God I get to you before somebody else does."

Beneath his anger, Stuart's relief was enormous.

The address was exactly where Stuart had thought—in the Tenderloin. Strip joints and triple-X movie theaters, drag bars and crack houses. Winos and drug addicts trembled from withdrawal on the sidewalks, and small-time drug dealers lurked in the shadows. The shadows there were darker than those in the rest of the city, deeper and more liquid, better able to hide people, and things. It was a place where the word "homeless" was redundant. Whether they lived in the filthy, crime-ridden tenements, one of the old rat-infested hotels, or on the diseased streets below, they were all homeless. The Tenderloin was not a place that could be called "home" by anyone. It was a place you did not visit at night unless you were up to no good. Some of the city's ugliest news stories came out of the Tenderloin, stories of stabbings, shootings, and rapes. And his son had skipped school to spend the day there.

Stuart gave the cabdriver the address he had written down on a page of the school's stationery back in the office. He was driven into one of the city's darker, more treacherous urban forests and came to a stop on Turk Street at the curb. James stood on the sidewalk in the rain, umbrella up, shoulders hunched. Three faces had peered down at them from a third-floor window. One dark, one pale, and one somewhere in between. Their features were blurred by the rainy pane's filth.

Quietly, Amelia asked, "Where did you go, James? What were you doing all day?"

James put his elbows on the dining table and cracked his knuckles one at a time. "I dunno . . . y'know, like . . . well, y'know. . . ."

"Jesus Christ, stop!" Stuart shouted, wincing at the boy's stammering verbal pauses. He lowered his voice when he said, "My God, James, what's happening to you? What kind of people have you been running around with who talk like this?"

"Stuart," Amelia said cautiously, "that's not what we're talking about, is it?"

He waved a hand gently at her once, nodded his head, but did not take his eyes off James as he said, "Yeah, I know what you're saying, Amelia, and you're right. But in this case, I think it matters. Who *are* you running around with, James? I've just now realized that I don't know, and I *should* know, dammit."

"You never asked before," James said, raising his voice nearly to a shout. He put his arms under the table and hunched forward, as if he were trying to hide.

Anger flared in Stuart's chest, but dissipated almost immediately. James was right. Stuart had been making no effort to stay up to date on his son's life. He nodded and said, "Yeah, I can't argue with you there, James. You're right, I haven't asked. I'm sorry. My bad."

James sat up slightly, his face twisting into the expression of someone who has taken a few gulps from an out-of-date carton of milk before giving it a sniff first. "My bad?" He shook his head. "Don't try to sound hip, Dad. You can't do it."

"Hey, don't push your luck, all right?" Stuart snapped. "I'm saying I've been wrong, here, and I'm apologizing for it. You should be enjoying this while it lasts. And I'm going to change, I promise. Starting right now, tonight, I'm going to show a lot more interest in your life, James. Who were the three guys watching you through that window? Were they your friends?"

James nodded.

"What are their names?"

More fidgeting, another sigh. "Um, well . . . there's Wolfman, the Phantom, and Dracula."

Stuart stared at his son for a long moment. He shrugged and said, "Okay. Is there a punchline?"

"We go by our Internet identities."

"Oh." Stuart nodded. "Okay. I guess I can live with that. What do they call you?"

"The Hunchback. We're The 4UMM."

"The Forum?" Amelia asked.

"The Four Universal Movie Monsters. The number four, capital you, capital em, capital em."

"Uh-huh. What does The 4UMM do, exactly?"

James shrugged. "I don't know. Computer stuff. Games. Hack—"

"Wait, you mean . . . they're all computer geeks?"

"Yeah. Like me."

Relief loosened the taut muscles in Stuart's neck and shoulders, and he smiled. "Well, I'm glad to hear that. Male? Female?"

"All guys."

"How old are these monster guys, anyway?"

"My age."

"What does that mean? How old are they?"

"One's a little older and one's a little younger."

"How old are they?"

James shook his head impatiently. "I don't know how old they are, you think I go around askin' everybody how old they are all the time, or somethin'?"

"Answer my question. How old are they? Take a guess. Live dangerously."

Another irritated wince passed over James's face. "Jesus, can't we just, like, drop this and—"

"We're not finished yet, James!" Stuart shouted. He shook his head immediately after his outburst and said, "I'm sorry, I shouldn't shout at you like that. But I'm frustrated. The question I'm asking you is very simple, and you don't even have to be accurate. Just give me some ballpark ages for these—"

James's voice grew louder as he said, "Okay, Jesus, this is such bullshit, one's eleven, one's nineteen, and the other guy's my age, awright?"

Stuart's mouth dropped open as he turned to Amelia. She looked back at him with wide eyes under a concerned but delicate frown. He thought it was amazing, the way she did that—the way she made such an unpleasant facial expression look so soft and feminine. Even with that haircut.

He pointed at James across the table as he looked at Amelia, to his left, and said, "Okay, I'm going to ask you, first. Do *you* think I'm out of line to be concerned about that?"

"No." Amelia turned to James. "Why don't you hang out with boys your own age?"

"What diff'rence does it make?" James snapped.

"At your age, it makes a lot of difference," Stuart said. "Do any of these guys go to the same school as you?"

James shook his head.

"Do they go to school at all?"

Again, he shook his head. "But they have jobs."

Stuart's eyes widened. "*Jobs?* An eleven-year-old and a nineteen-year-old who don't go to school and have jobs, but live in the anus of San Francisco? What kind of work do they do?"

"They're into computers," James said. "They do all kinds of work."

Stuart thought about that a moment, nodded. "Okay. That sounds good. I want to meet them as soon as possible." He turned to Amelia. "Do you mind if they come over for dinner tomorrow night?"

"No, I don't mind," she said. She looked at James. "I'll make something fun for dinner."

James's mouth dropped open for a second, closed, then opened again. "They won't come to dinner here."

"Why not?" Stuart asked.

"Well, because . . . because, like, they pretty much do whatever they want, and that don't include goin' to people's houses for dinner, y'know?"

"No, I don't know," Stuart said. "I have no idea what that means. But it doesn't matter, because this is the way it is from now on. Either we meet your friends, or you don't see them anymore. At all. Period. I talked to the vice principal today. You and I are going to meet him in his office tomorrow morning before your first class. He'll be keeping his eye on you from now on. So will your teachers. If you don't show up for school by the beginning of your first class, or if it seems you've left school before the end of your last class, I will be called immediately." He pointed a stiff forefinger at James, aimed directly between the boy's eyes. "You do *not* want that to happen."

James said, "But Mom's already talked to the—"

"Your mother had her chance to handle this, now it's my turn."

Stuart and James stared at each other for a long moment. Amelia looked back and forth between them. After a long silence, James spoke in a hoarse voice.

"Is . . . is that . . . it?" he asked.

"One more thing," Stuart said. "You have no computer access for a month."

"What?" James frowned. "What do you mean, no—but I can—how do you think you can—"

"You won't have any at school after we see the vice principal tomorrow, and you won't have any here," Stuart interrupted. "And those are the only two places you'll be spending any time for at least a couple weeks, unless you're with me."

James pushed his chair back and stood, releasing shocked, indignant explosions of breath. "What? I'm being *grounded*? Jesus! You act like I'm, like, ten years old!"

"You're thirteen!" Stuart said with exasperation. "That's not such a big leap from ten."

"I'll call Mom. Get her to come home."

"Won't matter. You're staying here for awhile. And if your mother fights me on it, I'll sue for full custody, and I'll get it."

James was aghast. "They won't give it to you. You're—" He stopped.

Stuart's nostrils flared as he stood. His teeth sounded like tectonic plates grinding together in his skull. "Crazy? That's what your mother tells you, huh?" he asked, quietly but with controlled rage.

"She can't be lyin' all the time, Dad," James spat.

Stuart nodded, as if some suspicion had been confirmed. He pointed at James. "Well, you can tell that vicious bitch I'll put my mental health up against hers any day of—"

"Hey, *hey*, wait a second, guys," Amelia said as she got up quickly, stepped around Stuart, and stood between them, arms outstretched at her sides, shoulder-level, a flat palm open to each of them. "Maybe now would be a good time to give this thing a break, huh? What do you say? James? Maybe you could go to your room and—"

James did not let her finish. He turned and left the dining room, stalked down the hall to his bedroom.

"Have you eaten?" Amelia called, but halfway through her question, James's bedroom door slammed hard.

"Can you believe that?" Stuart said. "She probably spends so much time telling him how crazy I am, she doesn't realize he's off playing in the city all day instead of going to school. I *will* sue for full custody. We could handle it, couldn't we, sweetheart?"

She propped a fist on her hip and shook her head. "Not if he keeps behaving like this."

"Oh, that won't be happening anymore." Electric anger

fizzed and crackled in his voice. "If I have to, I'll make him live with my mother—she'd love it, he'd hate it, and it would probably do him some good. Don't worry, I'll take care of that."

Amelia stepped close to him and whispered, "Whatever he was doing in the Tenderloin with those other kids, chances are it wasn't good, you know that, don't you?"

He nodded slowly, whispered, "I'm going to talk with him about that."

"Want me to give you a hand? I think it might help to have someone involved in the dialogue who has a—"

"Good grief!" Stuart interrupted with a sour face. "*Dialogue*? Have you been watching *Oprah*, or something?"

Amelia smirked, rolled her eyes. "All I'm saying is, I think I could bring a healthy perspective to the problem."

"Perspective?" He shook his head in short jerks, wincing. "How? Were you a teenage boy once?"

Amelia took a step back from Stuart. Her voice dropped low and struggled with tremors when she said, "Goddammit, Stuart, I want to help you. But not if you're going to take this out on me."

Stuart's head dropped forward, broad shoulders became slack. The same bone-weakening fatigue he had felt at work that morning suddenly fell over him again like a wet blanket. The instant he said the two words again, he was unsure if he had spoken them aloud, or simply thought them to himself—he seemed to say them so often these days, sometimes it was difficult to tell the echoes from the memories: "I'm sorry," Stuart said, and his words had meat on their bones. He meant them. He went to her and closed his hands gently on her upper arms, pulled her close. "You're right, that's exactly what I'm doing," he whispered, "and I'm sorry."

Amelia put her hands on his chest and rubbed in slow circles for awhile, then snaked her arms around his neck. "I know you've . . . got a lot on your mind."

"I do?" Stuart frowned. "What do you mean?"

"Well, um . . . James, for one thing. Isn't that enough?"

"Oh, God, yeah, let's hope so."

"So, would you like me to talk to James with you?" She nuzzled his neck. "I think it would be a good idea."

"Okay, let me get this straight," he whispered into her hair just above her ear as he wrapped his arms around her, moved his hands slowly over her back. "You want to talk to James with me because you think I'm . . . what? A clod? An idiot father?"

Amelia laughed, dropped her arms under Stuart's, and curled her long graceful fingers into talons. She dug them into Stuart's ribs and tickled him.

When they heard their laughter become too loud, they went into the kitchen. Stuart pulled her to him, tried to kiss her. Amelia turned her head, would not let him.

"Stuart, you know that's not what I meant, right?" she whispered, although they did not need to.

"What you meant about what?"

"About you being an idiot father, I don't think that. But I see James through different eyes than you. You're his father, but . . . well, I know how much you want to reach out to him, to get through to him. I'm afraid you might be a little lenient as a result."

"You think so?"

"It's possible. I don't think you should let this slide."

"Of course it's not going to slide," he said firmly. "I won't let it."

"Okay. Just . . . don't ignore any possibilities because . . . well, you know, just because he's your son and you want to be friends with him."

He frowned, slid his arms around her waist. "Possibilities? What's that supposed to mean?"

"Just that . . . it could be anything. Drugs or guns or . . . anything."

"You mean I should prepare myself for the worst?"

"Something like that." She gently kneaded each of his tense shoulders as they leaned against each other.

"He's a computer geek. How bad could it be?"

"You might be surprised."

Stuart closed his eyes and put his face into her hair. She smelled so good, felt even better. He was suddenly surprised by how little thought he had given to sex in recent months. When had he and Amelia last made love? He was not sure. But suddenly, it was all he could think about as his hands moved with more purpose over Amelia's back and nicely curved rear. He suddenly had a hyperadolescent need to get their clothes off and get down to business right there. She continued to rub his shoulders as they kissed deeply.

"You're so tight," she whispered when their mouths finally separated. "How about a nice long back rub?"

"Will you rub my front, too?"

"I'll work my way around there eventually, sure. We'll get you nice and relaxed."

"What, uh . . . what parts of me have to be relaxed?"

"The one you're pressing against me right now doesn't count."

CHAPTER NINE

After sex, Stuart always felt a surge of creativity and wanted to work. Amelia was the one who fell asleep, usually while Stuart was talking.

She snored gently into her pillow as Stuart slid out of bed and put on his baggy old sweats. He slipped out of the room, went downstairs to the kitchen.

He needed to talk to James some more, but did not feel like doing that right away. He felt too good for that. He felt healthy and strong and full of energy. It was not just the aftereffects of sex, either, although that had contributed. It was something else, something that had begun its trek through his system before he and Amelia had made love, and might even have been behind Stuart's sudden horniness. He had first noticed it on his way to pick up James earlier that afternoon. Something quietly building up inside, slowly filling him. It was settling in now and made him feel invigorated, but anxious. Not in a bad way, but anxious nonetheless, as if he were anticipating some upcoming event, something naggingly important and potentially life-changing, for better or for worse.

As he filled a glass with raspberry iced tea, he noticed that his hands trembled, not from weakness, but from pent-up energy, restlessness. He felt like going for a run in the rain, but chose instead to release his energy in his sketch pad. He took his drink with him to the card table in the garage. He sat in one of the two old kitchen chairs, sorted through the clutter on the table until he found a large sketch pad and a charcoal pencil. His hand went to work the instant it touched the pencil's tip to the heavy page. Straight lines stroked at an angle. More lines fell just short of joining with the first set at another angle.

Whatever Stuart was drawing, it made his chest feel tight. Made him nervously tap the toe of his right foot while bouncing the heel of his left. He drew for awhile, drained the cold tea from the glass, then drew some more.

Unsatisfied, though he was not sure with what or why, he flipped to the next page and started over. It wasn't right, that was all. Whatever it was, it just wasn't right. Before half a minute passed, he flipped to the next page. After he had drawn on page after page for awhile—Stuart had no idea how long—he got up and stretched, paced slowly for a bit as it gnawed at him. It still was not right, still would not work: He went back to it, turned another page in the sketch pad.

Stuart lost track of time, as he always did while working. The only sounds were the ongoing murmur of rainfall outside, the occasional passing car, his pencil whispering secretly to the page as he drew.

Suddenly, he sat up at the card table, looked around. It was dark outside the windows, but the light on the front corner of the house across the street fell through the garage's windows and cast deep, squat shadows in the corners. He wondered what time it was. He vaguely remembered Amelia knocking at the garage door—how long ago? She'd asked if he wanted dinner, but he had not been hungry and had declined.

He stood, stretched, and his body released a series of thick, muted pops, like small mines hidden in his own skeleton. The alarm clock on top of the old freezer had stopped at twelve twenty a few days ago and needed to be wound again, but he kept forgetting to do it. He picked up the empty glass and tried to remember how long ago he had emptied it, looked at the open sketch pad, at the plans he had drawn. Pages he had torn from the pad surrounded it on the table in a specific order. It would look like a disorganized mess to anyone else, but that was okay, because no one else would see it. He had not finished the plans yet, and really did not need to. He knew what he was going to do, and the plans were etched in his mind, each detail excruciatingly vivid.

It's insane, Stuart thought as he stared down at his work. But he could not allow himself to think about it. He had learned that while sitting there drawing the plans. Once he realized what he was doing, thinking about it—what it would mean, what it would require of him, what he would have to do, and what would happen if he were caught—seized him with an overwhelming feeling of throat-clenching panic, a gut-deep need to run and get help, tell others. The only thing that had kept him from hyperventilating had been a slapstick mental image of himself running through the house, flailing his arms, shouting, "Help! Somebody help! Laaaady! Heeelllp!" like Jerry Lewis in an old movie. The thought had made him laugh, kept him from gibbering. But it did not comfort him, and the unspent panic remained inside him, smothered and quiet for the time being, but struggling to break free and scream. From that moment on, Stuart avoided thinking about the actual purpose of what he was doing. *Because it's insane*, he thought again, then tried to think about it no more.

He left the garage, went down the hall into the kitchen and flipped on the overhead lights. No one was there. The glowing green digits on the microwave oven read 2:41 a.m.

"Oh, jeez," he muttered, surprised by how much time had passed since he had started drawing. He ran a hand through his hair as he looked around, wondered what he should do next. Should he go talk to James? "Not at this hour," he mumbled as he looked in the refrigerator. For what, he did not know. He poured himself another glass of iced tea and took a couple gulps. It was delicious and chilly going down his throat. He tipped it back and finished it off in a few more gulps with a pleasant sigh. He stared at the empty glass for a moment, thirst slaked. But that was not what he had wanted, not what he really needed. He needed something else.

Stuart needed to find Dr. Furgeson.

Before he gets his hands on James, Stuart thought as he went to the computer in the corner of the dining room. He waited through the chorus of muffled electronic babble as the modem connected him to the Internet.

He heard a sound upstairs. Movement? Amelia? He left the computer and went upstairs, moved slowly, quietly. He opened the bedroom door and leaned inside. The room was dark and he could see nothing but vague images. But he heard Amelia snoring softly, asleep.

Back in the dining room, Stuart printed up the telephone book listing for every Furgeson in Redwood City, in search of Gardner Furgeson. Normally, Stuart would be unlikely to remember the name of a doctor he had seen only a few times so long ago. But who could forget a name like *Gardner*? Unfortunately, there was no Gardner Furgeson listed in Redwood City. There were a number of G. Furgesons, and many that read simply "Furgeson."

Stuart knew doctors never had their telephone numbers listed in the phone book. But if Dr. Furgeson were retired—and his mother was right, he probably was by now—there was a chance he had loosened the fiercely protective hold most working doctors maintained on their private lives.

He took the list to the bar, removed the cordless telephone from its wall base above the small television. Stuart was not unaware of the rude hour as he keyed in the first number. He simply did not care.

A great sense of urgency cramped his insides, and it had nothing to do with going to the bathroom. It was obvious Dr. Furgeson knew a lot about Stuart—where to find him and when. For all Stuart knew, the doctor had him under constant surveillance. But Stuart knew nothing about Dr. Furgeson, not even where he lived. He wanted to remedy that, and quickly.

"Hello?" It was the voice of an old woman, but she was wide-awake. Stuart quickly recognized the loud babble in the background as a local talk radio program.

"Hello. Is this the residence of Dr. Gardner Furgeson?"

"*Who?*"

"Dr. Gardner Furgeson?"

"No." She promptly hung up.

He crossed the number off the list, punched in the next. An angry man who kept asking Stuart if he knew what time it was. A woman who spoke broken English and fluent, angry, obscene Spanish. A loud old man who was mostly deaf. None of them had ever heard of Dr. Gardner Furgeson. The next few were the same.

He stood and stretched, walked around the chair a couple times, took a few swallows of iced tea. Dropped back into the chair and punched in the next number.

"Hello, Stuart," a male voice said suddenly, before the first ring.

Stuart froze. Even his lungs became blocks of ice for a long moment.

"It's not very polite to call people at this hour of the morning," Dr. Furgeson said. He spoke quietly, but his voice seemed to fill Stuart's head like a crash of cymbals. There was a smile in the doctor's voice that brought to Stuart's mind an image of his large, ugly teeth.

Stuart had to peel his tongue from the dry roof of his mouth and cough before he could speak. "Why . . . why are you doing this to me?"

"Doing what to you?"

"You know what I'm talking about, dammit! Just . . . leave me alone, all right?"

"It's your son's health I'm concerned about, Stuart." Suddenly, his voice changed ever so slightly and he was the well-mannered doctor showing concern for a patient. "That problem you had when I saw you last—I'm sure you remember it, don't you? The small misshapen opening of your urethra? Well, I'm afraid that condition is hereditary, Stuart. We need to think of James. We want him to be able to pee right, don't we?" Dr. Furgeson chuckled, a series of rapid-fire, sharp, dry clicking sounds in his throat. Then, over the phone:

Snick-snick-snick. Snick-snick-snick.

Anger burned through Stuart as he shot to his feet and said loudly, "You stay away from him, you son of a bitch!"

The connection was severed with a soft click.

Stuart did not move for awhile, then slowly returned to the stool, lowered the cordless from his ear, turned it off. He looked down at the printed list on the bar, at the number he had just called, and quickly called it again.

Three electronic tones sounded, then a recorded female voice said, "The number you have reached has been disconnected and is no longer in service at this time. If you feel you have reached this recording in error, please hang up and try your call again."

Stuart tried the number three more times. Each time, the recording politely, monotonously repeated its message. He turned off the cordless, made a note of the street address listed with that telephone number.

We want him to be able to pee right, don't we?

He covered his mouth suddenly, pinched his lips between thumb and fingers and twisted them to hold back the sound of fear that was lodged in his throat. Probably a pathetic sound. That was how Stuart felt suddenly—pathetic. Helpless and lost. But he quickly pushed those feelings aside, sat up straight at the bar, told himself that was not him, and if it was, or ever had been, that would change soon. Everything would change soon.

He left the bar, went to the archway that led into the short hallway where James's room was located. He stood there for awhile, chewing on his lower lip, staring into the hall's darkness.

James already thought he was crazy. God only knew what kinds of things Molly had been telling him. What would he think if Stuart were to tell him all about Dr. Furgeson? If James harbored any doubts that his father was crazy, Stuart was sure an account of the phantom urologist would finish those off quickly.

He walked down the hall slowly, stopped at the closed door of James's bedroom. He stood there for awhile, listened for sounds of movement on the other side, then put his hand on the cold brass doorknob. His palm was slick with sweat. He decided he would be very quiet and just take a look, make sure James was safely asleep and nothing was wrong.

We want him to be able to pee right, don't we?

He turned the knob, pushed the door in slowly. A streetlight outside sent a glowing, gradually broadening sliver of dull light through the narrow space between the drawn curtains on the window. Other than that and the soft glow from the end of the hall that spilled through the opening door, James's bedroom was dark. The light from the window fell across James's bed, over the still lump beneath the covers.

Stuart stood still in the half-open doorway and listened. He heard no sounds but the rain outside, not even James's sleepy breathing. Stuart stepped inside the room, silently closed the door behind him. He took a few steps toward the bed, stopped and listened.

There was not a sound. No snoring, no gentle rhythmic breathing, nothing.

He's not breathing, Stuart thought with a surge of panic. He moved forward quickly, dropped to one knee beside the bed. "James?" he said gently. "James." He put his hands on the bed, searching for his son. But he was not there. All Stuart could feel were—

He stood, clicked on the bedside lamp.

—pillows. Three of them stuffed under the covers, manipulated into a shape that, in the dark, might look like a sleeping body.

James was gone.

Stuart spun around, rushed out of the room. He checked

every room on the first floor, called James's name a few times, even checked the closets. As he hurried up the stairs, his stomach twisted with the certainty that James was not in the house. Quietly, he checked every room on the second floor.

Amelia still slept deeply in the dark of the bedroom.

In the bathroom, Stuart found Hieronymus seated on the closed lid of the toilet, staring at the open door. The instant Stuart turned on the light, Hieronymus meowed loudly. Stuart knew the cat wanted him to lift the lid from the toilet seat so Hieronymus could lean into the bowl and get a drink. He ignored the cat.

James was not in the house.

"Oh, God," Stuart breathed again and again as he went back downstairs. He found Amelia's purse in its usual place, hanging by its long leather strap from one of the wooden coat hooks on the wall in the foyer. He struggled to get his hand inside the purse, groped through its contents blindly. "Son of a bitch," he hissed as he took the purse off the coat hook, turned it upside down and held its zippered mouth open wide. The purse vomited its contents onto the tile floor. Pens, breath mints, a hairbrush, chewing gum, tampons, a half-empty crumpled pack of Benson & Hedges—

When did Amelia start smoking again? he wondered absently.

—wallet, matchbook, lipstick, a compact—

He snatched the keys off the floor, stood, stepped over the mess, then grabbed his blue fleece cardigan off its hook and opened the door. He stopped, turned back, looked at the long black cashmere blend coat Amelia had given him for Christmas last year. He changed his mind and replaced the cardigan and grabbed the coat on his way out.

CHAPTER TEN

The night was cold, but Stuart felt hot and sticky beneath the heavy coat. Adrenaline hummed through his body and he had to will his foot to ease up on the accelerator as he drove away from the house in Amelia's gold 1998 Celica. Stuart hated driving, especially in the city, and took the bus or BART wherever he went. But at that hour, he assumed the traffic would not be very heavy, and he knew exactly where he was going.

Driving into the Tenderloin, the Celica seemed to pass through a thick, sticky web of darkness within the darkness. The glowing reds and greens and blues and yellows of signs over pawnshops, bars, thrift stores, and sex shops, most of them closed, seemed to be partially absorbed by the darkness and looked muted, depressed.

Stuart turned onto Turk, double-parked the Celica next to a sprawling old dinosaur of a Cadillac. He killed the engine, locked the car as he got out, opened his umbrella. The rain seemed louder, heavier. He stood outside the building a moment, looked up at the window in which he had seen three faces the previous afternoon. There were lights on inside, made a sickly yellow by whatever filthy shade had been pulled down over the window.

The latch on the building's double doors was broken, and one door hung open a few inches. Duct tape had been applied to long cracks in the glass panes in both doors. He carefully closed the door behind him, but with no latch, it creaked back a few inches and remained open.

The vague odors of cat feces and urine made Stuart's upper lip curl back in disgust. He went down a dimly lighted hallway until he came to an elevator. A circular window in the battered brown door revealed the dull, jaundiced light inside the the small elevator car. Its close walls were the color of rust, of dried blood. He decided to find the stairs.

They were just ahead, to the right. Narrow and unlit, Stuart could see nothing but blackness beyond the third step. He started up the stairs slowly. Fear tightened his chest, made it difficult to breathe. A loud racket—the growl and thump of rap music—came from upstairs, not too far away.

A few steps up, Stuart thought he could feel the darkness on his face, clammy and mistlike, as he passed through it. Sweat trickled down his spine. He stopped a moment to catch his breath.

He imagined Dr. Furgeson waiting in the dark ahead of him, holding his scissors. Smiling.

A thought came to him, and he began to relax immediately. His breathing slowed, he felt strong. He climbed the steps with more confidence and at a quickened pace. The thought was, *Just think of this as rehearsal for the real thing.*

He stopped midway at a small landing. To Stuart's left, the stairs doubled back and continued up to the second floor.

"Who the fuck're you?" a weak, phlegmy voice asked.

Stuart turned quickly toward the voice, and his long, unbuttoned coat spun around him like a cape. As his eyes adjusted slowly to the darkness, he saw a figure squatting in the corner of the landing. A butane lighter flicked to life and cast a weak glow. Hollow cheeks and deep eyes floated in a thin, pea green hood attached to a stained, threadbare jacket. He could not tell if the face belonged to a man or woman. It was neither male nor female, just pale and long and dirty. A few strands of greasy dark hair fell from beneath the hood and streaked the face. No lips were visible on the mouth, just a thin, bloodless, horizontal cut in the face. One hand held the butane lighter, the other a dirty glass pipe an inch from the mouth.

"You lookin' f'Floyd?" the figure asked. "Floyd's the super."

Stuart shook his head. "No. I'm looking for my son." He turned away from the figure and hurried up the rest of the stairs.

The phlegmy voice said, "Oh," then burst into a fit of laughter that sounded almost like vomiting. "Good luck!" the voice said with mossy sarcasm as Stuart reached the second floor. He stepped through the door and into the hall. The wet laughter faded as the door closed behind him.

Dim yellow light shone upward from the dusty brass sconces on the walls. The ugly red and blue diamond-print carpet in the hall was stained and worn, burnt in spots, and peeled away from the walls in places.

Stuart kept his bearings, knew exactly where he was in relation to the window he had watched for a moment before entering the building. He counted the doors on his left, stopped in front of one.

The loud rap music came from inside that apartment, number 202. Voices shouted at one another, laughed.

Stuart looked up and down the dim, dreary hall. Voices came from behind some of the doors—angry shouting, loud televisions, drunken laughter—but he saw no one.

He closed his hand on the doorknob of apartment 202, turned it slowly. It was locked. He touched the door with both hands. It was not solid, and the wood was old.

Might work, he thought, stepping back. Each kick hit the door just to the left of the doorknob. Wood crunched beneath the second kick. The third sent the dead bolt ripping through the weak doorjamb, snapped the chain lock on the inside. The door slammed against the wall with a loud bang.

A *rehearsal*, he thought again.

It was that moment that Stuart lost himself, became someone else in a way, someone who was afraid of nothing at all. Not even the gun pointed at his face.

A mocha-skinned boy with long, stringy black hair rushed toward Stuart, a Saturday Night Special in his right hand, aimed directly at Stuart's face. He shouted in Spanish as he got closer, closer.

Stuart grabbed his right wrist and twisted, pushed the arm upward as he buried his knee in the boy's groin. As the body went down, Stuart snatched the revolver from his hand. He turned away as the boy vomited onto the floor on all fours.

His eyes went to James first. He was relieved to see that he was okay. He had not been taken, he'd just ducked out to spend more time with his damned computer geek friends. He would deal with that later. The only thing on Stuart's mind was to get James out of there for the last time.

Behind him, the boy continued to retch and gag.

In front of him, no one moved. They stared at him as if he were a ghost. Someone turned down the rap music.

He took one step forward, gun down, then stopped to look around. The single room included a small, filthy kitchenette and a door that led, Stuart assumed, to the bathroom. The apartment was filled with computers and computer equipment, on tables, desks, chairs, shelves, on the floor, everywhere. Stuart assumed all of it was stolen. All of the equipment was in use, or had been torn out of boxes and was in the process of being installed. Most of the peeling paint on the walls hid behind posters of mostly naked girls with augmented breasts, of science fiction movies and television shows—geek culture, the icons of misfits.

A tall, thin teenaged boy, black, with his head shaved like James's, stood over an open computer, a small tool in his hands—clearly the nineteen-year-old. He glared at Stuart with a combination of surprise and rage. James stood frozen beside a desk. The eleven-year-old Asian boy seated at the desk peered around the computer monitor at Stuart, mouth open. The room reeked of marijuana, and Stuart noticed that James held a joint between the thumb and forefinger of his right hand. When James saw his dad looking at the joint, he quickly dropped it into an ashtray on the corner of the desk.

"You!" Stuart barked as he pointed a finger at James. He pointed the finger down at the floor and said, "Over here."

"Jesus Christ, Dad!" James shouted. "What the hell do you think you're—"

Stuart shouted, "Get over here!"

James glanced at his friends, but their eyes never left Stuart. The guy who had rushed Stuart with a gun earlier had stopped vomiting, but was still on the floor, groaning in pain. James walked reluctantly across the room, around the desks and tables and chairs to his father's side.

Stuart leaned toward him and spoke just loudly enough for James to hear, but not the others. "The Celica's parked right in front of the building. Go down there and wait for me by the car. I'll be down in just a few seconds."

"What're you—"

"*Now!*" Stuart roared.

James headed for the broken door, walking part of the way backward to stare at Stuart in disbelief. His amazement grew as he watched.

"Hey, you can't just bust in here den turn around and leave!" the black kid said. "Who da fuck you think you are? Nobody asked you here. We don't like no fuckin' visitors." He wore a black vest over a white T-shirt. He reached behind him, trying to be quick.

Stuart aimed the revolver directly at him. "What do they call you?"

The kid froze. "Phantom."

"Take your gun out, Phantom, put it on that table there, then take a few steps back. Move very slowly. Keep your hands visible."

The Phantom did as he was told, took the gun from under his belt in the small of his back. Once the .32 Magnum was on the table, he stepped backward, hands held out from his sides.

"Now turn around," Stuart said, "and put your hands on

that shelf—the one just over your head—and stay there until I say otherwise." He turned to the Asian boy. "Dracula?"

"No, Wolfman," the boy said. He raised his arms, as if he were being held up—tense, nervous, but holding together well. He nodded toward the teenager on the floor behind Stuart. "He's Dracula."

Stuart turned and looked down. Dracula was rising again, almost up on his knees. Stuart quickly stepped over and kicked him in the face. Dracula rolled over the floor and bumped the wall, unconscious. He breathed in a wheezy snore. Stuart turned to Wolfman again.

"You do the same. Put your guns on—"

He sat up straighter, raised his hands higher. "I don't have any guns. I don't like 'em. You can search me, if you want, but—"

"He don't got no fuckin' guns, man," the Phantom said angrily.

Stuart went to the table, picked up the Phantom's gun. He dropped it into his coat pocket without even glancing at it.

James left the apartment.

"You've seen the last of Hunchback," he said. "He won't be coming back here. And I'm here to tell you that you won't be coming after him, either. I don't know what you guys do here, and I don't want to know. But whatever it is, he's not involved in it anymore. If any of you try to contact him, I'll know, and you'll all be killed. It won't be me, it'll be somebody you won't recognize, when you least expect it, and he'll kill all of you, not just the one responsible. Do you understand that?"

Wolfman nodded quickly and said, "Yep, I understand it."

"Phantom?" Stuart prodded.

Phantom suddenly spun around and lunged at Stuart. "Who the fuck're you, anyway, you can bust inta people's homes and shit like dis, like you a cop, or somethin'?"

Stuart raised the gun so it pointed at Phantom's face.

"Don't act like you gonna shoot me wiffat, motherfucker, you din't come here to shoot nobody, so knock dat shit off!"

He was right. Stuart knew he could not pull the trigger. He was not certain he could use the gun even if the Phantom were armed. That uncertainty worried him. He lowered his arm.

"You ain't no fuckin' cop, motherfucker," the Phantom went on, coming closer. "Who you think you are, kickin' the—"

Stuart kicked him once in the stomach. When he doubled over, Stuart grabbed his neck, turned him, lifted him, then slammed his face down onto the corner of a desk. Then again. The Phantom did not move after hitting the floor.

Wolfman rose slowly from his chair, wide eyes staring at Phantom.

Stuart said, "You seem to understand the situation, Wolfman. Why don't you explain it to them when they feel better." He dropped the revolver into his other coat pocket as he quickly left the apartment.

On the stairs, he did not even pause when the wheezing figure in the corner asked, "Who the fuck're you?"

He was about to skip the last three steps when a voice from above stopped him.

"You have no right to come here and take one of my patients away!"

Dr. Furgeson peered down at him from the middle of the upper stairs. Backlit by soft light from the hallway behind him, the frames of his round glasses sparkled slightly, but the lenses looked black in the darkness.

Stuart clenched his teeth, his fists, and growled, "He's no patient of yours, and you know it." He took a deep breath and his voice trembled when he said, "*I'm* not even a patient of yours anymore."

The androgynous junkie in the corner of the landing began to laugh again, long, wet, wheezy laughs.

"I'm not concerned about you," Dr. Furgeson said. "It's your son who needs my help, not you." He took a step down, put both hands on the rail. Dull light flickered on his large teeth as he grinned. "We want him to be able to pee right, don't we? I might even go a little further with his treatment. Considering the fact that he's *your* son . . . he probably won't be needing those testicles, will he? It doesn't seem they've done you any good."

The junkie laughed louder.

Stuart went down the stairs sideways, staring at the doctor, heart thundering in his throat.

"I like to take care of these things before the patient gets too old," Dr. Furgeson said, still grinning. "He's already older than I prefer. We will have to do it soon."

Backing toward the door to the hallway, Stuart pointed a finger at the doctor and said, "You lay one finger on him and I'll kill you. Understand me? I'll kill you."

Dr. Furgeson laughed and the sound scraped down Stuart's spine.

But as Stuart went through the door and back down the hall toward the building's entrance, the only laugh he heard fading behind him was that of the phlegmy, sexless junkie.

CHAPTER ELEVEN

"What the hell do you think you're doing, sneaking out of the house and coming down here in the middle of the night?" Stuart shouted as he drove away from the building. He shook from anger, fear, and pure adrenaline. "What were you doing?"

"I—I can't believe you kicked the door in and—" James began.

"And what the hell was *he* doing there?" A tremor went through Stuart's voice as he asked the question, thinking again of Dr. Furgeson standing on the stairs.

"Who?"

"Dr. Furgeson!" he shouted.

"*Who?*" James squinted at his dad. "What're you talkin' about?"

Stuart had not seen the doctor in the apartment, had not seen him come out of the apartment. He remembered the closed door in the apartment and wondered if the doctor had been hiding behind it. Or was it possible he had been in another apartment nearby? Was it possible James was unaware of him?

"Dr. Gardner Furgeson. He was in there, I saw him, I talked to him."

"You're, like, on another planet, or something," James said, shaking his head and shrugging helplessly. "There was nobody else there."

"He's tall, skinny, bald, wears little round glasses, probably in his seventies now. He's got these big buck teeth and—"

When Stuart saw the wide-eyed look of amazement on James's face, he stopped. "What?"

"In his seventies? You think we, like, hang out with old men in their seventies?"

Stuart closed his mouth and faced front, stung by the boy's logic. James was right. What would a bunch of teenage boys be doing in a Tenderloin tenement building with an old urologist? It sounded like the setup of a sick joke. Something told him to say no more about it. For now. Until he had a better handle on things, knew exactly what was going on.

I know what's going on, he thought. *That son of a bitch Furgeson is screwing with my head.*

"You still haven't answered my first question," he said. "What were you doing there?"

"I toldja, we just hang out and do stuff on the computer." Suddenly, James sounded afraid, spoke quietly. "Mostly gaming, that kinda thing."

"Stolen computers, you mean."

"They're not stolen, *none* of that stuff was—"

"Where the hell do a bunch of punks with guns in the Tenderloin get brand-new expensive computers and equipment—"

"Wolfman's dad!" James shouted. His face screwed up as if shouting were painful. His voice dropped back down to a low monotone. "He writes for a computer magazine, gets all kindsa stuff for free, just to try out. He gives most of it to Wolfman."

"Well, why don't you go to Wolfman's place instead of that rat hole?"

"Because we don't *want* to go to Wolfman's place, Dad. The apartment belongs to Phantom's aunt. She's living with his parents now. We can do what we want there."

"Like what? Smoke pot, maybe?"

James turned his head, looked out the window, said nothing.

Stuart sighed. "I'm sorry for shouting. But I'm . . . upset, to put it mildly. I would like to point out, though, that a lot of fathers wouldn't bother shouting. A lot of fathers would have knocked you into next week by now. Mine would've—" He stopped, wished he had not said that. He chuckled coldly, thinking about it. "Jeez, I don't even want to think about what my dad would've done," he muttered.

Neither of them said anything for awhile. That was fine with Stuart, because he did not know what to say. He had warned James about drugs more than once, had tried to caution him against falling in with the wrong crowd. Had it not been enough, or did it simply not make any difference? Stuart remembered how little he'd listened to his mother's warnings when he was a kid.

Maybe he should wait till he got home and woke up Amelia—she always kept her calm. Lately, he felt more incompetent as a father than he had in thirteen years. The truth was, by the time he reached college, Stuart had decided he did not want to be a father, ever. He felt he would never be able to handle such a responsibility. Now, he thought he had been right. But when Molly became pregnant, he had done the right thing. Looking back on it, he realized it had not necessarily been his problem—knowing what he knew about Molly, she could have gotten pregnant with anyone.

That's it, he thought. *He's not mine. That would explain a few things.*

He hated himself for thinking it. Stuart loved his son with every fiber of his being. The problem was not with James. Stuart was his own worst problem.

James cleared his throat. "You, um . . . you were pretty cool in there," he said cautiously. "I mean, y'know, they're my friends, and I think it was a shitty thing to do, but . . . it was pretty kick-ass. Did you learn that in those karate classes you go to?"

Stuart was about to say, "No, not karate," but did not want to criticize James. He was touched by the compliment and did not want to ruin it. He smirked at James and said, "You think so?"

"Dracula's kind of a dick. He's always threatening to beat people up." He tried to hold in a laugh, but it snorted through his nose. "He didn't know what hit him."

Stuart smiled. "Well, let's hope his parents never find out what hit him, or I could have criminal charges and a possible lawsuit to deal with. Or worse, we could all end up on *Judge Judy*."

"Oh, you don't hafta worry about them," James said, shaking his head. "Dracula's parents are in prison."

"Why doesn't that surprise me?" Stuart muttered with a heavy sigh. "James, you're not going to like this, but you can't see those guys anymore. Period."

"What? Why?"

"We have to go through this again? You're smart enough to know why. Guns, marijuana . . . Jesus. Don't you have any friends at school? I mean, safe friends? Friends who are less likely to get you killed?"

James stiffened, turned away again and stared out the window to his right.

"If you don't," Stuart continued, "now would be a good time to make some, because you won't be hanging out with those guys anymore."

James's breath misted the glass as he said quietly, "They probably won't want me to."

"Fine, I hope they don't, that'll make things easier. Come on, James, after what I saw in there, you don't really expect me to say, 'Oh, sure, son, spend all the time you want with your thug friends, and smoke a joint for me while you're there!' Do you?"

He said nothing.

"Until I say otherwise," Stuart went on, "you do not leave the house without my permission, which you will not get anyway because you're grounded. I mean, you aren't even to go out to the backyard. If I have to go to school with you every day and tie you to your bed every night, you're not going anywhere."

James did not look away from the window and remained silent.

"And when I think you're able to handle the responsibility of coming and going whenever you want, you still won't be seeing those guys, and if you do, then maybe I'll have to do something a little more drastic. Maybe next time, I'll send the cops to kick the door down, and they'll be a lot more interested in your computers and marijuana than I was, I promise. You want that? You want to do some time in juvie? That's how serious I am about this, James. If I thought I couldn't get through to you, then I'd be willing to give the cops a try, because someone has to make you understand that—"

"They're the only friends I've got!" James shouted at the window. The glass fogged and spattered with saliva. His voice was angry, thick with unspilled tears.

Stuart stared at the wheel, thought his heart skipped a beat. He looked over at James, who was motionless. He wondered if the boy was crying, reached over and gave his shoulder a squeeze. James did not pull away, but neither did he respond.

"Hey, c'mon, that can't be true. You know people at school. Even if you don't know them all well, you're familiar with them, right? So, get to know them better. Find people who like the same things—"

"I don't want to get to know them," James said angrily. "I don't wanna be like 'em, I don't wanna be around 'em. And they don't want me around 'em, either, they let me know it. I don't fit. I'm a freak. When I'm at school with them, I'm a freak."

"Who are you talking about? Is this a group of—"

"It's *everybody*!" he shouted. He ran the back of his hand over his eyes and sniffled as a sob quaked through him. "Everybody. Even the teachers."

"What about the teachers?"

James shook his head wearily. "It don't matter, Dad. I'm just tryin' to tell you, those guys're the only friends I got, and I'm not gonna be makin' any at school."

Stuart's ribs cracked and splintered. His lungs collapsed and his heart imploded. The pain he felt for his son was so deep and intense, he expected to taste blood in the back of his throat. If he were not so close to the house, he would have pulled to the side of the road. Instead, he pressed a little harder on the accelerator, took a corner a little too fast, and zipped into the driveway. He stopped just short of the garage door, killed the engine, and removed his seat belt. He hoped he could keep his own voice steady as he put an arm around James, who resisted a little at first, and pulled him into an awkward embrace.

"You're not a freak," he said. He could think of nothing else to say. "You're not. Not at all. You're not a freak at all, James."

James rocked with sobs. He clumsily put an arm around Stuart and held him tightly. After about a minute, James took a couple deep breaths. Soon, the only sound was the rain on the roof of the car. Stuart did not let go, and James did not try to pull away.

"I know I sound like I'm full of crap when I say this," Stuart said very quietly near James's ear, "but it's all going to start changing in a few years, I promise."

"A few *years*?" James croaked into Stuart's shoulder.

"That's not as long as it sounds now." He pulled away, but stayed close, with his hands on James's shoulders. "Look, if anyone ever tells you that these are the best years of your life, you have my permission to punch that person right in the mouth."

James's shoulders hitched, this time with a laugh. But he kept his head tipped forward, embarassed by his tears.

"These are not the best years of your life. They might even be the worst. But once you get through them, you look back and see that they haven't taken up that much of your life, and you survived. You see that you've still got a whole lifetime to make up for them, and you move on. Some people don't. Some let this time chew on them for the rest of their lives. Like your uncle Dave." Dave was Molly's younger brother. "The one with all those trophies on his fireplace mantle. You know why he drinks like a fish? Why he's got that huge gut on him? Because he blew a play in some football game his senior year. No kidding."

As they talked quietly, both relaxed in their seats. The windows became opaque and rain continued to stampede on the roof. Stuart told him a couple stories from his days as the fattest kid in school. He tried to make James understand how insignificant all of this would be later, when he was busy making a life for himself.

"A few years after you graduate," he said, "you'll look through a yearbook and realize you can't remember all the names, and then you'll—"

"I don't know the names now, Dad."

"Well . . . maybe that's best. Lay low, concentrate on your classes, and get it all behind you. But I want you to be as happy as someone in high school can be, James. I want you to have friends. They can't *all* be that bad at school." Even as he said it, Stuart knew it wasn't true.

James leaned back in the seat and turned his head to the right again, looked out the window.

"We should get to bed," Stuart said as he took the key from the ignition. "We'll talk more, okay? Tomorrow. But I'm serious, you go to school all day and come straight home afterward. Tell me you're going to do that."

"I'll go," he said with a nod. "And come right home."

He opened his door and started to step out, but Stuart put a hand on his arm, gently pulled him back. "Hey, that guy I mentioned earlier . . . the doctor?"

"Yeah."

"Do you remember my description?"

He nodded. "Tall, bald, little round glasses, buck teeth."

"Have you ever seen anyone who fits that description?"

James thought about it a moment, shook his head. "Nope. Can't 'member ever seein' anybody like that."

"Well, if you do—" His chest tightened at the thought of how close James had been to Dr. Furgeson that night. Had he been watching James? Spying on him through a peephole in a wall while he was with his friends? "I seriously doubt that will ever happen, but if it does—please listen carefully, I'm very serious about this—if it does, I want you to stay away from him, okay? Don't talk to him, don't hang around him. If he comes toward you, go the other way. Run if you have to. And then let me know you saw him, right away. If I'm at work, call me. I'll give you a card with my phone number on it and I want you to keep it with you."

"Who is this guy?" There was suddenly more than a little concern in his voice. "Do you know him? What's he want with me?"

"Oh, don't worry, he doesn't want anything with you. You'll probably never lay eyes on him."

"Is he . . . after you?"

James's use of the word "after" sent an icy breath over the back of Stuart's neck. "No, he's not after anybody. He's just some guy I used to know, thought I saw him around a couple times the last few days."

"What kind of guy?"

"Not a very nice one."

"You didn't really see him in the apartment, did you? 'Cause he wasn't there, I swear—"

"No, not in the apartment. On the stairs. But don't worry about it." He opened his door, then said, "And don't mention any of this to Amelia, okay?"

"You mean about that doctor guy?"

"Yeah. It'll just worry her, and—" He shrugged, smiled. "—there's nothing to worry about. Now, let's get to bed before the sun comes up."

But Stuart did not go to bed. After checking on James one last time for the night—he was in bed, already drifting off with a radio playing softly—he went out to the garage and got back to work.

CHAPTER TWELVE

Amelia slept in an extra ninety minutes that morning, and Stuart and James were gone by the time she got up. She had a murky, sleep-soaked memory of Stuart telling her he was taking James to the club to work out with him, then on to school. She remembered with much more clarity what Stuart had told her at about five that morning, when she had gotten up to go to the bathroom and met him in the hall.

She had thought on more than one occasion that Molly simply was not a very good mother, but Amelia had never suspected such neglect. There had to be an explanation for it, she could not imagine Molly knowingly letting James hang out in the Tenderloin with strange kids. She decided to give Molly a call after she had some coffee. She probably would not want to talk about it, but Amelia could be pushy when she wanted to be, and it seemed to her that pushiness was perfectly appropriate in this situation.

Amelia read the comics in the *Chronicle* over a hot bowl of Cream of Wheat. When the telephone rang, she hoped it was Molly. Instead, she heard Betty Mullond's cheerful but timid voice.

"Hello, Amelia, honey, am I calling at a bad time?"

"Not at all. As long as you don't mind if I eat hot cereal in your ear."

They exchanged the usual small talk, mostly about what Betty was up to with her various church committees and church clubs and church projects. When she asked if Stuart was home, Amelia said he had gone to work.

"Oh, well. That's good. That he's gone back to work, I

mean. He might not want to talk to me, anyway. He seemed pretty upset with me yesterday. I'm not sure why, but . . . I almost never am." She laughed, but it sounded forced.

"I don't think he was upset with you, Betty. Stuart's feelings are always right there on the surface, you know? Especially when he's having a bad day. And he felt bad about it later," Amelia lied. "You know how he is."

"Oh, yes, I know, I know," she said quietly, voice heavy. "If anyone knows how he is, it's me. If he knew, though, how much he's like his dad . . . just like him in some ways." Her voice dropped to a harsh whisper and she spoke quickly when she said, "Don't you ever tell him I said that, do you hear me?"

Amelia blinked at the sudden change in Betty's voice. But before she could respond, it was gone.

"I have some information for Stuart," Betty said cheerfully, a smile in her voice. "Would you mind writing it down for him?"

"Sure," Amelia said, grabbing a Post-It pad and a pen from a small narrow drawer below the bar. "Fire away."

"Well, he was asking about Dr. Furgeson. Is he feeling okay, Amelia?"

"Uh, well, yeah. Sure."

"He's not having problems with his prostate, is he?" Betty whispered the word "prostate."

"Oh, no," she said with a chuckle. "I'm sure he would have mentioned that by now."

"Well, for some reason, he was asking about his old urologist, Dr. Furgeson. I called around to a few people and found out where he is. Are you ready with that pen?"

"Sure am."

"Dr. Gardner Furgeson is a patient at the St. Elizabeth Extended Care Center in Orangevale."

"Orangevale? Where's that?" Amelia asked as she wrote.

"Just outside of Sacramento, I think. Stuart probably knows."

"Okay. Anything else?"

"He's in room 310, bed B."

"Who is he?"

A two-heartbeat pause before Betty asked, "He's never told you about Dr. Furgeson?"

"Never heard of him."

"Oh. Well. That's too bad because I was going to ask if you knew why Stuart wanted to see him."

"You mean, he wanted to make an appointment with him, that sort of thing?"

"I . . . I don't know. Stuart got so angry while he was explaining it to me, and that always makes me feel so flustered and . . . and dumb, and then . . . well, I'm not sure what he said. But I was afraid he was having problems with . . . you know, with the things you go to a urologist for."

Amelia became distracted. Could Stuart be ill? Was he keeping it from her? Was that what had been eating at him? No, she did not want to consider that. If he were keeping an illness from her, their relationship had a grave problem that Amelia had never suspected until that moment. How could he keep such a thing from her? And why would he?

"Stuart told me James is with you for awhile," Betty said.

"Yes, he'll be here while Molly's out of town."

"I hope Stuart will bring him over while he's there. He said he would, but . . . I've got to have James do something with this computer of mine. The e-mail is on the fritz again. I'll never understand this machine. It just doesn't make any sense to me."

"Oh, come on, Betty, look how much you can do already!" Amelia said with a laugh. "You're sending and receiving e-mails, with attachments, writing and printing up your church bulletin each week, with graphics. You've learned so much in such a short time, you should be proud of yourself. And remember, learning new things keeps your mind sharp."

Betty laughed. "Tell that to Stuart. He thinks I'm about as dumb as a coatrack."

"No, he doesn't, Betty," Amelia said reassuringly. But she

was not sure how to reassure her. Amelia knew how Stuart talked to his mother, how he behaved around her. It was difficult to explain away, and she did not know why she was trying to cover for him. He was going to have to own up to it himself and then try to make amends. More than anything, she was trying to protect Betty's feelings. Amelia felt sorry for the frustrating but good-hearted old woman and did not want to see her hurt any further by her son. "Maybe if you could just tell yourself when he behaves that way that it's not because of you, he's not behaving that way *at* you. It doesn't matter if he's upset with just one person or if he's angry at the whole world, he doesn't seem capable of keeping it inside. He wears his feelings on his sleeve, and anyone within striking distance can get smacked by it."

"Yes, so much like his dad."

"Stuart's dad was the same way?"

"Well . . . the same way . . . kind of. Actually, Delbert was . . . well . . ." The line seemed to go dead for several seconds.

"Betty? You still there?"

"Yes, I'm just . . . thinking. Please, Amelia, promise me you won't tell Stuart I asked you this question? In fact, don't tell him about any of this conversation, would you do that for me, honey? Huh?"

"Sure, Betty. This is just between us."

"Okay, then. Has Stuart . . . does he ever . . . hit you?"

Amelia's eyes opened wide in surprise. "Hit me? You mean, like . . . does he ever knock me around, or—"

"Has he ever beat you, Amelia?"

Her own laughter caught her off guard. "No, he hasn't. And if he ever did, Betty, you'd hear about it because I'd put him in the hospital."

Betty's laugh was genuine, almost girlish.

Before they said good-bye, Betty reminded her one more time: "Now, you promised, Amelia. Not a word about this to

Stuart. He'd be angry if he knew we were talking about him behind his back."

The Cream of Wheat was tepid, but Amelia finished it, anyway. She tried not to think about Stuart and what might be wrong with him. A big red C flashed on and off in her mind—not just any c, but the Big One—like a letter flashing in a lewd neon sign. If he knew, how could he not tell her? She dumped her cold coffee and poured a hot cup, trying not to cry. But the idea of Stuart keeping such a horrifying secret from her made the back of her throat burn.

After eating the remaining spoonfuls of cereal, Amelia rinsed the bowl, went back to the bar and called Molly's cell phone.

"Can't talk long," Molly said breathlessly. "We're going to a—"

"I think this is important enough to be late for, Molly."

"What? Something wrong?"

Amelia told Molly everything that had happened. She was relieved when Molly expressed shock at the news that James had been spending time in the Tenderloin with heat-packing, pot-smoking computer geeks.

"He never said that was where he was going," Molly said.

"What did he tell you?"

"About what?"

"About where he was going?"

"Oh. He . . . well, he never said."

"And you never asked?"

Molly's sigh sounded defensive, but she said nothing.

"Don't you ever ask to meet his friends?" Amelia asked.

A long pause, then: "No. Are you going to give me a lecture about it now?"

Amelia said firmly, "I think it's a big mistake to be glib about this, Molly. Stuart says he's going to take you to court for full custody of James."

"What?" The bottom seemed to fall out of her voice and the word crumbled into a dry, throaty croak.

"After what happened early this morning," Amelia said, "I don't think he'd have any trouble getting it, either."

"Jesus, Amelia." Molly sounded hurt. "I thought you were on my side."

"I'm not on anybody's side. And if I were, I think Stuart's side would take precedence. But in this case, I think James's side is the one that needs the most attention, don't you?"

"How is Stuart taking this?"

"He's pretty upset."

Another sigh. "I'll come home right away."

"I don't know if that would be such a great idea," Amelia said.

"What do you mean?"

"You and Stuart shouldn't be together in the same room for awhile."

"We won't fight in front of James, we made a—"

"No. Not the way he is right now. Have fun skiing and I'll keep you up to date."

"Wait a second, hold it, something else is wrong. What's going on?"

"Don't worry about it," Amelia said wearily. "It's got nothing to do with James."

"Stuart, then? What's wrong?"

"I think I've found out what's been bothering him."

"He's seeing another woman."

"Of course not," Amelia snapped.

"Another man?"

"Molly!"

Molly laughed. "I'm sorry. Go on."

"I think he's sick, and he's hiding it from me."

Molly was silent for several long seconds. Then: "What kind of sick?"

"I don't know yet. But he's been looking for some doctor he used to see."

"Which doctor?"

"Furgeson." When Amelia heard a sharp gasp over the line, she said, "What's the matter? Do you know anything about him?"

"Only what Stuart's told me. You say he's been *looking* for Dr. Furgeson?"

"Yes. He talked to Betty about it."

"Ha! I can imagine what that conversation was like. Why does he want to find Dr. Furgeson?"

"Presumably because he needs to see a urologist. That's what Betty thought, anyway. What exactly do urologists cover, anyway? I mean, what kind of diseases?"

Molly laughed again, quietly. "Honey, trust me on this, there is no way Stuart is going to see Dr. Furgeson as a patient again. No way. If he's looking for him, my first thought is, he's decided to kill him."

"What? You've got to be kidding."

"Dr. Furgeson was not one of Stuart's favorite childhood doctors."

"Betty sounded very mysterious about it. So what's the deal with this Dr. Furgeson?"

"Oh, *I'm* not gonna tell you. Sounds like Stuart is pissed enough at me as it is. But now that Betty's brought him up, you're free to ask him about Furgeson."

Amelia was silent a moment. "What is *wrong* with you people?"

"You people?"

"You and Betty and . . . I don't know, it seems so juvenile to be keeping secrets and dropping hints, I mean, didn't we leave that behind with dollhouses and Easy-Bake Ovens? My God, it's amazing Stuart has stayed as sane as he is."

Molly was silent for a long moment. "You know, Amelia, it might not be a bad idea to get Stuart to a doctor if he's behaving weirdly."

"Weirdly?"

"Didn't you say he hasn't been himself?"

"Yes."

"Well, maybe you should talk him into seeing a doctor before it gets any worse. He doesn't like to go to doctors, but he will if you really—"

"You sound like you know something about it," Amelia said.

"Well, I-I-I just know that, you know, Stuart can be kind of . . . moody. Sometimes very moody, right? I mean, even his moods have moods. And if he's trying to find Dr. Furgeson . . . just get him to a doctor, okay?"

"Betty already found Furgeson. He's in a convalescent hospital near Sacramento."

"A home, huh? Doesn't sound like he's taking patients anymore. Probably has a urologist of his own. Just a sec."

Amelia heard Molly set the phone down, heard her talk with her ski instructor. Their voices low, they spoke stiffly. When Molly picked up the phone again, Amelia asked, "Is something wrong?"

Molly sighed. "I'll tell you all about it later."

"I looked in the cabinet."

"What cabinet?"

"Stuart's locked cabinet out in the garage."

"Aw, and I missed it. Couldn't you wait till I got back?"

"I'm still ashamed of myself for doing it."

"What'd you find? Guns? Drugs? Pornography?"

Amelia clenched her teeth and growled, "Molly, stop. I'm not in the mood for it now."

"Okay, no more Stuart-slamming. What'd you find?"

"Paintings. Beautiful paintings. So sharp, almost like photographs. But . . . odd. I'm serious, Molly, they're breathtaking, not like anything he's ever done before. But they're dark. The focal point of each painting—the ones I looked at, anyway—is Owl-Man."

Molly didn't respond for several seconds. "The doodle?"

"Yes, but he's not a doodle anymore. He's a grown man

with broad shoulders and a deep chest. Tall, and he's wearing this . . . owl suit."

"What do you mean, an owl suit?"

"Well, it's a very nice suit. You know, coat and tie. Dark brown, except, I think, in a few places where it's mottled with a tan color. There are dark feathers on the lapels, and from what I could tell, on the mask thing he wore, and on his cape, too."

"Mask? Cape? You mean . . . like in a comic book?"

"No, that's the thing. When he doodles Owl-Man, he's this cute, pudgy little guy with baggy-seated pants. But this is like a real guy. It doesn't look silly or comic bookish, or anything. Sure, it's comic book material, but that's not what these paintings are. They're pictures of Owl-Man standing on top of buildings looking out over San Francisco, and it's . . . it's like he's supposed to be there. Like it's perfectly natural for some guy in a suit and an owl mask and a cape to be watching over the city. And they're beautiful, Molly, you should see them. I think it's the best work he's ever done."

There was silence over the line for a long time. Amelia waited for awhile, then said, "Molly?"

"Yeah. You said he paints a lot?"

"Well, I told you, he's in the garage all the time. I'm assuming he's painting."

"Does he get any sleep?"

"Very little lately. Sometimes he doesn't even come to bed."

"Is he having nightmares?"

"Not that I know of. You asked that before. Why?"

"Look, sweetie, I gotta go, we're running late, but I want you to do me a favor, okay? I want you to promise you'll get Stuart to a doctor."

"You keep saying that, but you won't say why."

"If you can't do it, we'll sic Betty on him. That always

works. He'll do it just to get her off his back. I'll be there in a couple days, I can do it myself, if I have to."

"A couple days?"

"Yeah, we were going to cut this trip short anyway, and I want to get home to James."

"Molly, I told you, Stuart is—"

"We'll burn that bridge when we come to it. In the meantime, you take care of yourself. Make Stu take care of you, the way he's supposed to. He only pulls shit if you let him get away with it. If he locks himself up in that garage too long, go kick the door and tell him to pay some attention to you! Tell him to come give you some lovin', that'll do it. I don't care how depressed or paranoid he gets, Stuart never turns down sex, even if he—"

"Depressed or paranoid?"

A male voice spoke in the background, and Molly said, "I've gotta go, Amelia. Call me if anything comes up, and I'll see you in a day or two."

After putting the phone back on its base, Amelia stared at it for a long time as her coffee cooled.

I don't care how depressed or paranoid he gets . . .

She turned those two words over and over in her mind, like gems under a jeweler's loupe: *depressed* and *paranoid*. They had been spoken with familiarity, as if Molly had encountered them in Stuart before.

"Or am I the one being paranoid?" Amelia muttered.

Hermione hopped onto the bar with one of Stuart's socks dangling from her mouth, and responded with a garbled meow. The cat dropped the sock, settled her rear on the tile and licked a paw.

"For me?" Amelia asked with a smirk. "Aren't you sweet."

She got off the stool and stuffed the sock in the right pocket of her jeans. She left her coffee behind as she went down the hall to the door to the garage. Her attempt to describe the paintings to Molly had been a feeble one and had not done justice to Stuart's work. It was difficult for her to describe what she did not understand. She had been unable to identify whatever it was that made the paintings work so beautifully, that made a grown man in an owl suit look so perfectly natural, even mundane, against a cityscape at night. She wanted to look at them again, more carefully.

In the garage, Amelia moved with much more economy than last time. She had the cabinet open in less than thirty seconds after entering. She found a dusty old camp chair, brushed a hand over it a few times, and sat on it to study Stuart's paintings.

In each painting, Owl-Man stood atop some kind of structure beneath a night sky. In a couple, Owl-Man was only a silhouette. In one painting, he stood on one of the enormous cables of the Golden Gate Bridge, and in another, he stood at the top of the TransAmerica building looking down at the city below.

The colors were rich and deep, and the paintings had about them a sharpness, an immediacy she had never before seen in Stuart's work. There was something feverish about them, something frantic. They were, each one of them, vivid and beautiful.

The rain was much louder in the garage than in the house, but it faded for Amelia as she lost herself in the paintings, until a new sound startled her out of her reverie. Amelia stopped and listened. The loud rain, a siren in the distance, nothing else. She could have sworn she had heard someone pull into the driveway. She turned her head toward the large, heavy garage door. It was electric and was supposed to roll up when the remote was activated. Amelia had never seen the door's remote. She certainly had never seen the garage door opened.

She turned her attention back to the painting she was studying, but nearly fell off her camp chair when she heard the Celica's door slam shut just outside the big door. Amelia's insides clenched with panic as she hurriedly put the paintings back in place. She might make it, especially if he didn't come straight down the hall into the garage. What was he doing home? She thought he had gone to work after taking James to school.

Amelia was sliding the last painting into its slot in the cabinet when a loud, rattling hum nearly made her cry out. She turned toward the front of the garage as the electric door rolled smoothly, loudly upward. In all the time she had lived with Stuart, the garage door had not been used once.

But he had to use it today, she thought.

Stuart appeared before her from the bottom up—his feet, his legs, his abdomen. Before the door rose high enough for him to step inside, he ducked down and went under it, got out of the rain. He froze when he saw her, started to smile, then saw the open cabinet.

"Please don't be angry," Amelia said. "I can explain."

CHAPTER THIRTEEN

After a brief meeting with James and the vice principal—Stuart was pleased with the man's apparent no-nonsense approach—Stuart left James at school and went shopping for supplies. He had not made a list, because the things he needed kept changing the more he thought about them.

The combination of shopping and waiting in traffic ate up almost three hours. He had felt edgy all morning, and the traffic just made him feel worse—fidgety, twitchy, unable to follow a train of thought very far, and worried, but about nothing in particular. Most of all, he felt nagged by a sense of dreadful anticipation.

Stuart knew his developing plan was lunacy. He would argue that point with no one. It did not, however, as far as Stuart could tell, mean that he was a lunatic. People probably questioned Benjamin Franklin's sanity when they saw him flying a kite with a key tied to the tail in the middle of an electrical storm. It was an insane thing to do. But Franklin was not insane, he was a genius. Stuart did not believe himself to be a genius, but he knew people would say the same thing about him—that he was insane. *If* they found out. *If* he was discovered. As long as he kept those things from happening, he would be fine, and if he was indeed crazy, no one would know.

When he saw Amelia at the open cabinet in the garage, a feeling of utter defeat passed through him. He had not even begun, and already he had been discovered. Then he became angry and shouted and kicked the camp chair hard and high enough to send it clattering against the back wall of the garage. Amelia apologized repeatedly and he kept shouting, until suddenly they stopped simultaneously. Stuart took calming breaths as Amelia tried to muzzle her sobs. His anger passed rather quickly and he closed the garage door and said, "Let's go in the house."

Stuart was relieved he had not brought any of the supplies he had purchased into the garage. There was no telling what she would have made of them. He would say nothing about it until he was able to determine how much Amelia knew, or thought she knew, and how much of it was accurate. He would say nothing revealing if he could possibly avoid it.

They said nothing at first, while Amelia started a pot of coffee. She took a paper towel from the roll and dabbed it at her teary eyes as she joined Stuart at the bar, face-to-face.

"I thought you'd gone to work," she said.

"I didn't say I was going to work."

"I know, I just assumed."

"Is that what you do every day while I'm at work? Go through my things?"

"Stuart, you know that's not true."

"Well, I have to ask, I mean, I'm not here, how could I know? I come home and find you going through my things, naturally I'm going to wonder if—"

"I'm sorry. I really don't know why I'm crying. It's just that I've been worried about you lately, and my nerves are just—"

"You've been worried about me?"

"Of course I've been worried about you. You don't sleep much anymore, you spend all your time in the garage. You hardly talk to me. I don't know what's wrong."

Stuart smiled and put his hand on hers. "Thank you. That's nice."

Amelia blinked a few times, frowned. "What's nice?"

He shrugged. "I can't remember the last time anyone was worried about me. For any reason."

She took his hand between both of hers. "Don't be ridiculous, Stu. Even Molly is worried about you. In . . . her way."

He pulled his hand away and leaned back, away from the bar. "You've been talking to her about me? I thought we went over that, Amelia."

"Yell at me about that later, okay? We're not talking about that right now. I want you to tell me what's wrong, Stu. Please. What's going on? Are you . . . have you been feeling sick lately?"

"No. I should sleep more, I know, but I've been . . . getting a lot of work done. Of course, you already know that. What do you think of it?"

"The paintings? They're incredible, they're beautiful. I don't understand why you locked them up like that, they're, I'm not kidding, they're *stunning*."

"That's nice of you to say, but how do you think—"

"I'm not just saying it. I mean it."

"Any respect my work has garnered in the past would go right down the toilet if I let those paintings out."

"I don't agree. I think they would be wildly popular and your stock as an artist would go through the roof. I want to know what inspired them, where they came from, but I don't want to talk about the paintings right now. I want you to tell me what's wrong."

He could not tell her what was happening, what he was up against. He did not know why, but he had the strong sense that telling her everything would put her in even more danger than she was in already simply because she lived with him.

"It's . . . not really anything specific," he said. "A little bit of everything. Work, James. Work. I don't think I can stay there much longer. Every day, it seems to get a little worse. The tension is . . . you could drink it through a straw."

"That's why you haven't gone back to the office?"

"I hope Chalmers fires me. I want him to."

"What will you do when he does?"

"I don't know. I could teach. I haven't given it much thought."

"Why haven't you talked to me about this, Stuart? You've been so moody and distant, I've been afraid to ask what was wrong. You've got to open up, Stu. I'm not here just for the good stuff, you know. I want to help with the heavy lifting, too. But I can't if you won't let me."

"I'm sorry," he said. "To tell you the truth, I'm not used to having someone around who wants to listen. Guess I haven't made the adjustment yet."

She waited a moment before speaking again. "Who's Dr. Furgeson?"

Stuart's heart froze in his chest.

Amelia watched as what little color there was in Stuart's weary, drawn face quickly drained away. His forehead creased, eyebrows drew together over troubled eyes. She reached out and clutched his upper left arm to hold him on the stool.

"Stuart?"

His lips moved eratically, but he said nothing. He licked them, cleared his throat. "Was he . . . here?" His voice was sandpaper on stone.

"No. Your mother called. She said you were trying to find him."

His breath was sucked from his lungs, but it sounded like nothing more than a quiet sigh. His head dropped forward into his hands, elbows on the bar. "I should've known."

"She just wanted to let you know she'd found him."

He raised his head abruptly. "Found him?"

"She called a few people and found out where he is."

"Amazing. Where is he?"

"Orangevale. Know where that is?"

He nodded.

"Who is he, Stu?"

"What did Mom tell you?"

"She wouldn't tell me anything. Neither would Molly. It's a great big secret, it seems."

"Why do you go to them first?" he asked. He tried to conceal his anger, but failed. "You can't believe anything they tell you, anyway. Goddammit, Amelia, I don't like people talking about my personal problems. I'm not gossip."

"We weren't talking about your personal problems. Because no one would talk about them. And I didn't go to them first. Your mother called *me*. I don't know who Dr. Furgeson is, I've never heard of him before so I asked, but nobody will tell me anything about him. It's almost as if they're *afraid* to talk about him."

He spoke in a low, raspy monotone. "That's because I've told them never to talk about him. They have in the past. Right after I married Molly. Mom told her the whole story one day when I wasn't around. Molly . . . she thought it was the funniest thing she'd ever heard and had a big laugh. She joked about it. In bed. You wonder why I don't like the fact that you two are friends? You don't know the half of it."

"What did she laugh at? What happened?"

Slowly, and sometimes with difficulty, Stuart told her the story. Amelia listened with growing alarm.

"How could she do such a thing?" she whispered when he was finished. "How could *any* mother do such a thing?"

"It's not a problem for her," he said, "because she remembers it differently. That's how everyone in my family has always dealt with bad things. Anger, violence, anything they don't like, they just remember it differently. Like my dad. He dragged me through childhood by the hair, kicking me half the time. But when he got older, no, he'd never done that. He said his parents had pulled his hair when he was a kid and he hated it, so he'd never do that to anyone else." He shrugged. "He just remembered it differently, and he was off the hook."

"You don't talk about your childhood in any detail," she whispered. "You've told me a couple things here and there, but only bits and pieces."

"I will if you want me to, but frankly, I'd rather not."

"No, no. I don't blame you." Anger still burned in her chest for the apparently sweet old woman who would allow such a thing to be done to her son. "I just meant that this kind of explains some things I've never been able to understand. Like your relationship with your mother."

"Even I don't understand that."

"I can't believe Molly found that funny."

"Then you don't know her very well."

"I'll drop her, if you'd like."

"I can't tell you who to be friends with and who not—"

"No, really, I'm pissed at her. I'd like to slap her. It doesn't matter what you want me to do. The next time I see her will be the last. I mean, she doesn't need to come in and hang out here every time James comes over or she comes to pick him up. The thought of her laughing at—"

"Hey, hey, look, I don't want you dropping friends on my account, no matter *how* much I don't like having Molly around. And I didn't mean to make you angry."

Amelia realized how loudly she was speaking, how tense her voice was, and laughed with embrassment. "Sorry. I don't get angry very often, and when I do . . . well, I don't handle it very well. I wouldn't mind smacking your mother, too."

"Oh, be my guest. It would be interesting to see how she'd remember it in a year or two."

They laughed together, and much of the tension in the air dissipated. They kissed over the bar.

"I'm sorry that happened to you," she said.

"I'm sorry I didn't tell you sooner. It felt good."

They just looked at each other for a long moment, and Amelia felt her worries dissolving. Not all of them, but most.

"Are you really trying to get fired?" she asked.

"I don't know. I needed the break. I wanted to work. On the paintings, I mean. They were flowing so smoothly, one after another, I didn't want to slow down or stop. Until I started working on the—" Stuart froze up, stiffened, frowned. He thought a moment, then shook his head. "I don't know what I want to do."

"Are you working on something else, too?"

He looked at her with a weary smile. "No."

"What did you mean? Until you started working on what?"

He shrugged. "I don't know. I'm . . . tired."

"Coffee's ready. Are you hungry?"

"I was thinking about going upstairs for a little nap."

"Oh?" She grinned. "Can I go upstairs and nap with you?"

"Doesn't sound like much of a nap."

But they went upstairs, anyway.

CHAPTER FOURTEEN

He moves through the city streets with speed and silence. Through the rain and down one dark, filthy alley after another, through the stench of overflowing Dumpsters and past clots of shuffling street people. A white flap of coattails disappears around the corner up ahead. He runs faster to close the gap between them, whips around the corner, runs down the sidewalk.

Even in the wee hours of the morning, there is traffic on the streets. Horns beep and wail, tires scream over pavement as Dr. Furgeson runs into the street and zigzags to the other side. A bumper crunches against a fender. Traffic in both directions stops completely for a moment. He takes advantage of it and runs across the street. Angry voices curse, and more horns protest.

Someone gawks at him out a car window and shouts, "What the fuck is *that*?"

Down another alley. This one smells of rotting vegetables, peanut sauce, and something dead, a cat or a dog, maybe.

He does not know how long he has been running, but for the first time, he recognizes where he is. The Tenderloin, where he found James in the middle of the night.

Up ahead, Dr. Furgeson stumbles, and the gap closes a bit more. Suddenly, the doctor throws himself onto the rusted ladder of a fire escape and scurries up smoothly, like a lizard. The whole structure shudders and rattles.

Stuart hits the ladder as Dr. Furgeson disappears into an open window.

When Stuart drops through the window, Dr. Furgeson disappears around a corner up ahead.

The same ugly red and blue diamond-print carpet. The same dusty brass sconces bleeding dull, butter-colored light upward on the walls.

He runs down the hall, rounds the corner.

Dr. Furgeson is gone.

Stuart searches his memory for the room number. But as he hurries down the hall checking the doors, he sees that they have no numbers.

Except one, farther along. 202. Loud rap music comes from the apartment. The doorjamb is broken, and the door hangs open a few inches. He pushes it all the way with his foot, steps into the room.

Wolfman, Phantom, and Dracula all smile at him. After looking him over for a moment, they laugh. James is not among them.

"Where's James?" Stuart asks.

"What the fuck you s'posed to be?" Phantom asks.

"Where's James?" he shouts.

Phantom nods toward the door—the one Stuart assumed, during his previous visit to the apartment, led to a bathroom—and says, "The doctor wants t'see you, birdboy." He laughs again. "Are them real fuckin' feathers?"

Stuart does not respond or move.

Phantom goes to the door, pushes it open. "In there."

He moves slowly around the cluttered tables, past the computers and monitors and keyboards, scanners, and printers. He pushes the door the rest of the way open as he steps cautiously through it.

The room is badly lit by a lamp in the corner and a harshly bright bare lightbulb that hangs from the ceiling. A medicine smell gives the stale air a sting. Beneath the bulb, a tall white-coated figure hunches over a long table, his back to Stuart. The figure straightens and turns.

"What took you so long?" Dr. Furgeson asks with a grin. "I almost started without you. But I thought you'd like to watch." He walks around to the other side of the table.

"Dad, who is this guy?" James asks with a fractured voice. He is lying naked on the table, but tries to sit up when he sees Stuart. "What's he gonna do to me? Huh, Dad?"

Stuart's mother appears behind James, at the head of the table. She puts her hands on his shoulders. "Just hold still, honey," she says. "It'll be over before you know it."

Something explodes in Stuart. "Get your fucking hands off him!" he screams as he lunges toward his son and mother.

"No, no, Stu, please," Amelia says as she steps in front of him. She puts her hands on his chest and gently pushes him backward.

Stuart resists and moves to push her aside, but his resistance is weak and she does not move. Amelia pushes harder, and he can only move back, useless against her, until he is pressed flat against a wall.

In a low, breathy voice, Amelia tells Stuart how worried about him she has been lately, how concerned, on and on, while behind her, James is screaming, "No! No! Dad, please help me, help me, no, Dad, please—"

And Betty cheerfully says, "It has to be done, Jimmy, it'll all be over in a minute," as Dr. Furgeson says, "Gonna make sure you can pee right."

"Get off me, Amelia," Stuart says through clenched teeth. But she continues to press him against the wall with unchallengeable strength. "Get off me!"

Amelia says, "But I've been so worried about you because you've been so—"

James screams in agony, "*Daaaaaad!*" as Dr. Furgeson says, "You won't feel this at all."

"See?" James's grandma says happily. "You won't feel it, and it'll all be over before you know it."

Even in the chaos of voices and amid the pounding of the

rap music from the other room, Stuart can hear the small, steely sound:

Snick-snick-snick. Snick-snick-snick.

Past Amelia, Stuart sees his son struggling on the table, sees him lift his head. James's eyes become impossibly wide, and Stuart knows what they are seeing. He cries out as he fights with Amelia, tries to roll out from beneath her, but falls and hits the floor hard facedown and—

He rolled onto his back and realized he was lying beside a bed. Suddenly, Amelia peered over the edge of the bed, down at him.

"Are you all right, Stu?"

"No, get away from me, dammit, I've got to help James!" he shouted as he crawled clumsily backward.

She came off the bed, naked, and pursued him on hands and knees, but not in a rush. Almost patiently, like some pale and pretty spider looking forward to sucking him dry. Her lips moved frantically, but her words were garbled gibberish to him. When he became cornered between his dresser and the wall, she knelt beside him, leaned over him, put her hands on his chest.

"*No!*" he shouted as he swung his right arm out and slammed it into her chest.

Amelia's breath exploded from her as she tumbled backward.

Stuart struggled to his feet and rushed toward James—but he was not there. The table was gone. So were his mother and Dr. Furgeson. He stood, instead, in his own bedroom.

He looked down at himself. His suit, his gloves, the cape—they were all gone. He was naked. Bewildered, Stuart turned and looked down at Amelia.

She was getting up slowly, gasping for breath.

He realized suddenly that he had been dreaming, and hurried to Amelia.

They sat together on the edge of the bed. Stuart felt

horrible and apologized repeatedly, but she kept telling him it was unnecessary, she knew it wasn't intentional.

"You were dreaming, honey," she said as she put an arm behind him, stroked his back. "Didn't look like a very pleasant dream, either. Do you remember it?"

"Oh, yeah," he said. His face felt wet and he wiped a hand over the layer of perspiration on his forehead, cheeks, and throat.

"What was happening to James?" Amelia asked.

"James?"

"You said you had to help James."

He shook his head. "I don't want to talk about it."

"Do you have dreams like that often?"

He shrugged. The sensation of Amelia's hand sliding back and forth over his sweaty back was irritating and he pulled away from her. She took the hint, and put her hand in her lap. He gently squeezed her thigh. "Sorry. I'm not . . . I just don't feel . . ."

"Was Dr. Furgeson in the dream?"

"I said I don't want to talk about it," he replied, exercising restraint in his words and tone. He spotted a red bath towel draped over the chair beside his closet, got up and dried himself with it as if he had just stepped out of the shower.

"I don't mean to pry," she said, "but for one thing, I don't think it's very healthy for you to hold that stuff in. And for another, it's not very healthy for our relationship. What are you afraid of, anyway? Are you afraid I'm going to run around telling people? I'm not Molly, Stuart. I didn't realize until today just how *much* I'm not Molly."

He stopped scrubbing himself with the towel and looked at her. Her eyes were wide and sad and beautiful. He knew she meant it, that she would tell no one. He was ashamed that he had given no thought to how Amelia must feel lately, not knowing what was wrong with him, why he had crawled so far inside himself. He had hoped to satisfy her with what he had told her earlier. But she knew there was more now.

Stuart paced slowly, the towel around his neck, fists clenched at each end pulling it taut. "Remember the other night? When you found me in the backyard with the flashlight?"

"Uh-huh. You said you thought you'd seen somebody out there."

"Yeah, but I lied. I *did* see somebody out there. I was standing at the sink when I saw Dr. Furgeson. Right outside the window. He smiled at me."

"Jesus, Stuart, why didn't you say so? Why didn't you call the police?"

"I . . . I don't know. I don't think I believed it myself. I mean, all these years later, why would he—"

"Wait, you mean . . . you thought it was really Dr. Furgeson?"

He stopped pacing and looked at her. "Well, yeah, what did you think I meant?"

"I thought you meant someone who looked like him, or . . . but I . . . didn't I tell you?"

"Tell me what?"

"Where he is."

"Dr. Furgeson? You said he's in Orangevale."

She nodded once. "In a convalescent hospital. A rest home."

Stuart went to the bed and sat down because his knees were suddenly weak. He closed his eyes against a wave of dizziness.

"What's wrong?" Amelia asked in a whisper.

It made no sense. Maybe it was a different Dr. Furgeson. But that was unlikely. His mother knew how to find the juiciest grapes on the grapevine, and her information was probably very solid.

"Why?" Stuart asked.

"Why what?"

"Why . . . is he in a rest home?"

"Oh. I don't know. Your mom just gave me the name of the

place and the address. I wrote it down. It's downstairs on the bar. Want me to get it?"

"No, no." A piercing headache was sweeping in like a storm off the ocean, and he massaged his temples with the tips of stiff fingers. His eyes opened suddenly when he realized that the rest home might be nothing more than an address. Would Dr. Furgeson do something so elaborate just to torment Stuart? How much more elaborate would that be than the things he had already done? Not much. He had gone far out of his way to find Stuart, to follow him. And it was such a perfect cover. Who would think him capable of stalking Stuart if he were in a rest home? No one. Including Amelia. He could tell by the troubled, doubtful look on her face that she was thinking that very thing. He stood and began to put on his sweats. "On the bar, you said?"

"Next to the TV," Amelia said, standing. "I can get it."

"No, I'll get it."

She was putting her clothes on when Stuart left the bedroom, but she caught up with him downstairs.

He stood at the bar reading Amelia's handwriting on the pad when she approached him from behind and asked, "What are you going to do?"

Stuart removed the page from the pad, put it in his pocket. "I don't know."

In a moment, they had resumed the places they had taken earlier, facing one another across the bar.

Amelia asked, "You, uh . . . you don't think it's really him, do you? I mean, Dr. Furgeson? If he's in a rest home, it seems pretty unlikely that he could—"

"I've seen him other places, too."

"Where?"

"Around." Stuart put his trembling hands out of sight. "It's him."

"Look, if somebody's stalking you, you should call the police."

"It's not just *somebody*."

"Stuart." She put a hand on his upper arm. "He's in a rest home."

"Mom says he's in a rest home." He sipped his coffee and winced when he found it cold. He got up and found the pot was still hot, poured another. "Who did she call? How do you know she's right?"

"Okay, let's . . . let's say you're right. It's Dr. Furgeson. Why? I mean, all these years later, why would he do this?"

He put cream in his coffee but did not return to the bar. He leaned his hips against the edge of the counter, sipped from his steaming mug.

"I've got an idea," Amelia said. She went to him, tried to meet his eyes.

He was not in the mood for eye contact at the moment. His mind was racing with disconnected thoughts.

"Tomorrow, let's go to Orangevale, to the rest home," she went on. "It's Saturday, so James can come. We'll make a day of it, do some shopping, maybe see a movie, go out to eat. And you could see him, Stuart, you could even talk to him if you want. But you'd see that he's . . . well, he's probably not in any condition to travel, even from there to—"

"No, I've got too much to do," he said with an abrupt shake of his head.

"Do? What do you have to do?"

"Work." He stepped around her and walked away, still without meeting her eyes. He could almost hear doors slamming inside himself, locks turning, shutters clattering shut, windows sliding closed and latching. Preparing for a storm. A big one.

Amelia followed him out of the kitchen. "You're going back to work?"

He said nothing as he went down the back hall.

"Stu, could you wait? Please talk to me. I think we should—"

"Got work to do," he said as he went through the door at the end of the hall and into the garage. He closed the door, flipped the hook into the eye and turned the lock on the doorknob.

All his purchases were still in the car. He needed to bring them into the garage and get busy. He was not sure why, but Stuart suddenly had the feeling that he was running out of time.

He punched the button on the wall that sent the garage door humming open and muttered, "Good thing Mom taught me how to sew."

CHAPTER FIFTEEN

When Amelia awoke the next morning, Stuart's side of the bed was undisturbed and looked exactly as it had when she'd gone to sleep. She got up and showered, dressed, went downstairs. There was no mess in the kitchen, no music or television playing. The house seemed empty. For all she knew, it was and she was alone. She went down the back hall and stood at the door, knocked, listened. No response, no whispers of movement in the garage. Not a sound.

Amelia tried the door, but it was locked. A jolt of fear went through her chest. Stuart was in there, or the door would be unlocked, and if he was in there, why wasn't he responding or moving around? Unless he had become ill. It could have happened and neither she nor James would have known. The way he was behaving—not sleeping, not eating right— some kind of illness seemed not only possible but perhaps even likely.

"Stuart?" she called as she knocked on the door. She waited, listened. Nothing. She knocked harder, shouted louder. "If you're in there, just let me know, Stuart, I'm getting—"

She was going to say "scared," but a thought interrupted her.

He's using the garage door now, she remembered.

She had not heard the automatic door activated, but upstairs and on the other side of the house, she probably would not, especially while sleeping. Stuart was probably gone.

Amelia turned and went back up the hall. She went to one of the living room windows, pulled the drapes aside.

The rain had withdrawn to a drizzle. Across the street, a couple of little kids took turns jumping into a puddle at the side of the street while a small, ash-colored dog hopped around them and barked playfully. The Celica was parked in the driveway, as always.

"Doesn't mean he's here," she muttered as she let the curtain drop back into place.

Stuart seldom drove the Celica. He thought driving was a waste of time and preferred public transportation, which allowed him time to draw or read. He had probably taken the bus somewhere.

She went through the dining room, down the short hall, and knocked on James's door.

"Yeah?" he replied.

"Can I come in?" she asked as she opened the door.

James was sitting on the floor in boxers and an *Attack of the Clones* T-shirt, his back against the side of his bed, a laptop open on his pasty white thighs. He looked up at her with blank disinterest.

"Have you seen your dad this morning?"

He shook his head, turned his eyes back to the screen.

"Okay. What would you like for break—" She frowned and took a step into the room. "Hey, I thought your dad suspended your computer privileges."

James shrugged as he looked up again, impatient. "From his computer, yeah."

"No, I don't think that was the deal. Where did you get that?" she asked, nodding toward the laptop.

"A friend gave it to me."

She laughed suspiciously. "Uh-huh. I know how much those things cost, James. Most people in your age group can't afford to buy them, let alone go around giving them to people."

"Who said anything about—my friend's dad writes for a—jeez, do I have to go through this with you, too?"

Amelia immediately regretted saying anything. She held

up both hands, palms out, and said, "You're right. It's not my place. I'm sorry." She left the room and closed the door.

In the kitchen, she considered what to make for breakfast, but knew she could not eat. She had not been up a whole hour and already she felt tense. If things did not lighten up around the house soon, she would become as unpleasant as Stuart and James.

As she made coffee, she thought about Stuart and his insistence that Dr. Furgeson was following him around for some reason. It was ridiculous, of course, and the fact that Stuart could not see that was a bad sign. It was not the behavior of a stable person. He needed to see a doctor as soon as possible. But he would not go if he thought nothing was wrong.

Amelia thought that what the doctor had done to Stuart— what Betty had allowed the doctor to do—was horrible. It should have been done on the operating table. It clearly had been a traumatic experience for Stuart and still disturbed him.

She had not been humoring Stuart last night when she said she would stop seeing Molly. The fact that Molly could laugh at such a thing infuriated her, and made her wonder if Stuart had been right about her all along. But before she distanced herself from Molly, she needed to ask her a few questions. Had this happened before? Did Stuart have a history of mental illness? No, she decided it had to be something new. Stuart would have told her himself. Or Molly would have told her. Wouldn't *someone* have told her?

In college, Amelia's younger sister Daria had developed a crushing drinking problem. She had hidden it for about a year, but it became impossible to conceal and had been the source of a great deal of pain in their family. Daria had finally become convinced that she had a problem when she was arrested for driving under the influence. It turned out that Daria's drinking was a symptom of a greater problem. She was suffering from bipolar disorder and her drinking was a way of medicating herself. But it had caused new problems of its own, of course. Everything turned out fine—Daria was happily married with a son, took medication to control her disorder, and had not had a drink in years. But before her sister had admitted to and dealt with her problem, Amelia had lived with a feeling of fear for her sister, and a sinking helplessness that never went away, even during the quiet periods between the crises that repeatedly broke out around Daria.

Stuart's insistence that a retired urologist from his childhood was stalking him was a problem, but it was not *the* problem. It was a symptom of something bigger. Not knowing what that might be gave Amelia the same helpless feeling she'd lived with when her little sister had been in trouble. Short of making Daria realize she had a problem, there was nothing Amelia could do back then. Getting arrested had been the nudge Daria had needed.

She thought of Dr. Furgeson, probably wasting away in that Orangevale rest home. Seeing the old man there might be the nudge Stuart needed. But it would do no good if he refused to go.

Amelia leaned against the counter and ate a banana as coffee began to dribble slowly into the pot. She could go herself. But would he believe her if she came back and told him the scary doctor was a withered, arthritic, slobbering old man? He might if she had pictures of the doctor to show him. She imagined a nurse walking in while she took Polaroids of an emaciated old man in bed. It was a crude thing to do, but it might be worth the embarrassment. If she left right away, she could be back by early afternoon. It would be best to go before Stuart came back, anyway—she was a terrible liar, and she was afraid he would get upset if she told him her plans.

The clock on the microwave read 9:12. Traffic might not be bad on a Saturday morning, and she might be able to make the trip rather quickly. Afraid she might change her mind if she thought about it any further, Amelia hurried upstairs to find her Polaroid camera.

Stuart sat at the card table and listened to the Celica's engine idle. He wondered where she was going, if James was going with her. All that mattered was that he had some time to work undisturbed.

When Amelia had come to the door earlier, he'd heard her approaching and stopped what he was doing. He'd been removing the aluminum drawer tracks from a battered old three-drawer metal filing cabinet that had been in the garage for years. He knew every creak in the house and could hear her coming from the other end of the hall. While she knocked and called his name, Stuart had remained still and silent.

The tracks from the filing cabinet were too long to fit onto his forearms. He measured them, marked them with a pencil. The Celica backed out of the driveway as he took the tracks to the filthy, cluttered old work shelf against the back wall of the garage. It had been filthy and cluttered and old when he bought the place fifteen years ago.

The car's engine faded with distance as Amelia drove away. He fastened one of the tracks down with the shelf's built-in clamps, poked around in the pile of old tools and coils of wire and cable and other useless junk he had never gotten around to throwing out. He found a hacksaw and went to work on the first track. They might be too broad, in which case he would have to find something else. But he would not know until he tried them.

Once both had been cut, Stuart unlocked the door and left the garage. He went to the kitchen and poured himself a cup of coffee, got a packet of two brown-sugar-cinnamon Pop-Tarts. He unplugged the clock radio and took it with him back to the garage. He put the coffee and Pop-Tarts on the card table, the clock radio on the work shelf. He was tired of the silence and plugged in the clock radio, found a station playing Glenn Miller's "String of Pearls." Nice.

Stuart was afraid another minute of silence would have driven him insane. With the music playing, maybe he would stop hearing the scissors.

"Hello?"

"Hi, Betty, it's Amelia. Um, I wrote down the information you gave me yesterday, but I lost the piece of paper I wrote it on, can you believe it? What was the name of that rest home again?"

"Oh, I'll get it." She put the telephone down with a clank.

Amelia held her cell phone to her left ear, right hand on the steering wheel as she drove down Interstate 80.

The phone was picked up again and Betty said, "It's the St. Elizabeth Extended Care Center in Orangevale. Room 310, bed B."

Amelia repeated it quickly several times in her head. "Thanks, Betty, I really appre—"

"How's Stuart?"

"He's . . . not well."

"Oh, I've told him—for years I've been telling him—he needs a good multiple vitamin every day, and he should make sure he gets plenty of—"

"I don't think vitamins will help this, Betty."

"What's wrong? Is it the flu? He usually gets the flu two or three times a year because he doesn't take any vitamin C. I tell him he needs his C, but he doesn't listen."

Amelia was already angry at Betty. Hearing her rattle on about vitamins only made her feel worse. "Listen, Betty, I need you to answer a question for me, and I need you to answer it honestly. Has Stuart ever . . . in the past, has he ever had any problems with, um . . . with mental illness?"

The two words "mental illness" shattered over the line like breaking glass. Betty made a couple of stammering false starts before responding.

"Mental illness? Why on earth—what would make you ask that? Stuart is . . . he's moody. I don't have to tell you that, do I?" She laughed. "He's always been more sensitive and temperamental than most, but he's an artist, so I suppose it's not that surprising that he—"

She's not going to tell me a damned thing, Amelia thought as she said, "Okay, well, thanks, Betty. I've gotta run. See ya." She turned off the phone, dropped it onto the seat beside her. A moment later, she picked it up again and punched in the number of Molly's cell phone. There was no answer. A few minutes later, she tried again. Nothing.

She regretted not bringing James. He was going through a tough time right now, but he was a decent kid. She had liked him the first time they met. Before leaving, she had popped into his room and asked him, very politely, to please stay in the house until she or his dad got back.

"If for no other reason," she had said, "would you do this as a personal favor to me? Just to keep the peace, or what little of it we've got. Please?"

"Sure," he had replied, his tone sincere, even a little concerned by her question.

Fifteen miles before Sacramento, Amelia called Molly again. Still no answer. Once again, she dropped the cell phone in the seat and tried to focus her thoughts on what she would do once she arrived at the St. Elizabeth Extended Care Center in Orangevale.

Stuart found James slumped on the living room couch reading a comic book while a Godzilla movie played on television.

"Where did Amelia go?" he asked.

James shrugged. "Dunno. Didn't say."

Stuart put both hands on the back of the couch, leaned on them with elbows locked. He watched the Godzilla movie with James for several seconds, until Stuart laughed. "It's amazing," he said. "Movie special effects have become so sophisticated and realistic, and yet the Japanese still have a guy in a rubber suit stomping on toys."

"That changed with the American *Godzilla*," James said.

Stuart wrinkled his nose, shook his head. "Nah, that movie doesn't count. It's American. It doesn't have the same sensibility. Godzilla is uniquely Japanese."

"Whatta y'mean?"

He walked around the couch, plopped down next to James. "Have you ever seen the first Godzilla movie?"

"*Godzilla, King of the Monsters?*"

"That's the one. Midfifties, I think. The one with all those stupid inserts of Raymond Burr looking like he hasn't had a bowel movement in months. That movie was a big success in Japan, because it terrified audiences. The way *Jaws* and *The Exorcist* terrified American audiences back in the seventies, *Godzilla, King of the Monsters* terrified Japanese audiences in the fifties."

James turned toward his dad, interested, a little puzzled. "They were scared of a guy in a rubber suit?"

"No. They were scared of radiation. Remember, about a decade or so before that movie came out, we dropped two atomic bombs on Japan."

"We did?"

James frowned. "You should be in a private school getting a decent education. But no, your mother had to have her house in Pacific Heights. Of course, if you wouldn't skip school, you might—"

"Just kidding, Dad. I know about Hiroshima and Nagasaki. Grampa was always talkin' about it."

"Yeah, that's right."

"So, Godzilla was created by radiation," James said thoughtfully, "and he had, like, radioactive breath. And that's what they thought was so scary?"

"Yep. Because they'd seen the effects of radiation up close. Right there in their own country. So the idea of radiation raining down on their cities was terrifying stuff to them."

James looked at the television screen but did not seem to be watching the movie. He frowned thoughtfully, chewed on a fingernail. "Does that mean that, y'know, everybody's that way?"

"What way?"

"I mean, could I be scared of something that nobody else is scared of? Y'know, like, there's something that scares only me, and nobody else is afraid of it."

"Sure. We all have different fears. Sometimes they're instilled early in life, sometimes they develop over time. I knew a guy in college who was scared out of his mind by dust bunnies. You know, those clusters of dust that gather under the furniture, under the bed? He kept his dorm room spotless, perfectly clean at all times, just because he'd fall apart at the sight of a dust bunny."

James laughed.

"Yeah, I laughed, too, but it didn't take long to realize this was a really big fear for him. It was serious. I think we've all got at least one fear we're a little ashamed of, but it's no less terrifying. Like me."

"What are you afraid of?"

"Water."

James's eyes widened. "You're afraid to get wet?"

"No, no. Deep water. You've never seen me go swimming, have you?"

He thought about it a moment, then shook his head.

"Because I'm terrified of deep water, of drowning. Always have been, ever since I was little. I don't know why, but it scares the hell out of me. How about you? What fear embarrasses you?"

James bowed his head, then shook it. "Nothin'," he said quietly, opening the comic book again, reading.

Stuart sensed it was a good time to change the subject. "What's the comic book?"

"*Spawn.*"

"Mm. Heard of it, never read it." He leaned over and looked at the colorful panels on the pages. "It's been ages since I've read a comic book. Used to read them all the time, even as an adult, when you were a baby. *Batman, Spider-Man, The X-Men, Fantastic Four, Iron Man.* When I was a kid, there was a comic magazine called *Vampirella.* I read that, too."

James tipped his head back, looked up at Stuart and said, "Yeah, I've read *Vampirella.*"

"It's still being published?"

"It started up again as a full-color comic book back in the nineties. I got some, you wanna see 'em?"

"Well . . . I've got work to do, but . . . maybe for a few minutes. Yeah, sure."

While James went to his room, Stuart sat on the couch and watched the movie. James returned with a cardboard box filled with comic books and graphic novels. He sat on the couch and put the box between them, removed a stack and handed it to his dad.

"You've got so many," Stuart muttered.

James shrugged. "I got a couple more boxes of 'em at Mom's. I never get rid of 'em. I got some issues of *Vampirella* in here somewhere."

Stuart went through the stack slowly, a smile on his lips. There were many familiar figures on the covers, and some he had never seen before but which were no less intriguing. James filled him in on the changes that had taken place over the years in the titles that Stuart used to read regularly. For example, Superman had died at one point. Special editions had pitted Batman against the monsters from the *Alien* and *Predator* movies. Catwoman had her own comic book. He told him about characters unfamiliar to Stuart, like Hellboy and Sandman.

They talked superheroes and supervillains, comic book artists and writers. Stuart was pleased to learn that they liked most of the same titles and favored many of the same characters. James gave him a rundown of the newer titles, explaining heroes and villains that were totally unfamiliar to him.

Stuart thought of his Owl-Man paintings. He considered

toning down the lighter parts of the costume, wondered if he might try getting work in the comic book industry after he left Carnival.

Stuart's mouth dropped open as he removed from the stack a comic book called *Lady Death*, with a scantily clad and impossibly buxom woman on the cover. "Good Lord, this woman's breasts have their own weather systems!" he exclaimed with genuine amazement. "We never had comic books like this when I was a kid!"

James laughed. "I thought you had *Vampirella* back then. She's got a rack on her."

"Yeah, but it wasn't really a comic book. More of a magazine, black-and-white." As he went on, he spoke more slowly and his voice became gradually quieter. "I had every issue, though. Boxes of comic books. A neighbor gave me all his old ones, and then, when I started getting an allowance, I spent nearly every dime on comic books. I took good care of them, too. Kept them in those plastic envelopes, never let anybody borrow them."

"Still got 'em?" James asked. "They might be worth some money."

Stuart frowned as he thumbed through *Lady Death*. His eyes were on the pages, but they were seeing instead remembered images that flashed behind them. Images of his mother and Pastor Merckin leaning toward him, concerned faces close, voices urgent. "No. I don't."

James watched him, waited for him to continue. When he did not, James asked, "What happened to th—"

"My mother made me burn them," he said, nearly whispering.

"Grandma?" James screwed up his face for a moment in sympathy. "Yeah, I guess she's pretty religious. That sucks, Dad."

Slumped on the couch, head down, eyes on the comic book, he said, "Oh, yeah."

"Why'd she do that?"

"At the time, I'd decided I was going to be a comic book artist. I wasn't interested in anything else, my mind was made up. That scared her, I think. As far as she was concerned, I might as well join the Church of Satan, or something. She wanted me to go into the ministry. Wanted me to be a singing evangelist."

"A singing evangelist? Are you serious?"

Stuart smiled at James. "Yeah. Believe it or not, I used to sing a lot when I was a kid. I was the youngest member of the church choir. Sometimes I sang solos for church, that kind of thing. She wanted me to keep that up. I mean, for the rest of my life. Every once in awhile, she reminds me how disappointed she still is. So that was one reason she wanted to get me off comic books. The other, I think, was that she just got tired of having them around the house. Whenever somebody from church showed up unannounced—and they did that a lot because they liked to see if they could catch you doing something wrong—first thing she'd do was run through the house—and I am serious, she would *run*—to make sure I hadn't left any comic books lying around. Then she'd close my bedroom door so no one could see the posters on my wall—Batman, the Fantastic Four, other comic book characters. I don't know what she would have done if one of her church friends had come across a copy of *Swamp Thing* or *Creepy*. She probably would've died of humiliation. So she got the pastor to help her out. Pastor Merckin. A pudgy guy with a high voice. He came home with her after church one Sunday and she brought him to my room where, naturally, I was reading a comic book."

"Didn't she make you go to church?" James asked.

Stuart shrugged. "When I was younger. You know, a little kid. As I got older, she wouldn't say anything. Not with her voice, anyway. She said it all with her behavior, the way she looked at me. I usually went to Sunday school, but if there was any way to duck out of church, I'd do it. I guess I'd ducked that day. Pastor Merckin came into my room and my mom—you should've seen the look on her face. When Pastor Merckin walked in and looked around at all the posters on the wall and the comic books that were all over the place, Mom . . . she just wilted. She was mortified. The secret was out. Her son was an unrepentant, comic-book-collecting, science-fiction-reading heathen. She looked like she wanted to die. Like in her mind, she was praying that God would take her, right then and there."

Stuart regretted bringing up the story of his burned comic books. It was an ugly memory. Instead of continuing, he went on browsing through the stack of comic books on his lap. He was surprised by James's interest.

"What did the pastor guy do?" James asked. "They didn't, like, exorcise you, or anything did they? I saw that once on *20/20*."

Stuart chuckled. "No, there was no exorcism. But it was close. He started quoting scripture as he walked around my room and picked up a comic book here, an H.P. Lovecraft collection there. He had kind of a squeaky voice, but made up for it with words. He knew how to use words. Probably not to normal people who hadn't had religion pounded into their heads since birth. But I'd been going to church as far back as I could remember, and it had created all these . . . *buttons* in me. And Pastor Merckin knew how to push them. One after another. In less than twenty minutes, he had me sweating bullets. He'd convinced me those comic books were going to drag me straight down to hell sometime before lunch the next day. He used all the catch phrases and code words I'd been taught to respect and fear in church school and Sunday school, tried to convince me I could die at any second. Get hit by a car or die in a car accident, take a fall and break my neck, have an embolism in my brain. And if that happened, was I ready to face God? Was my life clean? Was I ready to be judged? Not if I was reading comic books, filling my mind with all that garbage." He shook his head slowly. "Scared the shit out of me. I couldn't stop shaking.

We made a fire in the fireplace, and I burned them all. Comic books, novels, posters. Even records and tapes. Mom on one side, Pastor Merckin on the other, leaning close and looking so . . . so *serious*. Afterward, I went into the bathroom and sat on the edge of the bathtub and shook like mad. My whole body, my arms, legs, even my head, I couldn't stop shaking. I even started to hyperventilate. And cried like a baby."

"Because you'd lost all your comic books?"

"Well . . . no, not that. Because, see, at the time, I was glad to get rid of them. Pastor Merckin had convinced me that any day now, I could wake up dead and in Hell. I was crying because . . . well, I'm not sure why I was crying."

"Sounds like you had a panic attack."

Stuart turned to James curiously. "A panic attack?"

He shrugged. "That's what it sounds like."

Smirking, Stuart asked, "How do you know what a panic attack sounds like?"

"My therap—" He cut himself off with tightly pressed lips, turned away slightly, feigned interest in a comic book.

"What? Were you going to say therapist? You have a *therapist*?"

James planted his right elbow on the stack of comic books in his lap and put his face in his hand. "Jeez, I . . . I wasn't supposed to tell you. Mom's gonna kill me."

"Not if I get to her first," Stuart muttered, teeth clenched. He put the comic books back in the box and stood, turned and faced James, hands on his hips. "How long have—" He reminded himself that he wasn't angry at James, so there was no need to shout. He lowered his voice. "How long have you had a therapist, James."

"Couple years, I guess. But really, Dad, I'm serious, Mom'll be *so* pissed if she finds out I told—"

"Don't worry about your mother, okay? I mean, if you really want to worry about her, I can give you some better reasons than that. You can worry about how pissed I am at her."

"Why?"

"Because I wasn't told you were going to a therapist. If I had been told, you *wouldn't* be going to a therapist. Why did she send you to a therapist?"

He shrugged. "I dunno. She started going to one and really liked it and she thought it'd help me get my head on straight if I went to one, so she sent me."

"Get your head on straight. Jeez, they've even got you speaking the language. What kind of therapist?"

James shrugged again. "Some woman named Leach."

"Hah! Dr. Leach. How appropriate. Do you like her?"

"She's . . . well, she's um . . ." He looked down at the comic books on his lap. "She's nice."

"Uh-huh. Well, I'm sorry if you like her, because you won't be seeing her anymore."

"Why?"

"Because I don't want her screwing you up. God, most therapists—no matter how high their fees get, most therapists will never be able to afford the amount of therapy *they* need." He stopped pacing, turned to James. "Is she sending you to anybody else? An accupuncturist? A psychic? Past life regression?"

James laughed, shook his head. "No."

Stuart continued pacing, anger snowballing inside him.

"It's okay, Dad. She's not that bad, really. All I do is talk to her and she listens, no big deal. She's not screwing me up, really."

Stuart sat down beside James again. "Hey, if you need to talk, you can always come to me, you know. And I won't charge anything."

James looked down at an open *Spider-Man* comic book in his lap, paged through it absently. He said nothing.

"Why don't we talk more?" Stuart asked. "We've been having a nice conversation here. What did I do right this time?"

James shrugged. "Talked about comic books, I guess."

"Why can't we talk like this about other things?"

After several seconds, James turned to him. "You mean like my weight? Or how I've got the wrong friends? Or how I spend too much time on the computer?"

Stuart sighed. "We can't talk about comic books all the time. Those things need to be discussed, too. I . . . I just don't want you to make any of the same mistakes I made."

"Maybe I won't."

After a moment, Stuart nodded slowly. "Yeah. Maybe you won't."

"Every time you talk to me, you're . . . I don't know, telling me about something I'm doing wrong, or telling me about something I should be doing."

"I'm your father. That's my job."

"I know. But sometimes can't we just talk about something other than the things I do wrong or the things I should be doing? Like . . . like now? Just sitting here talking about comic books?"

Stuart smiled. "Sure. This was nice." He stood reluctantly. "Look, James, I've got to get back to work. But this was fun. I want to look through those comic books and talk some more. Okay? Maybe this evening?"

"Sure," James said. "Um . . . are you still mad about Dr. Leach?"

"I'm not mad at you, James. Don't worry about it. It's no big deal." He started to turn away, but stopped and looked down at the box of comic books. "Would you mind if, um . . . if I borrowed some of those and read them?"

James shrugged. "Sure. Take 'em all, if you want."

Stuart smiled. "I'll take good care of them."

"I know you will," James said, and half smiled in return.

In the kitchen, Stuart dumped his cold coffee in the sink and poured a fresh cup, took it with him to the garage, the box of comic books held under his left arm. He put the box and his coffee on the card table, locked the door, and kicked a green plastic bucket the length of the garage. It hit the closed door in front, then bounced around a few times before settling in a corner beside the old ice-cream maker they never used.

He went back to work, hoping it would take his attention off his anger. It did not. So after awhile, he sat down and started reading one of the comic books.

CHAPTER SIXTEEN

The St. Elizabeth Extended Care Center smelled of urine and a sickly sweet industrial cleaner, and something else underneath those smells—the odor of decay, human rot. The corridors were bright and cheerful, but still, a dark gloominess fell like shadows on everything. Treacly Muzak played quietly from speakers in the ceiling. On the wall, posters of kittens and puppies and ducklings sported greeting-card captions, and seemed as inappropriate as clowns at a graveside service.

Amelia took the elevator to the third floor without stopping at the front desk. She passed what looked like ghosts sitting in wheelchairs outside their rooms, or slowly shuffling along the corridors with canes or walkers—tangled white hair, dying liver-spotted skin, and toothless mouths that mumbled nonsense. Bleary, sunken eyes clouded by cataracts and loneliness turned to her hopefully, then slowly fell when they realized she had not come to see them. Some reached out to her, tried to grab her and hold her back, so desperate for the attention of another human being that even a stranger would do.

The door of room 310 was closed. Amelia pushed it open and stepped into the dark room cautiously.

The drapes were drawn and the only light came from the television on a dresser against the wall facing the bed. A nature documentary was playing with the volume high. The bed closest to the door, bed A, was empty and neatly made. A curtain was drawn between the beds, and she stepped around it slowly.

"Dr. Furgeson?" she said.

At first, she could not tell if anyone was in the second bed—partly because of the dim light, partly because the figure in the bed was so painfully thin, swallowed up by the covers. Then she saw the face that stared up from the fluffy pillow.

The right eye was open and looking at her from its deep pit beneath a pronounced brow ridge. The left drooped sadly and the lid was almost completely closed. Sharp cheekbones protruded above deep valleys of sunken gray skin. The mouth was partially open and the left corner slanted downward sharply. A glistening tongue moved secretly inside. He still had his teeth, but they were not in the best of shape—long and yellow, no gums visible, the upper teeth quite large and prominent. His arms lay above the blankets, unmoving. At the cuffs of long blue pajama sleeves, two large, knobby hands rested on the blanket, mottled by dark spots of age, with thick nails in need of a trim. The left, unmoving, wore a lusterless gold wedding band, while the right tremored against the mattress.

Dr. Furgeson, if that was indeed who he was, looked impossibly old, but Amelia supposed some of that was due to the limp, melting, dead side of his face. It seemed to have been frozen in the midst of sliding off the skull. He was completely bald, with an oblong skull that seemed too large for the neck. The bare scalp was speckled with liver spots and small open sores, a couple of which were covered with Band-Aids. A triangular hole rimmed with scarred flesh was open where his nose used to be.

When Amelia realized what it was—that she was looking at a hole in his face where his nose should be—she had to look away for a moment. She cleared her throat, smiled and looked at him again. "Are . . . are you Dr. Gardner Furgeson?"

His mouth curled into a twisted mockery of a smile as he struggled to sit up.

"Oh, you don't have to—"

He waved his right hand dismissively as he managed to pull himself up and turn. He slid his legs out from under the covers and dropped them over the edge of the bed, reached over to the bed stand for a pair of thick, wire-rimmed glasses and put them on. Attached to the glasses was a false nose. Amelia could not tell what it was made of, but it looked remarkably real once the glasses were in place. The glasses had been resting in front of a black-and-white photograph of a younger, healthier Dr. Furgeson, standing with his arm around an attractive middle-aged blonde woman who Amelia assumed was his wife. A walker stood beside the bed and he rested his right forearm on it. He made a high, breathy sound, and his floppy lips tried to form it into words. When she asked him to repeat himself, he took a remote from the bed stand and turned down the television's volume. He had to repeat himself slowly a couple times before she realized he was saying, "Yes, I'm Dr. Furgeson. What can I do for you?"

"Uh, well, I was just wondering, Doctor, if . . . if I could ask you a few questions."

"Questions?" he said, mangling the word.

"Yes. Are you the same Dr. Furgeson who had a urology practice in Redwood City?"

He nodded his head unsteadily.

Amelia felt relief—and disappointment that Stuart had not come with her. "Do you remember a patient named Stuart Mullond? A little boy, maybe twenty-five years ago, who—" She laughed at her own question. "It was a long time ago, and I'm sure you don't, but I—"

Suddenly, the old man's head began to wobble, as if it were about to snap off the skinny, veiny neck. At the same time, he made a high, equally wobbly sound with his wounded voice.

She realized he was nodding and saying, with surprise, as if the memory had caught him off guard, "Yes, yes, yes, I remember him."

Amelia knew it was only a matter of time before he interrupted her to ask who she was, why she was asking all these questions. She was a terrible liar, but Dr. Furgeson had never met her before and would not know any better. She hoped. A lie quickly formed in her head. She was writing a column about local seniors for the Sunday edition of the *Sacramento Bee*. It was awful, ridiculous, and a little bit cruel because of the expectations it might raise in the old man, who probably would look forward to reading about himself in the paper. But it would give her a good excuse to take his picture. And it was the best she could do. She was just as inept at fabricating lies as she was at telling them.

Dr. Furgeson spoke, but Amelia shook her head, unable to decipher his words. He said it again, slower. "Terrible thing, what happened. I felt soooo bad." He stopped speaking, but continued to shake his head slowly for a few seconds.

Amelia forgot her lie entirely and quickly pulled a chair away from the wall toward the bed. She sat facing Dr. Furgeson and put her purse between her feet, leaned forward urgently. "What was terrible, Doctor?" she said. "What happened?"

He lifted his right hand and wiped away a bit of spittle that had gathered in the drooping, dead corner of his open mouth. Deep creases appeared on the right side of his forehead as half of it frowned. It was a nightmarish expression, as if he were in great agony and were about to scream. Finally, he said, very slowly, "Who are you? Why are you here?"

"Well, Dr. Furgeson, I . . . I'm afraid I owe you an apology. I was going to lie to you, give you some story that would explain why I came here. Because I didn't think the truth would work. But . . . well, maybe it will. I live with Stuart. And he's . . . um, lately, he hasn't been . . . well. I'm beginning to think his problems are . . . I hate to say this, but I think he may be having some kind of a breakdown. A mental breakdown. And it seems to have something to do with something that happened in your office when he was a little boy. Something you did, some kind of procedure. He seems to have become obsessed with it. Well, actually, with you. Now he thinks you're . . ." It was embarassing. "He thinks you're stalking him, Dr. Furgeson. I know that sounds . . . well, *ridiculous*, but I think it's pretty serious. I came here to meet you and . . . if you'd be kind enough to let me, I'd like to take a couple pictures of you to show him. So he'll know that it's just not possible."

Dr. Furgeson stared at the floor with a distant look in his good eye. He tucked his lower lip beneath his large front teeth for a moment. He turned to her and said, "Do you know what happened?"

She nodded. "He told me."

He shook his head sadly again, said something that was garbled.

"I'm sorry?"

Dr. Furgeson took a breath to speak again, then held up his hand as if to tell her to wait a moment. He reached over to the bed stand and opened the drawer, removed a spiral-bound notebook and a pen. He pointed at the rectangular bed table that had been pushed over next to the curtain.

Amelia stood and rolled the table over to him. He put the notebook on it and wrote with his trembling right hand. It took a few long minutes for him to finish. When he did, he put down the pen and pushed the table away. The effort seemed to have exhausted him. He reached back and adjusted the pillows, stretched his legs out on the bed as Amelia picked up the notebook and read his large, unsteady writing.

When I realized I had not performed the meatotomy in the operating room, I felt terrible. I told his mother I would be happy to do it under a general anesthetic in the operating room at my own expense, because I knew how painful and even traumatic it would be for the boy if I did it in the office. She was grateful for the offer but told me to go ahead and do it there and then. I pointed out to her that

*the injection to numb the area would be extremely pain-
ful, but she said she preferred he not be put under anes-
thesia again. I did it, but I never felt right about it. And
I've regretted it ever since. Not only did it hurt him, but it
terrified him. I had many, many patients during the 48
years I had that practice. They came and went, and I
probably could not name a dozen of them now. But he
has stayed in my memory. You say he's not well. I'm sorry
to hear it. If that procedure has anything to do with his
state of mind, I am truly, gravely sorry.*

Amelia's eyes stung as she finished reading the note and
she blinked back tears. What had Betty been thinking?
How would Stuart react if he knew? He still held it against
his mother all these years later for not putting a stop to it.
The full story would only make things worse.

She sniffed and said, "Thank you, Dr. Furgeson. I appreciate this very much." She glanced down at the note again,
then asked, "Did you . . . when you performed this, uh, meatotomy, did you use, um . . . scissors?"

He lifted his head and frowned again, made an unpleasant
noise in his throat as he emphatically shook his head. "*Scissors?*" he blurted. "No, no. Scalpel, a *scalpel.*" He shook his
head again and repeated the word, "Scissors," with disgust,
clearly offended by the very suggestion.

Twenty minutes later, Amelia was back on Interstate 80 and
on her way home. In her purse were three photographs of
Dr. Furgeson. In the first two, he was sitting up in bed. She
had taken the third without his knowledge. On her way
back down the corridor to leave, she had thought it might
be a good idea to get one shot of the doctor without his
glasses. Without his nose. If Stuart could see the man with
one side of his face sliding off his skull and an ugly hole where
his nose had been, maybe he would realize that it would be
impossible for the old man to go anywhere, let alone to San

Francisco to sneak around Stuart's backyard in the middle of the night. She had gone back into Dr. Furgeson's room to ask if he would mind, and found him asleep and snoring on his bed, television still on. His glasses and the attached false nose were back on the bed stand. Amelia had quickly snapped the picture and left.

Rain came down in sweeping sheets and a hard wind had come up that jostled the Celica as she drove. Even at high speed, the windshield wipers could scarcely keep up with the downpour. It made Amelia even more tense than she already felt, and she clutched the steering wheel with white-knuckled fists.

Amelia had expected to feel better after seeing Dr. Furgeson. She thought she would be relieved once she was certain Stuart was wrong in his fears that the doctor was stalking him. She had assumed she would tell Stuart about her visit with Dr. Furgeson, show him the pictures, and everything would be fine.

But it was not going to work that way, she was certain. Because it was obvious there was something very wrong with Stuart, something with which photographs and a story about a crippled old man without a nose in a rest home bed might not be able to compete.

By the time she passed Vacaville, Amelia had tied her insides into knots with worry. She picked up the cell phone and began to punch in Molly's number, but stopped, turned the phone off and put it back on the seat. She could not talk on the phone while driving in such a hard rain, so she pulled off the freeway and parked in front of an AM/PM mini-market. The rain falling on the car sounded like thunder as she punched in the number again.

"Hello?"

"Molly? It's Amelia."

From Molly's end of the line, Amelia could hear music playing, voices chattering and laughing.

"Where are you?" Amelia asked.

"In the lodge. Where are *you*? On a battlefield?"

"It's raining. I pulled off the freeway to call you. Molly, we've got to talk."

"About what?"

"About Stuart. He's . . . I'm afraid that . . ." She groaned, slumped in the seat.

The background noise faded and Amelia heard a door close loudly at Molly's end. "What's wrong?"

"Is there something you haven't told me, Molly?"

A long silence, then, "What do you mean? What wouldn't I tell you?"

"About Stuart."

"What about Stuart?"

"Well, I already asked Betty, but . . . I don't know if I believe her. Especially now after talking to . . . well, I'm not even sure how to ask it, but something's wrong, and I don't think it's the kind of thing that just shows up out of nowhere."

"Amelia, honey, you're babbling."

She took a deep breath and told her all about Stuart's fears about Dr. Furgeson, then about her visit with him that morning.

Molly became very quiet.

"There's something wrong with him," Amelia said. "But I can't believe that no one noticed before, that he hasn't had any problems with this before. He really believes he's been seeing Dr. Furgeson. Please, tell me, Molly. Has Stuart had any problems in the past with mental illness?"

Amelia watched water rush down the windshield as she waited for a response.

"Hello? Molly? Are you still there?"

The silence went on for several more seconds. "Look, Amelia, I'm coming home tomorrow," she said. "Right now, I want you to—"

"Didn't you say you were coming home today?"

"We're having a bad storm right now. But it's supposed to die down tonight. I'll leave the second I can, even if it's before sunup, but I doubt it. Now listen, Amelia, here's what you need to do. Go back to your place and get James. If Stuart's there, just make some stupid excuse. You're going grocery shopping, whatever. Then I want you and James to go straight to my place. You've got the key. Stay there until I get home. Got that? Don't go out until I get there. Don't answer the phone and keep the door locked."

"What aren't you telling me?"

"I'm telling you to get James and go to my house and wait there till I get home. I'm not telling you anything else."

"Jesus Christ, are you all crazy? *All* of you? You drop hints, you speak in riddles, you cover things up. You lie! What the hell *is* it with you people? You fucking well better tell me what you have to say *now*, Molly, or so help me God, I'll never speak to you again, I won't let you in my house."

Nothing but background noise. Molly said nothing.

"Start talking, dam—" Amelia ducked her head a moment. Took a deep breath. She had never been as angry as she'd been lately, particularly at that moment. It had never been a problem before. She did not like it. Her head rose and her voice dropped as she said, "I'm sorry. Just start talking, okay? Please?"

When she spoke, Molly's voice was soft and sounded as if she were cupping a hand to the receiver's mouthpiece. "Look, Amelia, I'm not saying he's going to turn into some kind of monster and kill you, or anything. But you're right, he's not well, and when he's *this* not well, he can get pretty ugly. Maybe even violent. And yes, it's happened before. But I can't tell you about it right now, okay? I'm sorry, but I'm standing in a bathroom and there are some people waiting for me to come back. I'll tell you everything when I get back, I promise."

Amelia did not want to sever the connection between them. Suddenly, she felt very alone. "If I call you later, will you tell me what the hell you're talking about?"

Molly sighed with frustration. "I might. Maybe. But it's

not the kind of thing I like to talk about over the phone. Hell, I'm . . . I'm not supposed to talk about it at all. Stuart made me promise never to talk about it, and I've stuck by that promise because . . . well, to be honest . . . I'm afraid of him. But I can't—"

"*Afraid* of him?"

"I can't talk now, Amelia. Please, will you promise to do what I told you?"

Amelia took a deep, calming breath. "Okay. I promise."

"Good. Tell James I love him. I'll see you as soon as I can. Gotta go."

Amelia turned off the cell phone and slowly put it back on the seat. Now that she knew what she was going to do next, she was afraid to move. Afraid to go home.

CHAPTER SEVENTEEN

After nearly ninety minutes of reading comic books in the garage, Stuart took them back into the house and joined James in front of the television again. Apparently, the Syfy Channel was having a Godzilla marathon, because the giant radioactive lizard was battling Ghidra, the three-headed monster. The people of Tokyo continued to find it difficult to get anything done as, once again, they took to the streets screaming and flailing.

Stuart and James talked more comic books for awhile. Stuart was astonished by the change in James. He listened to everything Stuart said, responded when he was finished speaking, didn't interrupt or ignore Stuart sullenly. It was almost as if they were having a normal—yes, they *were* having a normal conversation. It made Stuart feel almost giddy. It wasn't that Stuart had not wanted to find a common ground between them before, he simply had never taken the time or exercised the patience to try to find one. He was thrilled to have stumbled onto it, however inadvertently.

As they talked, Stuart decided he was going to subscribe to several comic book titles, some old, some new. He planned to have more conversations with James like this one. If they could communicate so well about comic books, there was no reason they could not communicate just as well about everything else. Start on comic books, work slowly into encouraging him to make new friends, casually find out if he's still seeing old ones. Maybe he could convince James that he was not crazy, no matter what Mom said. But that was for later.

For the time being, Stuart was having more fun than he could remember having in a long time.

That was when Amelia got home. She brought the chilly, damp air in with her. It seemed to hover around her, even after she'd removed her coat.

"Hi," Stuart said, smiling. "What have you been up to to-day?"

"Oh, just . . ." She stopped, mouth open. "Driving around."

She was lying, and seemed frightened as well. Stuart knew it immediately. Amelia was incapable of hiding things like that.

"What're you guys doing?" she said.

Half of James's mouth turned up in a smile. "I didn't know Dad was a comic book geek."

"What's wrong?" Stuart said.

Amelia tossed him a couple rapid-fire glances, a double, then triple take. It was something she did whenever she was trying to hide something from him. She did it a lot around Christmas and his birthday. But she still looked emotionally shaken, as if she had just seen something awful.

"Wrong? There's nothing wrong." As she headed out of the room for the kitchen, she said over her shoulder, "I'm starving, I'm going to get something to eat." And she was gone.

Stuart turned to James and asked quietly, "Did it look to you like something's wrong?"

"Yeah," James whispered with a nod.

Stuart stood and said, "I'll be back." He went to the kitchen, where Amelia was making a sandwich. He went to her side, gently placed his hand on the back of her neck, naked since she had cut her hair. "What's wrong, Amelia?" he whispered.

"Nothing." She smiled, kissed his cheek. "How are you? You didn't come to bed last night."

"No, I was working. Didn't want to stop."

"Are you hungry? I'm starving. Want a nasty bologna sandwich?" She spread mayonnaise on a slice of buttermilk bread, spread it too fast.

Stuart reached out to take her wrist, turn her to him. But the second he touched her, she gasped and jerked away from him. She dropped the butter knife on the edge of the counter, where it dropped to the floor. She turned her head away a moment, bent down to retrieve the butter knife. She tossed it into the sink and took another from the drawer. Still, she did not look at him.

The problem was clear to Stuart. "You've been talking to Molly," he said with certainty. It made him angry, but he would not show it, not now, when Amelia was obviously so upset.

"I talked to her on the phone," she said as she washed a couple leaves of lettuce, then put them on the bread. "She's coming back tomorrow."

"So soon."

"She didn't say why, but it sounded like they're not getting along, or something, I don't know."

"What else did you talk about?"

"Stuart, please. I'm not in the mood."

"What did she say that made you so afraid of me all of a sudden?"

Amelia turned to him and put a hand to her hip. "I'm not afraid of you, Stuart. I'm . . . if anything, I'm disappointed in you."

The word needled him. It was a word his mother had used often when he was growing up. Stuart almost would have preferred that Amelia say she was afraid of him. "Are you trying to pick a fight?" he asked.

"What haven't you told me, Stu?" she whispered. It wasn't an angry question—it was, instead, rather anguished.

The whisper was contagious. "What haven't I told you about what?"

"About anything. About you. About your marriage to Molly. What haven't you told me?"

He spread his arms from his sides in a gesture of futility. "I don't know what you're talking about," he said. He took a breath to try again, gentler this time. "Really, Amelia, I don't know what you're asking me about, you're not making any—"

"Okay, that's fine," she said. She slapped a couple slices of bologna on the lettuce. "I don't feel like talking about it now, either. I need to—"

"Oh, no-no-no, you can't do that. That's unfair. That's like Lucy pulling the football away just as Charlie Brown kicks, it's not fair."

She slapped a couple slices of American cheese on the bologna. "I don't want to talk now, Stuart, please, I'm upset."

"That's the best time to talk! You don't hold back then. You tell the truth."

She stopped whispering, spoke in a tense voice. "I don't like to talk when I'm upset." She squeezed a plastic mustard bottle over the cheese and bologna.

"Because you get angry. And you don't like to get angry because then you're just human like the rest of us."

Amelia squeezed the mustard bottle so hard, it slurped a fat glob of it onto her sandwich. She tossed the bottle aside and turned to him. "That's a rotten thing to say."

"I just calls 'em like I sees 'em," he said with a shrug. "If you don't want me to describe you as someone who behaves that way, then quit behaving that way. Like you just got back from some Vulcan group-therapy session. I mean, just be human, for God's sake, get *angry!*" He swung his fist and slammed it into the refrigerator door. Most of the magnets— pieces of fruit, characters from *The Simpsons*, and several different flowers—dropped off the door and scattered around his feet.

Amelia aborted a startled cry by slapping a hand over her mouth, and backed away from him quickly.

He looked down at all the magnets on the floor, hunkered down and quickly picked them up. "I'm sorry. I really didn't mean to do that." The magnets stuck to the refrigerator door with dull clicks. "I didn't mean it, I just got carried away and—"

When Stuart turned to her, she had not moved. Her hand was still over her mouth and she stood rigidly. The only movement was that of tears spilling from her wide eyes. The fear in those eyes was unchecked and raw.

He knew then, and he made an instant decision to deal with it in the best way possible.

"Molly told you about my . . . illness," Stuart said quietly.

Amelia relaxed a little then.

"Mental illness," he said reluctantly. The words stung him.

Her hand slowly moved from her mouth. "Why would you keep something like that from me?"

"I didn't keep it from you," he said defensively. "It just never came up."

"Your mother and Molly are *afraid* to tell me anything about you. It's like you've threatened them, or something."

"I haven't threatened anybody!" Stuart shouted. "And I haven't kept anything from you. I'm telling you now. It's not like we're married, or anything, for crying out loud."

"What does that mean?"

"It means what it means. We haven't exchanged any vows yet. And there's no law against having things in your past you don't want anybody to know about, things you're ashamed of."

"But why would you be ashamed of that?"

"Oh, please, spare me all the liberal bullshit about mental illness being just another disease, like arthritis or diabetes. It isn't, it never has been, and it never will be. It means you're crazy, and that kind of thing doesn't go over well at parties, and it sure as hell doesn't go over well with employers, either, no matter how understanding they may try to be. And nobody has to *tell* my mother not to talk about that. She'd rather be anally raped by demons from Hell than let anyone know her son was mentally ill, you know that. As far as she's concerned, no one in our family has ever suffered from mental illness. Unheard of. Whatever Molly told you—and I don't even want to think about what that might have been—it's probably not true."

"She hasn't really told me . . . anything. We're supposed to talk, but . . ."

Stuart sighed. "Good. Then I can tell you first. The whole thing. Before anyone else gives you their screwed up version."

It was beginning to get dark outside as they took their places at the bar between the kitchen and dining room. It was raining hard and there was an occasional flicker of bluish white light through the windows—lightning in the distant sky. Amelia nibbled on half of her bologna sandwich while Stuart talked. From the living room, they could hear the sounds of Tokyo being destroyed. Stuart was glad James had the volume so high. He did not want his son to hear any of what he was going to say.

"In a way," he said, "I really have told you about everything. I just haven't labeled it."

"What do you mean?" Amelia asked.

"I told you how miserable my childhood was. Well, part of it was because of my parents. But part of it was because of me. I was always so morose. All the time. It was like there was this little cartoon cloud over my head that followed me around everywhere, always raining. But it only rained on me, nobody else."

"You were suffering from depression?"

Stuart nodded. "I just didn't know it. I thought it was me. That there was just something wrong with me. Anyway, a doctor I went to once—Dr. Ruddy, I think it was for strep throat—he noticed it right away. Mom was out in the waiting room. After Dr. Furgeson, I never let her go into the exam room with me."

He could remember only vaguely what Dr. Ruddy had looked like, but Stuart remembered him being very concerned, interested in what he had to say. He had asked Stuart several questions, then stared at him thoughtfully for awhile.

He asked if Stuart felt bad most of the time, or maybe all of the time, a kind of bad that he couldn't explain to anyone else. When Stuart relucantly said yes, Dr. Ruddy explained to him that he was suffering from depression.

"The word wasn't used as much back then," Stuart said as he took the other half of the bologna sandwich from Amelia's plate. "These days, jeez, everybody's depressed. And doctors weren't handing out antidepressants like Pez the way they do now. I mean, these days, if you're having a bad day, you can go to your doctor and get a prescription for Prozac or Zoloft, I'm surprised they're not selling them over the counter, or in kiosks on every street corner. Prozac and Zoloft and all that other happy candy didn't exist then." He bit into the sandwich.

"Want me to make you one?" Amelia asked. "I will."

Stuart shook his head, chewing. "He told me about the chemical imbalance in the brain that can cause depression, and about the pill he wanted to give me, and said he'd like me to see a therapist." He laughed. "That's what I did then, too, I laughed. I told him there was no way my mom would allow me to see a therapist, and she'd probably never let me take that pill because she'd never believe that I was depressed. I remember, Dr. Ruddy said, 'I think you're being a little hard on your mom, Stuart. She'll want whatever's best for you.' And I shook my head and said, 'Not if I have to go to a headshrinker.'" He took another bite of the sandwich and put the remainder back on the plate. "So, he went out and talked to my mother while I waited in the exam room. He was gone for a long time. When he came back, he looked pretty pissed. He took a deep breath and said, 'Well, Stuart, it seems you were right.'"

"Your mother said no," Amelia said quietly, and with no doubt.

"'Course she did. Therapy's against her religion, and taking an antidepressant would be admitting there was something wrong with me. That I was a mental case."

"What about your dad?"

"She didn't tell him. And she never took me back to Dr. Ruddy."

"Did you ever get any treatment?"

"Eventually. If you can call it that. I got worse. The summer before I went to college, I had a talk with Dad. Hardest thing I ever did. I told him what Dr. Ruddy had said several years ago, and that I thought I should do what he had said, otherwise I didn't think I'd be able to handle college. He threw one of his fits. Just went nuts. Not because I was sick, but because Mom had never told him what Dr. Ruddy said. He spent the next day or so either not talking to anybody or yelling and throwing things around. But he told Mom to get me to a therapist. Before I turned eighteen and was no longer covered by his insurance."

Amelia finished the first half of the sandwich. "He must have been concerned," she said. "Even though he was abusive, he had to feel something about it."

Stuart took another bite of the sandwich and said, "Up to that point, he'd often called me lazy, useless, stupid. I could never do anything right, never had an idea that wasn't idiotic. I guess a doctor saying I was crazy didn't surprise him much, and he told Mom to take me to a therapist." He finished the sandwich half and brushed his hands together as he chewed.

"I saw a guy named Beacham, Dr. Beacham," Stuart went on. "He looked kind of like Mark Twain. Big bushy white mustache, white hair to his shirt collar, but he was bald on top. Had a little paunch and wore suspenders. He fooled me, I guess, because I liked him a lot at first. Nobody had ever listened to me that way before."

"What way?" Amelia slid the plate aside, folded her arms on the countertop.

"Well, I always knew he was really listening. He looked at me while I talked, right in the eye. He'd only interrupt me to ask a question, to clarify something, but it was always a question he couldn't ask if he wasn't listening, you know what I mean?"

"Why was that so surprising to you, Stu?" she asked.

He shrugged. "It just always seemed nobody'd ever listened to anything I had to say. At home, at school, at church. Everybody thought I was a weird kid because I was so quiet. But I figured, hey, if nobody's gonna listen, what's the point in saying anything, right?"

"Did Beacham put you on an antidepressant?"

"Oh, yeah. They didn't have dozens to choose from back then. No varying degrees. It turned me into a zombie. I was constantly in that weird state where you're just about to fall asleep. I couldn't think, I could hardly talk."

"Didn't he try others?"

"There were no others. That was the weakest thing they had. Either I could take it, or I couldn't. And I couldn't. I wasn't able to function. So we stepped up the therapy and I stopped the pills. After that, I felt worse than ever. I started having . . . thoughts." He stopped and licked his lips. Rubbed a hand slowly over his mouth. "See," he said with a chuckle, "this is why I don't like talking about this. You obviously think I'm some degree of crazy already, I could see it in your face earlier. This is just going to reinforce whatever Molly told you."

Amelia put her right hand over his. "Please, Stu, forget about whatever Molly said and—"

"Forget about it? That's why I'm doing this. To shoot down whatever melodramatic lies she's been telling you."

She sighed. "Okay. Go ahead. Nothing you say will change the way I feel about you, so don't worry about it, all right?"

He left the bar and walked over to the large green bowl of fruit on top of the dishwasher. He took an apple from it as he tore a paper towel off the roll over the counter, took a paring knife from a drawer, then returned to his seat across from Amelia.

"It made me feel differently about the crazy street people you see sometimes," Stuart said as he began to peel the apple over the paper towel. "You know, the ones outside donut shops, the ones who walk up and down Market Street with Reynolds Wrap on their head, or a collander? Something to keep the alien signals from getting to their brains, or whatever? Because these thoughts—they weren't mine. They were coming from nowhere, almost as if they *were* being beamed into my head."

"What kind of thoughts?"

"Thoughts of hurting myself. Killing myself. Hurting my parents. Even torturing them. I had these long, vivid dreams—" He smirked. "—wonderful dreams—of torturing them. They were so explicit, so real, I could still feel their blood on my hands and arms when I woke up. I thought I was going insane."

"Did you attempt suicide?"

"No. I went to Dr. Beacham. I called his beeper number late one night and we ended up meeting at his office. I told him how I was feeling, what I was thinking, whether I wanted to think it or not. It was like mind mutiny—my own thoughts were turning against me."

"What did he do?"

"He recommended that I spend a little time in the Raleigh-Higgis Neuropsychiatric Hospital in Walnut Creek. A mental hospital. Whoopee."

"Did you go?"

He nodded. "I was scared to death of it, but not as scared as I was of what was happening to me. Dr. Beacham made a deal with me. If, after spending five days there, I honestly believed it wasn't doing me any good, I could leave. I agreed. So, he followed me to my house, where I left the car and went inside to get some things I would need. While I was doing that, he explained everything to my parents, who had been asleep in bed. I kept waiting for my mother to start wailing, but she didn't. Maybe she was too tired."

A small pile of sliced apple skin lay on the paper towel. Stuart cored the apple, began to slice it slowly into sections.

"Dr. Beacham checked me in, talked with me awhile, then left," Stuart whispered. "Then he went on vacation."

"You're kidding. You mean he just left you there and—"

"For a month. He left some woman to take care of his patients."

"Some woman?" Amelia asked. "She wasn't even a doctor?"

"Oh, she was a doctor, all right," he said. "But she was awful. She'd walk into a room and the temperature would drop ten degrees. When I told her about the five-day deal I'd made with Dr. Beacham, she laughed and said, 'Well, he can't very well check you out from Ireland, so I guess you'll just have to wait till he gets back.' And I did. God, that place," Stuart whispered. "It was awful."

"When was this? The late seventies, early eighties? Even then, a lot of improvements had been made in—"

"No, no, it wasn't *One Flew Over the Cuckoo's Nest* or *The Snake Pit*. It was such a clean and cheerful place. The doctors and nurses were so friendly and were always smiling. Everyone but the patients. They gave us drugs that made us so wonky, it seemed like all that smiling and happy talk was normal. When really, it was like a nightmare. I realized that when I started palming the pills they gave me and flushing them down the toilet. They'd turned me into an old man in a rest home. I was sitting around staring at the television or playing board games with other patients. Very slow board games. All those smiling faces, all the time. It was unreal. A nightmare. That was the longest month of my life."

He offered her a slice of apple on the blade of the paring knife. Amelia shook her head and asked, "Did he get you checked out when he got back?"

"Yeah. He was very apologetic. Said he'd forgotten all about me. I'd completely slipped his mind, he said." He bit a section of apple in half, chewed slowly. "Yeah, he was really concerned, really listening while he sat there with me in his office. Sticks me in a nuthouse and then I slip his mind. All the way to Ireland. For a month."

"Did you find another doctor?"

Stuart laughed once. "Are you high? You couldn't get me to go to another one of those people at gunpoint."

"But you have to," she whispered, leaning toward him. "I can tell something's wrong, Stu, you're not yourself. That's not something you can leave untreated, any more than you can ignore . . . I don't know, high blood pressure, or heart disease."

"It's not untreated. I'm doing what I've been doing ever since I got out of the cracker factory. When I feel it coming on, I get plenty of exercise. Lots of exercise. It helps, trust me. And it doesn't hurt to—"

"But it's not enough." She left her stool with a sigh, went around the bar and sat on the stool beside Stuart as he ate another section of apple. She put an arm across his shoulders and whispered, "I went to see Dr. Furgeson today, sweetheart."

Stuart dropped a piece of apple onto the bar, stiffened his back. He turned his head to her slowly. "What? You did what?"

"I drove over to Orangevale this morning and saw Dr. Furgeson. In that hospital. I talked to him, Stuart. I even took—wait right here." Amelia dropped off the stool and disappeared, saying, "Don't go away, I'll be right back."

Stuart was struggling to control himself, to hold in the fear created by what she had done, by what could have happened to her, and the anger that rose in him as well. He took the paring knife in hand and slowly impaled the slices of apple skin on the blade, then the three remaining apple sections.

Amelia returned with her purse, put it on the bar. She removed three Polaroid photographs and handed them over to him.

"The nose is fake," she said. "He lost it somehow. I'm guessing skin cancer. He's not wearing it in the third picture."

Stuart spent a long time looking at each picture. His face grew steadily darker, harder.

"He's had a stroke," she continued. "Maybe more than one. His left side is messed up. You can tell on his face. On the left side, it just—"

Stuart turned his head to her suddenly. He said nothing at first, but startled her with the unexpected movement and the anger in his eyes.

He said quietly, "What are you trying to pull?"

"Pull?"

Stuart shook the pictures at her. "Who is this? Who is it?"

Amelia's mouth opened slowly as she pulled away from him. "I told you, Stu . . . it's Dr. Furgeson."

"Bullshit!" he shouted as he threw the pictures onto the bar. They scattered across the tile bar top, off the edge, and over the floor.

Amelia nearly fell off the stool, slowly backed around to the other side of the bar.

"I don't know who that is, but it sure as hell isn't Dr. Furgeson," he said. "I've seen him. And he might be older, but he's not a corpse, for God's sake!" He waved at the photographs on the floor and Amelia bent down to pick them up. "I mean, is that guy even alive? He looks propped up!"

She perched herself on the edge of the stool, facing Stuart, and put the pictures on the bar. "Stu, this man is the real Dr. Gardner Furgeson," Amelia whispered. "He's very old, very sick, and he's probably not going to live much longer. He's about a hundred miles away, and he can't drive. He can't walk without a walker. He can't even speak very—"

"Goddammit, why are you doing this?" Stuart shouted. But there was more anguish than anger in his voice. "Are you trying to say I'm hallucinating this guy? That he's not really there?" He kicked the stool hard as he stood and it fell backward, clattered as it rolled over the floor. "Then why the hell don't you just say so!"

Amelia flinched, bit her lower lip. She did not make much eye contact with him after that. Nodding at the pictures, she asked, "How do you explain this man in Orangevale, who even—"

"I told you, I don't know who that guy is." He leaned across the bar and she backed away from him quickly. "Come on, Amelia, why don't you just say you think I'm crazy instead of pulling this bullshit."

She stood and shouted, "I'm not pulling anything! He even remembered you, Stuart, he rememberd what he did to you, and he felt horrible about it."

"Goddammit, this is—"

"Your mother *told* him to do it in the office, Stu, he wanted to do it in the O.R., and he was even willing to pay for it himself to make up for his mistake, but your mother said no, she wanted it done there and then, in his office."

He slowly stood up straight, lifting his left hand to the side of his head as a sharp pain grew there. It came in a straight line behind his left eye, as if a laser beam were shooting through his eyesocket and searing its way through his brain.

"What's wrong?" Amelia asked.

Stuart closed his hand on a fistful of his own hair as his lips peeled back slowly over his teeth, eyes closed, then clenched.

"Stuart, what's the matter?" She still sounded afraid, but concerned now, as well. "Can I do something?" she said as she went to his side.

"Headache," he said in a raspy voice, pressing the heel of his right hand over his left eye.

Amelia tugged on his elbow and said, "Come on, let's go upstairs so you can lie down. You haven't gotten any sleep in—"

He jerked away from her unsteadily. "Don't touch me."

"Stuart, please stop this." Her voice quavered on the edge of a building sob.

But Stuart said nothing to her. He went upstairs, but only to the bathroom for a bottle of Vicodin left over from when Amelia's wisdom teeth had been removed and she had developed painful dry sockets. Orange pill bottle in hand, he went back downstairs to the kitchen, took the carton of milk from the refrigerator.

Amelia was talking again, crying now. He could not have listened if he had wanted to. The pain in his head had reached a level that made concentrating on anything impossible.

He took the painkillers and milk to the garage, locked the door. He turned off the lights and sat in the dark at the card table. He popped open the bottle of pills, took three with the milk. Then he put his head down on the table and hoped the pain would go away.

Chapter Eighteen

Amelia chewed her popcorn fast and slumped farther down in Molly's plush couch. She closed her eyes as the big guy in the leather mask carried the screaming girl toward the meat hook. She groaned as the girl cried and screamed in agony.

"Oh, James!" she said to her lap as she covered her head with both arms. "How can you watch these things?" A chain saw roared to life in the movie and Amelia put her hands over her ears. When the sounds of mayhem stopped and it became obvious the scene was over, Amelia sat up and turned to James.

Flames popped and crackled in the fireplace. Molly's beautiful Abyssinian cat Lucretia was curled up on the floor in the fire's warmth. James was slumped in the recliner, arms folded tightly across his chest, almost as if he were hugging himself, with a look of extreme distress on his face.

"You mean that bothers you?" she asked.

"Well, yeah. I mean, a meat hook? That's gotta hurt." He sat up, but kept wincing for several more seconds.

"Then why do you watch movies like this?"

"Horror movies?" He shrugged, ate some popcorn from the microwave bag in his lap. "I guess they're, like . . . the only movies that make any sense to me, y'know?"

His explanation made her heart clench. Was it possible that Stuart had passed his propensity for depression on to his son? Maybe that was James's problem, and no one had noticed. Amelia did not feel it was her place to approach the subject with James, but she would discuss it with Molly.

"If you don't like it," he said, "I can go downstairs to watch the rest."

Amelia stood with her bag of popcorn in hand. "No, go ahead and watch it on the big screen. But you'll have to do it without me."

"You sure? It's a classic."

Amelia laughed at James's use of the word "classic" in reference to *The Texas Chainsaw Massacre*, then said, "Not my cup of guts, I'm afraid."

He half smiled. "Okay, if you say so."

In the kitchen, Amelia put a kettle of water on the stove to boil. She spotted a boom box on the table in the breakfast nook. She brought it and the *Redbook* next to it into the kitchen with her, found some music on the radio. She sat on the wooden bench against the wall under several flourishing plants suspended from the ceiling and tried to read. But she was unable to concentrate, so she simply looked at pictures and read the brief captions. She should not have watched any of the movie. Already upset, it had made her feel only worse.

When the kettle began to whistle, she dropped a mint tea bag into a mug and drowned it in steaming water. She put the cup on the counter and stretched her tired limbs. It felt good, and gave her an idea. She took her tea down the hall to the room across from Molly's bedroom, flicked on the light and looked around, surprised.

In the living room, she said, "James, where's all the exercise equipment?"

"We moved it downstairs last week."

"Why?"

"Well, I started usin' it once in awhile, and Mom thought I'd do it more often if it was next to my room instead of hers."

"Hey, good for you, James. Have you told your dad?"

James shook his head.

"You should, he'd like that. He worries about your health."

"He worries about everything."

Downstairs, she found that a stereo had been set up in the previously empty room, as well as Molly's treadmill, stationary bike, and Bowflex machine. She turned on the radio, sipped her tea, and went to work on the Bowflex.

The last time Amelia had been in that particular room, it had contained a single bed, a bed stand and lamp, a dresser, and a couple chairs. All were gone except the dresser, which had been moved to the other side of the room. It was one of four bedrooms, two on the main level and two on the lower level. Upstairs, there were also a bathroom, living room, dining room and kitchen, and downstairs, a bathroom, and two other rooms, which Molly had not yet decided what to do with, even after three years. She had more space than she could use.

The house had been a source of raw contention between Stuart and Molly. She had purchased it after receiving an inheritance of just under one million dollars upon her father's death. The first thing she wanted to do was get a nice house in a safe neighborhood for herself and James. Stuart suggested she use some of the money to send James to a private school, where he would get a better education and would be less likely to get shot to death between classes. Molly thought that was a good idea, but did not commit to anything.

Then, while searching for a reasonably priced house in a good part of the city, she stumbled onto the two-story salmon-colored Spanish/Mediterranean in Pacific Heights. She fell in love with it and had to have it. It was a decision made quickly, with her heart rather than her head. Not only was the house gorgeous, but she loved the idea of living in the exclusive, toney neighborhood of Pacific Heights. It had swallowed up nearly the entire inheritance, but she had snatched it up immediately.

Her decision had infuriated Stuart, and he had held it

against her ever since. He brought it up at every opportunity. It had become a hot button he could push with just a few words, and he often pushed it when he knew he was wrong in an argument and needed a quick change of subject.

The worst Amelia had ever seen it was last year on James's birthday. The four of them had gone to Golden Gate Park for a picnic, with a German chocolate cake and thirteen candles. She had made Stuart and Molly promise to remain civil for the day—they planned to see the new Star Wars movie. They kept their promise for about thirty minutes. Then the prodding began. Even when they were not speaking to each other, they made references, emphasized certain words, things only the two of them would understand, things only two people who were married for several years could do. It reached critical mass and they began to circle each other like a couple of animals facing off.

"That house is a testament to the kind of person you are, Molly," Stuart had said, voice bubbling with controlled rage. "You are living in a statement. It's a statement of your self-ishness, your inability to—"

"James lives in that house, too! I was thinking of him when I bought it, thinking of his future. Kids don't leave home as fast as they used to. Things are different. Sometimes it's not as easy for them to get started as it used to be. That house is like two houses in one. James can have the downstairs, and he can live there as long as he likes. And when I go, he gets the house, which will only increase in value. And it was a good deal for—"

"For its price range, yeah, I know. Molly, why do you keep saying that? It doesn't make any sense. The price range that mattered was *your* price range, and that house wasn't in it. Pacific Heights," he spat with disgust. "Buying that house had nothing to do with anyone but you."

"Oh, fuck off, Stuart. Just fuck off. Talking to you is like beating myself over the head with a baseball bat."

"I would prefer you do that."

It had gotten worse, and Amelia had known it would only continue to get worse. She took James to the movie herself and left them in the park screaming at each other like a couple of lunatics.

On the way to the theater, James had been quieter and more morose than usual. She asked, "What did you wish for when you blew out your candles today?"

"Not s'posed to tell, am I?"

"Oh. Okay, then. I will rephrase the question, your honor. If you could have anything you wanted, anything at all, what would you wish for?"

James had not hesitated with his answer: "I'd wish Mom and Dad would never be in the same place together again for as long as they live." After a moment of pause, he added, "At least for as long as I live."

The thunder was much louder and lightning had been flashing in the window. The lights flickered for a moment as Amelia exercised on the Bowflex and she froze to see if they would go out. They did not.

She felt energized, which was not necessarily a good thing after eleven o'clock at night. But she was not expecting to sleep much, anyway—she was too worried about Stuart. He had responded to none of her knocks on the garage door before she left the house, until she'd threatened to get an ax and break the door down. Then he had said, "The ax is in here, Amelia. I'm fine. Go away."

Shortly after she and James had arrived at Molly's house more than three hours ago, the telephone had chirped. James had answered, but the caller hung up immediately. She had said nothing to James, but she wondered if it had been Stuart calling to see if they had gone to Molly's house. Would he really call just to hang up like that? She would not have thought so before the talk she'd had with him that evening. Now Amelia was uncertain of what Stuart might do.

She was anxious about what Molly would tell her when

she got home. The fact that she did not want to talk about it over the phone made Amelia nervous. She worried that Stuart would continue to refuse treatment and wondered what would have to happen before he finally decided to do something about his illness. Nothing good, she was certain.

Lightning flashed, a brief tremulous brightness in the window. She noticed the window's paper shade was up. Amelia got off the Bowflex and went to the window. She reached up for the narrow strip of wood at the bottom of the shade. When lightning flashed again, she screamed and stumbled backward, still clutching the strip of wood. The paper shade ripped and Amelia fell backward, still screaming, with half of it trailing her hand.

She had screamed because in the flash of lightning, a man appeared just outside the window, looking in. Tall and thin, bald, smiling, with small round glasses and a pair of scissors held up in his right hand. It was the man she had seen in the framed picture on the bed stand at the St. Elizabeth Extended Care Center. In the lightning's illumination, Dr. Furgeson appeared to be colorless, black-and-white, just as he had been in the photograph.

With half of the shade torn down, the lower half of the window went black when the lightning stopped, and Amelia's scream broke off. He was still there. She could feel his eyes on her, and something else. A sound, just outside the window.

Snick-snick-snick. Snick-snick-snick.

Confused and terrified, Amelia crawled halfway across the floor, struggled to her feet and hurried out of the room. She was shouting for James as she bounded up the stairs when the lights went out.

"Amelia?" James called. His running footsteps thumped closer on the hardwood floor, and they met in the hall.

James carried a flashlight, and its beam comforted Amelia a little. Normally, she did not mind the dark, but tonight was not normal. She panted, trembled. "Are all the doors and windows locked?" she asked.

"I don't know, probably. Why?"

"Because there's—" She covered her face with both hands. "Oh, God, this is going to sound crazy."

"What? What is it?"

"That doctor your dad talks about . . ."

"The bald guy? Yeah, what about him?"

She whispered, "He was just standing outside the window downstairs."

James's eyes widened slowly as a range of emotions passed over his face. Disbelief, suspicion, shock, terror. "Oh, shit," he whispered. "Are you sure?"

"You check the doors and windows while I call the police," Amelia said as she stepped around him.

He turned and said, "No, wait. I . . . I don't know if that'd be a good idea."

She stopped and turned to him reluctantly. "He's outside looking in the windows!" she hissed.

"Dad told me . . . he said if I ever see the guy, I should call him."

Amelia took a few steps toward him. "When did he say that?"

"Look, I think we should call Dad first. I think he might, like, be in some kinda trouble, and I don't know if it'd be a good idea to call the cops."

"What do you know, James? Please tell me."

He shook his head. "I don't know anything. I thought . . . I figured he was just . . . y'know, crazy. But if you really saw that dude . . ."

"He was there. I got a good look at him."

"Okay, I'm gonna call Dad." He started back up the hall and she walked with him. "You do whatever you want, but I think the cops're a bad idea."

The doorbell rang and Amelia gripped James's arm as

they both stopped and looked back. The flashlight beam moved to the brass dead bolt above the doorknob. It was locked.

The bell rang again, lingering for a moment.

Squeezing James's arm, Amelia pulled him with her to the kitchen, where she got a flashlight of her own. Then she called Stuart.

It had been a long time since Stuart had put thread to needle, and he was surprised to find he was still quite good at it. He had spent an hour plundering Amelia's studio for odds and ends off old blenders, toasters, typewriters, and other dated junk. He had even done a little welding. Pleased with his progress—he was nearly done with everything but the big stuff—he rewarded himself with a microwave-heated cup of stale coffee.

Stuart was pleased, but disappointed. He knew he would never be able to create precisely what he could see with his mind's eye. It might come close, but never close enough to suit him. But it would have to do, because he could not go to a professional. Not with this.

He was about to start welding again when the telephone rang.

His headache had begun to fade mercifully about an hour after he took the Vicodin, but a dull throbbing remained behind his eye. According to his watch, it was just after midnight. He wondered who would call so late? *No one with good news*, he thought. He left the garage and hurried down the hall. The answering machine picked up before he got to the phone.

He could not understand what Amelia was rasping over the answering machine at first, but the distress in her voice came through clearly.

"—the window, just a couple minutes ago, and now he's at the door, he's ringing the doorbell, Stuart, please pick up the phone, I know you're there, for God's sake pick up the—"

The terror in her voice cut like a razor through Stuart's dull headache. He snatched the cordless off its base. "Amelia? What's wrong? Where are you?"

"Dr. Furgeson is here," she said in a low, throaty voice, tight with fear.

The words punched him in the gut. "Where? Where are you?"

"I'm at Molly's."

"Is James with you?"

"Yes. Should I—"

Stuart heard James's muffled voice.

Amelia whispered, "Oh, honey, come here, come here. Don't cry, James."

Tears blurred Stuart's vision. He asked hoarsely, "Why is James crying?" He listened, could hear James near the phone.

"He started talking outside the door," James said. "To me. He was talking to me. He *knows* things about me. Things he can't know."

"Put James on the phone, Amelia." He listened as the phone changed hands. "Listen to me, James. *Listen* to me. He's not going to hurt you, I promise. I'm coming right over and—"

"You don't have a car!" James whispered. At that moment, he sounded like a frightened little boy.

"I'll take a cab. Now, listen. Take Amelia to a room in the house that has a good lock and no windows and stay there. Okay? Will you do that for me?"

James's voice dropped to a mere breath, barely intelligible. "Who is this guy, dad?"

"I'll tell you all about it later, okay? I promise. Now hang up and go to that room. Someplace where he can't get to you. Okay? Now, go!" He turned off the phone and took the phone book from a shelf just under that end of the bar. He flipped the Yellow Pages in search of taxicabs.

Afterward, Stuart left the kitchen and ran back to the garage for the .32 Magnum he had taken from Phantom in the Tenderloin. If he was not prepared to face Dr. Furgeson the way he originally had planned, he was not about to face him unarmed.

"You have inherited something from your father, James. Something bad. I can take care of it for you. I can fix it, and you'll never have to worry about it again. For the rest of your life. Are you listening to me, James? I can fix it for you. Don't worry, you can trust me—I'm a doctor."

The voice came from outside the door. Although muffled by the door and the falling rain, it remained clear and intelligible, words deliberate and clipped.

The doorbell rang again.

Amelia and James stood in the hall a couple yards from the front door, each with a shining flashlight. They had just left the kitchen to go to Molly's room, where James said they could wait in the bathroom until his dad arrived.

"What's he talkin' about?" James whispered. He turned to her.

Amelia put her arm around him and whispered in his ear, "Don't pay any attention to him. Come on, let's go to your mom's room." She led James away from the front door. They moved quickly, but tried to step quietly on the hardwood floor so Dr. Furgeson would not be able to hear them. They went into the bedroom and James locked the door.

The master bedroom of Molly's dream house was spacious, with a sliding glass door that opened onto a wooden balcony that looked out over the garden and backyard. It had become Molly's favorite place in the entire house. Fortunately, it was on the second floor and inaccessible from the ground level outside.

The bathroom, too, was large, but not large enough for Amelia to feel comfortable closed up in it. Her whole life, she'd had a touch of claustrophobia, just enough for a good-sized room to become much smaller than it really was if she had to be closed up in it for very long.

"Let's just wait out here," she whispered as she sat on the edge of the bed. "He can't get to the glass door, we're fine here."

James sat beside her and turned off his flashlight. "Don't want him to know which room we're in."

Amelia nodded distractedly.

The silence in the house was smothering. Outside, thunder occasionally rolled overhead and teasing flickers of lightning bled in around the edges of the curtain that covered the glass door. The storm was slowly moving away, but Amelia did not notice. Her mind was racing and she could not stop trembling.

"Who is he?" James whispered.

She thought about it awhile before saying quietly, "I wish I knew. He can't really be Dr. Furgeson. He just *can't* be! I saw the real Dr. Furgeson today. He's in a rest home, crippled by a stroke, with a hole in his face where his nose should be."

"What?" He sounded confused.

"It's a long story, honey, I couldn't begin to go into it now." She fidgeted, shifted her position on the bed. "What did he say to you, James?"

"He said . . . it was about my friends. He knew their names. And he knew . . ." He took a deep breath through his nose. "Other things. Just, y'know . . . things he couldn't know."

There was a sharp click from the bed stand, loud enough to make Amelia jump, and the numbers on Molly's clock radio lit up. Four green, blinking zeros.

"Power's back on," James said.

"I still think we should call the police."

"Dad said not to. I dunno why, but he sounded pretty firm about it."

Amelia put her flashlight on the bed and stood. Pacing slowly, she whispered, more to herself than to James, "What is he doing out there?"

"Maybe he's gone." James stood, still holding his flashlight, and went to the door.

"What are you doing?" Amelia hissed.

He turned the lock on the knob. "I just want to see if he's still talkin' at the front door like he was before."

"I don't think that's a very good idea."

But he was already on his way down the hall.

Amelia stepped out of the room and slowly followed him, and at a good distance. The television was still playing in the living room. A chain saw sputtered and roared as a woman released a blood-freezing scream. The faint sounds nauseated Amelia.

James approached the front door as if the door itself might be dangerous. He stopped a few steps from it and leaned forward precariously, put his eye to the peephole, silent and tense. A moment later, he pulled away and turned to Amelia.

"He's gone," he whispered.

Amelia watched the door fearfully as she went to James. "He's not at the door," she whispered. "But that doesn't mean he's gone. I think we should make sure everything is locked, especially downstairs." She put a hand on his shoulder and turned him around to face the stairs.

"Wouldn't it be faster if we split up?"

"Do *you* want to be alone?"

He smiled crookedly and shook his head.

They went down the stairs together, almost side by side, with Amelia a step behind. The stairs were dark, and James switched on his flashlight. The beam fell on the black tie against Dr. Furgeson's white shirt, neatly flanked by the lapels of his white coat. He was already coming up the stairs, smiling. The light glimmered on the chrome of his stethoscope, then flashed on the lenses of his small round glasses.

Snick-snick-snick . . . snick-snick-snick. It shone on his scissors, too.

The instant the flashlight beam fell on him, Dr. Furgeson said pleasantly, "I've come to help you, James."

At the same moment he spoke, Amelia screamed. She

and James stumbled backward up the stairs. Amelia fell on her side and James tripped.

Still coming up the stairs, still smiling, Dr. Furgeson said, "I've come to make sure you can pee right, James." Then he laughed.

CHAPTER NINETEEN

As Amelia and James were sitting on Molly's bed and whispering in the dark, Stuart was getting into an idling Yellow Cab in front of his house. He pulled the door closed and leaned toward the divider. The driver on the other side had crew-cut red hair, buzzed completely flat on the top, and three rolls of fat on the back of a beefy neck. Stuart recited Molly's address, then said, "Look, pal, my son and my girlfriend are in trouble at that address, and I *have* to get to them as soon—"

The woman turned to him with cold, narrowed eyes. In her early fifties, her face was round and she had two distinct chins. There was a smoothness around her mouth that suggested she did not smile much.

"I-I'm sorry," Stuart said nervously.

"It happens, it happens," she said, frowning as she looked his face over.

He dropped back in the seat, waved a hand urgently. "Just . . . go, please, hurry."

The cab pulled away from the curb. The driver's eyes spent half their time on Stuart's reflection in the rearview. "Were you serious just now? About your kid?"

He moved forward in the seat, leaned his face near the opening in the divider. "Dead serious. Can we go any faster? Please?"

The driver took her radio microphone from its rack. "I can have the cops there in just a few—"

"No!" Stuart barked. He quickly lowered his voice. "I'm sorry, but don't do that, please. I don't want the police involved." He removed his wallet from his pocket. "I just want to get there fast, please. I can give you an extra twenty? Forty? Let's see, I've got, uh, a little over ninety dollars here, you can have it all."

"For what?"

Stuart shouted, "For breaking some fucking traffic laws, that's what!" Ever since Amelia's phone call, his hands had been making involuntary, aborted reaches upward to pull at his hair. His nerves felt exposed to the night air, and he could hear them screaming in his head.

The cab increased its speed, but not by much.

Stuart's eyes found the cabbie's license posted just beneath the dash. Her name was Helen Penn. Above it was Helen's picture, in which she appeared to be biding her time, waiting for the right moment to attack and kill the photographer. At the wheel of her cab, she wore a black bomber jacket and had the radio tuned to a classic rock station.

"I drove a cab in New York City for eighteen years," Helen said as the cab idled at a red light. "These politically correct touchy-feely northern California pussies don't know what drivin' is. Everybody's so—" She suddenly pounded a fleshy hand onto the dash and shouted, "What's with this fuckin' light, over here? The other one turned green twice, goddammit!" She looked at him in the mirror again. "Everybody's so fuckin' polite around here, takes three or four hours to get through a lousy four-way stop sign. Everybody's goin', 'You go,' 'No, you go,' 'No, *you* go,'" she said in two alternating, equally whiny voices. "Judas Priest, it's like bein' in church, or somethin', it's enough to make ya crazy."

When the light turned green, the yellow Ford Crown Victoria vaulted forward and knocked Stuart back into his seat hard. The car swerved sharply to the left to pass the Volkswagen Jetta in front of them, with oncoming traffic ahead. She swerved back into the correct lane, barely missed contact with the Jetta it had just passed, and knocked Stuart over in the backseat.

"You don't have to pay me extra," she said. "I been feelin' kinda homesick lately." The cab went faster, and more swerving made it difficult for Stuart to sit up.

Helen shouted, "But you *do* have to put on your fuckin' seat belt!"

He got up, belted himself in on the passenger's side.

"What's wrong with your kid?" Helen asked.

"Nothing. It's . . . this guy. I think he wants to hurt my son."

"And you haven't gone to the cops? What're you, on drugs?"

"It's . . . personal."

"Personal? The hell does that mean? Somebody's after your kid, you don't fuck around. You think you're gonna—"

"Could you—"

Helen hit the brakes when a car slowed suddenly to make a turn. "You should shit scorpions the rest a your life, you Geo drivin' motherfucker!" she shouted, and her voice drove needles into Stuart's brain. She looked in the rearview as she drove on and asked, "You say something?"

"Could you please just drive, Helen?"

"Yeah, I know, I know. Shut up and drive, that's all I ever hear in this fuckin' job. I'm doin' this outta the goodness of my heart, you know!"

Helen stopped talking and went even faster. Stuart tilted his head back and closed his eyes.

The toe of James's sneaker connected just under Dr. Furgeson's chin. He had kicked as hard as he could, had felt the impact, had seen the doctor's head jerk backward. It bounced back and he smiled, unharmed. The smile broke down when he realized he was teetering, had lost his balance on the stairs. The doctor fell backward, arms swinging and groping, scissors *snicking* viciously.

The fall gave them time to run, and they did, to the front door, where Amelia fumbled with the dead bolt. With the door open, they rushed outside into the rain and James pulled the door closed behind him. They went down the concrete stairs to the driveway below, where Amelia had parked the Celica. They were soaked by the time they reached the car. She got behind the wheel, slammed her door and locked it. As James got in on the other side, she groaned, "Oh shit, oh *shit!*"

"What's wrong?"

"The keys! The damn keys!"

"What?" James said, his voice suddenly higher. "You mean we, we can't, um, get out of here?"

Amelia clutched the steering wheel until her knuckles turned white. "I'll have to go in for the keys," she whispered, surprised by how little fear could be heard in her voice. She looked up the concrete steps. The porch glowed softly, distorted by the rain on the windshield. It was light from inside the house. The door was open. But there was no sign of Dr. Furgeson.

"You can't go back in there," James said. "We'll just stay here till Dad comes, locked up in the car. We're safe here. Okay?"

Amelia sighed, leaned her head back. Her eyes fell on the rearview mirror, on the bleary dark shape standing between the Celica and the streetlight across the street. She breathed, "He's behind us."

James turned around in his seat, got on his knees.

Dr. Furgeson stood perfectly still a few feet down the sloping driveway. He began to walk slowly toward the car.

"Whatta we do?" James asked.

Amelia had no answer as she watched Dr. Furgeson approach. "There's something wrong with him," she said, dread rising like a tide in her voice.

James shouted, "No shit!"

"No, there's something wrong, he doesn't, he's not, he's not—"

A burst of movement behind Dr. Furgeson startled James and he said, "What's that?"

She squinted at the rearview. Someone was running fast to catch up with the doctor.

"It's Dad!" James shouted. He turned and unlocked his door, reached for the handle to get out, but Amelia gripped his arm, squeezed hard.

"No, James, stay in here and lock your door."

He did.

Dr. Furgeson turned away from them, but never quite saw what hit him. He was knocked headfirst into the back window of the Celica with the crunching shatter of safety glass.

Amelia screamed as James shouted, "Get out! Get out!"

They got out of the car and James ran around the front to Amelia's side.

"Go back in the house and lock the door!" Stuart shouted.

Dr. Furgeson's legs hung motionless from the back window for several seconds. Then he started to crawl backward out of the shattered window.

"Stuart!" Amelia cried.

"Go inside!" he shouted before she could say more.

Dr. Furgeson stood and brushed off the front of his white coat. He smiled at James and said, "It will have to be done soon. I want your father to watch."

Amelia pulled James by the arm, up the steps.

"They're not your problem right now, Furgeson," Stuart shouted. "You'll have to deal with me."

The doctor turned slowly. "Oh, Stuart, *you're* certainly no problem. Not at all. Please don't think that. I'll be with you in a moment." Dr. Furgeson turned toward James again, but he was gone. He and Amelia had already gone inside the house.

Amelia did not feel safe watching from the open doorway and closed the door, locked it. She leaned forward against it, forehead resting on her right forearm. "This is insane," she whispered. "It doesn't make any sense, it can't be happening." She pushed away from the door and ran a hand over her wet hair as she headed for the kitchen. James followed.

"Do you think, um, that Dad'll be able to take that guy?"

James said a couple steps behind her. He sounded younger than his age, like a frightened little boy trying to be brave and conceal his terror. "Whuh-what's he wanna do to me?"

She went to the breakfast nook and peered over the table, out the bay window that overlooked the driveway. "I don't know, James, I don't know. Oh, Jesus!"

"What?" He rushed to Amelia's side. "What's going on?"

Amelia's hands covered her mouth to muffle her cry as she watched a struggle between Stuart and Dr. Furgeson end with Stuart going down hard. She saw movement peripherally and her eyes darted to the left. She had not noticed the taxicab before. The driver had just gotten out—a large fat woman with a buzz cut—and hurried across the sidewalk diagonally, toward Stuart and Dr. Furgeson.

Stuart got up fast and landed a kick to Dr. Furgeson's stomach. The doctor stumbled back a step or two, but hardly seemed to care. They appeared to be talking to each other the entire time.

Amelia realized once again that something was not right about Dr. Furgeson. She went around the table and stood close to the window, watched the doctor as Stuart shouted at him.

Dr. Furgeson was perfectly dry. He stood in the pouring rain, but did not have a drop of water on his white coat, which moved freely, lightly. Stuart, on the other hand, was drenched. His long black coat sagged on his body, sopping wet, and swung around him heavily with each movement.

Looking across the street, Amelia saw people coming to windows and doors. The fact that others were seeing it, too, worried her. They would no doubt call the police, and the police would come quickly, as they always did to neighborhoods like Pacific Heights. They would go from house to house, asking if anyone had seen anything. When they came to her, what would they think if she were the only one who had not called the police? Especially when the disturbance had taken place right outside in the driveway?

The cabdriver stepped into the picture and Amelia gasped when she raised her right arm. The cabbie aimed a gun, but Stuart and Dr. Furgeson stood so close together, it was almost impossible to tell at whom.

She could not watch, and quickly turned away.

Helen shouted, "Looks like you're havin' a hard time takin' a hint, baldy!"

Dr. Furgeson turned to her slowly as Stuart shouted, "Stay outta this, Helen! Just get back in the cab and go!" He took advantage of Dr. Furgeson's distraction to take the gun from his coat pocket.

"Don't look like you're doin' so well on your own, fella." She did not take her eyes off Dr. Furgeson, who slowly walked down the driveway toward her, smiling. "You take one more step, and I start squeezin' this thing."

"Get out of here, Helen!" Stuart shouted.

She ignored him and fired her gun. Three shots in rapid succession.

Dr. Furgeson's narrow body flinched each time he was hit, but he did not miss a step.

"What the fuck!" she shouted, and backed up quickly. She turned and ran for her cab, shouted over her shoulder, "You're on your own, buddy!" Her door slammed and the cab's tires screamed against the pavement as she sped away.

Stuart stared agape at the doctor, still standing, unhurt. Somehow, it did not surprise him.

"We've called the police!" a woman's voice called from across the street.

Dr. Furgeson turned to face Stuart, who was up the driveway from him. The doctor walked toward him. "Well," he said, "that won't do, will it? The last thing we need is the attention of the police. This is not a police matter, now, is it? It is a medical matter."

"Go. And don't come back," Stuart said. He held the gun

down at his side, but the doctor saw it. "You want my son, you'll have to go through me."

"I look forward to going through you, Stuart."

"It won't be as easy as you think. I'll be ready for you."

Something happened inside Stuart's head, in his mind. It made him jerk his head back as if slapped, squeeze his eyes shut, and shake his head hard a few times.

Dr. Furgeson grinned around his large protruberant teeth. "Yes, you've been busy, haven't you? I will be ready for you, too, Stuart." He stopped suddenly, then walked sideways across the driveway, *snick-snick-snick*ing his scissors. Up onto the concrete retaining wall with its overlay of salmon stucco, which matched that on the house. Across the lawn, to the far corner of the yard, where the dark got darker. A rustle of bushes, and he was gone.

Stuart could *feel* that he was gone.

He turned and looked up at the front door when Amelia hissed his name. She stood in the doorway.

"Go around to the laundry room, and I'll let you in. People are watching. Don't let anyone see you come into the house."

Stuart nodded once and went around the garage.

"Does your mother have any men's clothes in the house?" Amelia asked on her way down the stairs.

Behind her, James sounded embarassed. "You'd know better than I would."

"Yeah, I guess I would, huh?"

Down one hall, then another, to the narrow laundry room behind the garage. She flicked on the interior overhead light, then the yellow antibug light just outside, and unlocked the door.

Stuart was waiting on the other side and came in at the sound of the lock.

"Get those clothes off," she said to Stuart. Then to James, "Go grab a robe or something for him to—"

"No, don't," Stuart said. "The police are on their way. If they haven't gotten here yet, you've got to drive me home."

"Not just yet," she said. "While you were playing in the yard with your friends, I called the police."

He started to shout, but held back. "I told you not to," he growled, teeth together, quiet but furious.

"It occurred to me that if everyone in the neighborhood called to report a shooting in front of this house, it would look a little strange if I didn't, don't you think? I don't even *live* here."

After thinking about it a moment, he nodded.

Her voice became hoarse when she said, "But don't make me change my mind, Stuart, by talking to me like that again. The way you talked to me just now? It was dripping with hate."

"I'm sorry, Amelia," he said quietly, "but I was nearly killed out there, and now I'm starting to wonder if maybe I've got some internal bleeding, so etiquette wasn't really on my mind. I'm sorry."

Hurt and, as much as she hated to admit it, angry, Amelia spun and left the laundry room. She went upstairs to wait for the police.

After Amelia left, James said, "That woman shot him and it didn't do a thing."

Stuart's gut ached, his back hurt, and another bad headache was coming down the tracks hard. "Where does your mother keep her prescription medicine?"

"The bathroom in her bedroom."

He started to hobble out of the laundry room.

"Hey, Dad?"

Stuart turned to his son. "Yeah?"

"What just happened out there?"

"Oh. That."

"Yeah, that. You said you'd tell me all about that guy."

"I will, James. But not right now." He went upstairs in

search of relief from his pain. He had to take the stairs slowly. His head was still reeling.

As Dr. Furgeson had walked slowly toward him up the driveway, just before he had disappeared into the dark, Stuart had experienced something that had jarred him to the core of his soul. It was something he had never even imagined before, let alone felt: the sensation of no longer being alone in his head. Invisible fingers had dipped into his brain and felt around in his most intimate of places—his very mind. It had been brief, but left a residue, like the last drippings of a bad dream in the first seconds of waking. He was still queasy from it. If he never felt it again, he knew he would never forget it, and feared that residue might never go away.

There was no doubt in Stuart's mind about the identity of the trespasser. If it was possible for Dr. Furgeson to violate him in such a way, why couldn't Stuart do the same in return?

Because I don't know how, he thought. *Not yet.*

Until he learned, if that were possible, he was never safe. That meant James and Amelia were never safe as long as they were with him—and as long as he knew where they were at any time.

None of them spoke as Amelia drove back to the house with Stuart seated beside her, James in the back. A smooth, unconcerned male voice on the radio warned of fallen power lines here, a flooded street there. Amelia wanted to scream at Stuart, to scream that she believed him, that she did not think he was crazy. Stuart wanted to tell them both everything, but he did not understand everything yet. James had questions, nothing but questions. But none of them spoke.

Amelia had spoken briefly with a police officer at the door. She said she was a visitor, not a resident, that she had heard a commotion outside, but hadn't seen anything. She feigned surprise when the officer told her the back window of her

car had been shattered. She agreed to go into the police station the next day and file a complaint.

Stuart sat in the passenger seat with his head back and
eyes closed. He wondered if they could hear his confused
and swarming thoughts through the walls of his throbbing
skull. His experience in Molly's driveway, which had been
rerunning itself in his mind ever since, had left him paranoid. That, in turn, frustrated him, because he had no time
for distractions.

The Celica's headlights splashed over the garage door of
his house and the car jerked to a stop. Amelia turned to him
and waited silently for him to say something.

"Inside," he said, opening the car door.

As soon as he was inside the house, he went through the
dining room to the kitchen bar, took the phone off its base
and clicked the redial button. He asked for a cab at his address as soon as possible. He doubted Helen would come back.

Stuart turned to Amelia and James. "Pack whatever you
absolutely need. I have to keep the car, Amelia. In a few
minutes, a cab will be here to take you wherever you want to
go." Amelia tried to interrupt, but he raised his voice and
spoke over her until she stopped. "I don't want to know
where you're going. Don't tell me. If you call, don't call col-
lect, or in any way that might tip me off to where you are."

"Dammit, Stuart, quit talking like that, I'm not afraid of
you!" Amelia said. She was trying to sound angry, but doing
an unconvincing job.

"It's not me I'm talking about. It's him."

"Could you please explain that?"

He shook his head. "Not now. Get your things."

"Dad?" James stepped toward him. His eyes were red and
puffy from crying silently in the backseat. "Please tell us
what's goin' on, okay?"

Stuart looked at neither of them as he whispered, "He
can get inside my head. If I know where you are, he'll be able
to find you."

He was startled at first by Amelia's quick move toward him, and expected her to shout in his face, perhaps even slap him. But instead, Amelia embraced him, held him tightly.

"I believe you, Stu, I believe you." She shook her head against his shoulder. "I don't think you're crazy. I'm sorry, okay?" She pulled back and met his eyes. "If you're crazy, then so am I. You're right, it's Dr. Furgeson. It doesn't make any sense, but it's a younger Dr. Furgeson. And one who stays completely dry in the pouring rain."

A corner of Stuart's mouth twitched and he chuckled. "Really? I hadn't noticed."

"I noticed. I'll do whatever you want, but I need to be able to reach you and make sure you're okay."

Stuart nodded. "Call me anytime. Just don't let me know where you are."

James went to his room and Amelia hurried upstairs, both to pack a few things. James returned in less than a minute with a small blue suitcase he'd had since he was a little boy.

"You gonna be okay, Dad? I mean, that guy's not gonna . . . he won't—"

Stuart took him into his arms. He said nothing, and James said no more. When he returned his dad's embrace, he did not need to speak. They stood that way until a horn honked twice in front of the house.

He saw them to the waiting cab—Helen was not at the wheel—kissed Amelia good-bye, and waved once as he went back inside. He made coffee and put a frozen dinner in the microwave. He would not be sleeping again anytime soon, but he needed to get some food into his stomach.

While the coffee brewed and the dinner rotated in the humming microwave oven, Stuart went through the entire house. He checked every door and window, even the small bathroom windows that no one could ever fit through. But even when he was sealed up like leftovers in a Tupperware dish, he knew it would make no difference. If Dr. Furgeson could get into Stuart's head, locks would not keep him out of the house. But Stuart could see no point in handing out an invitation to the son of a bitch.

He drank coffee and ate his hot dinner out of its plastic tray. He tried to enjoy the food, tried not to shovel it in so fast that he did not taste it. But he had too much work to do, and not a clue as to how much time he had to do it.

CHAPTER TWENTY

Amelia and James ate breakfast in a Waffle House near the Motel 6 where they had spent the night. She was not hungry, but nibbled and picked at a cheese omelette she could barely taste. For James's sake, she tried to keep up a conversation about whatever she could think of that had nothing to do with the previous night.

The city was gray and drenched, and the rain continued to fall. It had been raining so long, Amelia felt like it had always been wet and always would be, even though it was only November. It seemed everything was broken or on the fritz, everything in Amelia's life, everything in the world, including the weather.

"Did you know that you snore?" she asked.

James looked up from his scrambled eggs and hash browns. "I do?"

"Like a gorilla."

"Sorry. I kept you awake?"

"No. I slept. For a little while."

"I had bad dreams."

"What kind of dreams?"

"Nightmares. About that doctor. Those scissors."

"Your mom will be home sometime today, if she's not already. We're going to sit down with her and talk about all of this."

"You mean, somebody's gonna tell *me* what's goin' on?" James asked with mock amazement.

"I don't think any of us know what's going on."

After leaving the house in the cab, Amelia and James

had discussed where to go. James wanted to go back to his mom's house, reasoning that his dad would never expect them to go back there. Amelia did not like the idea of spending the rest of the night in the same house in which she and James had been pursued by the grinning Dr. Furgeson about an hour earlier.

Who stays perfectly dry in the pouring rain? she thought. It was an image she could not shake from her mind.

Amelia suggested they go to a motel, get some sleep, then go back to Molly's after a good breakfast. When James pressed his suggestion, she insisted, and remembered a Motel 6 not far from Molly's house.

Amelia put down her fork and opened her purse to find her credit card. "Let's call it a meal and go wait for your mom at her place."

They took a cab to the house and found Molly at home, smoking a cigarette and staring wearily at a morning talk show on television. Her eyes looked heavy, with dark half-moons of puffy flesh beneath them.

"You quit smoking," Amelia said when she saw Molly on the couch, cordless telephone in one hand, cigarette in another.

"Not this week," Molly said. She put down the phone and stood. "Where the hell have you been? I told you to stay here. I was scared to death. I called your place, but—"

"Did Stu answer?" Amelia asked urgently.

"No. What's happened?" Molly sat up straight on the couch, suddenly concerned. "Something's happened, I can tell by your voice."

"Some guy came in here last night," James said as he entered the living room.

Molly's eyes widened. "What guy?"

"Don't panic," Amelia said. "Everything's fine, and we'll tell you all about it."

"I've been up all night worrying about you two, and . . . well, the trip didn't go as well as I'd hoped," she said, rolling her eyes. "God, I need a glass of wine." She stood and headed for the kitchen.

"It's nine thirty in the morning," Amelia said.

"For you it's nine thirty in the morning. For me, it's the first time I've been away from that jerk in a couple days, and I need to unwind."

"Told ya," James said as he dropped himself into the recliner. His voice was a low mutter.

From the kitchen, Molly shouted, "I heard that!"

"Well, I did," James whispered. "I knew the guy was an asshole when I met him."

"We all did," Amelia said. "All but your mother."

Molly came back into the room with a glass of wine in hand and returned to the couch, where Amelia joined her. "I didn't hear *that*, but I didn't like the sound of it. I assume you're questioning my taste in men. Kindly wait until I'm out of earshot, would you?" She sipped her wine, put the glass on a coaster on the end table.

Having ignored her craving for a cigarette all morning, Amelia got one from her purse and lit up.

"I thought *you* quit," Molly said.

"I did. And I will again. I've just been kind of . . . anxious lately."

James sat forward until he was on the recliner's edge. "Hey, Mom? Maybe you didn't hear, but some crazy dude with a pair a scissors came in here last night. And he was after *me*."

Molly's face fell a little and she stood, went to the recliner. "Stand up, dammit, so I can hug you." He stood and she embraced him, but looked at Amelia. "What happened?"

Together, Amelia and James told Molly what had happened at the house the night before. As she listened, Molly paced a bit, finished her wine, told them to hold the story until she returned and went to the kitchen for another. She returned with the bottle in one hand, her glass in the other, asked a few questions, then let them continue. But she could not hold still as she listened. She fidgeted and shifted on the couch, got up and paced, rearranged some knickknacks on a shelf, went back to the couch and finished her wine.

As Molly lifted the glass to her lips, Amelia saw her hand trembling.

"I don't think Dad's as crazy as you thought, Mom," James said. He tried to sound firm, but recalling the frightening events of the night before had shaken him.

"I thought you were right," Amelia said. "I thought he was . . . not well. That he'd become obsessed with some imaginary figure that represented someone from his past. I thought showing him the pictures of Dr. Furgeson in the rest home would put his mind at ease, make it stop. But it didn't. That's when I really became convinced he was sick. But then this happened. I agree with James. Stuart might have problems, but he's not crazy."

Molly stared silently at the glass of wine in her hand, finished it off.

"I watched Stuart fight with him in the rain," Amelia said. "He never got wet, Molly. The guy was in the rain, and he never got wet. He's real, I know that now. But I don't know . . . what . . . he is."

"That woman," James said, "the cabdriver who brought Dad over here—she shot him, more than once, and he didn't even go down."

Still no response from Molly, who fondled her empty wine glass.

Speaking slowly and deliberately, as if to be sure she were heard and understood, Amelia said, "I would appreciate it, Molly, if you would tell me everything you know."

Molly fidgeted, looked at neither Amelia nor James. Finally, she said, "James, why don't you go to the kitchen and whip up some breakfast for yourself, and Amelia and I will—"

"I've already had breakfast," James said, anger edging into his voice.

Amelia said, "Molly, after what James went through last night, I don't think it would be fair to exclude him from—"

"Fine, then." She poured more wine for herself.

"Did you become an alcoholic while you were gone?" Amelia asked.

"No, I became very miserable while I was gone. After we're done talking, I'm going straight to bed." She raised the bottle as she sat on the couch. "This is the only way I'll be able to get to sleep." She took a sip. "And it's probably the only way I'll be able to tell you what I've got to tell you."

A chill passed through Amelia. Suddenly, she was not so sure she wanted to hear whatever it was Molly had to say. But she said nothing and let her friend talk. She had no choice.

The studio audience on television was in the middle of a big raucous laugh when Molly took the remote control from the end table and cut them off. She found a comfortable position on the couch—left knee on the cushion with her ankle tucked under her right knee, one elbow propped on the back of the couch. She put out her cigarette in the black plastic ashtray on the couch between her and Amelia, took another from its pack and lit up. Finished off her wine, poured another glass.

"When Stuart and I got married," she said, "I was with child." She pointed the two fingers that held the cigarette between them at James. "This child, to be specific."

"What?" James sat forward, frowning at his mother. "You guys had to get married because of me?"

She shook her head. "No, no, honey. The news that I was pregnant made us both very happy. We were planning to get married, anyway. We just had to do it a little sooner, that's all. Otherwise, your grandmother would have exposed her core and melted a hole through the earth to China."

"Tell me about it," Amelia said with a chuckle. "I think the only reason she's able to tolerate us living in sin together is by pretending we're married."

"Oh, I'm sure she tells all her friends you're married," Molly said before continuing. "We had a nice little wedding and bought the house on Lake, Stuart got his job at Carnival, and we had you, James."

"I've heard all this," Amelia said, frustrated.

"I don't have any proof of anything I'm going to tell you," Molly said. "All I know is what happened, what I saw. A couple times, I came close to telling a doctor. But I knew no doctor would believe me. They'd want to lock *me* up. So I just kept it to myself and lived with it. Lived in fear of it."

"In fear of what?" James whispered. "Of Dad? Did he hurt you?"

"No, James. Your dad never hit me, or anything like that. He's not that kind of person, never has been. But there were times when I was afraid he might. He would fly into these rages and break things."

James nodded. "Those used to scare me. I even used to have nightmares about 'em. He hasn't done that in a long time, has he?"

"No," Molly said, shaking her head. "But no matter how bad it got, he never hurt me. I used to wish he would so I'd have a good reason to leave him. I figured if he gave me a black eye or a few bruises, something people could see, nobody would be surprised if I left him. But everyone liked Stuart. I've always had to work hard to get along with people, make friends. But even people Stuart didn't like liked him. I knew they'd all understand my leaving Stuart if they could tell I'd been knocked around a little."

"He never hurt me, neither," James said.

"He'd have these terrible headaches," Molly went on. "But I couldn't get him to see a doctor. I don't know if he's told you how he feels about doctors, especially of the psychiatric variety."

"He told me all about Dr. Beacham," Amelia said with a nod.

"Who's Dr. Beacham?" James asked his mother.

"That was before I met him," she said. "I'll tell you later, James. It's only important because Stuart hates doctors and has refused to go to them ever since. Whenever he got one of those headaches, he would take aspirin, sleep. Sometimes they got so bad, he'd vomit. But he wouldn't go to a doctor."

"He's having them again," Amelia said, frowning. "The last day or two. He's been holding his head a lot. He's never been to a doctor since Beacham?"

"Only once while we were married. Appendicitis. He didn't have much choice and was in too much pain to resist. Other than that, no."

"What's this got to do with Dr. Furgeson?" James asked.

Molly drank a little more wine, took a final drag on her cigarette before killing it among the broken remains of its predecessors. She nodded to James in a way that said she was getting to that. "He'd have these periods of depression, too. I knew that about him before we were married. He'd get very quiet and inward, and it was almost like he wasn't there, like he'd left his body. I figured it was because he's an artist, you know?"

"That's how he's been over the last several months," Amelia said. "And it's been getting steadily worse."

Molly nodded. "That seemed to be when the headaches came on, when he was depressed. And that was when things happened."

"What things?" Amelia asked.

"Things that didn't make any sense."

The sounds of the streets outside bled into the house. A siren cried in the distance, and someone persistently honked a car horn. Beneath the sound of the rain was the thrum of the city itself, low and constant, all around them.

While drinking her wine and smoking one cigarette after another, Molly told them about a time Stuart had become very depressed after they were married—it was not the first time, but the worst up to that point. It was the Christmas of their second year together, the first Christmas they'd had enough money to afford to buy lots of gifts. They spent most of it on James, and splurged on an enormous tree.

"But Stuart wasn't enjoying himself," she said. "He was distant and kind of brooding, and it was just getting worse. See, he'd been working on Christmas cards early in the year, and by Halloween, he was sick to death of Christmas. And he got on this kick. For weeks and weeks, he'd been talking about Santa Claus. Saying what a cruel prank it is to play on children. You know, telling them there's a fat elf living in the North Pole who brings toys to children all over the world every Christmas, all that happy crap. He became fixated on it. And everywhere you look in San Francisco from October to January is Santa Claus. This was back when they still *waited* until October to drag out the Christmas stuff. He started doing these Santa Claus doodles. I tried to put them all out of sight." She turned to James. "You were only two, and I didn't think you should see them. They were . . . pretty ugly."

James's elbows were on his knees and he sat forward, tense, mouth open as he listened, frowning. "What kind of ugly?" he asked.

"Stuart's Santa Claus had a mangy beard. A rotten old cap, a lumpy drinker's nose. Horrible rotting teeth. Those were just the doodles. Sometimes he'd take a little more time with one and add gin blossoms on the nose, or pockmarks on the face, or maybe he'd give him a hairy mole or an ugly goiter. And somehow, he always gave his Santa a . . . I don't know, a very slimy look. Like a child molester, or something."

James's face grew darker. "Why'd he do that?"

Molly shrugged. "He was just hung up on this Santa Claus thing. On how the whole concept was damaging to children. That's what he kept saying, anyway."

James nodded slowly and said, "Well, it *was* a real letdown. It felt like, y'know, like everybody had, like, played this trick on me all those years."

"Why did you say the Santa Claus looked like a child molester?" Amelia asked.

Molly replied, "It was something Stuart said to me."

Stuart had gotten onto the subject of Santa Claus while

he and Molly shopped for Thanksgiving dinner. The grocery store was already decorated with Santas and reindeer hitched to sleighs.

"We don't tell children it's fun to play in the street, do we?" he'd asked. "We don't tell them the best candy is the kind you get from strangers, or that child molestors make great friends. Do we? Of course not. But everybody gets a big tickle out of telling them the same lie every Christmas, which stays with them all year long, and then messes them up for the rest of their lives when they learn the truth."

After that, Molly had thought of Stuart's doodled Santas as fat, sweaty, sneering child molesters. They made her uncomfortable and she disposed of any she found around the house.

"Then he started getting the headaches, and they got worse each time," Molly said. "He'd go to bed early with a headache, then wake up in the middle of the night, unable to go back to sleep. So he wasn't feeling so good. But it was a nice Christmas season, anyway. It felt so cozy and comfortable, and James was old enough to start appreciating it." She smiled at James. "You loved all the decorations and the department store Santa Clauses." She looked down at the wine glass she held between both hands. "It was a great time in our marriage, and a great Christmas season. Until Christmas Eve. James came down with an ear infection and he was miserable, in bed most of the time. And Stuart had one of those headaches. My mom had given him some codeine pills she had in the medicine cabinet, so he took a couple of those and went upstairs for a nap around dinnertime. I didn't expect him to come back down that night, though. He was in a lot of pain, I could tell."

Molly picked up the bottle of wine from the floor at the end of the couch, poured herself another glass. "You want some, Amelia?" she asked.

"I can't believe you'd even ask at this hour," Amelia replied.

"I'll ask again in a few minutes, and you'll want some, I promise."

James groaned and rolled his eyes as he flopped back in the recliner. "Jesus, Mom, are you getting drunk?"

"No, James, I'm not getting drunk," Molly said. "I'm getting relaxed. You have no idea what I went through the last couple—" She stopped, shook her head and sighed. "You were right, sweetie. He was an asshole. I should've listened to you. I will from now on."

"Yeah, sure." He sounded dismissive, but his smirk revealed how much his mother's words pleased him.

Molly turned to Amelia. "And don't give me that church-lady look, either. I'm fine, really." She raised her glass in a silent toast and took another drink. She squirmed around on the couch until she was comfortable again. "Anyway, I was making cookies that evening while—"

"You *baked?*" Amelia tried to imagine Molly in the kitchen making Christmas cookies. She could not.

"I baked a lot," Molly said.

James asked, "When?"

"When you were two," Molly replied somewhat defensively. "I didn't do it for long. I finally quit pretending I could bake or cook and just stayed the hell out of the kitchen. I can't boil eggs. But I was trying back then, and I think those cookies turned out pretty edible, too. I was the only one up, but I wasn't going to let that keep me from enjoying Christmas Eve, so I played Christmas carols on the stereo and sang along as I worked on the cookies. When I was done with those, I checked on Stuart and James. Both asleep. I fixed myself an egg nog with rum, started a nice fire in the fireplace, turned on the television and watched an old Christmas movie." She nibbled on a thumbnail for a moment, thinking. "*The Bishop's Wife*, I think, with Cary Grant."

"Molly, are you *trying* to drag this out?" Amelia asked, smiling but impatient.

Molly ignored her, lit another cigarette. "Somebody knocked on the door during the movie. I usually asked who it was, looked out the peephole, but it was Christmas Eve, you know, and I was feeling good, a little lonesome, maybe, and I just got up, went to the door, and opened it. . . ."

It was a cold night, and biting winter air gusted in as Molly pulled the front door open. It brought with it an offensive odor that Molly scarcely had time to register. An avalanche of red and white fell through the door, and a white-gloved hand covered her face and pushed her backward hard. And a deep, moist, throaty voice growled, "Ho, ho, ho."

CHAPTER TWENTY-ONE

Molly went down hard and her head hit the wall as Santa Claus closed the front door behind him, grinning. Molly gulped air to scream, but she was too late. In a blur of dirty red and white and a wave of sweaty stench, he engulfed her field of vision and stuffed something violently into her mouth. It was soft and sticky and hairy and he shoved it to the back of her throat, shoved it in farther and harder, until her breathing was restricted and she gagged. She rolled her eyes downward and saw that Santa had stuffed most of his filthy red white-trimmed cap into her mouth.

Santa leered down at Molly as he reached behind his back and locked the door. Time slowed, almost stopped, as she took in her assailant.

He was no department store Santa. A round crescent of pale, hairy belly was exposed beneath the bottom of his filthy red coat, hanging in front of his sagging red pants. The Santa costume looked like it had been dragged through a gutter. The beard dangled from his face in limp strands of dirty white that could not conceal the large, deep-red goiter bulging from his throat. The only mustache was the black and silver one growing over the man's mouth. His fat cheeks and broad, bulbous nose were cratered by the ghosts of severe acne, and stubble darkened both his chins behind the flimsy beard. A mole almost the size of a thimble grew on his right temple and black hair sprouted from it in all directions. Damaged capillaries glared a painful red on his lumpy nose, from which mucous dribbled into his mustache. Fat, glistening lips trembled over yellow teeth, some blackened by rot. A cloying body odor surrounded him, and his breath carried the same smell that had sickened everyone on the block after an injured cat had crawled under their house and died the previous summer. When he moved, the exposed scoop of his belly swung pendulously.

Santa's white glove slapped onto her head, closed tightly on a fistful of hair, and lifted Molly to her feet. It felt like her scalp was tearing away from her skull and she screamed as loudly as she could. The cap absorbed much of her voice, and although it roared inside her head, it did not get much farther. Molly began to fight then, to punch and scratch and kick. But Santa was very big—not just fat but tall—and his large hands quickly seized her wrists. He spun her around and twisted her left arm painfully against her back, pushed her into the wall.

He pressed his body against hers, put his face close to hers. His moist odor clung to her, clogged her nostrils.

"Where's the kid?" he breathed into her ear.

Molly screamed again, then coughed, gagged.

"How old is it? One? Two?"

As he chuckled, she screamed and struggled, but only made herself cough more against the cap in her mouth. His soft glove squeezed her wrists together behind her in a steel grip. The other hand closed on the hair at the back of her head and jerked her away from the wall, pushed her toward the stairs.

Molly continued to resist, but she could not shake his hold. At the foot of the stairs, he pulled her around until she faced the staircase. Standing at the top of the stairs in his pajamas, James sucked on three tiny fingers of one hand and held the other over his sore ear as he stared down at them. Molly tried to make soothing sounds through the Santa cap stuffed into her mouth, but she was sobbing too hard. And James was not looking at her, anyway. As he stared at Santa Claus, James's face slowly twisted into a round, fat-cheeked mask of fear, and he opened his mouth and wailed.

She wanted to break away from Santa and run up the stairs to her son, take him in her arms and run from the reeking fat man. But he squeezed her wrists together so hard that pain radiated up her arms, and her scalp felt scalded where he pulled her hair.

Santa pushed Molly up the stairs, held her up when she tripped over the steps, pulled harder on her hair whenever she stumbled.

James turned and ran away from the stairs, screaming.

Suddenly, Molly was thrown down on the stairs like a stuffed toy. Her wrists were free. She scrambled on the steps to get away from Santa, to find James and hold him, keep him safe.

The cap was gone from her mouth. When Molly glanced over her shoulder, Santa was gone as well. She became still on the stairs, looking back at the spot where Santa Claus had stood. She could still smell him. But he was gone.

"Whassamatter?" Stuart asked sleepily from the top of the stairs. He held James, who was crying.

But Molly could not answer.

Wind blew the rain onto the windowpanes of Molly's house, groaned around the corners like a sick old woman.

On the couch, Molly rocked slightly, arms wrapped around herself as if in the sleeves of a straitjacket. Lips sucked between her teeth, her eyebrows dug down toward her nose.

James whispered, "I don't remember that. Were you . . . seein' things, Mom?"

She let her lips go and smiled. "That's what your dad said. I was drinking, I fell asleep on the couch, had a nightmare. That's all. And I agreed. That had to be it, that was the only explanation for it. Except I could still taste that cap in my mouth. For the rest of Christmas Eve and most of Christmas Day, I could taste that furry, stinking thing. My wrists and shoulders ached, too. And my scalp felt like it was sizzling."

Curled into a ball at her end of the couch, Amelia felt

tense, tightly coiled, ready to get up and run out of the house before she heard anymore of what Molly had to say. The Christmas story had been more than enough, and Amelia did not need to hear anymore because she knew where it was going. She had already figured out what Molly was getting at, and it was something she could not process, not without some of her sanity crumbling away like loose dirt dribbling down a rapidly eroding embankment.

Molly turned to her and said, "You want some wine, Amelia?"

"Yes, please."

As Molly got up to get Amelia a glass, James asked hoarsely, "Can I have some?"

"You most certainly *cannot*," Molly replied.

After she was gone, he turned to Amelia and whispered, "Does Mom think that, like, *Dad* did that? I mean, that creepy Santa Claus? Is that what she's tryin' to say?"

Of course it is, she thought. *She thinks Stuart can bring his drawings, his doodles, to life, that he somehow created that Santa Claus with his mind while he was asleep. I've been trying to get someone in this family to tell me what they know, and when Molly finally does, it's this nightmare.*

Amelia already believed whatever Molly was going to tell her, no matter how outlandish or bizarre. She had no choice but to believe it, because she already knew they had gone off the map and were in dark and unfamiliar territory—she had known that the moment she had seen the somehow younger Dr. Furgeson in Molly's house, and it had been confirmed when she saw him stand in the rain without getting wet. She simply did not want to admit it, because it meant she really knew nothing, as intelligent as she liked to believe herself to be. It meant she knew nothing at all about anything.

When Molly returned with a wineglass and poured the wine, Amelia finished her first glass in a couple swallows.

"You want a water glass?" Molly asked.

"Very funny." She took the bottle and poured more into her glass.

Once Amelia and Molly were settled again, James asked, "So, who was it?"

"Who was who?" Molly asked.

"The Santa Claus. Who was he?"

"For awhile, I tried to convince myself he was a bad dream. But I just refused to believe that. The next year, I was—"

"Please, Molly, get to the point," Amelia said with unconcealed impatience and fatigue. "Just say what you're going to say."

Molly's hands trembled, and her quietly cheerful disposition seemed brittle and forced. It finally broke and fell away. She quickly set her wineglass on its coaster as she shook with sobs. Amelia moved to her side, put an arm around her. Molly turned toward her, leaned on her as she cried.

Clearly embarassed and uncomfortable, James squirmed in the recliner, then shot to his feet and headed out of the room.

"Are you coming back?" Amelia asked.

He nodded. "Just gettin' something to drink."

"Bring some tissues, okay?"

When he was gone, Molly sat up and tried to compose herself. "You don't know what it was like," she said. "Being married to him. To Stuart. He was such a good father. A good man. But I was terrified almost every minute of my life. That's why I haven't told you any of this before now. He made me promise to tell you nothing about his . . . problems. So I didn't. I didn't understand it—that Santa Claus, where he had come from—so I didn't know what brought it on, but when I finally came to the realization that *he* was doing it, I lived in fear of it happening again."

"Of what happening again. Santa Claus?"

"Oh, that wasn't the only thing that happened. I haven't finished yet. There were other . . . incidents. Like the time Stuart got really depressed again and became obsessed with the fact that some rare, deadly virus had been found in a couple rats in the Bay Area. Some little girl caught it and died, and Stuart panicked, thinking the same thing would happen to James. For a couple weeks, all he talked about were rodents. He scattered rat poison all over the house, set a dozen or more traps."

"I remember that," James said as he came back in with a Coke, handed a box of tissues to his mother. "He was afraid I was gonna get bit by a rat. Wouldn't even let me go into the pet store one day, 'cause they had, like, all these rabbits out in the open for kids to pet. He freaked. Like it was, y'know, a phobia, or somethin'."

Molly nodded, dabbed her eyes with a tissue, blew her nose. "One evening, Stuart took a couple pain pills and went to bed early. His head was hurting. James was—" She turned to him. "I think you were at camp then, but I'm not sure. You weren't home, thank God. I was upstairs, doing something, and as I was going down the stairs, I noticed the floor down there was . . . it was moving." She took a quick drink of wine. "There were . . . the floor was . . . rats covered everything. They climbed the curtains and crawled over each other on the floor and furniture. And then, something seemed to move through them like a kind of wave. And I realized they were all turning, all these rats were turning to look up at me. All their tiny little eyes looking right up at me. They all moved at once, very smoothly. Like water. It was like the floor was flooded, and suddenly the water started to flow up the stairs. The sound of their little claws on the hardwood floor was . . . I can't describe it. It was such a small sound, but such a loud sound. And on top of that, they started making little squealing noises as they climbed over each other to get up the stairs. I turned around and started running, but my toe caught the top step. I hit the floor crawling. Screaming the whole time, I mean, I don't think I've ever screamed that hard before or since."

Molly sighed and emptied her wineglass. "I crawled

halfway to the bedroom before I finally got up and ran the rest of the way, screaming. Stuart was already coming down the hall, but that didn't make me feel any better because, really, I mean, what the hell is *he* gonna do? There were—it looked like a thousand rats. And they were right behind me, so I didn't think it was necessary to stop and explain things to Stuart, I figured he'd *see* them, but he just looked at me, looking tired and really worried, and he opened his arms to hug me and kept asking, 'What's wrong, honey? What's wrong?' I tried to go around him—I don't know where I was going, I might have thrown myself out a window if he hadn't reached out and grabbed me and held me. But I couldn't stop screaming. And then he said, 'Holy shit!' and I thought he'd finally seen them. But when I looked back over my shoulder, a single rat was running along the wall away from us. Wasn't even very big. It made Stuart crazy, of course. He went nuts, said he was going to the store for more poison right after he found that rat and killed it, and then he took off and left me standing there ready to wet myself. They were gone. I was scared to do it, but I went back to the stairs and looked down and . . . they were all gone. Not a sign of them, not even those little black turds they leave, and with that many rats, you know there's gotta be rat shit *some-where*, but there wasn't."

"Did you tell Dad?" James asked.

Molly lit another cigarette. "I've never told this to anyone, not even your dad. I knew what would happen. I wasn't about to say I'd hallucinated or had a dream again when I knew damned well I hadn't. I hadn't been drinking that time. I didn't think I was crazy anymore. But I knew Stuart was dangerous."

"Dangerous how?" Amelia asked.

"I wasn't sure. I'm still not. After that Christmas, though, I was watching for it. It wasn't always something big and horrible. Sometimes it was just little things around the house. At first, I thought it had something to do with his sleep. That maybe his dreams were . . . oh, this sounds so ludicrous. That maybe his dreams were becoming real," she said quickly, as if to get it over with. "It seemed to happen only when he was asleep. But it happened when he was awake, too. Then I thought it might have something to do with his work, his paintings and drawings, because the things that happened always seemed to be connected to that. I finally realized that the only connection between all these things, all they had in common, was his depression. It only happened when he was depressed."

"Whatta you mean?" James asked. "Dad did all these things?"

Molly said, "James, you have to promise me you won't tell any of this to anyone, and don't *ever* bring it up with your dad. Okay? Will you promise me that? And I'm *serious* about this."

He nodded, but looked uncertain.

Pouring more wine into her glass—Amelia declined—Molly said, "I begged Stuart to see a doctor. If for no other reason, he should've gone for the depression, it could have been treated so easily. But he refused. I tried for . . . I don't know how long I tried to convince him. He accused me of nagging, got angry. I stopped. It terrified me when he got angry because I didn't know if that would trigger it or not."

"Trigger what?" James asked.

"I don't know!" Molly snapped. "Look, honey, why don't you leave me alone with Amelia for awhile. When we're done here, I'll come talk to you privately, okay? Please?"

He was frustrated, and a little angry, but he got up and left.

"Why didn't you tell someone?" Amelia asked.

"Oh, please. Who was I supposed to call? Mulder and Scully? Scooby Doo and the gang?"

A little anger rose in Amelia's voice as she asked, "Why didn't you tell me?"

Molly seemed to wilt on the couch and more tears rolled

down her cheeks. "You wouldn't have believed me, and . . . because I was afraid to."

"Why were you afraid?"

She cried quietly for a little while. Pulled another tissue from the box and dabbed. "Because, like I said, Stuart told me not to," she whispered. "He told all of us not to. Me, Betty, maybe even James, but I don't know, I haven't asked him. He . . . Stuart hates to be talked about. The idea of people talking about him behind his back, even if they're saying good things about him . . . it just drives him crazy. But it wasn't just that. I mean, he didn't even know what it was he didn't want you to know. He just told us—his mom and me—not to tell anyone about his *problems*, that's how he referred to his depression and moodiness, his *problems*."

"You mean, he's been completely unaware of these . . . *things* he's been doing? He hasn't known about it all these years?" Amelia asked.

"Yep. Doesn't know a thing. I don't think he does, anyway. He might suspect something, but he's got it buried pretty deep if he does and he's not aware of it consciously. He told me I was to tell you nothing personal about him. He was very firm about it. 'If there's anything to tell her,' he said, 'I'll tell her when I want to, in my own way. And if I ever find out that you have . . .' He didn't finish the sentence, but as far as I was concerned, he didn't need to. We were divorced by then, of course. A lot of water under the bridge by then, and my feelings for Stuart weren't—aren't—as charitable as they used to be. I've said some pretty rotten things to Stuart in anger. You've heard us plenty of times, you know how we talk to each other. But there are lines I still don't cross. Things I don't say. Because I'm afraid of him." The cigarette between her fingers trembled as she lifted it to her lips, drew on it. "Well, not really him. I'm afraid of what he can do."

"We don't know what he can do."

Molly smiled. "Why do you think I'm so afraid of him?"

"Why didn't you just leave him?"

Shrugging, Molly said, "There didn't seem to be a good enough reason to leave him. I mean, a good enough reason I could *give* for leaving him. I couldn't very well tell people the truth. Look how long it's taken me to tell you."

"You sound like Betty."

Molly's eyes widened. "I *beg* your pardon? Them's fightin' words, lady."

"You do. You put yourself and James in danger because you were worried about what other people would think. Just like Betty."

"Jesus Christ, what an awful thing to say. But . . . you're right." She poured herself more wine. "I started partying with friends, drinking too much. Then sleeping around. I wanted him to dump me. I couldn't do it myself. Partly because of what people would think. Partly because I wanted James to grow up with a father. And partly because . . . I was afraid to leave him. I didn't know what he would do, what would happen."

"You screwed around on Stuart on purpose?" Amelia asked. She found it hard to believe. Ever since Amelia had known her, Molly had spoken badly of her own behavior during her marriage to Stuart, as if she regretted it. It required quite an adjustment in Amelia's thinking to accept the fact that Molly had done it all with the intention of getting Stuart to divorce her.

"Even that didn't work," Molly said with a bitter chuckle. "I finally had to tell him I was unhappy. Bored with him. That I wasn't cut out to be a wife. If I hadn't done that, I might still be married to him." She sniffled as tears filled her eyes again. "I really did love him, Amelia," she whispered. "We would have had a great life together if it hadn't been for . . . for that *thing*."

Amelia sighed. Molly lit another cigarette. Neither of them spoke for a long while.

Finally, Amelia said, "I've got to get him to a doctor."

"You think a doctor's going to figure out what's wrong with him?"

Amelia did not reply. Molly was right—there was little chance of a medical doctor being able to fix whatever was wrong with Stuart. She could not imagine finding any doctors who specialized in that particular field, whatever field that might be. "What about Betty?"

"What about her?"

"You said he'd go to a doctor if his mother nagged him into it."

"Yeah, probably. I don't know."

"Have you ever tried to find out if she knows anything about this?"

"If she knows anything, it would have to be removed from her surgically."

"She has to know something. I doubt it started when you two were married. It was probably going on long before that, when Stuart was a kid."

"Short of getting her drunk, I don't know how you'd get it out of her. She'd never talk about it."

"Well, I have to try. She wants James to help her with her computer. Maybe I'll take him over and while I'm there try to talk to her about Stuart. I should take her something, a peace offering. I was kind of abrupt with her on the phone the last time we spoke."

"Bake her some brownies. She's a sucker for brownies."

"Mind if I use your kitchen?"

"Be my guest. I've got a package of Betty Crocker brownies in the cupboard. I'm going to bed."

CHAPTER TWENTY-TWO

The Bay Area was drenched, and the gunmetal sky gave no sign of clearing. Streets flooded, both the Russian and Napa rivers had overflowed, and mudslides wreaked havoc in the hills of Marin County, above Saratoga and Los Gatos, and around the flooded town of Guerneville. Houses were being damaged, some destroyed, and four people had been killed by flooding and mudslides. A male voice on the radio in Molly's Saturn reported the various rain-related problems in San Francisco and throughout the Bay Area.

"California's not going to fall into the ocean," Amelia muttered. "It's going to slide in."

"Mind if I find some music?" James asked.

"As long as it's not country or rap."

He found a station playing heavy metal, then went back to playing his GameBoy. Amelia tuned it out and focused on the rhythmic sound of the windshield wipers.

Molly had not gone directly to bed. She'd sat in the kitchen awhile, still sipping wine while Amelia made brownies.

"This is probably going to be a waste of time," Amelia said.

"Hey, who knows, she might accidentally come up with a way to help Stuart."

"If she knows how to help him, why hasn't she by now?"

"Have you forgotten who we're talking about, here?"

Amelia nodded, muttered, "Sometimes she's the sweetest little old lady, and sometimes I could strangle her."

"Welcome to the family."

"I'm not too happy with you, either," Amelia said, standing.

"Me? What'd I do?"

"When you found out what Dr. Furgeson did to Stuart, you laughed. You actually thought it was funny. That was a cruel thing to do, Molly, and you hurt Stuart."

"Want to hear my side?" Molly said.

"Of course, but I can't imagine it'll change how I feel."

"His mother told me the story, so I only got her version. I didn't think it was a big deal. I mean, I didn't know the guy used a pair of scissors on him. I didn't think it was anything traumatic until Stuart told me the whole story."

"I'm afraid Betty might have been telling the truth about that," Amelia said. "Dr. Furgeson told me he used a scalpel. From what he said, I got the impression scissors are never used in that procedure. And when you think about it, a scalpel would make a lot more sense."

"Why do you think Stuart would lie about something like that?" Molly asked.

"I don't think he's lying. I think that's how he remembers it. I don't think Betty's the only one in the family who remembers things her own way."

"Think it's got something to do with his problem? His mental illness?"

"The more I learn about Stuart and his problem, the less I realize I know about him." Amelia sighed heavily. "I've got to get him to a doctor. I think he should see a medical doctor, then he can refer Stu to a psychiatrist, or whatever."

"Well, if you can get his mother to start nagging him about it, he might go just to shut her up."

As Amelia turned the Saturn onto Betty Mullond's street, she said, "I think it would be a good idea for you to help Grandma with her computer right away, okay? Then when you're done, I want to talk to her about your dad."

James shrugged. " 'Kay. What'sa matter with it?"

"I don't know. Maybe nothing. I think she just needs you to show her how to do a few things."

He nodded, but didn't look up from the game.

Amelia realized she was as nervous as a child going to the dentist. She'd never had a serious talk with Betty about anything, and she doubted her ability to get around the old woman's smiling defenses.

She parked at the curb in front of the house and turned off the radio, then the engine. She smiled at James, who stuffed the game into a pocket of his denim jacket. "Ready?"

"Yeah." He opened his door, took his umbrella from the floor. "Just hope she don't play none of that creepy religious music."

Amelia did not bother with her umbrella and hurried across the small lawn with her head down, the foil-covered Pyrex dish of warm brownies cradled in one arm. A soggy brown mutt in the next yard had started barking as soon as she parked the car. It ran back and forth along the chain-link fence that separated the lawns and madly barked without pause.

On the small covered porch, Amelia rang the doorbell. Betty was home—her white Ford Taurus was parked under the carport beside the house. When the bell got no response, she pulled open the screen door and knocked hard on the front door.

"It's Sunday," James said. "She might not be home."

"Her car's here. And it's after two, church is over."

"Yeah, but she might've gone somewhere with them old . . . um, them ladies she hangs out with."

Amelia sighed. "Or she just doesn't hear me." She knocked again, harder than before, and called, "Betty!"

The dog went on barking up and down the fence.

James reached around Amelia and tried the doorknob. It was unlocked and the door opened a few inches. "She's home," he said as he pushed through into the house.

Inside, Amelia closed the door and called, "Betty, you've got company!" No response. She turned to James. "Why don't you go see if you can find her."

James headed down the hall while Amelia carried the brownies to the kitchen. Her right foot caught on something on the kitchen floor and she nearly fell. She looked down at the white object on the old brown and tan linoleum. A purse. Betty's white purse, smeared with something red.

Amelia lifted her head and her eyes fell on Betty, stretched out on the oval kitchen table and covered with blood. She dropped the Pyrex dish—it hit the floor with a heavy, sharp sound, but did not break—and spun around to rush back through the door and into the dining room. But in that instant, the sight of Betty Mullond lying on her back—arms stretched out at her sides, dress torn down the middle and crumpled around her, throat grinning redly, abdomen yawning—was seared into Amelia's mind. And there was something else, something red and wet in Betty's mouth. It had been stuffed in until her cheeks looked ready to burst, and what would not fit into her mouth was piled on her face.

Amelia slapped a hand over her mouth and pressed her back to the wall just outside the kitchen door. She breathed rapidly through her nose as tears pixilated her vision.

"Grandma?" James said from down the hall. "You here?"

She was unable to think, unable to find her voice. She could not even move.

"She's not here, Amelia," James said as he came back up the hall. "She prob'ly went with—hey, whassamatter?"

She closed her eyes, shook her head. She knew there was something she should do immediately. Call the police? That was probably it. But for some reason, that idea set off klaxons in her head. Her hand dropped from her face. "Get in the car," she said in a raspy monotone.

"Whuh-what? Is somethin'—"

"Just get in the car, James, go, now." She was afraid to meet his worried gaze, afraid he might see in her eyes what she had just seen. "Go!"

James hurried out of the house.

Amelia tilted her head back against the wall, tried to

think. Thoughts shattered before they were fully formed. Fragments of the image of Betty Mullond's eviscerated corpse on the kitchen table flashed behind her eyelids.

She pushed away from the wall, forced herself to remain upright as she hurried through the dining room, living room, foyer, and finally outside, where she drank in the cold, damp air. The dog was still running back and forth along the fence, barking, barking. James was already getting into the car. Amelia fumbled with her keys as she got into the Saturn, started it up and drove away.

"What . . . what happened in there?" James asked.

Amelia said nothing.

"You look . . . sick. You're real pale, Amelia. Is something wrong with Grandma?"

"Wait till we get home, James," she said, horrified by the forced, synthetic cheerfulness in her voice.

He said nothing more for the rest of the drive.

CHAPTER TWENTY-THREE

It had been a long and productive day and Stuart decided it was time for a break. He had gone shopping for more supplies many hours ago, but other than that, he had been working nonstop for . . . he was not sure how long. All he was sure of was that he needed a shower and was hungry. He felt sticky and gritty with dirt, and his stomach growled.

After showering, he searched the refrigerator and cupboards for something to eat, but found nothing appealing. He had a craving for red meat, something greasy and deliciously unhealthy, like a cheeseburger. Even better, a buffalo burger from Tommy's Joynt on Van Ness. He put on his jacket and went out into the darkening late afternoon.

The rain had turned daylight to dusk. The streetlights had already come on, their glow reflected on the wet pavement below.

The air felt good and he breathed it deeply. He got into the car and pulled the door closed, slipped the key into the ignition, pulled the seat belt across him and fastened it. As he started the engine, the door on the passenger side opened. Stuart's head jerked to the right with a startled jolt as Dr. Furgeson bent down and leaned into the car. His stethoscope dangled from his neck and he smiled.

"I saw your mother today, Stuart," he said. "She sends her love." He wore a pale surgical glove on his right hand streaked with something dark, and held in his hand what looked to Stuart, at first, like a lump of raw meat. Dr. Furgeson tossed the object at him and it landed between his thighs with a wet squish. Slightly larger than a baseball, it was surprisingly heavy and a number of rubbery tubes protruded from it. Stuart gawked at the object.

A heart. A real human heart.

His legs kicked involuntarily as he opened the door and tried to get out of the idling car. The organ fell from the seat to the floorboard between his feet. He could not get out, he was trapped in the seat, held back by something, someone. He feared it was Dr. Furgeson, leaning in and holding him, pinning him to the seat, but he heard the doctor laugh and the sound came from outside the car, some distance away. When he realized he still had his seat belt on, he made a high whimpering sound, teeth clenched. He clawed at the latch, released it, fell out of the car. On his way out, he inadvertently kicked the heart on the floorboard and knocked it out with him. It hit the concrete with a heavy squashing sound and wobbled a few inches as Stuart tumbled onto the wet grass.

He scrambled to his feet and spun around, stared at the heart. Both of the car doors were open. Dr. Furgeson was gone.

Stuart looked around to see if anyone was watching. He saw no one, but that did not mean no one was there. There were a lot of windows across the street. He stared down at the heart, tried to catch his breath. Moving without thought, he leaned into the car and killed the engine. He took an old newspaper from the floor behind the driver's seat, closed both of the car doors, then returned to the heart. Hunkering down in the rain, he put the newspaper over the heart, closed the paper around it and picked it up.

In the house, he put the soggy newspaper on the dining room table and it fell open. The paper bore dark stains on either side where the heart had dribbled onto the newsprint. Stuart had never seen a human heart before outside of photographs, but the one before him appeared to have been freshly removed.

He's bluffing, he thought.

Stuart could not believe it was his mother's heart. That was what Dr. Furgeson wanted him to believe.

He's screwing with my head again. That's all.

But he could stir up no confidence in that assumption. He turned away from the table and went to the phone, started to punch in his mother's number. He stopped before he finished and put the receiver back on its base. What if Dr. Furgeson had not been bluffing?

Stuart's mother had caller ID, although she still had no idea how to use it. If he called, there would be a record of it, and if something had happened to his mother, he would most likely be a suspect. The two combined would not look good. Maybe that was what Dr. Furgeson wanted. Stuart looked at the heart again. Dr. Furgeson could be trying to set him up, get him out of the way so James would be more accessible.

He pulled a chair from the table and dropped into it, stared at the organ on the table. He thought, *It's her heart. She's dead.* But he could feel nothing, because he could not believe it was true.

If it were, someone would call him soon. Stuart decided to do nothing just yet, to wait and see what happened.

Amelia opened her eyes to see an unfamiliar, fair-complexioned woman looking down at her. She had short dishwater-blonde hair and wore oval-shaped glasses with brown tortoise-shell frames. A black bag hung from her shoulder on a strap over her knee-length beige coat. Beside her stood an equally unfamiliar man with brown skin, shiny black short-cropped hair, and a pleasant smile. He wore charcoal-colored pants and a gray sportcoat over a yellow shirt with a black, red-striped tie. A long gray coat was draped over his left forearm.

"Hi," the woman said.

Amelia sat up on Molly's sofa quickly, clumsily.

"You don't have to get up if you don't want to," the man said.

"Maybe she wants to," the woman said.

She wanted to. Amelia had been so hysterical when she got back from Betty's that Molly had given her a Xanax, and she'd had another glass of wine. She had told Molly everything once James had left the room, then had fallen asleep on the sofa. Her head felt heavy, tongue swollen. She had no idea how long she'd been asleep, but wanted to go back as soon as possible. She sat up, rubbed her eyes.

"Do you feel up to answering a few questions, Miss Randall?" the woman asked.

Amelia squinted up at the woman. "Questions?"

"They're detectives," Molly said as she sat beside her.

The woman smiled, but only for a moment. "I'm Detective Scherber. This is my partner, Detective De la Rosa. We're here about Mrs. Mullond."

Molly put an arm around her and said, "I told them everything I could. They want to know what you saw."

Once Amelia had told her everything, Molly had called the police immediately in spite of Amelia's protests. Amelia had been able to think only of Stuart. Once the police learned he was having mental problems, he would be their primary suspect, and she knew he could not have done something so savage.

"But Stuart is responsible, Amelia," Molly had said. "You know who did this. It was Dr. Furgeson. And that means Stuart is responsible, even if he didn't do it with his own hands."

"How do we know it was Dr. Furgeson? I mean, it could have been . . . I don't know, just some anonymous psycho."

"That's pretty unlikely, don't you think?"

Amelia had nodded slowly. "But what do we tell the police? If I tell them about Dr. Furgeson, they'll think *I'm* crazy."

"Just answer their questions. When they ask why you left and came all the way back here before calling them . . ." Molly had taken a deep breath, run a hand through her hair as she blew it out with puffed cheeks that reminded Amelia of Betty's face, bloated with something red and wet that snaked from her mouth. "Just tell them you wanted to protect James, that you panicked, you were hysterical. We'll tell them you and Stuart are having problems and you were on edge to begin with."

"I have to tell Stuart," Amelia had said.

"Don't worry about that now."

Detective Scherber was taller than Detective De la Rosa and seemed restless, fidgety. He, on the other hand, was quite calm and still and continued to smile pleasantly as he casually looked around the room.

"Would you like to sit down?" Molly asked them.

"No, thank you," Scherber said. "We won't be staying long. What's your relationship with the deceased, Miss Randall?"

"She's my . . . she's the mother of my . . ." Amelia shrugged, a little embarassed. "I'm sorry, I'm not sure what to call him. 'Boyfriend' sounds so juvenile."

"Amelia lives with Betty's son," Molly said.

Scherber removed a black notebook and pen from her bag. "His name is . . . ?"

"Stuart," Molly said. "Stuart Mullond."

"And where is he today?"

"At home, far as I know. He's . . . not feeling well. He's missed the last couple days of work."

"Is this Mr. Mullond?" Detective De la Rosa asked. He stood before the fireplace looking at a framed photograph of Stuart and Molly and James as a toddler.

"Yes," Molly said.

Detective Scherber went over to the picture, got a good look at it. "Does he still look like this?"

"Pretty much," Molly said.

"He's in better shape," Amelia said absently.

Scherber came back to Amelia and asked, "Where is home?"

Amelia gave her the address and, when she asked, the phone number.

"Where does he work?" Scherber asked.

"Carnival Greetings. He's an artist."

"Any siblings?"

Amelia shook her head.

"Does he know about this yet?"

"No. I . . . I need to tell him."

"Don't worry about that," Molly said. "I can tell him."

Scherber asked, "What about the senior Mr. Mullond?"

"Dead."

"Why did you go over there today, Miss Randall?" Scherber asked.

"I took James over to help Betty with her computer."

"James?"

"That's my son," Molly said. "Mine and Stuart's. We're divorced."

Scherber's eyes moved back and forth between Amelia and Molly. "You two're friends, are you?"

They both nodded.

"Well. Isn't that nice." She wrote in her notebook, absently sat on the edge of the coffee table.

"That's very rude," Officer De la Rosa said.

She started to stand again, but Molly said, "No, go ahead, it's okay."

Scherber sat on the coffee table, shot De la Rosa a cold glance, then asked, "What did you see while you were there, Miss Randall?"

Amelia described everything, from knocking on Betty's door to finding her body on the kitchen table. As she spoke, De la Rosa wandered slowly around the living room, casually looked at the knickknacks and books on shelves.

"I . . . I didn't want James to see," Amelia said, "so I got him out of there right away. And came here."

"Why didn't you call the police right away?"

"I should have, I know. But when I saw her like that, I panicked. I-I freaked out, all I wanted to do was get away from there, I mean, for all I knew, the killer could still be there, and I didn't want to, I mean, I couldn't—"

Amelia started to cry again and Molly squeezed her shoulder, whispered, "Calm down, honey, just calm down."

Amelia lowered her head, forced herself to stop crying. But she could not stop thinking of the gaping hole where Betty's abdomen and chest used to be, the ropey objects trailing from her unnaturally bloated face. "I'm sorry," she whispered.

"I understand," Scherber said, though she did not sound very understanding. There was a chilly detachment to her voice. "That was a horrible thing to discover. It's natural for you to be upset."

Amelia took a tissue from the box on the floor, dabbed her eyes. She realized De la Rosa was no longer in the room.

Scherber asked her again what she had seen, took her through the details one at a time. She made notes in her notebook as Amelia repeated her story. Once they had gone through it again, she asked, "How did Stuart get along with his mother?"

Amelia fought the urge to turn to Molly for help. "Fine. They got along fine." She shrugged. "They had the usual squabbles, you know. Like all mothers, Betty still seemed to think of him as a child even though he's thirty-seven years old. But they had a good relationship." She turned to Molly. "Don't you think?"

"Oh, sure. If they'd been next-door neighbors, they might have had some problems, but they got along fine."

Scherber nodded. "You know of anyone who *didn't* get along with her?"

Amelia frowned. "No, not at all. She was very sweet, had a lot of friends."

"She was active in her church and did a lot of charitable work, volunteered a lot," Molly said.

Amelia looked up at Scherber and hesitated a moment before asking, "What . . . what was . . . done to her?"

"Her heart was removed. It hasn't been found yet. It appears the killer took it."

"Oh, Jesus," Amelia said tremulously as she put a hand over her mouth. "Did . . . did she suffer?"

Scherber said, "We don't know all the details yet. Forensics people are working on that now."

The next question that came to Amelia's mind was one she did not want answered. At the same time, she had to know. "What . . . what was in . . . her mouth?"

Scherber hesitated. "The killer removed some of her intestines and put them in her mouth." Standing, Scherber said, "I'm going to let you get some rest, Miss Randall. But I'll need to talk to you again in the next couple of days. You'll be at home?"

"Either there or here," Molly said quietly.

"Here?"

"They're, um . . . having a little disagreement. Know what I mean?"

Scherber nodded. "I'd like to speak to James, if I—"

"That's okay," De la Rosa said as he came into the living room with James. He held a notebook and pen in his hand. "I talked to James."

The boy was pale and looked a little stunned.

De la Rosa smiled and put a hand on James's shoulder. "He's a real computer game wizard." Turning to James, he added, "I've got a nephew you'd get along with real well."

"We can go, then," Scherber said. "For now."

Molly asked, "Are you going to talk to Stuart next?"

"I'm afraid we'll have to."

"He doesn't know. Can you give us a chance to talk to him first?"

Scherber checked her watch. "I'd like to talk to the forensics people. That'll take a little time. What's wrong with him, by the way? Is he sick?"

"The flu," Molly said before Amelia could respond.

Standing, Scherber reached beneath her coat and produced

a couple business cards. She gave one to Amelia, one to Molly. "Call me if anything occurs to you that you think we should know."

After seeing them out, Molly hurried back into the living room, where Amelia remained on the sofa. James sat beside her, but with one sofa cushion between them. He almost seemed afraid of her.

"We have to tell Stuart," Molly said.

"I'll tell him."

"You can't drive."

"You can drive me."

"What happened to Grandma?" James asked, his voice hoarse and frail.

Molly sat between them, put an arm around him. "Sweetie, somebody killed Grandma."

"Why? Who?"

"Well, we're not sure—"

His voice lowered when he said, "Dr. Furgeson."

"You didn't mention him to the detective, did you?" Molly asked.

"No. Why didn't *you?*"

"I don't think that would've gone over too well with the detectives," Molly said. "Remember, Dr. Furgeson is . . . well, what*ever* he is, he's not . . . real."

He nodded. "We gotta tell Dad right away. He shouldn't hear it from them."

Molly gave him a brief hug. "You're a good kid, you know that?" She turned to Amelia, who was dabbing her eyes again. "Let's go."

CHAPTER TWENTY-FOUR

The rain had receded to a lazy drizzle and the artificial dusk that had lasted all day, created by the black clouds, slowly darkened as night fell. Amelia's stomach churned, but not with hunger. The raw-nerves tension she was feeling nauseated her.

Molly slowed the car as it approached the house on Lake Street. Amelia sat beside her, and James leaned forward in the backseat, too distracted to play his GameBoy.

"Oh, shit," Amelia said, glaring at the two detectives who stood on the front porch. "She lied. They're already here." As they stood facing the front door, Detective Scherber pushed the doorbell, then knocked.

"Doesn't look like they've talked to him yet, though," Molly said. Her words were hopeful, but her voice was angry. She parked at the curb behind a tan Ford Crown Victoria. "You stay here, honey," she said over her shoulder as she and Amelia got out.

"But Mom, I wanna—"

"Stay here for now. No argument."

Scherber turned as they crossed the lawn, smiled at them.

"I thought you had something to do," Amelia said. She hated the tremor in her voice.

Scherber shrugged. "Couldn't get ahold of the guy I needed to talk to, so we came here. Just doing our job."

Amelia pressed her lips together tightly to hold back an angry remark.

"Is that his car?" Scherber asked, pointing at the Celica.

"No, it's mine," Amelia said as she stopped on the front

step just below them. Molly stood beside her, one step down. "Is he gone?"

"Seems to be. I thought you said he was sick."

Amelia shrugged. "I haven't seen him since yesterday. He might feel better."

"What happened to the car's back window?" Scherber said.

"It was vandalized recently," Amelia said.

"Wouldn't he take the car if he went somewhere?" Scherber asked, cocking her head curiously, right hand propped on her hip.

"No, probably not. He prefers public transportation. He doesn't care for driving. Prefers to draw or read."

"Ah, I see. Well, while you're here, I thought of a couple more things I'd like to ask you. Mind if we go inside?"

Amelia put her knuckles against her right hip, tilted her head. "I didn't bring my purse, so I don't have the keys. Sorry. What are your questions?"

The smile dissolved on Scherber's face as she came down the steps and stood before Amelia. "You know, Miss Randall, if you're trying to delay or obstruct our interview with your boyfriend, I'm afraid it doesn't look good. Do you understand? And on top of that, it's against the law."

"That's the furthest thing from my mind, Detective Scherber," she said, slowly shaking her head. She clenched her teeth. "I just don't want him to be told his mother has been sliced open like a fish by two complete strangers. Do *you* understand? I think he should hear it from someone close to him, don't you?"

Scherber's smile returned as slowly as it had disappeared. "Well. Since you don't have your purse—" She slipped a hand beneath her coat and removed another business card. "—here's another one of these. Give me a call after you've told Mr. Mullond about his mother's misfortune." The smile disappeared and Scherber headed for her car.

De la Rosa followed, smiling at them both. "Have a good evening," he said with a nod.

Amelia went up to the door, opened the screen, tried the doorknob. It was locked. She knocked hard and called, "Stuart?"

"I've got my key," Molly whispered.

"I'm sure he's in there."

"Let's go back to the car. Drive around the block, if we have to. C'mon."

As they went down the steps, the doors of the Crown Victoria slammed shut. Scherber was at the wheel.

Amelia and Molly got into Molly's Saturn.

"What'd they say?" James asked urgently. "Is somethin' wrong? Where's Dad?"

"Quiet, James," Molly said.

"They're not leaving," Amelia whispered. "She hasn't even started the—"

The Crown Victoria's engine started. The lights came on. Molly started the Saturn.

Amelia put a hand on Molly's arm and said, "Wait, they're going."

"I know, but we want them to think we're going, too. They might drive around the block a couple times, see if we're still here." She pulled away from the curb when they did, but made a quick U-turn. An oncoming sedan braked and blared its horn at the Saturn. "Yeah, yeah, yeah, bite me," Molly muttered.

Ten minutes later, Amelia slipped Molly's key into the lock, turned it, and opened the front door. She pushed the door open, held it for James and Molly, then closed it and turned the lock.

They had passed the two detectives in their Crown Victoria twice, circling the block in opposite directions.

"They'll see us!" Amelia had said.

"I want them to see us," Molly had replied. "I want them to know that we know that they're fucking with us. What're they gonna do, arrest us?"

The house was silent inside. For a moment, Amelia was afraid Stuart really might be gone. Then she heard a high-pitched whine, like a mosquito flying around her ear. She went through the dining room into the kitchen and realized it was muffled, tinny music coming from the garage at a low volume.

When James started to follow his mother and Amelia through the kitchen, Molly turned to him and said, "Why don't you go play on the computer, honey?"

"I'm not s'posed to play on the computer!" he snapped, irritated.

"Well, we're making an exception today, okay? Go on."

With an annoyed sigh and a roll of his eyes, James turned and went to the computer.

Amelia heard Molly catching up to her in the back hall as she approached the door, knocked hard several times. "Stuart? It's me. Please let me in, we have to talk."

Big-band music was playing on the other side of the door. There was a rush of movement, a couple of clumsy bangs.

"Just a second," he said. The music was turned off.

"Stuart?" She knocked again. "Stu, honey, this . . . this is important. Please let me—"

The door was unlocked and pulled open, and Amelia looked down at Stuart, who stood beside the three concrete steps that went down into the garage.

"What's wrong?" he asked.

He looked sick. Amelia frowned as her eyes moved over Stuart's pale, drawn face. His dark hair was wildly mussed and the skin beneath his eyes had a sickly shade to it. His cheekbones seemed more prominent than they had been the last time she had seen him. His mouth hung open as if he were too weary to hold it closed, surrounded by a thin beard and mustache of stubble that stood out harshly against his pasty skin. He looked exhausted, drained. In his eyes, along with a scorched-out lack of sleep, she saw a cold detachment, as if he were looking at a total stranger, or at nothing at all.

She knew as soon as she laid eyes on him that whatever was wrong with Stuart had gotten much worse since she had seen him last.

He said nothing, just looked at her blankly.

Amelia reached out cautiously and pushed the door all the way open, stepped down into the garage. She glanced over her shoulder, glad that Molly was staying in the hall.

"Um, Stu," she said quietly as she approached him. "I've got some, uh . . . bad news, honey." She gently placed her hands on his chest. "There's been a . . . someone has—"

"Mom," he said. It was more of a noise than a spoken word, hoarse and breathy.

"How did you know?" she whispered.

Stuart shook his head. "I didn't. Just a guess. He hasn't been able to get to James, so he's punishing me."

Amelia turned to Molly a moment, standing in the doorway. Molly's expression frightened her. She was looking past Amelia and Stuart at something that made her look like she was about to scream, or vomit. Following her gaze, Amelia gasped when she saw the heart on the card table, on an open, bloody newspaper. She reflexively took a step backward as she turned her horrified eyes on Stuart.

He shook his head slowly. "I was about to drive to Tommy's Joynt. Furgeson came and tossed it into the car. Said he'd seen Mom." He turned to the heart. "So I guess . . . that really is . . ."

Amelia spoke quickly, urgently as she said, "Jesus, Stuart, if the police find that, if they know you have it, they'll arrest you on sight!"

"Fuck the police. I want you to pack your things and go away. Get out of the city. Out of the state."

"Whuh . . . where do you expect me to go?"

"I don't know, and I don't want to know. Just go." He looked up at Molly. "Both of you. And James."

Amelia shook her head. "If we just leave, the police will—"

"Dammit, I'm not going to argue with you," Stuart said

with quiet anger. "Get out of San Francisco, as far away as you can. Now, go upstairs and—"

"What the hell is *that?*" Molly asked, pointing a finger at the aluminum frame leaning against the locked cabinet.

"Never mind, just go." Stuart waved Amelia toward the open door.

Amelia immediately recognized the spare aluminum frame covered with brown silk as the one Owl-Man wore on his back in the paintings. When folded up, it fit neatly beneath his cape, until he jumped off a building. Then he opened it up with the pull of a small lever and rode the wind.

A mottled tan and brown suit hung just above the down-sized hang-glider frame. And a cape.

"My God, Stuart, I am *not* going to leave you here to kill yourself with *that* thing!" Her voice trembled with a mixture of anger and fear.

Molly came slowly down the steps, mouth gaping as she stared at the suit and cape.

"It's not finished," he muttered.

"Even when it's finished, it's still going to kill you! Think about what you're doing, Stuart! *Think!* You need help. You know you do. You're only going to get worse if you don't get help. But I'm not letting you dive off a bridge with *that* thing on your back!"

He pushed a breath through his nostrils, stared at the floor a moment. He lifted his head and asked, "Where is James now?"

"Here," James said, and all three of them turned to where he stood in the open doorway.

Molly said, "I thought I told you to—"

"Shut up," Stuart said, shooting her a burning glance. "Listen to me, James. Your mother and Amelia are going to take you out of town. You need to do me a favor, okay?"

James nodded.

"Do what they say and never leave them." He turned to Amelia. "Never let him out of your sight. Understand?"

"I'm not going anywhere, Stuart. Not unless I take that thing with me." She pointed at the glider frame.

He turned to Molly. "You. Out."

Molly hurried from the garage and disappeared down the hall, but James stayed in the doorway. Amelia made no move to leave.

"You have to go," Stuart said quietly. "He could be watching this place right now."

That weakened her resolve. The very thought of seeing Dr. Furgeson again made her want to break into a run. She put her hands on Stuart's shoulders and said, "I'll go if you'll see a doctor."

"This is not a negotiation."

"I'm serious, Stu. Let me take you to a doctor. We'll go together. We could—"

He took in a deep breath, then shouted, "I am not going to any fucking doctor!"

Amelia stumbled backward and James's entire body jolted in the doorway. She took another step back, away from the rage in his eyes. It filled the space between them, made the air quaver as if with hot vapors.

"Now, get out of here," Stuart said quietly. He turned to James. "Both of you."

Amelia was impressed with the resolve in James's face. Neither of them moved.

Stuart's eyes shot back and forth between them as he shouted, "Listen to me, this guy is *serious*!" He settled his gaze on James. "He killed your grandmother, James. And he brought me her heart. You hear me? He did that. Now, he wants *you*," he said as he pointed a finger at his son. "If he gets you, he's going to do to you what he—"

"No, don't, Stuart," Amelia said as she hurried to him, put a hand on his arm and gradually lowered it. "Don't take this out on him." When he turned to her, she flinched. His face had changed, looked puffy and red, as if he'd been hanging upside down.

"If anything happens to James," he said quietly, "I'll take it out on you."

He could not have shocked her more had he backhanded her in the face. But far more hurtful than his words, or the tone of his voice, was his animal-like face and eyes, animal because he looked about to pounce on her and go for her throat.

Lowering his voice to a hoarse whisper, he added, "Forget about me and take care of James." The puffy redness was gone suddenly, perhaps had never been there. The look of animal fury had disappeared, if it, too, had been there in the first place. "Please."

"What's he gonna do to me?" James asked nervously.

Stuart went up the steps and embraced James. "He's not going to do anything to you, because he's not going to find you. I want you to do what Amelia and your mom tell you, okay? And stick together."

"Where are we going?"

"Right now, you're going to go in the house with your mom, okay?" He held him tight for a moment, then pulled back, looked him in the eyes, hands still clutching the boy's upper arms. "No sneaking off, you got that?"

James shook his head quickly. "Don't worry. Not gonna do that."

Stuart said nothing and did not move for an uncomfortably long time. James began to fidget under his gaze.

"I love you," Stuart said. "And I'm proud of you. You've got good taste in comic books." His hands smacked onto James's shoulders and gave him a shake. "Now get going."

The ring of finality in Stuart's voice clearly bothered James, and he stared at his dad with dismay, unmoving. It had sent a little shudder through Amelia as well.

James's eyes welled up. Stuart moved close to him and spoke quietly.

"Do it for me, okay?" Stuart said. "I'll take care of Dr. Furgeson, I promise. But in the meantime, I need you to stay with your mom and Amelia and lay low, okay? Will you do that for me?"

"Okay," James said with a nod. He backed slowly down the hall.

"I love you, James."

"I love you, too, Dad," he said. Then he turned and walked away.

Stuart came down the steps to Amelia. "C'mon, you too. Get your things and go."

"I told you, I can't leave. I don't *need* to leave if you'll get help."

Stuart's head tipped forward suspiciously. "What do you mean?"

Amelia struggled with it for a moment. After all the bizarre incidents Molly had told her about, it seemed Stuart should, at the very least, have an inkling of what was going on. Surely he had made the connection and was aware, to some extent, of his strange abilities. But all she saw in his face was pain and anger and fear.

His voice was a mere exhalation of breath when he asked, "You still think I'm just making this up?"

"No, that's not what I mean at *all*. Don't you know what I'm talking about, Stuart? Don't you know what's happening?" She took his hands in hers.

"What are you talking about?"

She clutched his hands, shook them, angry and frustrated. "Dr. Furgeson is real, but he's coming from *you*, dammit. He's coming *out* of you. I don't know why, I don't understand any part of this, I don't even understand why I believe it, but it's connected to your depression, somehow. It happens when you get depressed. You've done it before."

He took her hands from his and clutched her wrists tightly, but said nothing.

"Your second Christmas with James. Molly got a black eye."

Stuart's eyes narrowed. "She fell on the stairs."

Amelia nodded. "You *know* that's not what happened. You and James were both asleep. Somebody knocked on the door and when she opened it, a big, fat, smelly, filthy Santa Claus came in and knocked her around. The kind of Santa Claus you'd been doodling. With characteristics that matched the things you'd been saying about Santa Claus. And when you woke up and came out into the hall, he disappeared, and you found Molly lying on the stairs. He disappeared because you stopped . . . doing whatever it was you—*ah!*" she cried when his grip on her wrists became painful.

"Are you saying that I killed my mother?" As he shouted the last word, Stuart pushed her away from him.

Amelia's heels connected with something—the camp chair, it turned out—and she fell, hit the concrete floor on her back. Her lungs imploded and for a moment, she could not breathe. Pain shattered her back as she rolled over, got up on one elbow, struggled to her feet. She expected Stuart to come to her side, help her, tell her how sorry he was. He did not.

"Get out," he said quietly.

Gasping for breath, she stood, wondered if her fear showed on her face. She decided to say no more for the time being and went up the steps slowly without taking her eyes from Stuart. Finally, she turned away from him and started to go through the door. A cold and despairing fear made her stop. It was more a dreadful certainty than fear, a feeling she had never experienced before. But Amelia felt fear as well—she was afraid it was a moment of prescience. The certainty that had overwhelmed her was that, once she left the house, she would never see Stuart again. She turned to him silently.

Stuart's face had softened. His eyes did not quite meet hers.

"I'm going to call you," she said.

He nodded once. "Thank you." He made eye contact long enough to say, "I love you, Amelia." Then: "Get out."

She put the garage behind her and went upstairs, packed a few clothes. She sniffled a little and shed a few tears, but kept herself together long enough to leave the house with Molly and James.

Molly drove away without asking where they were going. James was silent in the backseat. And Amelia could not shake the feeling that she would not see Stuart again.

But she was wrong. She would.

CHAPTER TWENTY-FIVE

"Zit ever gonna stop rainin'?" Shavonna said.

Amaze shrugged her narrow shoulders. "Weatherman on the radio says no. Maybe that means it'll stop. They're always wrong."

"Z'd have us out here if it was hailin'."

Amaze laughed and nodded. "If it was hailin' the size of baseballs."

"'Somebody out there wantsa fuck, baby, so you gotta be there for 'im,'" Shavonna said, imitating Z's high voice.

Amaze laughed again. She was small and blonde with wholesome caucasian looks. She had been known as Cynthia Mott a hundred years ago back in Michigan, but she'd been calling herself Amaze—Mazie to her friends—ever since she'd started stripping in a biker bar called Hog Heaven in Modesto four years ago at the age of fourteen. Even that bar seemed like a long time ago, and far away from the rainy sidewalk across from the Whitman Hotel in San Francisco's Tenderloin District.

They stood together under a large red umbrella Shavonna held in her left hand. Shavonna was a few years older than Amaze, taller and heavier, with skin the color of dark chocolate and long black hair in thin ropy braids.

Z—Prince Z if anyone else was within earshot—was their pimp. Their "manager," he preferred.

Amaze and Shavonna stood near the edge of a pool of yellowish light cast by a nearby streetlight. They both wore miniskirts, Shavonna with black net stockings, Amaze barelegged, both in stilettos, and they were cold. The rain was loud on Shavonna's umbrella. They sometimes caught a whiff of the garbage in a nearby alley.

It had been a slow night. Amaze had not turned a trick for two hours and she eyed with hope a man crossing the street toward them.

He wore jeans and a dark green down jacket zipped up the front, his hands buried in the pockets, shoulders hunched forward against the rain as he walked. His head was down and he wore a dark baseball cap with the bill pulled low. He stopped in front of them and lifted his head. He wore glasses with tinted lenses.

"Hey," he said.

Amaze flashed all her wattage. "Hey, honey."

Shavonna said, "Don't *chew* look like a man knows what chew want."

The man looked back and forth between them a few times, then settled his stare on Amaze. "You," he said. "How much?"

Shavonna laughed and Amaze said, "Whoa, sweety, hold on, what—"

"A blow job, how much?"

Shavonna laughed again, and the man's upper lip curled as he turned to her. "Shut the fuck up," he said with quiet force.

Propping a hand on her hip, Shavonna said, "Fuck you, motherfucker!"

"Hey, hey, c'mon guys," Amaze said, still smiling. She tossed a look at Shavonna that said, *Gimme a break.* She turned to the man and said, "You wouldn't be a cop, would you?"

"No, I'm not a fucking cop. How much?"

Shavonna said, "You better hurry up, honey, 'fore he pops off right here, 'cause this boy's in a *hurry*."

"I said *shut up*."

"Fifty," Amaze said. "I've got a room across the street in the hotel."

"No hotel," the man said as he grabbed her elbow. He

jerked her away from Shavonna so suddenly and hard that Amaze released a small cry of surprise and pain.

Before Amaze had a chance to realize he was leading her somewhere, they were entering the alley's darkness, walking into its foul odor.

"Hey!" Shavonna shouted. "Hey motherfucker, you don' wanna do that, you fuckin'—"

A moment later, Amaze heard Shavonna blow the whistle. Z had given each of them a silver whistle. Either Z or someone who worked for him was always across the street in the hotel, and when they heard the whistle blow, one or more of them rushed over armed with guns and knives.

It occurred to Amaze that she should be afraid, but fear had not caught up with her yet. She heard the man unzip his fly. He put a hand on her shoulder and pushed down hard.

"Look, I'm not doin' this in no alley," she said, trying to step back. "I got the room across the street, I'm not gonna—"

He touched the broad side of a cold blade to her cheek, then held it in front of her face. Her eyes were adjusting to the deeper darkness of the alley and Amaze saw the large hunting knife in the man's hand.

Fear caught up with Amaze and landed with a cold explosion in her chest.

The whistle stopped, started again, then stopped.

Trembling, Amaze began to bend her knees when a hand gently settled on her left shoulder. She knew immediately that it wasn't Z or any of his boys—they wouldn't be able to keep their mouths shut long enough to sneak up on anyone so quietly, and none of them had any gentleness in them. The hand firmly pulled her back away from the man.

She turned and saw a tall, broad-shouldered man beside her. Amaze rapidly blinked her eyes several times. The large man wore a mask covered with dark feathers. A sharp, curved silver beak glinted where a nose should have been.

The angry john said, "What the fuck're you—"

The large masked man threw a single punch and hit the john in the throat. Warm blood spattered Amaze's right cheek as the john collapsed and made a horrible sound on the ground. He gurgled and gasped as the masked man put a hand on Amaze's shoulder again and turned her around, steered her out of the alley. By the time they reached the sidewalk, the gurgling sounds had stopped and the alley was silent.

Amaze looked at the gloved hand on her shoulder and saw the four sharp blades that curved out from the knuckles.

"What the fuck're *you* s'posed to be?" Shavonna said with a laugh as she stared at the masked man.

Amaze stepped away from him and looked him over. He wore a suit with what appeared to be feathers on the lapels, and a long cape. Her eyes were wide as they settled on the sinister beaked mask.

"The fuck's goin' on?" Z shouted as he hurried across the street. He wore a long black coat and a wide-brimmed hat. He laughed as he approached the costumed man with the shiny beak. "Dis freak fuckin' wichew?"

"No, Z, wait, he's not—"

"Whyn't you get the fuck outta here 'fore I cut your ass, birdman?" Z took a switchblade knife from his coat pocket and flicked it open.

The costumed man punched him in the face twice, first with a right cross, then a left. Z dropped the knife and staggered backward, and his hands went to his face as he screamed. It was a high, shrill sound that was cut off abruptly when the man punched Z in the stomach. Z doubled over with a wet coughing sound, then dropped to his knees. As Shavonna began to scream, Z fell on his right side.

The man with the beak looked down at Amaze and she stared up at him with her mouth hanging open.

"Call your parents," he said. "At least let them know you're still alive."

Gooseflesh spread over Amaze's back. She turned and

watched him walk away. His cape flapped behind him as he disappeared around a corner at the end of the block.

Kneeling beneath the umbrella beside Z on the sidewalk, Shavonna was hysterical. She kept screaming, "He's bleeding! He's bleeding!"

Amaze looked down at Z and saw strips of flesh dangling from his face. His blood was pooling on the wet sidewalk, black in the glow of the streetlight. Z made long, high-pitched whining sounds.

As she stared, Amaze was secretly pleased by the sight. After all the times Z had beaten her until she dropped to the floor, it gave her a sense of satisfaction to see him down and bloodied on the concrete. She turned and headed across the street.

"Call an ambulance!" Shavonna screamed. "He's bleeding! He's bleeding!"

But Amaze had no intention of calling an ambulance. She was going to call her parents.

In spite of the rain, it had been a busy night for twenty-two-year-old Rocky. They came in bursts, mostly regulars, looking for heroin or crack or ecstasy. Word got out when Rocky's pockets were stocked. He paced in the shadows under his black umbrella in front of a boarded-up storefront, just a few yards down from an adult bookstore that advertised 25 cent video booths. He had been there for only ninety minutes, pacing slowly in the dark, and had sold almost everything he had.

Rocky's buddy D.J. leaned against the wall and stared at nothing in particular. He did not have an umbrella and was soaking wet, but he was flying too high to care. Rocky had a buzz from the flask of rum he carried in the back pocket of his jeans, but that was all. He knew better than to sample the wares.

"You ever go in that place?" D.J. asked, jerking his head toward the adult bookstore.

"You kiddin'? Buncha fags in there suckin' each other's dicks in the booths in back."

D.J. released a slurred laugh and muttered, "Buncha fags."

Rocky said, "Who wantsa watch videos, anyway? I get a hard-on, I'd rather go a couple blocks and see one a Z's bitches. If I hadda pay for it. But I don' hafta pay for it. I never paid for it."

"I paid for it once."

"Only once?"

Another slurred laugh. "Only once. Bite me."

Rocky laughed. "You sure paid for it widdat Korean chick."

A frown grew slowly on D.J.'s brow. "That bitch gave me the fuckin' clap."

"S'what I mean, dickweed."

Rocky was approached by two of his regulars, a couple guys referred to him by another customer, both in their late teens. They were looking for ecstasy, all business, as usual. They were nervous and hardly spoke. Each had an umbrella and wore an overcoat. They looked too clean for the neighborhood, and Rocky figured it probably scared them. They wanted to get out as soon as possible and wasted no time on small talk.

Rocky was taking their money when a large hand reached from his left and grabbed his wrist with an iron grip. The hand pulled Rocky's arm until his elbow locked, and a knee swung up under his arm and made hard contact with his elbow. The arm broke with a sharp crack and the pain made Rocky scream and throw his umbrella into the air. The money and the pills in their little baggies scattered over the sidewalk as the two shocked young buyers stumbled backward away from Rocky and the tall, broad, masked man who had broken his arm.

Rocky collapsed unconscious onto the concrete as the two young men turned and ran across the street, leaving their money and their drugs behind.

The tall man spun around to face D.J., who stood rigid with his back pressed against the wall. D.J. trembled all over as he looked the costumed man up and down.

"Are you with him?" the man asked, nodding toward the still heap that was Rocky.

D.J. stammered and fidgeted, but did not reply.

The man stepped closer and said, "When your friend gets better, you tell him to find something else to do for a living. Tell him Owl-Man will be watching. Understand?"

"Ow-Owl-Muh-Man. Owl-Man. Wuh-watching."

Owl-Man turned and walked at a quick pace down the block through the rain and disappeared around a corner.

D.J.'s fidgeting became a kind of dance as he jittered over to Rocky's side. He tossed glances over his shoulder to make sure Owl-Man was gone. Shaking his head with disbelief, he repeated the name to himself quietly—"Owl-Man . . . shit, Owl-Man . . . Owl-Man, fuck *me*"—as he bent forward and stared down at Rocky for a moment. D.J. looked all around to see if anyone was watching, then quickly gathered up the damp cash and the baggied ecstasy pills. Still quaking with fear, he ran in the opposite direction Owl-Man had taken and left Rocky behind, sprawled unconscious and alone on the sidewalk.

The rap beat thundering from Phantom's stereo was felt throughout the apartment, in the floors and walls. It almost drowned completely the sharp wailing of the sniffly, puffy-eyed baby in the closed bedroom. Each boy sat at his own computer.

On the night of their deaths, they waited for the two piz-zas they had ordered almost thirty minutes ago. Phantom and Wolfman were breaking into popular online game web-sites, a favorite pastime of the 4UMM. Once inside, they extracted passwords, magic crystals, talismans, and other symbols of passage that led to higher levels in the games from which the boys stole them. They were valuable in the gaming subculture, allowing users to skip ahead in a game rather than spending the days, weeks, or even months it might take to proceed on their own. With the money they made selling them, the boys bought marijuana, new games, and whatever software and hardware they were unable to get from Wolfman's dad.

They divided all their money three ways—unless Hunchback returned, then it would be quartered. They hung out together more for the company than to do any damage online. Although they had hacked into Wolfman's school's computer once and changed a few of his grades from Fs to Ds just before report cards went out. They had offered to change Hunchback's grades, too, but he had said no.

Phantom had told his aunt that someone had broken into the apartment and done permanent damage to the door. She had sent a repairman over the same day with a new door and he had installed it. Reinforced with steel plates and held fast by a couple of heavy-duty dead bolts, it was no longer a door that could be kicked in easily. It was a door that probably would break the foot of anyone who tried.

They did not like Hunchback's dad, and they worried about their friend. They had discussed contacting him, helping him out of his prison. But the fact that his dad knew where they were and had promised to kill them if they tried to reach Hunchback—no, he said somebody else would do it, somebody they would not recognize—kept them from going through with it.

All three boys heard it at the same time—the pounding.

"Pizza," Wolfman and Dracula said simultaneously. Wolfman turned to him and said, "Your turn."

Dracula rolled his chair back, picked up a joint from the ashtray on his desk. He took a quick hit, then got up and made his way to the phonebooth-like foyer. He put his eye to the peephole, but only for a second before pulling back and turning the first lock, because he knew it was the pizza guy. But he took his hand off the lock and put his eye to the peephole a second time. Something had caught his attention on the other side of the fish-eye lense, something small, quick, and odd.

A small brown feather danced a fluttery downward waltz through the air just outside the door. Someone pounded on the door again, three rapid blows, and Dracula jerked away from the door, so startled he dropped the money from his hand.

"Pizza?" he asked, hunkering down to retrieve the bills.

"Yo."

Money in hand, Jamal Winston—Dracula to his friends— drew the locks, turned the knob, and pulled the door open. A dark figure filled the doorway. He had no pizza, but wore a costume that made Dracula blurt a single loud laugh just before he saw the flash of an oncoming fist. It was visible for less than a second, but long enough for him to see the dull flash of the small, sharp blade that curved out from each of the four knuckles.

The fist punched him just beneath his jaw, in the throat. He fell backward as a spray of red jetted from his throat, and was unconscious shortly after hitting the floor. Dead seconds later.

Phantom was on his feet the instant he saw Dracula go down. He reached for the gun he now kept ready on his desktop. But the figure that stepped out of the small foyer caught him by surprise and he froze a moment. Before he had time to understand what he was seeing—the tall, muscular man wore a cape and had feathers, Phantom couldn't get past the feathers—the man flicked his right hand, snapped his wrist, and a gun appeared from his sleeve. It wasn't there, and then it was. The man fired once, put a bullet into Phantom's skull, killing him instantly.

Wolfman was under his desk by the time the dark, feathered man turned the gun in his direction. He was small, wiry, and had crawled from one end of the room to the other beneath the tables and desks before, more than once.

The rap beat still made the floor vibrate deeply, so Wolfman moved fast, not caring about making any noise down there because the music would eat it all up. But he could not find the man's feet and had no idea where he was, or even if he were still in the room. After crawling under his own desk, he passed beneath a card table, then Hunchback's desk, then a longer table. There he remained, watching for the intruder. Maybe he had left the apartment already. When Wolfman looked back, he saw Phantom on the floor, his blood pooling around his head. Across the room, the blood of Dracula had spread like wings over the floor on each side of him. Wolfman seemed to be the only one in the room still moving. Still living, maybe.

He crawled out from under the long table and was still on hands and knees when two feet landed heavily directly in front him after jumping off the table. A hand closed on his hair, lifted him to his feet, and the fire that burned over his scalp made him cry out in pain. Wolfman's feet left the floor and he was flopped onto the long table on his back. The feathered face descended on him, moved in close. A fist appeared against the left side of Wolfman's face. The tips of the curved razors on its knuckles gently touched the skin at the top of his cheekbones. The man's mouth moved in the pointy shadow of his mask's chrome beak.

"Is he here?"

Wolfman's breathy voice trembled as his words fell out in a rush. "I don't know who is it who are you I don't know who you're—"

"The doctor. Is he here now?"

The man's voice was very quiet, difficult to hear with the stereo playing so loudly and yet impossible to shut out. There were fine black screens in the mask's round owl eyes, and beyond them, Wolfman could see a glimmer of the man's eyes. But no more than a glimmer. He was glad. If the man's eyes looked the way his voice sounded, Wolfman was very glad he could not see them, because whatever it was he heard in the man's voice, it scared the piss out of him and he did not want to hear it again, so he started talking, and found that he could not stop, could only get louder and louder as he said, "I don't know any doctor mister I don't know what doctor you talkin' about I mean there's no doctor *here* we don't have one *here* there's no doctor no man no we don't have a—"

"Dr. Furgeson. Is he in there now?" The man nodded his feathered head toward the bedroom door. "Is Dr. Furgeson in there?"

Wolfman's voice left him and his throat clicked.

The man put his left hand on Wolfman's scrawny neck, thumb over his throat, and squeezed.

"It's just a baby," Wolfman rasped. "Don'tcha hear the baby?"

His feathered head turned in stiff, jerky increments, tilted as he listened. "He's got a baby in there?"

Wolfman's head bobbed up and down.

He released Wolfman and stepped back from the table. "Get out of here."

"Huh-what?"

"Get out of here. And tell the others. It stops tonight. Now. It's over."

"Over," Wolfman whispered. He dropped off the table, sidled toward the door.

"Tell them to leave me and my family alone. Repeat it."

"Repeat it?"

"*Repeat* it."

"It stops now, tonight, right now, and it's over. And they're supposed to . . . leave you and your family alone." Closer to the door.

"That's right."

Closer to the door, closer.

"Now, get out."

Then Wolfman noticed that sound again, the sound he'd been listening to for hours, for so long that he hardly noticed it anymore. The baby was still crying. The boy had not been named yet because the mother—Shatter, a fourteen-year-old Mexican girl who spoke only a little broken English and whom Dracula had met at a goth club—wanted the father to participate in naming him, and Dracula insisted he was not the father. Wolfman had heard of Shatter before but had only met her that night, because while Dracula enjoyed having sex with her, he didn't like having her around. She'd shown up that evening in need of a place to stay for the night. Dracula had taken her into the bedroom, where they had bumped and grunted for awhile as the baby cried. Dracula had come out and behaved as if she weren't there the rest of the night. Shatter and the baby had remained in the bedroom ever since. Had she heard the gunshot? Did she know something was wrong?

Wolfman stopped taking sideways steps toward the apartment's open door and looked at the bedroom door, and said, "Wait, I gotta—"

"Go!" the man shouted.

"But there's—"

He aimed his gun at Wolfman. "Go spread the word, or I'll kill you now, understand? I've got no problem with killing you guys. I know you're not human. You're one of them. One of him."

The boy glanced at Phantom, dead on the floor. At Dracula, drenched in his own blood. Wolfman continued moving carefully toward the door. He placed his hand on the door-jamb as he turned to look back over his shoulder. He took in a deep breath and tried to shout a warning before darting out of the apartment: "Shatter, there's a—"

The gun fired and Wolfman hit the floor, ears ringing. He tried to sit up, could not breathe well, wheezed and coughed. A shimmer of red sprayed from his mouth. Still coughing, Wolfman looked down at the small bleeding hole in his chest. His last thought was, *This is my favorite Babylon-5 T-shirt!*

* * *

A baby was crying. Somewhere. Crying and crying. Owl-Man tried to determine whether it was an aural hallucination, but it was difficult to tell. The baby continued to cry, its voice growing ragged but no less piercing.

Owl-Man stood at the door inside the apartment, listening to the baby cry on the other side. There was no other sound beyond the door, none he could hear through the deafening pounding of the rap music. Pounding, pounding. It irritated him, but he let it play, hoping it would mask any sounds he made.

Gun in his right hand, he opened the door with his left and dropped to a crouch. He swept the gun across the small room until it stopped on a little figure sitting on the edge of the bed. She wore a long baggy T-shirt, still as a department-store mannequin as she stared at him with round eyes. Right knee up high, bare foot resting on the edge of a straight-back chair in front of her, right hand holding the nail-polish brush over her third toe. Her left foot was on the floor, cottonballs between the metallic green–nailed toes. Her dark eyes were huge on her plump face, mouth open, a glistening pink wad of bubblegum resting in the bed of her tongue. Tattoos on her arms marred smooth cocoa skin, and she wore too much makeup on her face. She also wore a set of tiny headphones on her ears that were plugged into a Discman on the bed beside her.

A fat, naked, squawling baby boy slouched against a pillow on the bed. He was alarmingly fat, not just plump or chubby, but rather grossly obese for such a small creature. He looked like a doll sculpted out of soft butter.

"Where is he?" Owl-Man asked.

The bottle of nail polish dropped from her left hand, thunked onto the floor. It bled metallic green on the brown throw rug at her feet. She raised her hand slowly and hooked a finger beneath the headphones, peeled them off her head and dropped them onto the bed.

"*Que?*" she said, staring at the gun. "*Que?*"

His arm relaxed a little at his side, but he kept the gun on her. "Uh . . . *sprechen*—no, shit, that's German. Um . . . *se habla* . . . English?"

The girl's eyebrows drew together as she shook her head, muttered something in Spanish. Her eyes remained on the gun.

The baby continued to squawl, stopping only when it became necessary to breathe. His mouth looked impossibly large as it yawned open beneath a flat nose that was all nostrils.

"Dr. Furgeson," he said. "Where is *Doctor Furgeson?*"

She flinched when he shouted the name the second time, but kept talking. In Spanish, faster, louder. And then she came apart. She sobbed and tears wet her face as she pushed the straight-back chair away and rose to her feet. She babbled on, louder and louder.

He spoke deliberately, enunciated succinctly: "Doc . . . tor Fur . . . ge . . . son." He sighed. "No English at all?"

"A leetle," she said. "Jus' a leetle." Her face was wide with panic as she looked back and forth between the gun and his face. "Pleez don' hurt me, pleez!" Then she continued to rattle on in Spanish.

"Shhh, please don't do that," he said, shouting to be heard above the rap music, as well as the girl's shrill babble and the baby's unrelenting yowl.

She dropped to her knees and pleaded with him.

"No, stop it, please," he said. "Don't do that, there's no reason—could you please stop—"

She stretched out her arms to him, hands upturned, pleaded with him.

"No, no, I can't—look, I can't understand you!" he shouted, frustrated. "Would you please just calm—stop *shouting*, stop—would you just—"

He lifted the gun and hit her on the forehead with the butt of it. She dropped to the floor in a limp heap.

He went to another door, opened it. A tiny bathroom

with a filthy bathtub and a dripping faucet in the sink. Empty. He closed the door as he left the bathroom, looked into a cluttered closet. No room in there for anyone to hide.

Dr. Furgeson was not in the apartment.

The bedroom had no windows and was so small it made Owl-Man feel claustrophobic. There was no reason to stay now. He had made his point, and one way or another, it would get back to Dr. Furgeson. As he turned to leave, his eyes fell on the screaming baby.

Suddenly, Stuart's weak, shuddering knees gave way beneath him and he dropped onto the edge of the bed. Owl-Man was gone for the time being. Stuart stared at the round baby. Its entire body quivered and rocked with its cries.

He looked down at the girl on the floor and his insides withered. A knot had risen on her forehead the size of a golf ball. He waited to hear the sound of his own screams, to feel the unravelling of his mind from the inside out. But he heard nothing but the rap music coming from the boom box, felt nothing but nausea.

Stuart was reluctant to leave the baby there, all alone. It did not feel right.

She'll wake up soon, he thought.

It was difficult to look at a baby, any baby—even this fat, ugly shrieker with its snotty nose—without thinking of James. It had not been so long ago that James had been a baby. It suddenly seemed like just last week.

Stuart slid the gun back up the sleeve of his suit coat until it latched and was safely out of the way. He pushed his cape back and opened his arms, leaned over and picked up the crying baby boy. The infant was even heavier than Stuart had expected. Through his gloves he felt the baby's pliant flesh move, saw it undulate over the baby's torso.

A wave of movement passed over the baby's fat belly and chest.

Like clay being sculpted by invisible hands, the flesh bunched and flattened, pulled and stretched, all very quickly, until two rolls of fat pressed together to become thin lips, and the crease between them became a mouth that spread across the baby's belly as it smiled up at Stuart. Beneath the lips were the familiar protuberant teeth.

Stuart dropped the baby as if it had burst into flames. The infant bounced once on the mattress. His arms flailed and legs kicked as he wailed on, apparently unaware that he had been picked up, dropped, or disturbed at all. The baby's nipples lifted like eyelids to reveal Dr. Furgeson's gray eyes. And from the front of the baby's fat, naked body, the doctor grinned.

It's not real, Stuart thought. *It's some kind of trap, a trip, a trap*—

"You do not come to me, Stuart," Dr. Furgeson said. "I come to you." The doctor's voice sounded thin and wavering, as if he were talking through a spinning fan. The nipples blinked over the eyes. On the baby's chest and abdomen, Dr. Furgeson had no nose. "You will never find me, no matter how hard you try. But there is no place you can go where I am not with you."

A trap, he thought. *A trip, a trap.*

He turned away from the screaming baby on the bed and left the bedroom, then the apartment.

CHAPTER TWENTY-SIX

He had started coming apart very quickly after he got the news about his mother. Before that, his decay had been progressing at a steady but slower pace. He was aware of it now, the declining state of his mind, but he still considered it a single problem among many, probably caused by the stress of all his other problems. He'd had a headache for two days, and that evening it only grew worse. It changed the shape of his head, made his eyes pop out of their sockets and dangle by bloody stalks, caused his teeth to soften and flop in his gums. It made him feel like he was trapped in some nightmarish *Gumby and Friends* episode. Painkillers did not help. It had not occurred to Stuart that his usual regimen of more rigorous exercise and proper diet at the first sign of a mood swing might not be working. It had never crossed his mind that his poor mental health might be the cause of all his other problems, including his headaches. It was not that he refused to believe such a thing was possible—he simply had not considered it. Until Amelia had stabbed him in the gut with her words.

Dr. Furgeson is real, but he's coming from you. He's coming out of you.

He knew she was right, had known the instant she said it, although he had behaved otherwise. But he did not know how she was right, or how he knew she was right. Only that she was. And his mind had been gnawing on it ever since, like a slobbering dog with a bone. There was plenty of meat left on that bone, too, and the biggest, juiciest piece was this: If Stuart was, indeed, responsible for Dr. Furgeson, then he was responsible for his victims, too, and that meant he was responsible for his mother's death. He had killed his mother.

Stuart's mind had thought in dizzying circles after Amelia, James, and Molly left the house. Literally dizzying—he'd fallen over twice when the floor tilted beneath him, and had felt sick from seeing the walls turn around him as if he were at the hub of a giant spinning wheel.

He had lost track of time and had no idea how long ago they had left the house. Sometimes it felt like only a few hours ago, and other times it seemed like days had passed. He'd spent all that time working, putting on the finishing touches, preparing, while the headache stretched his skull into a long oval, then a lopsided blob, a squashed lump at the end of his neck. He had tried to sleep once, but was unable to keep his eyes closed. Stuart's mind gnawed on his mother's death while the headache gnawed on him. He was never more than a glance away from her heart, resting on its bed of bloody newspaper on the card table.

Stuart had begun to hallucinate sometime after his family's departure. At first, he had recognized them as hallucinations— like when the animated figures of comic book superheroes and supervillains from some of James's comic books chased each other around on the card table while Stuart nearly wet himself laughing at them. Or the bats that flew through the house while *Dracula Has Risen From the Grave* played on television. Or his mother. They had to be hallucinations. He supposed they had something to do with the chemicals that were out of balance in his brain.

But when he put on the suit for the first time and stood before the full-length mirror he had removed from the back of the door in the master bedroom and brought down to the garage, the line between hallucination and reality began to blur.

Stuart was unable to make the suit look exactly as it appeared in the paintings, which had never quite looked the way he saw it in his mind, anyway. He knew he would never be perfectly satisfied, and even if that were possible, he did not have the time to spend striving for it. He did not have the physique of his creation, but the costume effectively fulfilled its purpose. It was dark and imposing, frightening. As he stared at his reflection in the mirror, a powerful shudder moved through his entire body and cramps briefly twisted his insides, doubled him over for a moment. When he stood and looked at the mirror again, he gasped.

He was taller. Stuart laughed at first, because it was such a ridiculous notion, but after he reached beneath the mask and rubbed his eyes with his fingertips and looked again at the mirror, nothing had changed. The top of his head was cut off in the mirror, when seconds before there had been plenty of room between the crown of his head and the top of the mirror. Now his reflection ended just above the mask's frowning round eyes. Several inches had been added to his height.

Stuart laughed again, because his whole body had changed, become larger. His shoulders were broader, chest deeper, and the suit was filled out much more impressively than before. He stared openmouthed at the reflection that was not his. He raced his hands over his body to feel the powerful muscles beneath his suit. Stuart had been in good shape, but these muscles were *much* larger and fuller than his own. Beneath his shirt, he felt a flat washboard stomach, enormous pecs. Even his neck was thicker. They were the muscles of a serious bodybuilder—the muscles of a comic book hero.

Moving quickly, he undressed, nearly falling a couple times in his rush. He placed the costume over the back of a chair for now, in too much of a hurry to put it back on the hangers. Wearing only his boxers and socks, he stepped before the mirror again.

The space between the mirror's top edge and the top of Stuart's head had returned. The abs and pecs were his.

He thought about it until his mind wandered to other things. To his mother. He dropped into a chair at the card table, overwhelmed by an exhausting guilt that drained him of more energy every time he allowed himself to think about it.

Amelia was right. In some way that Stuart did not understand, and did not particularly care to understand, he was Dr. Furgeson. The doctor was part of him, drew his strength from Stuart. He felt as if he had known all along, but secretly. So secretly that even he had been unaware that he knew. It was something he had carried with him but never noticed, until Amelia had brought it up.

It happens when you get depressed, she had said. *You've done it before. . . . Your second Christmas with James. Molly got a black eye.*

He had known it then, too. But Molly's explanation—that she had fallen on the stairs—sounded perfectly reasonable, and he had believed it.

No, no, he thought, *I didn't believe it, I seized on it. I accepted it. Because it worked.*

It worked in keeping those secret thoughts locked away in a hidden part of his mind, hidden even from Stuart.

He got up and put the suit back on slowly, waited until he had everything in place, then stepped in front of the mirror. There was less discomfort this time, no cramping. It happened more abruptly and with greater ease. But this time, Stuart was watching when it happened.

Suddenly, he was a much larger man. A different man. He was Owl-Man.

Stuart went to the mirror, bent down to look closely at his reflection, and in a fair impersonation of Michael Keaton, said, "I'm Owl-Man." He laughed as he backed away from the mirror, then turned a cocky profile to it, hunched a little. "You talkin' t'me? Huh? Are you talkin' t'me? If you ain't talkin' t'me, then who the fuck you talkin' to? Huh? Who? Who. *Hooo!*" He laughed some more, struck a few poses in the mirror. Something about his new body struck Stuart as funny. His laughter became a low, nervous giggle, which he was unable to control for almost a full minute. He took off his gloves and tossed them onto the card table. Lifted his mask to wipe away tears from his laughter, but there were more right behind them. Once he had stopped laughing, Stuart could not stop crying. He went to the table and sat down, took off his mask, ripped the Velcro that fastened it to the inside of his collar. Stuart cried for his mother as he held his head in his hands. He cried for the countless times she had been good to him, had doted on him, spoiled him, had been such a wonderful mother to him. She had even made an effort to compensate for the affection Stuart did not get from his father. Worst of all, he cried for the shameful way he had treated her, for focusing only on her faults and weaknesses, for always being so impatient and intolerant. He put his head down on the tabletop and cried himself to sleep, even continued for awhile as he slept, quietly. For twelve minutes.

Invigorated by the short nap, Stuart got up, put the mask and gloves back on, and went into the house. He had things to do, but could not remember what they were.

He found his mother standing in the kitchen. Posture perfectly straight, as always, head tilted back in that church-lady way of hers. She had on one of the housedresses she wore when doing housework. Checkered in pink and white, it was dark red in front. The red speckled and spattered in all directions from the great splash of it over her abdomen. All the buttons on the dress were gone, and she held it together just beneath her throat with her left hand, her right pressed flat over the large stain. Caking dribbles of blood went down her bare legs like runs in her stockings and puddled at the edges of her furry pink open-heeled mules.

"If you would only take the vitamins I give you, the way you're *supposed* to take them," she said, "you'd look that good all the time, Stuart."

Stuart looked down at himself. He had forgotten about his new body since his nap. He thought of it as his "costume body."

Costume, he thought. *My costume. It still fits.*

"Why does my costume fit?" he whispered. His body had changed, become larger, but the costume still fit.

"There are many things we don't understand, Stuart," she said. "Things we'll never understand till God Himself explains them to us."

How many times had she said that to him when she did not have the answer to a question?

"Some people will never have that chance," his mother went on. "I don't want you to be one of them, Stuart." A familiar, emotional quaver went through her words. The same quaver she got in her voice at church altar calls and baptisms. Her lips trembled the same way they did every year at the Christmas sermon, and every year at the Easter sermon. "I want you to be there with me, sweetheart, when we see Jesus."

Stuart was not in the mood for it. He sighed and rolled his eyes. "Mother, what makes you so sure *you'll* be there?"

Her reaction was so predictable. The little backward toss of her head, the delicate intake of breath. She lifted her right hand to her face to place it against her cheek, and something dropped from beneath her dress. It landed between her feet on the tile floor with a wet slap. A deep-red, gelatinous blob.

She quickly put her right hand back over her abdomen and said, "Oh, no. Oh, dear, I've dropped my . . . oh, what *is* that?"

"Oh, God," Stuart breathed as he turned to leave the kitchen.

"Stuey, sweetheart, could you please help me with—" There was another wet slap on the floor. "Oh, no."

He turned to see a fleshy, blood-mottled rope of intestine hanging from under his mother's housedress, coiled on the floor between her feet.

Stuart covered his eyes with one hand and clenched his teeth. "You're not real," he muttered. "I'm imagining you.

Creating you. You're not real." He left the kitchen quickly and headed back to the garage.

Suddenly brimming with confidence, he was ready to try out his suit, his new identity. All he'd wanted to do at that moment was get out of the house, go out into the city for the first time as Owl-Man. And he had known exactly where he wanted to go: the Tenderloin.

He left the Tenderloin apartment and walked quickly through the rain, head down. He ducked into the alley where he had parked the Celica.

He had not found Dr. Furgeson, but the doctor had found him. Dr. Furgeson had come out of Stuart's own head, and yet Stuart had no idea where he was, could not find him. But he would continue to try, because every minute that passed increased the chances that Dr. Furgeson would find James.

If he comes from me, Stuart thought, *does that mean I secretly want to hurt James?* He knew that was not possible. If that were the case, he would not be so desperate to keep the doctor away from his son.

It was still early, plenty of night left. Owl-Man decided to keep looking.

CHAPTER TWENTY-SEVEN

"We're making a big mistake," Amelia said.

Molly asked, "What do you mean? We're not doing anything wrong."

"No, not wrong. I just feel like we should be doing something *else*."

They stood outside the Castro Theatre the following night, smoking cigarettes as they watched the passing traffic through the rain. A soggy melange of greasy aromas from nearby restaurants traveled on the cold wind.

Around them, the theater's display cases were filled with posters and publicity stills of zombies with rotting flesh and filthy teeth, blood dribbling down their chins. The Castro was finishing up a three-night festival of zombie movies.

"If I'd watched another minute of that movie," Molly said, "I would've thrown up."

Amelia thought, *But it's okay for your thirteen-year-old boy?* It made no sense to her, but she did not say anything. She had other things on her mind. Although she had sat through the first feature and part of the second, she had seen neither movie. She had kept her eyes away from the screen and burroughed so deep into her own thoughts, she had not even heard the gruesome soundtracks.

"Don't you think we should at least check your answering machine for messages?" Amelia asked.

"We will. But not now. There's no rush."

"But we haven't talked to anyone about Betty's funeral, and I can't reach Stuart, I mean, for all I know, he's been arrested for his mother's murder and—"

"A little louder, hon, I don't think the guy at the snack bar inside heard you."

Amelia sighed, took another drag on her cigarette. "Sorry. I'm . . . tense."

"Believe me, if Stuart gets arrested, you'll hear from him. He'll call your cell phone."

"How do you know?"

"Because he'd need you to put up the bail."

"Don't even say that," Amelia whispered. Her cigarette trembled between her fingers as she lifted it to her lips. Its flaring ember bobbed slightly as she took a drag. "You've got me hooked on these damned things again, Molly."

"You're more likable that way. I hate nonsmokers. Self-righteous health police. Everyone on my mother's side smoked, including my mother, who is still very healthy at the age of sixty-nine."

"Yeah, but she sounds like Larry King."

"Maybe so, but she's healthy. My grandpa smoked since he was thirteen years old and died at the ripe old age of ninety-three."

"Of lung cancer."

"Hey, would *you* want to live any longer than that? He was senile, practically blind, in pain all the time from arthritis. The lung cancer put him out of his misery."

Amelia turned to her. "You know, Molly, sometimes you can be pretty cold."

"I'm not cold. Just practical. You could use a little practicality, too, you know."

"I could use a drink." Amelia shook her head again. "I can't believe it. You've got me drinking, too."

"Yeah. I got in your face and put a gun to your head and made you drink. Next, I'm going to force you to shoot heroin into your veins."

Amelia's shoulders dropped as she sighed. "I'm sorry. Don't pay attention to anything I say. I'm not myself," she said with a dismissive wave of her cigarette. She had not been herself for a few days. Molly had held up much better than she, perhaps because Molly was so practical. Or so cold. Amelia had always thought it was a front Molly put up to conceal her own insecurities, but she was no longer so sure.

The last couple of days had lasted forever. Amelia had spent every minute expecting to get some bad news from one direction or another. A phone call, a report on the television or radio, something about Stuart. Or worse, another visit from Dr. Furgeson.

Molly had been leading Amelia and James around the city all day, keeping them busy, trying to keep their thoughts off Stuart and Dr. Furgeson. She had gotten them a couple rooms at a Travelodge the night before because none of them wanted to return to her house for fear the doctor would come looking for James again. Molly had not seen the pale, toothy doctor in the long white coat, and there was no sign of fear or dread in her behavior. Everything that had happened lately seemed to bounce off her without sticking. But Amelia had not stopped feeling jumpy and agitated since she'd seen Stuart last. James did not talk about his dad, but he was clearly worried and afraid, and while he typically put as much space as he could between himself and adults, he'd been staying close to them.

For the whole day, Molly had been behaving like a guide, leading them around like tourists who wanted to go to all the places they'd seen in the complimentary videotape from the travel agent, the kind of places people who lived in San Francisco never visited. They seemed perfectly appropriate to Amelia, who found herself feeling more than a little like a tourist. Part of it came from waking up in a hotel room that morning. Most of it was due to the sudden changes in her life. Nothing seemed familiar anymore, as if she were a tourist visiting a stranger's life.

After breakfast in the hotel restaurant, Molly took them to the Exploratorium, an interactive science museum in the Palace of Fine Arts, where they spent the morning. Afterward, they went to Fisherman's Wharf to lunch with the tourists. Even on such a rainy day, the wharf was crowded and noisy, the air permeated with the smell of seafood and car exhaust. From there, they went to Pier 39 and browsed the overpriced shops, rode the carousel. The day was a blur of gift shops and clowns and cameras hanging from necks. For patiently putting up with so much shopping, Molly promised James she would take him to see the zombie movies at the Castro. Amelia had no choice but to go along and keep her eyes low to avoid seeing the carnage on the screen.

But no matter where they went or what they did, Amelia had been unable to think of anything but Stuart. He did not answer the telephone and had not called her.

People began to file out of the theater, talking and laughing. James wore a broad, satisfied grin as he broke away from the crowd and joined his mother and Amelia, a half-empty tub of popcorn hugged to his chest.

"Are you happy now?" Molly asked. "Did you see enough people get eaten, or do we have to stay for the next showing?"

"Thanks, Mom. And thanks Amelia. I know you don't like horror movies."

Amelia gave him a halfhearted smile.

Molly had parked a couple blocks away on a side street. They walked back through the rain under umbrellas. James, who had not brought one, moved back and forth between the two umbrellas and munched popcorn.

In the car, Amelia took her cell phone from her purse.

"Are you callin' Dad?" James asked from the backseat.

"No, I'm calling the answering machine to check the messages."

Molly shook her head. "There won't be anything there. Not from Stuart."

"We'll see. How do I play the messages?" Molly gave her the code and Amelia punched the numbers and waited. Several seconds later, she said, "Your mom called. Said she wants to get some pattern from you. What kind of pattern?"

"A tablecloth."

"Pete called."

Molly rolled her eyes. "What did he have to say for him-self?"

"Says he wants to talk."

"Yeah, he always wants to talk. His mouth should have a meter on it."

"He wants you to call him tonight."

"He wants a lot of things."

The next message made Amelia's chest and throat ache.

"Amelia?" Stuart said. "If you're there, pick up. I wanna . . . I need to talk to you." His voice sounded like glass being ground to powder. He waited a moment before continuing. "Okay, guess you're not there. Um . . . I wanted to tell you, uh . . . whatever happens . . ." He made a sound that could have been a sob, covered it with a few coughs. "I don't know what's happening to me."

Molly started to speak, probably to ask what was wrong, but Amelia waved her hand spastically between them. Molly pulled her head back and frowned.

"What's wrong?" Amelia muttered. "Tell me what's wrong."

"I'm sick, but it's not anything, uh—" He laughed a couple times, a painful sound. "Well, it ain't the flu. I'm . . . well, forget about that. I don't know what's going to happen, that's what I'm trying to say. So I wanted to say good-bye, just in case. And I wanted you to know how much . . . oh, I don't think you'll ever know how much I love you." He said noth-ing for a few seconds, and the answering machine automati-cally cut him off.

The machine's robotic voice said, "End of messages."

Amelia slowly lowered the cell phone from her ear. Tears dropped from her eyes when she blinked. She turned to Molly suddenly and said, "Get to the house. Now, go."

Pulling away from the curb, Molly asked, "Which house?"

"Ours."

"Stuart called?"

Amelia nodded. "Something's wrong, he sounds awful. He said he called to say good-bye. In case something happened." She quickly punched in her home phone number, waited for an answer.

"Oh, Jesus," Molly muttered.

James's head appeared between them. "Where's he goin'? I mean . . . that's what that means, right? He's . . . goin' somewhere?" He made no attempt to hide the fear in his voice.

Molly said, "We don't know, sweetie, now sit down and put on your seat belt."

He reluctantly sat back.

The answering message on the machine at home seemed to last forever. When she heard the beep, Amelia said, "Stuart, please pick up the phone. We're on our way over right now, we're going to come in whether you like it or not, understand? I'm serious, we're in the car now. Dammit, Stuart, pick up the phone!"

There was no answer. Before she could speak again, the machine cut her off. She took a deep breath, dropped the cell phone into her purse. "He's got to be there," she whispered.

Molly shrugged. "The way he is now, he could be anywhere, do anything. Nothing would surprise me."

"Thanks. You really know how to cheer a girl up." She rubbed her eyes with two knuckles.

"Oh, don't look to me for cheer, hon. I don't do—oh, shit." The car slowed to a stop on Mission.

"What?" Amelia blinked her eyes, saw the backed-up cars ahead. A block or so up, red and blue lights pulsated like silent heartbeats. "A car accident?"

"Probably." She brought the car to a stop behind a pickup truck with a camper shell on the back. When she heard the seat belt unfasten behind her, Molly said, "Sit down and put the belt back on, James."

They waited.

Amelia said, "Dammit, isn't there any way to get around this?"

"If we were in the right lane," Molly said, "we might be able to get to that side street up there. But we're not."

"Mom, since we're not moving—"

"Yeah, okay."

He leaned forward between them. "What's goin' on up there?"

"Whatever it is, we've got to get around it," Amelia shouted.

"Hey, c'mon, Amelia, you've got to relax a little." Molly reached over and took her hand, squeezed it. "There's nothing we can do about this. It happens all the time, you know that. Stuart's gonna be fine. Well, maybe not fine, but . . . there's nothing you can do for him, anyway, Amelia, you might as well face that now."

Amelia wanted to scream back at her friend that she had to find Stuart, he wanted to say good-bye, and she was going to be there for him to say good-bye to. But she sucked her lips between her teeth and gulped back the words. Molly was right. There was no sense in beating herself up.

"Holy shit!" James said, pointing. "There's somebody on the roof of that building up there! See where they're shining that spotlight?"

"Oh, God, there is," Molly muttered.

Amelia's eyes followed James's finger out the windshield, up through the rain to a figure standing on the edge of the roof of a ten-story basalt-block building. If not for the lights below, Amelia doubted it would be visible at all. Something behind the figure moved slightly, heavily in the wind. When she realized it was a cape, she gasped.

"What's he wearin'?" James asked, leaning farther forward.

"What's wrong, Amelia?" Molly asked.

Amelia could not move or speak or even think for a moment as she stared at Stuart up there in his Owl-Man costume. Then a loud, crazy-sounding laugh exploded from her chest. At least, the laugh sounded crazy to her, and it frightened her, but what she was seeing was, she thought, insane.

Astonishment raised the pitch of James's voice. "He's got *wings!*"

"Oh, Jesus," Amelia said. She fumbled with her seat belt, opened the door. Molly shouted something as Amelia threw herself out into the rain. She stumbled around the front of the car and ran down the street between two rows of stalled traffic.

Stuart surveyed a crowd gathering around all the flashing, spinning lights below, then lifted his eyes to look at Dr. Furgeson on the roof of the building directly across the street.

He had come up to this place because Dr. Furgeson had been on the roof, waiting for him. The doctor had called down at him, taunted him, and had laughed when he saw Owl-Man, laughed and pointed.

"*Look* at you, Stuart. You look . . . positively . . . *ridiculous.* You're not ready for me yet. It would not be a fair fight."

Along with slipping in and out of Owl-Man's head at will, Dr. Furgeson was capable of disappearing and reappearing somewhere else in the blink of an eye. That was what he had done. He had disappeared in a blink, then reappeared on the roof across the street, an efficient-looking twelve-story building of concrete and glass. Owl-Man had been standing at the edge of the roof watching him ever since.

Stuart reached down for the stubby lever at his side that would spread his aluminum-frame wings beneath his cape, gently wrapped his fingers around it.

On the street below, someone aimed the spotlight at the doctor, and there was a loud reaction from the crowd. His white coat flapped in the wind like a long cape. He held up his right hand and a shimmer of light sparked off the silver scissors. Flashes of red and blue from below glinted off the lenses of his round glasses.

"The time has come, Owl-Man!" Dr. Furgeson shouted. "Just the two of us! Mano a mano!"

Snick-snick-snick. Snick-snick-snick.

The voice and the sound were in his head, he knew that—Dr. Furgeson was putting them there. Anger and hatred burned in Owl-Man's guts. All else disappeared as his eyes focused tightly on the figure across the canyon of Mission Street.

Dr. Furgeson lifted his left arm, beckoned with four fingers. "You want me, Owl-Man? You want me?"

Owl-Man's lips pulled back over his teeth as his fist clenched on the lever. He pulled it as he dove off the ledge, and his wings caught the wind.

But it lasted only a moment. Cold, damp air slapped him in the face as he rapidly spiralled downward. The crowd screamed and the world spun in a multicolored blur as it rushed up to meet him. Everything disappeared in blissful blackness.

The last thing he heard, deep in his head, was Dr. Furgeson's bitter cackle.

Chapter Twenty-eight

When Dr. Biederman entered the waiting room in turquoise scrubs, the knuckles of Amelia's right fist became milky as she clutched the wadded tissue in her palm. She and Molly and James stood from the couch where they had been waiting in silence so thick and tense it was smothering. They had waited more than seven hours while Stuart was in surgery.

Dr. Biederman was in his late thirties, slender, with thick, short black hair and mustache, a pale complexion. White hairs streaked his mustache and the hair over his ears. His smile was weary and somber as he pulled a chair over to face the couch. They all sat down and the doctor leaned forward, elbows on his thighs, fingers intertwined between his knees.

Amelia wanted to ask how Stuart was, but she did not speak for fear of crying again. She had been crying so much that her head throbbed. Her cheeks glistened and her eyes were puffy and red.

Dr. Biederman spoke quietly. "Stuart has sustained a severe head injury," Dr. Biederman said. "He's comatose right now, and in critical condition."

"Is—" Amelia's voice broke on the word and she stopped, cleared her throat and took a breath. The fingers of her left hand flitted around her mouth a moment, then her hand dropped in her lap. "Is he in pain?" Once she had learned he was still alive, that had been her biggest concern.

"He's receiving pain medication and he doesn't seem to be uncomfortable. But it's very difficult to tell how aware a comatose patient is, so I can't really say. We do encourage the families of comatose patients to talk to them, read to them, to behave as if they're fully conscious of their surroundings."

"Can we see him?" Molly said, her voice thin and quavery. She had not shed any tears, but her hands had been trembling and fidgeting uncontrollably all night and morning.

They had walked around the stalled traffic of Mission Street and watched him, a ghostly figure on the roof of the ten-story basalt-block building, standing on the very edge looking directly across the street at something. They had followed the spotlight as it was turned on the white figure of Dr. Furgeson.

"Do you see that?" Amelia had asked as they stopped walking and stood in the rain staring up at the doctor.

"Of course I see it," Molly had said.

"And so does everyone else." Amelia had been relieved—finally, she and Stuart and James were not the only ones who had seen the white-coated doctor.

Dr. Furgeson had disappeared then. The spotlight searched for him a moment, but when it could not find him, it swept back across the street to Stuart. They had watched as he tipped forward and his wings spread. It had looked so hopeful at first, as he caught a gust and swept upward for a moment. Then he had spiraled down to the pavement.

Afterward, the spotlight had returned to the other building across the street and searched again for the tall, thin figure in the long, flapping white coat. But Dr. Furgeson was gone.

Dr. Biederman nodded. "You can sit and talk to him, but don't expect a response. Not for now, anyway."

"What are his chances?" Molly asked.

Dr. Biederman paused a moment, as if choosing his words carefully. "His condition is grave. The chance of permanent brain damage is high, but to what extent is impossible to say.

In situations like this . . . well, anything can happen. He sustained a closed head injury on impact. An artery was torn, causing a hematoma, which has created—"

"Hematoma?" Molly said.

"A blood clot, which has created swelling and put pressure on his brain. We've relieved some of that pressure and inserted monitors that will allow us to maintain constant—"

"You mean you had to cut his head open?" James said, his voice a high, rough whisper. His eyes were wide, round face even paler than usual. He looked more like a scared little boy than a teenager.

"Just a small hole to help relieve the pressure," Dr. Biederman said. "And we have him on medication to control the swelling and prevent convulsions. He's on a ventilator and IV, and his face is bandaged. He has fractures in both arms, his right shoulder, and left leg. What I'm saying is, he's not a pretty sight. I want you to be prepared."

"What are his chances of coming out of the coma?" Amelia said.

"It's too soon to tell. Our main concern right now is keeping him alive. His condition doesn't seem to be worsening at the moment, but the longer he stays on life support at this level, the weaker his chances of pulling through. We need to get him off the ventilator and have him breathe for himself. If we can manage that, his chances will be a lot better. But I warn you, even if he does recover, he's probably sustained permanent brain damage from that injury, the extent of which I can't tell yet. His EEG—the electrical activity of his brain—is showing serious abnormalities."

James asked, "Is that really bad?"

"Well . . . it's not good."

Amelia looked away, ran a hand through her short hair. After hours of crying, the muscles of her chest and throat ached. She knew there were more tears ahead, but for the moment, she felt numbed to what Dr. Biederman was telling them. She absorbed the bad news but did not react to it, not yet. She said, "Is there anything . . . does he, um . . ." She lowered her head and sniffled, but said no more.

Dr. Biederman's thick eyebrows rose questioningly. "Yes?"

She lifted her head again. "Nothing."

"I want you to feel free to ask questions, anything at all. I'll answer them as best I can."

Amelia was not quite sure what she wanted to ask, how to express her concerns. She turned to Molly, and when their eyes met, Amelia knew they were wondering the same thing. Would Stuart's coma bring an end to Dr. Furgeson? Molly looked as uncertain as Amelia felt.

The monstrous Santa Claus that had attacked Molly a dozen years ago had appeared not only while Stuart was in a depressed state, but while he was sound asleep. So had the rats that had covered the floor of Stuart and Molly's house. Amelia wondered if there was a connection between the two, a connection to Stuart's state of consciousness. Would a comatose state make any difference? And if so, how? How could Amelia ask Dr. Biederman about or explain such a thing?

Molly turned to the doctor and said, "Is there anything . . . you're not telling us?"

Dr. Biederman frowned. "I'm not sure I understand. You mean, am I withholding information about his condition? No, not at all. I'm happy to answer any questions you might have."

Molly nodded once. "Thank you."

Dr. Biederman opened his mouth, hesitated a moment, then said, "There is something else we need to discuss, just so the staff here understands your wishes. I've already explained to you the seriousness of Stuart's condition, and he is currently on . . . well, just about *maximum* life support. If his condition worsens significantly, there really isn't too much more we can do. Are you familiar with the term 'no code'?"

Amelia thought about it, closed her eyes a moment. She

thought she knew what it meant, and it sent a sharp pain from her chest up into her throat. "Do you mean . . . letting him die?"

"Well," Dr. Biederman said, "that's what it amounts to. A 'code blue' is the emergency response medical personnel perform when a patient has a cardiac arrest. You've probably seen it on TV . . . the CPR, the cardiac shocks, things like that. With patients who have a good chance of surviving and making a good recovery, it's just automatic to do these things. But with patients for whom surviving an arrest just means continued coma or suffering, such as terminal cancer, for example, a choice *can* be made by the patient, or by his family if the patient cannot make those decisions, to decline what we call 'heroic measure.' If this choice is made, we make sure all the staff are aware of these wishes and put it in the patient's chart."

The doctor paused and looked from Amelia to Molly and back again. "Right now," he said, "I cannot tell you with any certainty what his chances of regaining consciousness are, much less what kind of recovery or life he would have. It's possible that, with more time, we'll have a better understanding of what his chances are. On the other hand, his condition could remain as it is now indefinitely. You don't have to make this decision right now, but I want you to be aware of it, and to know that we will support whatever decision you make."

A dry, harsh sob erupted from Amelia's chest and she pressed her lips together tightly against it. But she did not cry. She took a deep breath before speaking in a tense whisper. "You said his EEG was abnormal. What does that mean?"

"Typically, it is a sign of brain damage. But like I said, I don't know the extent of that damage yet."

She lowered her head, nodded.

Dr. Biederman sat up straight in the chair as an uncomfortable silence fell on the small waiting room. It was broken when James spoke.

"Have you met Dr. Furgeson?" he said.

Amelia gasped and started as if she had been stabbed with a pin, and Molly reached over quickly and clutched James's hand.

Dr. Biederman said, "Dr. Furgeson? Is he Stuart's doctor?"

"No." Amelia realized she answered too quickly, and she tried to smile to smooth over it.

Dr. Biederman said, "I can contact him if you want, especially if he's familiar with—"

Molly shook her head. "No, no, he's . . . nobody. Really."

"The name doesn't sound familiar, does he work in this hospital?"

"He's retired," Molly said, also too quickly.

Dr. Biederman frowned as his gaze moved back and forth between Amelia and Molly. He seemed about to speak for a moment, but then stood. Amelia, Molly, and James stood with him.

"He's in ICU," the doctor said. "I'm going back there now, so I can take you, if you'd like."

"Thank you," Molly said.

They followed Dr. Biederman out of the waiting room and down the corridor in silence.

The Shock/Trauma Intensive Care Unit was circular, with a round, brightly lighted nurses' station at the hub of a wheel of patients' cubicles separated by pale green curtains. The cubicles, dark and shadowy compared to the bright light in the center of the ring, were arranged so each patient was visible from the nurses' station.

Amelia saw nothing in the cubicle but Stuart for some time. She did not even see, at first, the machinery that was keeping him alive. She went directly to his side, placed her right hand on his—gently for fear of hurting him—and silently stared at him. He was covered in bandages every-where, even his hands resting on his abdomen, and the left side of his face. Even his nose was bandaged, nostrils rimmed with caked blood. A dark crust of it ran along the edge of the bandages that covered the left side of his face.

After a few minutes of standing silently by his side, touch-ing his hand, Amelia looked at all the tubes attached to him, so many that he looked like a lab experiment. A tube as big around as her finger came out of the corner of his mouth, anchored by adhesive tape that went all the way around his head. Two long blue accordion hoses connected it to the ventilator, which clicked and wheezed quietly in the corner of the cubicle. Amelia noticed moisture condensing inside the blue hose and hesitantly touched it to find that it was warm. A smaller tube came out of one nostril and was con-nected to yet another tube connected to a canister with graduation marks on the side and partially filled with an emerald green fluid that was being drawn out of the tube in Stuart's nose. On the right side of his neck, an IV line emerged from under a clear plastic dressing, then split into four separate lines, each connected to more tubing coming from a small forest of IV poles and pumps. Another tube was connected to his head, not far from a sutured, crescent-shaped incision on a shaved section of his scalp.

Amelia's foot bumped something and she looked down at a large plastic rectangular box standing upright, like a big book standing on end. Water bubbled gently inside and a yellow latex tube went from one corner of the box up under the sheet spread over Stuart. Amelia lifted the sheet slightly and saw that the yellow tube was attached to a clear plastic tube as large as the one in Stuart's mouth, except that it came out of his chest, between two ribs on the lower right side. A small amount of bloody fluid was inside the tubing, and there was more of the fluid in the box on the floor. A large plastic bag hung from the side of the bed and was half filled with urine. She knew where that tube went. There were others that attached to the monitor mounted on the wall above the ventilator, wires attached to various places on his chest, a glowing red clamp attached to the index finger of his right hand.

Amelia knew intellectually that it was Stuart, and she felt a deep ache for him in the pit of her stomach. But looking at him on the bed, attached to all the tubes and machines, wrapped in all that gauze, he did not look even vaguely familiar. Fresh tears sprang to her eyes, transforming Stuart's image into a blur of gray in the dark cubicle. She resisted the urge to squeeze his hand, as much as she wanted to. She parted her lips to speak, but could not. Her throat burned all the way down to her stomach, as if she had swallowed fire. She could not shake the gnawing certainty that there was something she could have done, that she had made the wrong choices, that she should have done or said something else, something more, something sooner. Something.

"Hello, Stuart. It's Molly." Standing on the other side of the bed, Molly poked James with an elbow.

"Hey, Dad. How's it going?" His voice hitched on the last word and a tear made its way down over his cheek. Then he rolled his eyes when he realized what he had just said.

Molly put an arm around James and squeezed him.

"Stuart, it's Amelia." The words were followed by a gush of breath, a sniffle.

Molly took a small package of tissues from her purse and handed it across the bed to Amelia, who quickly blew her nose with one and dabbed at her eyes with another, then tossed them both into a wastebasket beside the bed near her feet. "I'm sorry for crying, Stu," she said, "but I-I'm . . . I'm worried about you, that's all. I know you're gonna be fine, but you really scared me."

"I'm pissed at you," Molly said. "What the *hell* were you doing on the roof of that building, anyway?"

Amelia flashed an angry look at Molly, but it dissolved quickly when she saw Molly's sad, tired smile.

"We want him to come out of it, right?" Molly whispered. "I'll bring him out of it." She looked down at Stuart and said, "You'll never guess what I found in my garage last week. That box of old Batman trading cards you lost so long ago? Must've gotten mixed in with my stuff when I moved. It's been under a couple boxes of old paperbacks and photo albums all these years. You don't come out of this, Stuey, I'm going to have a garage sale and sell them all to some snot-nosed kid with sticky hands."

The throat-to-stomach pain did not go away, but Amelia found herself laughing.

James turned to his mother and whispered, "You did?"

"What?" Molly said.

"Find a box of old Batman trading cards?"

She gave him a silent no with a couple shakes of her head.

There was a chair on the other side of the bed from Amelia, just behind James, but no one sat down. They stood beside Stuart's bed, looking down at him almost as if they expected him to levitate.

Amelia said, "I'm going to stay here as long as it takes, okay, Stuart?"

"I think we should go get something to eat first, Amelia," Molly said.

"Go ahead. I'll see you later."

"No, I mean all three of us."

"I'm not going to—"

"Look, he's out of surgery, we know he's stable," Molly said. "I know you're gonna stay here day and night from now on, but before you do that, let's go get a hot meal and a breath of fresh air. Then you can move in here. I'll bring you food, and I won't pester you about leaving. But I think it might do you some good right now."

The thought of walking around outside for awhile, even though it was still raining, was appealing. Her muscles ached from tension, from sitting in the waiting room for so long. But she was afraid she would be too busy worrying about

Stuart to enjoy it. She was about to tell Molly to bring her a hamburger when Dr. Biederman spoke up as he came to the cubicle from the nurses' station.

"That would be a very good idea, I think," he said. "If you've been waiting here since he was taken into O.R., you should all go out, get a little exercise, and some sleep, if possible."

It would feel good to move around a little, and Amelia decided not to argue. She looked down at Stuart and said, "Okay, you heard the doctor. We're gonna go out for a little bit. Not very long, I promise. No more than an hour."

"We may be gone longer than that," Molly said.

Amelia said, "Don't listen to her, Stuart."

"Stuart never listens to me."

"Okay," Amelia said. "Let's go. I don't want to be gone long."

It was still dark outside and the rain had become a dreary drizzle blown by a cold wind. By Amelia's watch, it was 5:23 a.m. They stopped at a Denny's.

Amelia did not know how hungry she was until they stepped into the restaurant and she smelled eggs and bacon and pancakes, and her stomach seemed to collapse a little. They ordered Grand Slam breakfasts and coffee and sat silent in the booth for a couple minutes. James broke the spell.

"Can we stop by the house before we go back to the hospital, Mom?"

"Why?" Molly said.

"The doctor said we could read to him. I wanna get some comic books."

Molly frowned. "You're going to read him comic books?"

"Yeah." One corner of his mouth turned up. "I found out we like a lot of the same ones."

"I think Stuart would like that," Amelia said. She nodded to Molly. "We'll stop and pick up the comic books before we go back."

Their breakfasts came, and while Amelia and Molly wasted no time in eating theirs, James merely picked at his. Seated beside him, Molly noticed and said, "Why aren't you eating? You've been up all night, you should eat."

"Do you think it's safe to go back to the house?" James said.

Amelia and Molly looked at each other across the table, each chewing a mouthful of food. Amelia swallowed first and said, "I think that's a good question."

"He's in a coma," Molly said. "You don't think that'll put a stop to it?"

"Why should it? Look what happened while he was asleep. It happens when he's depressed, and it also happens when he sleeps. It's almost as if the more cut off from the world he is, the more inward he draws, the worse it becomes. So what about a coma? You can't get more inward than that."

James said, "I think it'd be a mistake to think that just 'cause Dad's in a coma, Dr. Furgeson is gone."

"I'm with you, James," Amelia said.

Molly sighed and went on eating her breakfast. So did Amelia, and James finally began to eat his. Finally, Molly whispered, "I have a gun at home. I think I'll start carrying it."

"You have a gun?" Amelia said. "What are you, a rap star, now, or something?"

"It's a Ladysmith revolver, registered and fully legal," Molly said. "You remember Harvey Petievich, the cop I dated for awhile? He showed me how to get a permit, and I did. He taught me how to use it, and I'm perfectly happy to if necessary. I don't have a permit to carry it, but under the circumstances . . ." Her sentence remained suspended in midair.

"It won't do any good," James said. He turned to Amelia. "That cabdriver shot him outside the house, remember? It didn't make any difference."

Amelia nodded. "I remember." It seemed so long ago now. She felt as if she had spent a week or more in the hospital waiting for some word about Stuart's condition. She turned to Molly. "Molly Mullond, urban warrior."

They ate in silence until the food was gone, but they did not get up. The waitress came and filled their coffee cups.

James said, "What about that . . . that thing the doctor talked about? That 'no code' thing? Are you gonna tell them to try to save Dad if he has a cardiac arrest?"

Amelia and Molly looked at each other for a moment.

"What do you think?" Molly whispered.

Amelia's upper lip curled back for a moment and she put four fingers over her mouth, cut off the urge to cry again. For a moment, she was afraid her breakfast was going to come back up. She sipped some ice water. "I don't know," she said. "Maybe . . . maybe it's too soon to decide that. Do you think?"

James responded immediately: "Yeah. I think you should wait. He might get better."

"Dr. Biederman said we didn't have to decide right away," Molly said.

"Okay," Amelia said. "We'll wait. And see."

From Denny's, they went to Molly's house. Amelia went downstairs with James to get the comic books while Molly went to her bedroom to get her gun. They met again at the front door, all three tense and jumpy. But they were alone in the house and there were no surprises.

As Molly drove them back to the hospital, the eastern sky glowed with the dull gray light of a new day behind the steel-colored clouds. Rain continued to fall and it suddenly made Amelia feel slightly claustrophobic. She craved sunlight, the warmth of it on her skin. She could not remember the last time the sun had broken through the clouds. It seemed ages.

In the car on the way back to the hospital, Molly called

Betty's pastor on her cell phone and explained the situation to him. In light of Stuart's condition, he offered to take care of Betty's funeral arrangements himself, and Molly accepted his offer. Betty had paid the plot and burial costs years ago, before Delbert had died, and all that was left to be done was to make the arrangements.

Molly parked in the lot in front of the hospital. Amelia and Molly each opened an umbrella when they got out of the car. Amelia's was bigger, so James walked beside her with a large manila envelope stuffed with comic books tucked beneath his left arm.

Inside, they took the elevator up. As they went down the curved corridor, they met Detectives Scherber and De la Rosa walking in the opposite direction. De la Rosa wore his pleasant smile. Scherber turned up the corners of her lips for a moment.

"Sorry to hear about Mr. Mullond," Scherber said.

Amelia frowned. "You came to see him?"

Scherber said, "We came to see if he was in any condition to answer questions. Obviously, he's not. We talked to Dr. Biederman, who agreed to notify us should Mr. Mullond come out of his coma. Did you have a chance to talk to him before . . . he was injured?"

Amelia nodded. "We told him about Betty. He was . . . distraught."

"Did Mr. Mullond have a history of mental illness?"

"I said he was distraught, I didn't say he was mentally ill."

"Was his mother's death the reason he put on a feathered bird suit and jumped off a building?"

"Is Stuart a suspect?" Molly asked coldly.

"He hasn't been ruled out as a suspect," Scherber said. "You, um . . . you don't have any plans to leave town, do you?"

"Of course not," Amelia said.

Scherber nodded once. "All right, then."

As they walked away, Detective De la Rosa said, "Again, we're very sorry about Mr. Mullond. I hope he recovers."

"Yeah, I bet you do," Molly muttered as they continued down the corridor.

They passed through a pair of doors that swung slowly closed behind them, and into the Shock/Trauma ICU.

CHAPTER TWENTY-NINE

James spent the morning and the first couple hours of the afternoon reading comic books to Stuart. He described the pictures and read the dialogue dramatically, using different voices. Molly had brought a couple more chairs into the cubicle and Amelia sat next to her on one side of the bed while James sat reading on the other side. Between comic books, Amelia talked to Stuart. She told him that he had a good doctor, that it was still raining. She told him what they'd had for breakfast, about all the things they'd done in the city the day before. Then, when James continued reading again, Amelia and Molly nodded sleepily when they weren't whispering to each other.

At two thirty, Molly anounced that she could keep her eyes open no longer and needed to go home to get some sleep.

"Remember," she said to Amelia, "you've got to sleep, too."

"I will when I need to," Amelia said.

Molly gave her a hug. As they were leaving the cubicle, Amelia stopped them when she noticed the manila envelope stuffed with comic books on James's chair.

"You left your comic books, James," she said.

"I know," James said with a nod. "I want to come back later and read to him some more."

Amelia smiled. "Okay."

Once they were gone, Amelia turned on the TV and tuned it to CNN. She pulled her chair close to the bed and sat down. She lowered the bed's rail and placed her left hand on the upper part of Stuart's right arm.

"They'll be back later, Stu," she said. "I think James enjoyed reading to you. You've got to come out of this now, honey. Now that you've gotten through to him, you two can get to know each other a lot better."

Her voice was hoarse and she realized she was slurring her words slightly. Her eyes burned with fatigue.

"Hope you don't mind if I grab a few winks," she said. "I'm exhausted."

Amelia leaned forward and rested the side of her head on her left hand. In less than a minute, she was asleep.

When Molly and James got home, she went to the kitchen, called Amelia's cell phone and told her she was going straight to bed. "Sorry I woke you," she said. "I'll give you a call when we get up." She left the cordless phone on the kitchen counter and went to bed. James stayed up only long enough to eat a banana, then went downstairs to his room, put on a baggy pair of blue elastic-waisted shorts and an old T-shirt and went to bed. They slept the rest of the afternoon, and might have slept longer had the doorbell not rung a few minutes after six. It rang several times before waking Molly.

She sat up on the edge of her bed in T-shirt and panties, rubbed her eyes and listened to make sure she'd heard the bell. It rang again. She slipped into a pair of sweatpants and went down the hall to the front door.

"Who is it?" she said.

"Detectives Scherber and De la Rosa."

Molly opened the door. She was groggy and not at all in the mood to talk with them, but she could not very well tell two homicide detectives to go away. She opened the door, but did not step back to invite them inside.

"What can I do for you?" Molly said.

"We need to speak with your son, Mrs. Mullond," Scherber said.

"Why?"

"Regarding some friends of his."

"Does this have something to do with Betty?" Molly asked.

"We're not sure. That's what we're trying to find out."

Although she did not want to—what she wanted to do was go back to bed—Molly stepped back and let them in. "Wait here," she said, then went downstairs.

She woke James, who was sound asleep and snoring, and told him the detectives were waiting in the foyer to talk to him.

"Something about some friends of yours," she said as he followed her groggily up the stairs.

Detective De la Rosa smiled and said, "Hi, James."

Scherber gave him a brief smile. "We have some questions for you, James. Are you familiar with any of these names: Jamal Winston, Eric Lee, or Emilio Ramirez?"

James's mouth dropped open. "What about them?"

"Your name was found on a school binder discovered in a Tenderloin apartment where they were staying. Do you know them?" Scherber said.

James nodded once. "Yeah, I know 'em. Why?"

De la Rosa's smile disappeared. "We have some bad news, James. Your friends were killed night before last."

James's mouth dropped open and Molly immediately put her arm around his shoulders.

"You want to sit down, honey?" she said.

He shook his head without taking his eyes from De la Rosa. "What happened to them?"

"They were murdered," Scherber said. "It wasn't even our case, until we heard a description by a witness."

"Witness?" James whispered.

"A girl named Rosa Esposito. Otherwise known as Shatter?"

"Shatter," James whispered.

"You know her?"

He nodded. "I never met her, but . . . she was Dracula's girlfriend."

"Dracula?"

"Jamal. Jamal Winston. She was his girlfriend."

"She claims she saw their killer," Scherber said. "The description was what intrigued us. He was wearing a feathered bird costume. In fact, a couple feathers were found in and just outside the apartment." She turned to Molly. "The costume described by Rosa Esposito fit the description of the costume Mr. Mullond was wearing when he jumped off—"

"Now wait just a *second*," Molly said angrily, "Stuart is lying in a coma in the—"

"These murders occurred the night before Mr. Mullond jumped off the building on Mission. He had plenty of time to commit them."

"But why *would* he?" Molly said.

"Did your dad know your friends, James?" De la Rosa asked.

After several seconds, James nodded slightly. "He met them. Once. He . . . he didn't want me to hang out with them anymore."

"Did he ever threaten them?" Scherber asked.

James, mouth still hanging open, glanced at Molly, then said, "I . . . I don't know."

To Molly, Scherber said, "This gives us probable cause. We've obtained a warrant to search Mr. Mullond's house. We called, but there was no answer. Is Miss Randall at the hospital with him?"

Suddenly, the indignation drained out of Molly. From the expression on James's face a moment ago, she felt a nauseating certainty that Stuart was guilty of murdering his friends, although she had no idea why. And she knew what Scherber and De la Rosa would find if they searched Stuart's house—Betty's heart on the table in the garage. Unless Stuart had disposed of it. Suddenly, she could not speak. She had nothing to say. She simply nodded her head.

"She won't leave his side," Molly finally whispered.

"That won't be necessary," Scherber said. She turned to De la Rosa. "We should go."

De la Rosa opened the door and they stepped out onto the porch.

"We'll be in touch," Scherber said as she pulled the door closed.

A moment after they were gone, Molly put her arms around James and whispered, "Did he ever threaten them, James?"

"I . . . I'm not sure. He beat the crap out of Dracula."

Something finally broke in Molly and she sobbed into her son's shoulder, and he put his arms around her. She cried for Amelia, James, and herself, for Betty and James's friends. But mostly, she cried for poor Stuart. Something had finally gone terribly wrong with him and he was beyond their help now. If he came out of the coma, he would be arrested. But only if he came out of the coma—from what Dr. Biederman had said, the chances of that were not so great.

Minutes passed as they stood there, both of them crying, James quietly, Molly with loud, racking sobs—two minutes, three, four. Finally, Molly calmed down. They turned and started down the stairs, each with an arm around the other.

The doorbell rang again.

Molly pulled slowly away from James and wiped her eyes with the heels of her hands as she went back to the door. She took a deep breath and brought an end to her sobs before turning the doorknob.

"What is it *now?*" she said, and the door was kicked open so hard the knob flew from her hand and slammed against the wall.

Dr. Furgeson stepped into the foyer with a grin, scissors in hand.

Snick-snick-snick.

CHAPTER THIRTY

Molly's scream was cut short when Dr. Furgeson backhanded her in the face with his left hand and sent her spinning into the wall.

"Downstairs, James!" Molly shouted, her voice hoarse. She tasted blood in her mouth. "Lock yourself in your room!"

Standing on the stairs, James said, "I'm not gonna—"

"*Go! Now!*"

He turned and hurried down the stairs.

Molly ran into the kitchen, where she had left her purse on the counter. Her lower lip was cut and blood dribbled down her chin as she plunged her right hand into the purse. She took from it her Ladysmith revolver and cocked it as she turned to the kitchen doorway, gun aimed, ready to fire. But Dr. Furgeson was not there.

Feeling dizzy, she went down the hall and back to the foyer, which was now empty. She saw the back of Dr. Furgeson's bald head bobbing down the stairs. She took two steps down and stopped, held the gun in her right hand cupped in her left palm, and fired three times.

Dr. Furgeson twitched with each shot and three small black holes appeared in the back of his white coat. He stopped at the bottom of the stairs and turned to grin up at her.

Molly saw two larger holes in his chest and one in his stomach already closing when he turned to her. The material of his white shirt seemed to grow back together like a living membrane. In a matter of seconds, they were gone.

"Save your bullets," he said. He turned and left the stairwell, heading for James's bedroom. "James, my boy. I am afraid we've put this off long enough."

Snick-snick-snick.

Molly started down the stairs, but with another wave of dizziness, she lost her footing. She fell on her back and slid down a few steps. Sharp pain shot up her spine and she clenched her eyes shut, bared her teeth and cried out. She rolled over, got up on her knees, stood and went down the remaining stairs. She rounded the corner into the hallway and gasped when she ran headlong into Dr. Furgeson. It was not the surprise of the doctor suddenly swallowing up her field of vision that made her gasp, but the sharp pain she felt.

Grinning, Dr. Furgeson pulled the three-inch blade of the open scissors out of the left side of her lower abdomen. He stabbed her again, slightly higher and to the left, just above her navel.

Molly looked down and saw her blood on the shiny blade and stumbled backward. She landed on her ass, her left arm stretched upward, hand flat against the wall, fingers curved into claws. Pain exploded inside her.

"This doesn't concern you," Dr. Furgeson said, still grinning. "Now, if you'll excuse me. I have work to do." He turned and went down the hall to James's bedroom door. He knocked hard on the door several times. "James, open up."

"Don't open the door, James!" Molly screamed, her voice filled with pain. "Go out your window! Get out of here!" She got on her knees and leaned on her right hand, her left flat over the lower of the two stab wounds in her abdomen. She tried not to think of them as she stood. She fell again, and did not try to stand a second time. Instead, she crawled on all fours into the stairwell and up the first few stairs.

Waves of nausea moved through her and she vomited onto the stairs with both hands on her belly. She waited a moment as dizziness made the staircase tilt to the left, then the right.

There was a wooden rail on each side of the staircase.

Molly grabbed the one on her right with both hands and pulled herself to her feet, smearing blood on the rail. The pain only grew worse with each movement, but she tried to ignore it. She had to get to the phone to call Amelia. Maybe Amelia could get Stuart to make it stop.

James took his laptop from his desk and put it on his bed, then swept everything else off the desktop—notebooks, a couple paperback novels, a few comic books, a twelve-inch-tall plastic Godzilla and a stuffed Opus the penguin, a *Star Wars* mug filled with pens and pencils, several computer disks, a few CDs and DVDs, all of it gathered in the crook of his sweeping arm and tumbled to the floor with a clatter. He pushed his chair out of the way, clutched the corners at one end of the desk and pulled it away from the wall beneath the picture window that looked out over the backyard. He got in front of the desk and shoved it with a grunt over the carpet. It was an old wooden desk that his mother hated because it was covered with scuffs and nicks, but James, who had found it at a yard sale with his mother one summer Sunday, loved it because it was so broad and had three roomy drawers on each side. He had already locked his bedroom door, but did not trust it. He kept shoving the desk, putting all his weight into it, until it slammed up against the door.

"Your father was a patient of mine, too, James," Dr. Furgeson said on the other side of the door. "He was much easier to deal with, though. He didn't put up much of a fight. Of course, his mother was there to hold him down for me." He chuckled. "You need to stop putting this off, James. We want to make sure you can pee right."

Panting, James stared at the door and wondered what the hell Dr. Furgeson was talking about, wondered exactly what he had done to his dad.

Dad's creating him, remember, James thought. *He's a figment of Dad's imagination.*

But that seemed so far-fetched that, even though James

knew it to be true, he could not accept it as fact at the moment. Not with that whispery metallic sound coming from the other side of his bedroom door.

Snick-snick-snick. Snick-snick-snick.

Molly groaned as she reached the top of the stairs. Burning pain blossomed outward from each wound, nausea made her gag. Still on hands and knees, she crawled down the hardwood floor of the hall to the kitchen. Her stomach roiled hotly until she had to stop and vomit again in the hall just outside the kitchen. Her knees slid through her own blood, a trail of which was streaked behind her.

In the kitchen, she went to the counter where she had left the cordless phone. She reached up over the edge of the counter, felt around for it, and inadvertently knocked it off. It hit the floor beside her and the cover over the battery popped off the back of the phone. Molly sobbed as she picked up the phone, then crawled over to the plastic rectangle a few feet away on the floor. Her hands were slippery with blood and she fumbled with it for several seconds, dropped it a couple times, before finally sliding it back into place.

Molly's hand shook as she hit the directory button with her thumb. Amelia's name appeared in the LED display and she punched the PHONE button. Seven beeps sounded. As she waited for Amelia to answer the phone, Molly lay on her side, curled her knees up to her chest and groaned.

When her cell phone chirped, Amelia was reading to Stuart from the Op-Ed page of the *San Francisco Chronicle*, which he read every morning on his way to work. The ventilator softly whispered in the corner of the cubicle as it went about the business of breathing for Stuart. She took the phone from her purse on the floor beside her chair.

"Hello."

There was a horrible gurgling sound on the other end of the line.

"Hel . . . he*llo*?"

" 'Melia. S'Molly."

Amelia stood. "What's *wrong*?"

"I'm hurt. Dr. Furg . . . son . . . is here. He stabbed me. With his scissors."

"Oh my God." When she spoke, Amelia looked down at Stuart, still and lifeless. His heartbeat was marked by muted beeps from the monitor. She clutched the phone in her left hand, knuckles white.

"You've gotta make him stop," Molly said, her voice a groan. "He's going after James. Make him stop, Amelia."

"You've been—are you going to be okay, Molly? Did you say you've been *stabbed*?" Amelia's thoughts were suddenly in a jumble and she was uncertain of what she'd heard.

"With his scissors."

"Do you want me to call an ambu—"

"Just . . . make Stuart stop. Make him stop. Now, make him stop now."

Amelia bent forward, put her right hand on Stuart's right shoulder and shook him. She spoke loudly and firmly. "Stuart! Stuart, listen to me. Can you hear me? Dr. Furgeson is trying to—" She stopped and looked out the cubicle's opening in front. The curtain was pulled back so Stuart was visible from the nurses' station. Daisy was eyeing Amelia suspiciously.

Still holding the phone to her ear, Amelia went to the curtain and pulled it aside until it completely enclosed the cubicle, then returned to Stuart's side. She leaned over the bed's rail and put her mouth close to his ear, lowered her voice, but spoke with great urgency.

"Stuart, you *have* to do something. Dr. Furgeson has stabbed Molly, he's after James, you've got to make him stop, Stuart, he's at Molly's house and he's after *James* and you've *got* to—"

A wail of pain and fear came over the cell phone and Molly said, "He's screaming, James is screaming, my baby's screaming!"

Amelia's vision blurred with stinging tears. The agony and horror in Molly's voice sickened her, made her feel utterly helpless.

"Oh, Jesus, Stuart," Amelia said, "you have to make it stop, James is screaming, you've got to make Dr. Furgeson *stop*."

"Kill him!" Molly screamed. "Kill him, Amelia, you have to kill him!"

James had heard his mother shout to him to go out his bedroom window, but he decided to stay put for the time being. Inside his room, he knew where Dr. Furgeson was, and with the door locked and barred by the heavy desk, he knew he was safe for the moment.

A full minute had passed since he'd heard the *snick*ing of Dr. Furgeson's scissors on the other side of the door, followed by the doctor's voice: "You don't think a door will keep me from doing my job, do you?" Since then, there had been only silence out in the hall. Somewhere in the house, he could hear his mother's voice speaking loudly, although he could not understand her words. The only sounds in his bedroom, besides the sound of the rain outside the window, were those of his own breathing and his own heartbeat.

The silence disturbed him. Nearly two minutes passed before it was broken.

Snick-snick-snick.

It came from directly behind him. James spun around and when he saw Dr. Furgeson's grin a mere two feet away from him, he screamed.

As she shook Stuart's shoulder and quietly urged him to stop Dr. Furgeson, trying to avoid attracting the attention of anyone outside the cubicle, Amelia's eyes kept going to the two blue accordian tubes coming from the ventilator. They were joined to a single accordian tube, which was connected to the endotrachial tube that went into Stuart's mouth and down his throat.

Molly's sobs came over the phone sounding pinched and metallic, softened by an aura of static. Between sobs, she kept repeating, "Unplug him, James is screaming, make him stop, unplug him, make him stop, kill him, James is screaming."

Throat burning, eyes bleary with tears, hands trembling, Amelia put the cell phone on Stuart's chest. She closed one hand on the blue ventilator tubing, another on the endotrachial tube, and pulled them apart.

A shrill beeping came from the ventilator the moment the tubes were disconnected.

Up close, there was an odd sheen to Dr. Furgeson, almost a faint glow, as if he were some kind of projection—like a hologram. But his left hand was perfectly solid as it came to rest on James's shoulder and squeezed hard.

"I hope you'll take this like a big boy and not give me any trouble," Dr. Furgeson said. "We want to make sure you can pee right."

James swept his arm up and knocked the doctor's hand away, stepped backward until he bumped into the front of his desk. He made a small, frightened sound in his throat as Dr. Furgeson rushed him.

"This is for your own good," Dr. Furgeson said, lips peeled back in a sneer. "Think of it as a chance to prove yourself to be the man your father never was."

James hopped up on the desk and pushed himself back over the desktop until his back was pressed against the bedroom door.

"It's called a meatotomy," Dr. Furgeson said. "A simple procedure to enlarge a urethra that is too small. Just a little snip." He held up the scissors.

Snick-snick-snick.

Horrified, James began to kick and flail his arms, hands doubled into fists, but Dr. Furgeson ignored the blows to his face and shoulders and neck as if they were being delivered by a child and rushed forward. James froze when he felt the point of one of the scissors' bloody blades press against his throat. His pulse throbbed against the sharp blade.

Leaning his weight on James's legs, Dr. Furgeson curled the fingers of his left hand around the elastic waist of James's shorts and pulled as he said, "Struggling will only make this worse."

CHAPTER THIRTY-ONE

The curtain that cocooned Stuart's bed swept aside with a thin hiss and Daisy hurried toward the ventilator. She clutched Amelia's upper arms from behind and shoved her aside.

"What are you *doing?*" Daisy said as she closed her hand on the stray ventilator tube on the pillow beside Stuart's head and reached for the endotrachial tube to reconnect them.

Amelia grabbed Daisy's left shoulder with one hand, her left elbow with the other and violently pulled her back away from the tubes. "No, don't, please, you don't understand."

Daisy brought her left elbow back hard and pushed Amelia away. The small round woman turned, red-faced and incredulous. "What are you trying to do?" she said, suddenly breathless. She turned and reached for the tubes a second time.

Molly's insectile cries chattered from the cell phone on Stuart's chest as Amelia bounded forward again and grabbed the fleshy upper half of Daisy's left arm with both hands and pulled her once more away from the tubes. They spoke at once:

Amelia said, "Please don't do this, please, you don't understand—"

"Let *go* of me. I need some help in here!" Daisy shouted.

Someone was already on the way—a tall, broad-shouldered male nurse in his midtwenties with short curly blond hair wearing green scrubs. His badge read OLIVER BLEDSOE, R.N. He entered the cubicle already speaking. "Hey, hey, hey, what is going *on* in here?"

"*Hold* her," Daisy said. "She's disconnected the ventilator from the ET tube."

As Daisy reached for the tubes again, Amelia tried to stop her, but Oliver gripped her right elbow and pulled her back. As Daisy reconnected the tubes, Oliver said, "What are you trying to do? Aren't you the patient's girlfriend?"

Amelia turned around and tilted her tear-streaked face up to him and said, "You don't understand, I was trying to—" She pulled away from him suddenly, went around the foot of the bed to the other side, Stuart's right, and leaned over the rail. She gripped his shoulder and shook him again. "Stuart, you have to make it stop. He's after James, he's in the house and he's after James."

With the tubes reconnected, Daisy turned to the male nurse as Amelia continued to speak frantically to Stuart.

"You keep an eye on her, Oliver," Daisy said. "I'm going to call security and have her removed." As she hurried out of the cubicle, she said over her shoulder, "Keep her away from that tubing."

As Amelia continued to plead with Stuart, Molly's tiny, fuzzy sobs chittered from the cell phone's earpiece.

Dr. Furgeson's right fist held the open scissors near James's throat. The doctor leaned close, his toothy grin just a few inches from James's face. His body leaned on James's legs, but the boy's arms remained free and he pounded his fists on the doctor's shoulders and neck and head. James's struggle accomplished no more than to knock Dr. Furgeson's round spectacles askew on his narrow face. He became still and grunted in pain when the point of the blade pierced the skin on the left side of his neck. Blood trickled warmly down his neck and onto the collar of his T-shirt.

"You're being childish, my boy," Dr. Furgeson said. His voice was quiet and calm, as if he were not involved in a struggle at all but speaking gently to an uncooperative patient.

James was momentarily distracted by the fact that, as close as their faces were, he felt no breath from the doctor's mouth. The doctor had no odor, no warmth about him at all. He felt substantial, but in the way that a mannequin might feel leaning against him, not a person of warm flesh and blood.

"I would have been done by now if you weren't such a baby," Dr. Furgeson said. "No lollipop for *you*."

He pulled again at the elastic waist of the James's shorts. He dropped his right hand down to James's lap and gave the shorts a single snip, then tore them the rest of the way. They ripped down the left leg, then fell open, exposing his genitals.

James wanted to struggle further, to keep fighting until he knocked the doctor away long enough to get off the desk and back on his feet. But the overhead light glinted off the flat edge of one of the scissors' blades, poised open less than an inch above his penis.

"You don't want to move now," Dr. Furgeson said. "You wouldn't want me to take more than what's necessary, would you?" His laughter sounded like the snapping of dry twigs.

"If you don't cooperate, ma'am, I'm going to have to call the police," the security guard said. He was a graying, balding man with a belly that spilled over his belt and strained the buttons of his uniform's shirt. He stretched his left arm across her shoulders while his right hand firmly held her right elbow.

Amelia had pushed the guard away twice as she continued to talk to Stuart—"Please, Stuart, you've got to make this stop, for James, before he gets hurt, before he does something to James, you've *got* to!"—but once his arm was around her and he had hold of her elbow, she gave in. She snatched the cell phone up as he led her away from the bed, then out of the cubicle.

"Now, I don't want to do that," the guard said. "I know you're upset, and I know there's really no reason for me to call the police. Isn't that right?" He stopped once they were standing at the curved counter of the nurses' station. "Isn't that right, ma'am?"

"Please call the police," Amelia said as she put the cell phone to her ear again. "Molly, I'm sending the police over right away."

Molly was still crying, but her voice was considerably weaker than it had been a minute ago.

"You *want* me to call the police?" the guard said. Confusion narrowed his eyes and drew his bushy eyebrows together.

She turned to Daisy, who was behind the counter. "An ambulance, call an ambulance. My friend has been stabbed and her son is in danger. There's an intruder in the house." Then, into the phone: "Hang on, Molly, we're going to get an ambulance over there right away."

Oliver, the male nurse, stepped up behind Daisy and they both stared at her with a mixture of suspicion and confusion.

"Is that your friend on the phone?" Oliver asked. "The one who's been stabbed?"

Amelia said, "*Yes*, now *please*, call nine-one-one and give me the phone so I can tell them the address!"

Daisy and Oliver looked at each other a moment, then turned uncertainly to the security guard.

He shrugged and said, "What are you looking at me for? Call nine-one-one like the lady says."

Daisy picked up the phone and punched in the numbers, handed the receiver over to Amelia. As she waited for an operator to answer, Amelia wiped her eyes with a knuckle.

"If you knew your friend was being stabbed," Oliver said, "why were you trying to unplug the ventilator tube in—"

Amelia was relieved when the operator answered—"Nine-one-one, what is your emergency?"—so she did not have to try to explain herself, because that, of course, would have been impossible.

* * *

James was frozen on the desktop, slouched against the bedroom door with his legs bent over the desk's edge at the knees. His lower legs were held in place by the weight of Dr. Furgeson leaning against them. His elbows rested on the desktop at his sides, hands clenched into fists. And his eyes were trained on the pair of scissors poised just above his penis. He wanted to throw himself forward with all his weight and knock Dr. Furgeson over, but he was afraid to move a muscle because the scissors were so close, so close.

"This is going to hurt, James," Dr. Furgeson said. "You may scream, if you—"

The bedroom exploded with the sound of shattering glass. A figure hit the floor, but was upright in an instant.

Dr. Furgeson pulled away from James and spun around. The instant the doctor turned his back, James rolled off the desk, stumbled away from it and nearly fell into his open closet. He shook all over as adrenaline coursed through him like lava. Once he had his footing, he stood in the doorway of the closet and turned to see who had come through his bedroom window.

James stopped breathing when he saw the tall figure standing in a scattering of broken glass. He blinked his eyes repeatedly as time slowed.

Owl-Man towered over Dr. Furgeson, standing, at the very least, six and a half feet tall, but probably taller, James estimated. Like Dr. Furgeson, there was a dull shimmer to the hulking figure. But he was solid enough to have shattered the bedroom window.

The feathered hood ended halfway down his face where a shiny chrome beak curved down over his nose. At first glance, James had thought, impossibly, that he was looking at his dad, but the lower half of the face visible below the hood dispelled that thought immediately. The jaw was firm and square with a mouth that formed a straight line—the only line in the smooth bronze face—above a confident, jutting chin. Although it appeared to be flesh and blood, something about the face was stiff and masklike—it did not move, not even slightly. The feathered lapels of the mottled tan, white, and black suit jacket were smooth and unmussed over the broad, deep chest, the matching leggings snug over powerful thighs. The tan cape fell almost all the way to the floor. James's eyes were drawn to Owl-Man's enormous fists in black gloves, to the shiny silver blades on the knuckles.

Owl-Man threw his first punch before Dr. Furgeson could speak. The blades on the glove tore through Dr. Furgeson's left cheek and left behind four diagonal rips in the flesh that exposed, for a moment, the doctor's teeth. The cuts did not bleed and began to close immediately, but Owl-Man struck again before they could finish. He attacked with such raw ferocity that James stumbled backward until his back was pressed against the clothes hanging inside the closet.

The blades on Owl-Man's knuckles made soft crunching sounds as they cut into Dr. Furgeson's face and throat and neck. He moved forward as he threw punch after punch with such speed that his fists were a blur, until the backs of Dr. Furgeson's legs hit the desk. He pushed the doctor down flat on his back on the desktop and pounded his right fist repeatedly into the doctor's face. Owl-Man closed his hand on Dr. Furgeson's right wrist, lifted his arm and slammed it down hard on the doctor's abdomen, driving the scissors into him.

Dr. Furgeson convulsed on the desk as Owl-Man continued to pummel him with his fists. With no blood, the wounds were clearly visible. The blades on Owl-Man's knuckles shredded Dr. Furgeson's features, broke his large protruding teeth, drove his glasses into his eyes.

When Owl-Man finally stopped and stepped back, Dr. Furgeson slid to the floor like a torn and battered doll. There, his convulsions became a weak tremble. Owl-Man watched him closely for about fifteen seconds. Before those fifteen seconds were up, something happened that made James gasp.

Owl-Man became transparent.

"What—what—what—" The word blurted from James's mouth repeatedly like a cough. He looked down at the fallen doctor and saw that he, too, was fading.

Owl-Man turned to James. His face had remained motionless throughout the beating he had given Dr. Furgeson, but now the lips parted slightly. When he spoke, the voice made James gasp again. It was his father's voice.

"Take care of yourself, James."

He faded to little more than a shadow and lingered for several seconds.

"Dad?" James said. His throat suddenly felt hot and tight and the word came out as a croak.

Owl-Man was gone. James looked down at the floor and saw nothing to indicate that Dr. Furgeson had been lying there only seconds earlier, torn and beaten.

A heavy silence fell over the room as James continued to stare at the space occupied a moment ago by Owl-Man and Dr. Furgeson. He realized he heard nothing at all, and he remembered his mother. He bent down and picked up a crumpled pair of sweatpants from the floor of the closet and quickly stepped into them. Still unable to digest what had just happened in front of him, he moved to the desk, pulled it away from the door with effort and left his bedroom.

He hurried up the stairs, careful not to step in the trail of blood left by his mother. There was so much of it—he retched once, then swallowed repeatedly as he went down the hall to the kitchen.

She was lying on the kitchen floor on her left side, both arms stretched out before her. The telephone lay on the floor beside her open hand.

"Mom? Mom!" He touched her shoulder. "Mom, he's gone, it's okay now, he's gone, he's—" He stopped talking when he realized she was not hearing him. Her eyes were closed, her mouth open. James placed two fingers on her neck just below her jaw. Her pulse was faint. He picked up the phone and put it to his ear. The line was open and he could hear someone crying some distance from the phone. It was Amelia. Between sobs, she repeated one word:

"Stuart . . . Stuart . . . Stuart. . . ."

James knew at that moment that his dad was dead. That was why, he realized, the two figures in his bedroom had faded away like a couple of ghosts.

He sat on the floor beside his mother, the phone still held to his ear, and cried. He was vaguely aware of the approaching siren. It grew steadily louder until it stopped outside the house.

James realized Amelia had called the police and he was going to have to tell them something to explain why his mother was lying unconscious on the floor bleeding from stab wounds in her abdomen. He decided the best thing to do would be to tell them as much of the truth as he could without making himself sound crazy. When they asked for a description of the assailant, he would describe Dr. Furgeson.

The doorbell rang and a second later someone pounded on the front door, then rang the bell.

Unable to stop sobbing, James stood and hurried to the door. He opened it and said to the police officer who stood on the porch, "Please help my mother."

Within the first few minutes of the search of Stuart Mullond's house conducted by Detectives Scherber and De la Rosa, Betty Mullond's heart was found on a card table in the garage. But by that time, Stuart was already dead.

CHAPTER THIRTY-TWO

Amelia was startled out of a doze by a scream. It came from the television set in Molly's living room—an old black-and-white movie, something James was watching. But when she sat up on the couch, where she had been curled up on her side, she saw that he was asleep in the recliner. He had done a lot of crying that day, and his face was puffy. She looked at her watch—it was a minute before eleven o'clock. She got up and went to James's side, put her hand on his. He stirred.

"Why don't you go to bed, kiddo," she said.

He slowly lifted himself from the big chair, reached his arms above his head and stretched as he yawned. "Yeah. Okay."

They exchanged good nights and James shuffled downstairs to the exercise room, where he laid out his sleeping bag.

Amelia's neck and back ached and she was exhausted, but she did not want to go to bed. While dozing on the couch, she had dreamed of Stuart, and she knew she would go on dreaming about him if she went to bed. She was not ready for that just yet. Instead, she went into the kitchen and found a bottle of brandy. She poured some in a glass and returned to her spot on the living room couch and sipped it. She aimed the remote at the television and tuned to a local news broadcast.

A female Asian reporter stood outside Molly's house, talking into her microphone. There were others, too, maybe a dozen of them out there, all staring into cameras and reporting live. When they had come home from the hospital late that afternoon, Amelia and James had passed through the clot of reporters in front of the house. Amelia had put her arm around James and said repeatedly, "No comment, we have no comment."

Amelia had been waiting in the Emergency Room when Molly arrived by ambulance. James was brought to the hospital in a police cruiser after answering the police officer's questions. While Molly was being treated in the ER, they took seats in the waiting room and Amelia told him that Stuart had died.

"He went into cardiac arrest," she said. "They tried to revive him, but couldn't."

She expected an emotional reaction from him, but instead, James's eyes took on a distant look and he frowned, but he said nothing for almost a minute. Then: "I knew he was gone. I knew when I heard you crying on the phone. But I think I knew before that . . . when they faded away in my room."

"When who faded away?"

He explained everything that had happened, then told her what he'd said to the police. As soon as Molly was able to see them, they told her what to tell the police so her story would match James's. But it was essentially an accurate account of what had happened in the house—except for the fact that James had left Dr. Furgeson's stethoscope, and his name, out of the description. He had told the police that when the white-coated attacker—whom he had never seen before—could not get into James's bedroom through the door, he had gone outside to the backyard and broken through the bedroom window. James said he had struggled with the man, who had poked him in the throat with his scissors just enough to break the skin and draw blood. Then, frustrated by the struggle, the man had hurried back out the window and run away.

"They're going to hunt for him, you know," Amelia said. "And they'll never find him."

"I know. But it's either that or tell them the truth. You want to try to explain *that* to them? How do you think they'd react if I told them I was saved by Owl-Man, and that he and Dr. Furgeson just faded away like . . . I don't know, like a couple of digital effects?"

"You're right."

Footage of Stuart in his Owl-Man suit jumping off the roof of the Hartwicke Hotel on Mission—a run-down old hotel that housed mostly senior citizens—had been rerun on local newscasts ever since it happened. It had been picked up by CNN and Fox News. Stuart was big news since he had been posthumously accused by police of the murder of the three boys in the Tenderloin as well as that of his own mother. The footage included a glimpse of Dr. Furgeson on top of an office building across the street from the Hartwicke—that was also shown repeatedly since the release of the description of Molly's and James's assailant. Reporters had set up camp both outside Molly's house, hoping for comments from Amelia and James, and outside Betty's house, now a cordoned crime scene.

It was a bizarre, lurid story and local news outlets were milking every drop of airtime possible from it, using it to lead and close each newscast.

Amelia silently shed tears as she sipped her brandy and watched the reporter on TV, who was just outside the house. The Asian woman's lips moved on the screen, but her words were an aural blur to Amelia, who was sorry James had gone to bed—she realized she did not want to be alone.

She lifted the remote and channel-surfed until she found an old Gene Kelly musical. She got up and went to the kitchen, got the bottle of brandy and took it back to the living room. Amelia was not much of a drinker, and she knew it would take little to make her drunk. That was what she wanted—to drink herself into a dreamless sleep on the sofa with the television on. If she had to be alone, she did not want to be left in silence with her own thoughts. She allowed herself to be absorbed by the colorful musical.

Amelia was on her second brandy when she heard rapid knocking. She turned her eyes from the television and listened. Somewhere in the house, someone spoke, then knocked again. The knocking stopped and, once again, Amelia heard the voice.

A sob erupted from her chest because the voice, although muffled, sounded like Stuart's.

More knocking.

She put her drink on the end table and got up, left the living room and went out to the foyer. The knocking was coming from downstairs. She hurried down the stairs—

"James?" the voice said with concern. "James? Are you in there? Are you all right?"

—and stepped into the hall, turned to her left toward the exercise room. Amelia reached out her left hand and pressed it to the wall to hold herself up because her legs suddenly felt weak and watery.

The hall was dark, lit only by light that glowed down the stairs from the foyer above.

Stuart stood at the door, hand raised, fingers curled, poised to knock again. He wore his old gray paint-spattered sweatshirt, a pair of sweatpants and sneakers. His head was tilted forward and a frown etched lines into his forehead.

"No," Amelia whispered to herself. She put a hand over her face and closed her eyes. "No."

She opened her eyes again when she heard the exercise room door open.

Stuart was gone. James stood in the open bedroom doorway in a pair of boxer shorts. His eyes squinted against the faint light and he blinked rapidly several times.

"Amelia?" he said. "Were you knocking? I was asleep. I was dreaming. About Dad."

RAY GARTON

Author of *Ravenous* and *Live Girls*

Something very strange is happening in the coastal California town of Big Rock. Several residents have died in unexplained, particularly brutal ways, many torn apart in animal attacks. And there's always that eerie howling late at night...

You might think there's a werewolf in town. But you'd be wrong. It's not just one werewolf, but the whole town that's gradually transforming. Bit by bit, as the infection spreads, the werewolves are becoming more and more powerful. In fact, humans may soon be the minority, mere prey for their hungry neighbors. Is it too late for the humans to fight back? Did they ever have a chance from the start?

BESTIAL

"Garton has a flair for taking veteran horror
themes and twisting them to evocative
or entertaining effect."
—*Publishers Weekly*

ISBN 13: 978-0-8439-6185-0

"If you've missed Laymon, you've missed a treat!"
—Stephen King

RICHARD LAYMON

The legendary Beast House, once home to unspeakable acts of agony and murder, is now a decrepit tourist attraction where the curious go for cheap thrills and daily tours. These days few actually believe the stories of slaughter and sexual torture are true, or that the beast really exists. But in the silence of the night, the cellar door of Beast House opens once again. . . .

Mark and Alison snuck into Beast House after the tours were over for a midnight rendezvous. Mark hopes to get lucky but Alison seems more interested in the gruesome legends. But if the beast is only a legend, who's responsible for the mutilated carcass of a dog outside? And why is the padlock missing from the cellar door? Will this be the date of a lifetime or a date with death?

FRIDAY NIGHT IN BEAST HOUSE

ISBN 13: 978-0-8439-6142-3

Ronald Malfi

When a brutal snowstorm shut down all the flights in and out of Chicago, Todd Curry and a few other stranded passengers rented a Jeep to drive the rest of the way to their destinations. But along a forested, isolated road, they picked up a disoriented man wandering through the snow. His car wouldn't start and his daughter had vanished. Strangest of all were the mysterious slashes cut into the back of the man's coat, straight down to the flesh....

"What horror should be! [Five stars]"
—*SF Reader* on *The Fall of Never*

When they arrived in the nearest town it seemed deserted. Cars sat in the streets with their doors open. Fires burned unattended. But Todd and the rest of the travelers will soon learn the town is far from deserted, for they're being watched ... and hunted. Soon they will discover the inhuman horrors that await them in the ...

SNOW

ISBN 13: 978-0-8439-6355-7

INTERACT WITH DORCHESTER ONLINE!

Want to learn more about your favorite books and authors?
Want to talk with other readers that like to read the same books as you?
Want to see up-to-the-minute Dorchester news?

VISIT DORCHESTER AT:
DorchesterPub.com
Twitter.com/DorchesterPub
Facebook.com (Search Pages)

DISCUSS DORCHESTER'S NOVELS AT:
Dorchester Forums at DorchesterPub.com
GoodReads.com
LibraryThing.com
Myspace.com/books
Shelfari.com
WeRead.com

✂

❏ **YES!**

Sign me up for the Leisure Horror Book Club and send my FREE BOOKS! If I choose to stay in the club, I will pay only $8.50* each month, a savings of $7.48!

NAME: _____

ADDRESS: _____

TELEPHONE: _____

EMAIL: _____

❏ I want to pay by credit card.

❏ VISA   ❏ MasterCard   ❏ DISCOVER

ACCOUNT #: _____

EXPIRATION DATE: _____

SIGNATURE: _____

Mail this page along with $2.00 shipping and handling to:
Leisure Horror Book Club
PO Box 6640
Wayne, PA 19087
Or fax (must include credit card information) to:
610-995-9274

You can also sign up online at **www.dorchesterpub.com**.
*Plus $2.00 for shipping. Offer open to residents of the U.S. and Canada only.
Canadian residents please call 1-800-481-9191 for pricing information.
If under 18, a parent or guardian must sign. Terms, prices and conditions subject to change. Subscription subject to acceptance. Dorchester Publishing reserves the right to reject any order or cancel any subscription.

GET FREE BOOKS!

You can have the best fiction delivered to your door for less than what you'd pay in a bookstore or online. Sign up for one of our book clubs today, and we'll send you *FREE* BOOKS* just for trying it out... **with no obligation to buy, ever!**

As a member of the Leisure Horror Book Club, you'll receive books by authors such as **RICHARD LAYMON, JACK KETCHUM, JOHN SKIPP, BRIAN KEENE** and many more.

As a book club member you also receive the following special benefits:
- **30% off all orders!**
- **Exclusive access to special discounts!**
- **Convenient home delivery and 10 days to return any books you don't want to keep.**

Visit www.dorchesterpub.com
or call 1-800-481-9191

There is no minimum number of books to buy, and you may cancel membership at any time.
*Please include $2.00 for shipping and handling.